A
AT

Books by Melissa Jagears

A Bride for Keeps
A Bride in Store
A Bride at Last

A *Bride* AT LAST

MELISSA JAGEARS

BETHANYHOUSE
a division of Baker Publishing Group
Minneapolis, Minnesota

© 2015 by Melissa Jagears

Published by Bethany House Publishers
11400 Hampshire Avenue South
Bloomington, Minnesota 55438
www.bethanyhouse.com

Bethany House Publishers is a division of
Baker Publishing Group, Grand Rapids, Michigan

Printed in the United States of America

Library of Congress Cataloging-in-Publication Data
Jagears, Melissa.
    A bride at last / Melissa Jagears.
        pages ; cm
    ISBN 978-0-7642-1170-6 (pbk.)
        1. Mail order brides—Fiction. 2. Frontier and pioneer life—Fiction.
    3. Kansas—Fiction. I. Title.
    PS3610.A368B74 2015
    813'.6—dc23   2015005745

Scripture quotations are from the King James Version of the Bible

Cover design by Dan Pitts
Cover photography by Mike Habermann Photography, LLC

Author represented by Natasha Kern Literary Agency

15   16   17   18   19   20   21   7   6   5   4   3   2   1

To my husband, children, mother, and mother-in-law, who helped me carve out enough time to write this story, since a newborn and novel writing don't go together like peanut butter and jelly.

To my critique partners, Naomi Rawlings and Glenn Haggerty, who have helped me become a better writer over the years and poured hours into helping me with this story. Thank you for sticking with me on this wild journey of authorship amidst the ups and downs of life.

Chapter 1

At the sound of running footsteps, Kate Dawson glanced up from dumping mop water in the alleyway outside the school building.

Anthony Riverton skidded to a halt in front of her, his little chest heaving as he drew in gulps of air.

"Why weren't you in school today?" She frowned at his tattered clothing. She needed to find him a decent coat before winter.

"Mother's dying." Dread strangled his words. "Tonight. I just know it."

A lump pushed against Kate's high collar. "She seemed better yesterday." Lucinda didn't have many days left, but Kate wasn't ready for her to leave yet—wasn't ready to assume responsibility for this boy all on her own. She hadn't saved enough money, hadn't figured out where they would live . . .

"She coughed so much last night I couldn't sleep, and this morning she begged me not to leave." The nine-year-old swallowed hard, but his eyes were dry. "Said she'd be the one going. I thought she meant back to the laundry." His ragged voice barely registered. "And she's mumbling things about Pa."

Kate's breath stopped. "Your pa?"

The boy's arms hung limp at his sides. "Said he's coming."

She shook her head vehemently. "No."

"Said she wrote him."

"Wrote him? Whatever for?" She'd helped the two of them escape Anthony's father years ago—or at least the man Anthony had known as *Pa*. Had Lucy contacted him?

"Let's go." Kate leaned the mop against the schoolhouse door. She'd yet to clean Miss Jennings's classroom or the Widow Larson's, but a boy needed somebody with him when his mother took her last draught of air.

She sprinted after Anthony, her long-legged stride easily keeping pace with his. They darted down the convoluted streets of Breton, one of the many towns surrounding Independence, Missouri—a sprawling city they could get lost in, and where Richard Fitzgerald could never find them.

Surely Anthony had heard wrong. Lucinda had to have written someone else. She'd told Kate that Richard wasn't Anthony's real father months ago, but she hadn't thought to pry any further. The only other man she knew of in Lucinda's past was the husband who'd kicked Lucinda out penniless—who'd driven her to Richard. Was he Anthony's father or was there a third man?

Winding their way between factories and dilapidated apartments only impoverished factory workers would bother to live in, they ran for the boardinghouse where Kate paid for the Rivertons to lodge. The giant structure leaned, and its walls contained more bugs than the building had bricks, but Mrs. Grindall's was the only affordable place available. Lucinda's sickness had stolen her ability to work, and the landlord of the miserable shack they'd once lived in had not been gifted with compassion.

If only Kate could find them someplace better. But as long as she taught in the rundown section of Breton, that would never happen. Not only was the schoolhouse and surrounding neighborhood lacking, but so was the pay.

Lately, Lucinda had bemoaned the baubles and luxurious life she'd left behind so much that Kate had to keep reminding her of how her lover had treated her to snap her out of whining.

As a teacher, Kate wouldn't be able to provide Anthony with much, but he'd have enough. And most importantly, he'd be loved—which was better than anything Richard could give him.

But what if Richard was on his way to Breton right now? What if he was already here?

The wintery air, like a cold, sharp knife, sliced in and out of her lungs as she breathed deeply with each stride. She sped up to tighten the distance between her and Anthony. Dodging a pile of litter, she darted around the sharp corner into—

"Oof."

Her shoulder slammed hard into a man in the boarding-house's alleyway. She stumbled, arms flailing to save her balance.

"Are you all right, miss?" He reached for her, but she righted herself without his help and shook her head. Good thing she wore sensible boots. Heels would have sent her sprawling.

"I'm fine." She waved dismissively at him, then ran the last few strides to the steps by the back door. She grabbed the balustrade's rounded newel, increasing her pivoting speed to gain the steps faster.

Anthony turned the knob and barged through the board-inghouse's sticky side door, which released a puff of hot air. At least Mrs. Grindall kept the place warm—overly warm, but better than the alternative.

A spooked mouse skittered across the stair landing, and Kate shuddered in the dim light despite the heat. The tiny rodent disappeared into a crevice in the wall.

Even though Anthony's quick thumping on the staircase probably woke anyone who might have been napping, she didn't want to annoy any residents, so she slowed. Although, considering the thin, grayish walls, the boarders likely dealt with all kinds of unwanted noises.

Once Anthony's pounding steps ceased, the boardinghouse seemed eerily quiet. A dog barked outside, a baby cried somewhere down the corridor, pots and pans banged downstairs, and a lady sneezed across the hall, but what she didn't hear was coughing. . . . Lucinda's ceaseless lung-emptying hacking.

Anthony stood in front of his room's closed door, his eyes open with alarm and his lips pressed tight, his nostrils flaring with each frantic inhale.

Kate took a gulp of the hot, stale air and put a hand on his shoulder. "Let's go in quietly. We don't want to disturb her sleep." At least she prayed the lack of coughing meant sleep.

She opened the door. "Lucinda?"

No answer.

The stillness was palpable.

Kate approached the bed. "Are you awake?" *Please, Lord . . .*

The woman's matted blond curls lay limp against her pillow, the purple beneath her eyes darker than Kate remembered.

Lucinda's eyelids were relaxed despite being half open. Her mouth slack, her body restful. An unusual peacefulness pervaded her face.

With a trembling hand against her mouth, Kate focused on the threadbare, disintegrating quilt covering Lucinda's chest.

Not even a flutter.

Anthony crept up alongside Kate and pressed against her heavy wool skirt and thick petticoats.

She put her arm around him, and they both watched Lucinda. The clock ticked unmercifully slow.

"She never said it." His scratchy voice warbled with tears.

"Said what, honey?" His tense muscles tightened as she slowly rubbed his arm from elbow to shoulder.

"That she loved me." He swallowed audibly. "Do you think she wanted to tell me that while I was gone?"

Warmth flooded Kate's eyes and throat so quickly she barely kept from crying. She tightened her grip on Anthony's shoulder. To lie or not? "I don't know."

She kissed the top of his head and walked him to the hard chair beside the single drafty window. She sat and tugged him into an embrace, but his body refused to soften. He stared out the window, and she held her tears.

Her heart fractured into painful shards as the quiet seconds ticked by. If only he'd allow himself to cry. . . .

<hr />

Silas Jonesey rubbed his eyes as he stared up at the front door of the boardinghouse on Morning Glory Street for the seventh time. It wasn't as if the two-story structure had the stability of the walls of Jericho. He could probably push the building over without circling it once, but his feet had refused to cooperate when he first arrived. So he'd marched around . . . and around. However, his heavy traveling bag wearied his left arm and his boots had started rubbing his heels after several circuitous trips.

It was time to go inside.

Would she forgive him? He set his bag on the sidewalk and rotated his shoulder as he stared at the cracked windows. She'd only written him to ask for money, and no wonder—this boardinghouse was likely the worst building he'd ever seen that hadn't already collapsed in upon itself. The towns surrounding

Independence had grown a lot since he'd last been in the area. Surely there were a hundred better places for his wife to lodge.

Had she known he grew up near here, only a day's ride away? Surely not. Independence was one of the largest cities in Missouri, so she'd likely come to this area looking for a job—just a coincidence.

He rubbed his chest pocket, the letter inside his shirt crinkling. She'd asked him to send her money, but he had to apologize in person and plead for a second chance. But if she declined to return to Kansas with him, was he obligated to keep her housed in Missouri? He wasn't wealthy. This autumn's rain deficit and summer's myriad insect infestations had bit into his savings—and that was before he'd bought the train ticket to Independence.

He rolled his shoulders. No sense getting ahead of himself. He'd come to confess his sins and ask for forgiveness—that's all he really wanted. If she forgave him, then he'd worry about what to do next.

He swallowed, grabbed his bags, and forced his feet up one stair at a time.

The grimy window beside the front door obscured his view inside, so after two knocks and no answer, he tried the doorknob. Open. Stepping inside, a shiver stole over him, despite the relief the cloying heat gave his body. He crossed to the desk in the back of the room but couldn't find a bell, and nobody lurked in the dimly lit interior.

Overhead, a baby cried and footsteps squeaked on warped boards, both sounds muffled by kitchen clanging noises coming from somewhere down the hallway.

"Hello?" Should he pound on something or search for the proprietor? He set down his bag and pulled off his scarf. He raised his voice. "Is anyone available to help me?"

A ruddy-faced woman with a stained apron and gray hair

falling from an untidy bun stepped out of a door near the back of the hallway. "Whaddya want?"

"I'm here to visit Lucinda Jonesey. Do I—"

"There's no dallying with any of my guests. I don't run a—"

"No, ma'am." He cleared his throat. His face flamed hotter than the stifling room. "She's my wife."

"Lucinda who?" She lowered one brow, turning her head a bit to give him an unconvinced glare.

"Jonesey."

"Then you got the wrong place."

He glanced at the letter in his hand. "Is this 402 Morning Glory? She was here a month ago."

"All I've got is a Lucinda Riverton."

Riverton? She was using her maiden name? "That's her."

"She ain't got no husband." The lady took a menacing step forward, brandishing her wooden spoon.

"Not for the last ten years, no—at least we haven't lived together." Not as if *he'd* been the reason for that. "I promise if she's not the right Lucinda, I won't stay. Even if she is the right one, I'm not sure I'll be here long."

"Second floor, last door on the right." She waved her dough-covered spoon at a dark stairwell. "If I hear screaming, I'll thrash you."

He worked hard not to smile at the image of the round, flour-covered lady charging at him with a spoon. "That won't happen. She asked me to come."

Now, as for yelling? That might be a different matter. . . .

"Fine." She turned and charged toward the door she'd left earlier. "Myrtle! If those potatoes aren't done peeled, I'll whip you within an inch of your life!"

Did this woman threaten everyone with a beating, or did she actually do it?

No voice responded from the back. Perhaps this Myrtle

person knew the proprietress's threat was idle or she kept quiet to avoid confrontation.

Nothing but the sound of sliding pots and clanging bowls sounded from the back, so he grabbed his bag and headed to the stairs.

Carefully testing his weight on the splintered boards, Silas pushed himself upward, his heart pounding harder with each step closer to his wife.

Nearing the last door, he pulled off his hat and stuffed it deep into the pocket of his heavy coat. He cleared his throat and knocked on the door, which gave way under his fist. Something fluttered inside, but no one bid him enter nor asked his name.

"Hello?" Would he even recognize his wife? Ten years could certainly change anybody's looks, disposition . . . wants. "Lucy?"

He looked behind him to make sure this indeed was the last door. If she wasn't inside, where should he wait? Would his estranged wife view his entering her empty room as an invasion?

He pushed the door, and his eyes lighted upon the bed where his wife lay, her blond curls as long and sensuous as they'd been during the seven months he'd known her.

But the rest of her? Tightness captured his chest, and he took a shuffling step over to lean against the metal pipe footboard. He dropped his carpetbag and reached out to jiggle her foot. "Lucy?"

Her eyes remained closed. Could he have come all this way to miss her? He'd only wanted to ask for forgiveness. She didn't have to actually give it.

He slipped around the corner of the bed and reached for her hand. Limp and pale but not exactly cold. Perhaps her slack jaw was from deep sleep.

He felt her forehead, then placed his hand against her breastbone. No heartbeat, no rise and fall of her chest. He blew out a breath, and his shoulders slumped as he carefully sat down on the dirty mattress.

Why hadn't he written his apology last month when her letter first arrived? Why hadn't God allowed him to ask for forgiveness? He barely knew the woman he'd spent a few hours with each night for seven months after a long day of homesteading. Six years he'd wasted hating her for leaving him irrevocably alone, and the last four years he'd lived in agony waiting for a chance to—

"She's not there."

He startled and shot off the bed. The woman who'd smacked into him in the alley sat in a rickety chair with her arm around the urchin he'd sidestepped in an effort to avoid being run into.

Had they been racing to Lucy's side at the announcement of her death? He glanced around but saw no one else in the room. He swallowed against the stone lodged in his throat and blinked against the warmth hazing his eyes. "How long has she been dead?"

The woman's escaped dark auburn locks were wild about her face, her cheeks pink from either crying or her brisk run. "My guess would be no more than fifteen minutes."

"Your guess?" He turned to face his wife's motionless, emaciated form. "Was no one with her?"

"No, we found her this way, though death wasn't completely unexpected." She stood and shoved the boy behind her. "And you are?"

"Her husband." He cocked his head at her sudden defensive posturing. "And you?"

The woman's eyes narrowed. "Miss Dawson."

Which meant nothing to him. "A friend of Lucy's?"

"Yes."

That's all she was going to say?

She stepped forward. "Why are you here?"

He pulled on his collar. *Yes, why am I here, Lord? Why now?* He'd spent over ten years alone when his mother had abandoned him at the orphanage, seven months a semicontent but delusional groom, and ten more years as an estranged husband.

And now he was alone again.

"I suppose the Lord wanted me to know of her passing." Not the greatest comfort, being that he was completely abandoned once again, but it was something. "She'd written for help." And she'd definitely needed it. How long had she suffered? Her haggard face indicated a lengthy illness.

"Why didn't you come for her earlier?"

He returned the woman's glare. If her eyes weren't scrunched with accusation and her lips curled with scorn, she'd be heaps prettier. "I suppose you fault me for the month I took to get here? I live in Salt Flatts, Kansas. I couldn't leave my homestead unattended without ruining everything I've worked for. I got somebody to take care of my property as soon as I could, and yet I still . . . missed her."

He'd been walking outside for half an hour.

Was Miss Dawson right? Had he missed apologizing to his wife by fifteen minutes because he'd dragged his feet attempting to settle his nerves?

And why must this strange lady look at him so? What right had she to be mad at him? "Besides being named Miss Dawson, who are you?"

She took one step back, but her chin tilted higher. "So you're not here for any other reason?"

"Do you find evading questions amusing?"

Her eyes narrowed. "I need to know."

"Why must I inform you?" He set his jaw. He'd told her Lucy was his wife, yet Miss Dawson hadn't bothered to offer condolences, just a biting glare.

Her son leaned over to peer at him from behind her, and

Silas sighed. He couldn't chide the boy's mother in front of him. Nor should they be arguing beside a dead woman's bed. He swallowed his pride, something he'd become good at these last ten years, and shrugged. "I came here for no other reason than my wife asked me to." He held out his open hand indicating the door. "Why don't we talk outside?"

He led the way out, holding the door open for the mother and son to follow.

Turning around in the middle of the hallway, Miss Dawson returned to glaring. "Did she say *why* she wanted you to come?"

"I'm assuming now it's because she was sick." He glanced back into the room, noting the blood-speckled handkerchiefs, the tonics on the washstand, the disheveled cot below the window. Who slept there? "Was she not alone?"

"Someone had to care for her. She was dying of consumption. Penniless. Unloved. Beaten down by the life you tossed her into."

He straightened. "I tossed her into?"

"Do you deny sending her away?"

"I do." Why did this woman he'd just met think so poorly of him? "I don't know what she told you, but I never asked her to leave. I wouldn't have. She's all I have in the world." He swallowed hard. "Or had, anyway."

Miss Dawson relaxed, and he frowned. Why would his becoming a widower calm her? Her countenance hadn't struck him as unkind. In fact, she was rather attractive. Maybe not like Lucy—her looks had enamored him from the moment she'd sent him her photograph—but this Miss Dawson's face was pleasing enough.

Well, more than pleasing if he were honest, with her pert nose and softly colored lips. Less than an hour ago, she'd flown past him in a sea of petticoats, hardly slowed by a jarring hit to the shoulder and a near tumble. She didn't look strong, considering her soft feminine form, but her straight back, tilted chin, and peppery words would make any man cautious.

"Well, Mr. . . . I'm sorry, I didn't ask your name."

"Jonesey. Silas Jonesey."

"Ah. Jonesey." She smiled even more. "Mr. Jonesey, I'm sorry if I caused any offense. I wasn't certain you were—"

"Then you're not my real father?"

Miss Dawson stiffened, and the boy came out from behind her.

Silas licked his lips, watching the color drain from Miss Dawson. "I thought he was yours?"

"He is." She glared at the boy and gave him a quick shake of her head. The silencing gesture only made the boy cross his arms.

Silas glanced at Miss Dawson's fingers. No ring. Not that a lack thereof meant anything if they were as poor as they looked. He took a glance at the two of them again. Besides dark-colored hair, there wasn't much resemblance—and the boy's hair had no hint of red. Miss Dawson couldn't be much more than twenty-five maybe, and the boy had to be . . . around nine.

Nine.

If the boy had blond curls, he'd have looked exactly like Lucy must have at that age.

Silas put a hand to his neck and tightened his abdominal muscles against the slurry in his stomach. "I have a son?"

Chapter 2

"If you have to ask whether or not you have a son, I think that answers your question." Kate glared at Anthony to shush the boy—he'd never been good at keeping his mouth shut, but he'd been awfully quiet while Silas had held his dead wife's hand and called her Lucy as if he cared.

But a man who only showed up at his wife's deathbed couldn't care. And if Lucinda had meant this man when she'd told Anthony she'd written his father, he would've known the boy was his.

Mr. Jonesey's eyes flashed fire. "I wouldn't have known if she deliberately kept the information from me."

Had that blaze of anger in his pupils driven Lucinda away? She'd said he kicked her out . . . which he'd denied.

But with Lucinda dead, he could say anything he wanted to.

"Maybe there's a reason you don't know about the boy." Kate glared back at Silas, with his big muscles and scruffy face. She hadn't expected him to be so good looking, not after the way Lucinda described her husband from Kansas as a dirt-poor farmer. She'd need to keep from letting his attractive features make her forget what kind of man he really was.

The muscle under Mr. Jonesey's eye twitched as he held her

gaze. Suddenly his posture softened and he turned to Anthony. "How old are you, son?"

As though calling Anthony *son* proved anything. She tried maneuvering Anthony behind her, but he wouldn't budge.

"Nine almost ten."

Silas stared blankly, likely calculating the plausibility of his fatherhood.

Anthony crossed his arms. "And I'm not going anywhere with you."

That's right, he wasn't going anywhere if she could help it. But he shouldn't sass an elder, even if what he said was true. She steered Anthony to the stairwell. "Why don't you go downstairs and see if Mrs. Grindall has dinner ready?"

"I don't feel like eating." His slumped shoulders and red eyes tore at her, but she needed to talk with Mr. Jonesey alone.

"I know you don't, sweetie. Maybe you can find a cookie?"

He shrugged but turned toward the dim stairwell.

"We should talk while Anthony eats." But no matter what Mr. Jonesey said, she'd not change her mind—the boy wasn't going anywhere with him.

"Should we not fetch someone for . . ." He gestured toward Lucinda's open door but then let his hand drop. The hopeless gesture might have indicated heartbreak, except he'd abandoned his wife for a decade.

"I asked Mr. Sandwood down the hall to find the undertaker so Anthony could have some time to grieve." Yet she'd just sent the boy to eat alone . . . she wasn't starting her parenting off on a stellar foot. "I'm sorry for your loss, Mr. Jonesey." Though he probably didn't view it as much of one. She positively ached to kick him in the shins on Lucinda's behalf.

He moved to lean against the rough wooden wall and looked up at the shadowy ceiling with a glint of wonderment in his eyes. "A son."

"Now, wait a minute." She held out an accusatory finger, which did nothing to gain his attention.

A man shouldn't look all . . . gushy like that. Especially not the kind of man Lucinda described.

She'd not let an innocent-looking expression cause her to let some stranger claim the child she'd grown to love as her own. Silas Jonesey might be just as bad as Richard. "You've no proof he's yours."

"Doesn't matter to me." He shook his head. "I'd take him anyway."

What?

Oh right, Lucinda had said her husband was a taskmaster. One who'd worked his wife into the ground. An orphaned boy would substitute nicely for that thankless position. "No, Lucinda left him in my care."

"I can assume his care." He looked toward the stairwell as if he could see Anthony dragging his feet to the dining hall.

"If you've no proof of being his father, I mean to keep the boy."

He frowned. "Are you married?"

She drew up. "That matters not."

"Sure it does." He glanced back into the room, full of broken furniture and the scant belongings Lucinda possessed. "How could you provide for him better than I?"

She compressed her lips. She'd not tell him she'd been paying for this room for months. The boardinghouse was not impressive, by any means, but Silas hadn't seen the shack they'd lived in previously. "As a teacher, I'm housed with different families every year. Regardless of whose roof might be over our heads, Anthony will be with someone who loves him."

"That's kind of you to be willing to step in, but a boy needs a father."

"Only if he's a loving father. I love Anthony with all my

21

heart. I've sacrificed a lot for him already." She fisted her hands, wishing she could've strangled Silas a decade ago for Lucinda. "No man who marries a woman, makes her his slave, and then kicks her out when she doesn't pass muster should be raising a boy, blood relation or not."

"Now wait a minute." Silas pushed away from the wall. "I don't know what Lucy told you, but that's not me." He puffed his thick chest as if making himself look bigger would scare her.

"She told me you worked her night and day. Barely taking time for her. Treating her worse than her parents' servants."

He flung out his hands. "I don't want to sully your regard for a dead woman, but Lucy's expectations of homesteading were childish. She'd been spoiled in Virginia. Why, she'd never even helped in the kitchen before she came to me, and I certainly didn't force her to answer a mail-order-bride advertisement. She could've stayed in Virginia and found a husband there."

Silas took a step toward her, all broad shouldered and masculine, but she wouldn't back down. She tilted her head to glare up at him. Why did men think mail-order brides should accept whatever fate awaited them? "She was your bride, not your slave."

"She insisted on coming at planting season, and I . . ." He glanced back through the doorway into Lucinda's room, then shook his head. "When I saw the photo she sent me, I couldn't deny her." His eyes snapped back to hers. "Have you worked on a farm, Miss . . . What's your name again?"

"Dawson. Kate Dawson."

"Well, Miss Dawson. I know teachers work hard to keep children disciplined and learning, but have you ever been at the mercy of the land for your existence? Where weather, insects, coyotes, and grub-infected dirt could cause you to starve during the winter if you aren't diligent to till enough land or sow enough seed?"

"No."

"Then you don't know what real work is. And neither did Lucy."

Her fists tightened, nails biting into her palms. "Don't presume my past from a tidbit of personal information." She forced her clenched jaw to soften before her teeth shattered with the pressure. "I've worked far harder in my twenty-five years than most, down on my hands and knees, dawn to dusk, against my will."

All because of a man like him.

Silas cocked his head.

"And so has Anthony." She was done with men who thought they could run weaker people's lives. "When Lucinda took to her bed over a year ago, Anthony worked at the laundry for a time to help me keep a roof over their heads. I'll not allow him to quit school to labor like that again. He's got a bright mind, not to be wasted on—"

"I know what it's like to work as a child. I worked at Wilson's Mill when I was ten until twelve—no child should work the hours I did, or the jobs. But since the beginning of time children have helped parents with farm chores. It's not anything like how they're treated in factories. . . ." He closed his eyes. His hand, seemingly shaky, rubbed at his brow.

"Wilson's? The huge woolen mill the next town over?" He was from this area?

Silas nodded.

She let out a breath. So he'd had a hard time of it as a child. But if that were so, how would he know what a childhood should be like? She'd had a great one until her twelfth year—she wouldn't let Anthony lose his the way she had hers. "Farming might not be terrible altogether, but many of my students struggle to attend school regularly because of their parents' need for them to work."

"I won't deny him school."

Wait. Why were they even debating? Arguments were mere words; they proved nothing. He might not even be Anthony's father. "Maybe so, but as you heard, Anthony wants to stay with me."

Silas put a hand to his jaw and rubbed.

Had reminding him of Anthony's desire given him pause, or was he preparing a different argument?

If her sister had been here, she'd be sending her evil glares. Violet had always accused her of arguing for argument's sake and chastened her to hold her tongue, and maybe avoid another beating from Violet's heavy-handed husband.

Of course, losing an argument with her brother-in-law only landed her in the attic with a bruised body. If she couldn't win this one, Anthony's life was at risk. Mourning his mother was more than enough for him to deal with right now. "So we agree. Anthony's desire to remain with me needs to be adhered to—"

"No, we don't agree. I was just trying to figure out how I'd earned your ire."

"You don't think Lucinda would've told me about you?"

"I don't think she *could* have. She didn't know me."

Didn't know him? What did that mean? She was his wife. "So I'm to ignore everything she ever said about you and pretend you're a saint?"

"I'm no saint."

She crossed her arms. "Well good. We agree on something."

He chuckled, and she blinked. Her brother-in-law never would've laughed during an argument.

"I do believe you could sear off skin quicker than a firebrand."

"What?"

"Right. You're not a farm girl." He rubbed his hand over his face. "Look, I think we've gotten off the tracks and bogged ourselves in a mud pit. Let's start over. I know you've feelings for the boy, and Lucy probably did ask you to see after him, but he's likely mine. The fact of the matter is, I'll be the most capable of providing for—"

"Children need more than food and clothing. They need to be loved for who they are, not what they can do."

"Of course they do—"

"I can provide for Anthony. I assure you." She straightened, trying to add at least an inch in height. "I can offer him what he needs most."

"In the future, he'll need more than love, Miss Dawson. He'll need to learn how to work, and —"

"Exactly why he can't go with you!" She sliced her hand through the air. "I won't let you get ahold of Anthony and *teach* him how to work the way you taught his mother. Over my dead body."

Silas flinched at the dead body reference.

Kate slapped a hand over her mouth.

He tried not to imagine Lucy's form lying beneath her thread-bare sheet on the other side of the wall, but failed.

She dropped her hand and cleared her throat. "I think I might have gotten a little carried away there."

He'd heard redheaded women could be spitfires, but this woman only had a hint of auburn in her tangled locks. Good thing God saved the world from the wrath of a full-blown red-headed Kate Dawson.

He wasn't close to righteous—he basically fouled the air standing beside anything godly. Still, that didn't mean he wasn't right for the boy. But how to convince this pretty little firebrand to give up her claim?

"I know I'm a stranger to you and Anthony, but if you consider

25

the situation practically, a man's protection and provision will give him the best future."

"I don't worry about tomorrow. 'For the morrow shall take thought for the things of itself.'"

A Scripture-spouting woman. "True. We shouldn't worry about tomorrow, but that doesn't mean we shouldn't plan for it."

"I won't let Anthony live with a man who treated his mother so poorly. Do you deny it?"

"That I treated her poorly?" He sighed and ran a hand through his hair. "No."

"Then Anthony won't be a part of your future. Excuse me." Kate marched toward the stairwell, where a flicker of movement caught his attention in the shadows.

Anthony.

The boy's eyes narrowed before he disappeared down the stairs.

Had they said anything the boy shouldn't have overheard?

His feet urged him to go talk to the boy, but what could he say right now, when Miss Dawson was clearly not in the right frame of mind to hold a genial conversation? Whatever had he done to make Lucy paint him so badly to her friend and son? He might not have been the best husband, but he certainly hadn't been an evil one either.

When the sound of both of their footsteps faded, he entered Lucy's room and crossed over to her bed, taking a long look at her sad, still form. Would Kate return with Anthony, or would she take him away so he couldn't find him? He shouldn't have let them out of his sight.

But he couldn't abandon his wife with the coroner on the way either.

Nothing about Anthony's features shouted that he was his offspring, but if his praying for the last four years hadn't gained him the forgiveness he'd sought from his wife, surely God was consoling him with the one thing he wanted even more.

A family.

He pulled the threadbare sheet up to cover his wife's motionless form.

If this Kate Dawson thought heated words would deter him from raising the boy, she was mistaken.

Chapter 3

Shivering in the ice-cold drizzle, Kate eyed Silas across the open grave. He wasn't the tallest person in the small group gathered to see Lucinda interred, but he certainly was the broadest. Farm work had to be demanding to bulk up a man like that.

The pastor called for silent prayer while the gravedigger covered the coffin. Kate squeezed Anthony's cold hand and stared at their feet.

Lord, please help me figure out how to deal with Mr. Jonesey. I can't let Anthony go unless I know he's going with someone who'll care for him—I just can't.

A flicker of movement across the way made Kate peek from her prayer. Silas wasn't praying like the rest of them—he was walking. Was he leaving? Hopefully.

She pulled Anthony closer, his right shoulder damp from jutting out from beneath her small umbrella, his little frame shivering. She rubbed her hand briskly against his well-worn, too-short sleeve, keeping her eye on Silas.

Please help me know what to do. I mean, Lucinda knew who Anthony's father was, yet she wanted him left in my care. That has to mean something. How can I let a stranger take a boy who's already escaped one man's loveless household, to live with another who's more likely to give him a hoe than a hug?

Last night, she'd found Anthony in the stairwell though she'd told him to go downstairs. She couldn't chastise him for eavesdropping though; the poor kid was likely more uncertain about his future than she was.

He hadn't been impressed with Silas and had begged her not to let him take him home.

She'd fully expected Silas to put up a fuss when she told him she was taking Anthony to stay with her at the Logans' last night, but he'd said that was a good idea.

What if he wasn't the man Lucinda had painted him to be? Or what if he truly was Anthony's father? Could she let this precious boy go? She held Anthony tighter with each step Silas took.

He walked straight toward Anthony while pulling off his slicker.

"What are you—" Kate bit her lip. Her strangled voice had ruptured the reverent silence and drawn people's narrow-eyed glares.

Silas walked behind them and wrapped the coat around Anthony. The boy tried to shrug the slicker off with exaggerated movements, but she squeezed his hand.

"Be civil," she whispered into his ear. They shouldn't cause a scene, and well, Anthony needed the warmth. He was too skinny and his coat inadequate.

"Thank you for coming." Reverend Beasley finally nodded from his reverie. "I'm sure Lucinda's son would welcome your prayers and condolences, and her husband as well."

A few looked at them in surprise. Their gazes locked onto Silas. Did they wonder why he'd bothered to come when he'd left Lucinda alone for so long?

Yet there he stood, coatless with no umbrella, acting as if the rain and cold didn't bother him, staring at his wife's resting place, his hands shoved deep inside his pockets, as if warmth could be found inside his pants' soggy fabric.

What a pitiful sight he was. If she had a hat, she'd have handed him her umbrella.

Mr. Yi, the owner of the laundry, walked over first. He held out his hand to Silas. "I'm sorry for your loss, Mr. Riverton."

Silas grasped the man's hand but said nothing to correct Mr. Yi about his name.

"Sorry about your mother." Mr. Yi laid a lye-scarred hand on Anthony's shoulder. "I wish I could have employed her for longer time, but it is good thing you have an angel." He grasped Kate's hand and pressed something into her palm. He threw a glance at Silas before leaning closer, the smell of onions and cloves residing in his skin. "Please use this for care of boy," he whispered. "I wish I had more to give you."

At least Mr. Yi knew who the boy should stay with. "Yes, sir. I'll do my best."

"I'm sorry, young man." Mr. Kingfisher, the school superintendent, appeared next. After clapping Anthony on the shoulder, he turned to her. "I need to talk with you, Miss Dawson."

"Now? In the rain?" Kate's heartbeat ramped up at the tone of his voice. The two times Mr. Kingfisher had condescended to talk with her was to award her the teaching position despite her lack of credentials and to complain about her classroom's lack of tidiness.

She'd left her school chores unfinished to run to Lucinda's deathbed, but surely Mr. Kingfisher wouldn't chastise her for dusty classroom corners at a funeral. Unless Miss Jennings complained again. "This isn't the most convenient time for me to talk—"

"We can just step aside here." He threw a sidelong glance toward Anthony.

Silas stepped closer to Anthony. "It's all right." He nodded at them both, as if they were in agreement.

"Miss Dawson?" Mr. Kingfisher held out his elbow.

A couple stood dripping in front of them, staring at her as they waited patiently to talk to Anthony.

Kate squeezed his shoulder. "I won't be long."

Under a nearby oak, Mr. Kingfisher shook off his umbrella. "Nasty weather we're having for the end of September."

"Yes." She didn't care about the weather. Every funeral should be dreary. "I'm sorry, but why do we need to talk so badly you pulled me away from a grieving child?"

He shifted his weight. "The Logans came to me this morning wanting to be clear on what they'd signed up for."

"What they'd signed up for?" Her stomach tightened into a knot. This didn't sound promising.

"It's difficult to get families to take in our teachers. We don't have enough money to raise your salaries, so rooming with families is your best option."

Was he trying to make her feel like a burden?

"The Logans signed up to keep and feed you—just you, not a little boy as well."

She stared at her hands. The Logans had been nicer than the Ishams last year, but they definitely acted put out with her presence. "I haven't told them yet, but I intend to compensate them for Anthony's food."

"They aren't excited about entertaining a boy with a house full of daughters either."

So if they'd had a son, they would've allowed Anthony to live with them? "I suppose I'll move into the boardinghouse, then." There went the money to buy him a new coat and shoes and updates for her wardrobe.

Mr. Kingfisher sighed. "I know you've grown attached to the boy, but since his father has shown up—"

"Did Mr. Jonesey tell you he was the father?"

Mr. Kingfisher's mouth puckered. "I'd assumed."

"He didn't even know about the boy." She glanced back at Silas and froze.

Behind Silas loomed a man she'd never wanted to see again. *Richard.*

"Excuse me." Could this nightmare get any worse? She picked up her skirts and sprinted toward them.

Silas stood behind Anthony as a woman tried to squeeze the boy in two.

Richard moved toward Anthony the moment the woman let go.

Sliding in mud, Kate almost tripped over a headstone. "Silas!"

He startled and looked at her in surprise.

Who cared that she'd used his Christian name? Didn't he hear the alarm in her voice?

Richard doffed his well-worn felt hat, leaving his dark hair a bit ruffled, and gestured toward the fresh grave. "Sorry about your mother, son. Say good-bye to your friend now, so we can get you packed."

"What?" Silas pulled Anthony to him.

Finally he did something worthwhile.

"Mr. Fitzgerald." Kate rushed between them. "Don't you lay a finger on Anthony."

The man's smile melted into a scowl. "Forgive me, but I have no idea who you are."

"That hardly matters."

He slapped his hat back onto his head. "Seeing that you're standing between me and my son, it does."

Despite her heart leaping in and out of her throat, she worked to make sure her breathlessness wouldn't mar her voice. "He's not yours."

"Of course he is."

"No, Lucinda told me different."

The man took a menacing step toward her, and Silas's hand grasped her shoulder.

Richard stopped, taking in the sight of Silas's hands on both Kate and Anthony. "Who are you?"

That was the question, wasn't it?

"Lucinda's husband," Silas said.

"He's Anthony's father," Kate added. The only thing that could possibly send this man back to where he came from.

Richard blinked.

Kate stepped forward, hands on hips. "Now leave."

His glassy eyes reminded her of her last intended—bright with drink. "I don't know who you are, lady, but you've no right to keep my boy."

"As I said, he's not yours. Besides, the way you treated Anthony and Lucinda is plenty enough reason to keep him from you."

The man's face screwed up. "I treated the boy no worse than my own father did me." He glared at Anthony. "Come here, son."

Kate shoved him between her and Silas.

The man's eyes narrowed. "I said come here." He tried to dodge Kate to reach for the boy, but Silas blocked him.

"Excuse me?" All of them startled at the reverend's voice. "Is something the matter?"

Richard pointed to where Anthony now hid behind Silas's broad frame. "That boy's mine and they're refusing to give him to me."

Silas shook his head. "We need proof he's the father before we hand him over."

"Hand him over?" Kate scoffed. "Never." She'd not let him go with Richard, even if he paid her.

The reverend held out a hand. "Let's think things through here."

33

"There's nothing to think through, Reverend." Kate shook her head. "Richard abused Anthony and his mother, and he's not an upstanding citizen considering he . . ." She glanced back at Anthony and grimaced. He knew his mother hadn't been the best parent, but she didn't want to explain too much either. "Well, Lucinda is . . . was married to Silas. He's her husband, not this man."

"Doesn't negate the fact that the boy's mine," Richard blustered.

"No, he's not, and even if he was, you can't have him," Kate said, reaching behind her to grasp onto Anthony. She caught his upper arm and squeezed, hoping the pressure felt reassuring instead of desperate.

"Seems we've got quite the tangle."

"No tangle, Reverend." Richard glared at Silas. "You really think you're his pa?" His sneer made her skin prickle. "You weren't man enough to keep Lucinda happy, so she came to me. And I took quite good care of her."

The suggestive expression on the man's face needed to be knocked off.

"I'm not going anywhere with you." Anthony's voice trembled but held conviction.

"It might not be what you want, kid, but it's how it's going to be."

"You'll not strong-arm the boy anywhere when your claim to Anthony is as shaky as . . . as it is." Goodness, she'd almost admitted Silas had no proof of him being the father either—which he didn't, but maybe they could find something . . . anything.

Lord, if there's any way I can keep Anthony from going back with Richard, even if it's by proving the boy belongs to some other man, lead us to it.

"I think it would be best if you don't play tug-of-war with

34

the boy." The reverend stepped closer to Richard. "Why don't we take this matter to the law?"

The law? She licked her lips. Would simply informing the judge of the stories Lucinda had told her be enough to keep Anthony away from Richard?

"A court would see things my way." Richard crossed his arms over his chest. "I've raised the boy, even my wife knows about him. Just because Lucy fed these people lies doesn't mean I'm not the father."

She began to tremble. Was he right? She glanced at Anthony, who looked as worried as she felt. No, the stories about how he treated them were true, otherwise Anthony wouldn't look so pale.

"There should be no trouble, then, but the boy seems to want to stay with the lady." The reverend threw a sympathetic glance toward Anthony.

"She's intent on keeping him from me."

As a gambler, Richard likely knew what a sure bet that was.

The reverend looked at her. "Will you give your word you'll not take off with the boy?"

She tensed. A pastor asking her to give her word quelled the lie about to roll off her tongue. She'd defy the law if she thought it better for Anthony, but to defy a man of God?

Her muscles ached to rush off with the boy that very instant. She couldn't outrun Richard with Anthony in tow though.

Silas touched her on the shoulder. "It'd be best for Anthony to have a definite answer about who he belongs with."

Was there a chance that they'd get such an answer? But if a court declared Richard had no right to the boy, then she'd only have to worry about Silas, who just might be convinced to leave the boy with her in the end. She nodded. "We'll wait for a court decision, then."

Silas didn't know whether to smile or frown. Kate might have agreed to wait for a judge's decision, but he didn't doubt she'd run afterwards if the decision was in Mr. Fitzgerald's favor. Was there a chance the judge would rule in Silas's favor?

Would she run away with the boy if that happened?

"If I have to get a judge to settle this, then so be it." Richard ducked his head and caught Anthony's eye. "I'm getting a room at the boardinghouse. I'll catch you if you run from me again."

"Fine. You do that." Kate snagged Anthony from behind Silas and marched toward the street.

The boy certainly had broad shoulders, and his rain-slicked hair revealed two cowlicks much like Silas's own. But the boy looked more like his mother than him or Mr. Fitzgerald.

His insides flopped. The boy probably wasn't his . . . but if Kate wanted to keep him away from this man, he'd not mention his doubts. He trusted her love for the boy over any man's word.

The reverend cleared his throat. "I'd suggest you two go to the authorities tomorrow morning and get yourself a date for a hearing."

Silas nodded. "We'll do that."

The shorter man's mouth twitched and turned into a sneer. "Going to tuck your tail between your legs now and cower behind your woman?"

Silas swallowed a retort. He'd not let the man goad him into an argument. And it might be a good thing for Richard to think Kate belonged with him. "I'm going to see them safely home."

The man rolled his eyes and snagged a flask from his coat's inner pocket.

The urge to ask him for a drink welled up within Silas, but he tightened his hands and pressed his lips together.

Richard took a swig, then wiped his mouth with the back of his hand. "Tell that woman she better spend all the time she wants with Anthony, because she won't be seeing him again."

36

He screwed the flask's cap back on and tucked the container away. "You and I both know he ain't yours."

"We'll see." Silas turned to the reverend and shook his hand. "Thanks for coming to help us."

"I'll be praying for you both." He turned to offer his hand to Richard, but the man ignored it.

"Your prayers are worthless, Reverend."

"Would you care to enlighten me over dinner?" The reverend smiled. "The wife's cooking a pot pie. I've heard the boarding-house's fare leaves something to be desired. Might as well have something good before you get yourself a room."

"Don't want a sermon with my dinner."

"Then I won't offer one." He turned and gave Silas a small smile before he gestured for Richard to follow him. "The parsonage is this way. Please join us."

The man grunted. "Fine."

Silas ran after Kate, who was about to turn the corner three blocks ahead. Anthony trudged beside her, Silas's coat hanging off his shoulders, dragging in the mud.

When he caught up, Anthony turned to look at him. "Is Pa right? Will a judge tell me I have to go back with him?"

Kate hugged him against her. "I won't let you go."

"But if they say I have to?"

He needed the whole story from Kate before he could answer. After his encounter with Richard, he certainly had no good feelings toward the man.

But the boy needed hope at the moment. "Maybe they'll rule that you should go home with me."

Anthony stopped and shook his head. "I don't want to go with you neither. I want to stay with Miss Dawson."

He took in a deep breath. "I'm afraid a judge would probably choose between me and Mr. Fitzgerald."

"Why do you want me? So I can do your chores?"

"No. I've done them alone for years. I don't need someone for that." Silas put a hand on Anthony's shoulder. "I'd love to have a son. I've never had a family. Your mother was the closest I ever got."

Anthony jerked his shoulder away. "I'm Pa's only son, but he still treated the dog better than me. Mother said you weren't any better than him anyway."

A sucker punch right to the gut. He knew he hadn't been the best husband, but had alcohol corrupted him more than he remembered? Had his eyes been as empty as Richard's while he discussed people as if they were pawns to manipulate instead of loved ones to care for? "No, that can't be true," he rasped.

They turned the corner and Anthony ran toward the boardinghouse stairwell, tripping on the overly long coat. "Leave me alone."

"Wait." Silas jogged after him but stopped at the bottom of the steps as the boy disappeared inside. He likely needed time alone.

Silas rubbed his hand along the smooth handrail and waited for Kate to catch up.

She stopped near him, her reddish tresses fallen and plastered against her cheeks. "Is it true? Did you treat Lucinda no better?"

He shook his head. "I don't know how Mr. Fitzgerald treated them, but I never hurt her, not with my hands anyway, but . . ." Above the crowded rooftops, the smoky remnants left by a train maneuvering through the many towns surrounding Independence hung low and wispy. He needed Kate on his side if they had any hope of a judge choosing to give the boy to him.

But anything but the truth would be a lie. "I drank. I don't know if I remember everything I did while drunk, but I don't drink anymore."

"How long since you drank last?"

Oh, God, please keep me from drinking ever again, especially if Anthony comes home with me. "Four years this time."

"This time?"

He swallowed. "Yes."

She only looked at him. Did she believe him? Considering he could almost feel her abhorrence for Richard, who obviously drank, would she lump him into the same category?

He likely deserved it if she did.

But he still needed to hear what she knew about Lucy and this other man. Was there a chance Richard wasn't Anthony's father, or was he just latching on to the hope that he indeed had one person in this world to call family? "If we want to keep Anthony away from Mr. Fitzgerald, you better tell me everything you know."

"Fine." She sighed and lowered herself onto the stoop. "I met Lucinda and Anthony in Hartfield two years ago."

"Where's Hartfield?"

"A two-days' ride north of here. Richard gambles a lot. He was good to her whenever he was winning, gave her dresses and jewelry, whatever she wanted. We figured we could always sell Lucinda's things if needed, but we never expected her to get sick. The medicines she needed, the medicines she kept trying . . . nothing worked." She pulled her shawl tighter. "The doctors started demanding payment before they'd even come to see her. We ran out of stuff to sell."

"So she must have written Mr. Fitzgerald to request money, like she did me."

"How could she?" Kate shook her head as if trying to convince herself he was wrong. "It would've been better if we'd let Anthony steal."

"What?"

"Anthony's a pickpocket, a good one—though I won't let him do it. Lucinda and I didn't even know he was until a few months ago. We didn't have enough to pay the landlord, and Lucinda cried when I told her we had to sell her last ring. I took it to sell, but I lost it—or at least I thought I did. Anthony stayed home sick and when I came back after school to see if I'd dropped it, they were counting a stack of money, and two men's pocket watches lay on the counter and . . . and I thought the worst of Lucinda."

Given Lucy's situation with Richard, he'd have thought she'd sold herself too.

"When I got upset, Anthony said, 'Maybe I shouldn't have picked so much.'" Kate tipped her head back and looked blankly at the clouds. "Evidently whenever Richard lost, he'd get drunk and go into a tirade . . ." She sighed, the simple action dripping with weariness. "So Anthony figured if he made up for the losses, Richard wouldn't hurt them anymore. But from then on, Richard expected him to always make up for his losses."

"So even if we prove I'm Anthony's father—"

"I'm not so sure Richard would leave him behind without a fight."

Chapter 4

Silas trudged up the boardinghouse's front stairs. He'd sent a telegram to Lucy's parents, so now he'd go through her things looking for some hint that he was Anthony's father.

After going to the courthouse with Richard, he'd consulted a lawyer who told him without proof of parenthood or abuse, Anthony was at the mercy of a judge's discernment.

Surely God had orchestrated his being here to rescue the boy. If not, he was going to be in the same position as Miss Dawson next week: emotionally attached to someone he couldn't keep.

He'd attached himself to Lucy far too quickly—and she'd left him heartbroken.

But how could he not want to help this little boy?

If the judge ruled for Richard, having to pickpocket to keep his father happy was not a position any boy should find himself in. Though would that be better than being abandoned at an orphanage as Silas had been?

Maybe. He'd certainly longed to have known just one relative—to feel loved.

Should he bring up the boy's pickpocketing in court, or would that cause Anthony more trouble?

Stepping inside the stifling boardinghouse, Silas shrugged off his coat lest he die of heat exhaustion.

A young black maid, slumped over with firewood, entered through a side door.

"Good afternoon, miss."

She startled and cast her eyes to the ground. "Sir." A log on top rolled forward, and she barely tilted back fast enough to keep it atop the stack.

"Let me get that for you." He held out his arms, but the maid, who couldn't have been much older than Anthony—twelve, maybe—took a step away from him.

Her big dark eyes blinked as if he'd asked her the impossible, wariness seeping from her every pore. "I've got it just fine, mister."

He pried the load from her anyway, tempted to take the wood right back outside since the building needed no more heat, but he headed for the kitchen and dropped the logs by the stove. "There."

She'd followed him in, her full, almost plum-colored lips fidgeted with worry. "Obliged." The girl scuttled back out into the hallway.

He went after her. "Excuse me, miss."

She stopped short and submissively hung her head.

He reached into his pocket and pulled out a silver dollar. "I'd like to give you this."

"I don't want your money." She took a step back, her eyes narrowing. "I only work downstairs."

His face grew hot. "That's not what I meant. I'd intended to give this to you earlier . . . but I got sidetracked. It's in appreciation for your kindness. I noticed you cleaned my wife's room while we were at the funeral—I know that's not your job and Mrs. Grindall wouldn't pay you to do so."

"I didn't do it for money, sir. I only figured Anthony'd be too sad to clean. He shares his candy with me, so I figured I could do it. Wasn't too much work."

"I'd still like you to take it." He held out his hand, the silver coin smack in the middle of his palm.

She looked over her shoulder before stuffing it in her pocket. "Are you his father?"

"I hope so."

"I hope so too. Mrs. Riverton didn't treat me so nice. Maybe you're where Anthony gets his friendliness."

He gave her a sad smile, not certain if he should apologize on his wife's behalf or not.

"And you both got that dimple."

He frowned. "I don't have dimples."

"No, just one—shows up when you smile."

"Myrtle!" The proprietress's screechy yell startled them both. Mrs. Grindall barreled out of the kitchen doorway and scowled. "Don't be pestering the boarders. Get back to work."

"Yes, ma'am." Myrtle ducked her head and disappeared down the hallway.

"Can I help you with something?" Mrs. Grindall swooshed toward him like a big ugly crow, the harsh black of her skirts swinging stiffly.

He refused to back up for a woman more than a half a foot shorter than him, no matter how permanent her scowl. "Do you know when school's out?"

"Soon, I suppose. Never had little ones."

He pulled out his timepiece. Five past two. He should've asked Kate when they'd return. "Thank you anyway."

After going up the stairs, he knocked on Anthony's door, though he didn't expect him to be inside. He'd walked the boy to school that morning despite his protests.

Anthony had the right to grieve . . . but he also had to live. So Silas had prodded him out the door despite the boy's grumbling and exaggerated scowl. Perhaps it was wrong to send a mourning child to school, but he wanted him to have as much time as possible with Miss Dawson before he had to leave . . . hopefully with him instead of Richard.

Silas pushed against the slightly open door and took a seat on Anthony's small cot. He'd spent the Lord's Day in prayer, but today, he needed to start looking for the answer to those prayers.

He rifled through the rickety end table's drawers but found no papers. The battered chest held nothing but the boy's clothing. The wardrobe was half empty.

Peeping under the bed, he reached for several dark lumps. He pulled out a writing desk and two shallow boxes covered in cobwebs. One contained several books. Dust fluffed the air as he flipped through them, but nothing was tucked within their pages. How miserably sick she must have been to not even be able to read.

How wretched for a little boy to watch his mother die.

Silas set aside the books and checked the desk. None of the papers were written on, and the paper compartment was dustier than the books, yet the writing surface had been recently wiped clean. Must have been for the letters she'd written him and Richard. Had her parents told him the truth about never hearing from her during all the years he'd written from Kansas? The writing desk seemed to confirm she wasn't much for writing.

The other box contained what appeared to be journals.

His jittery fingers opened the pages of the book atop the pile and turned to the last page.

September 15, 1885

Things wouldn't be so terrible if that sorry excuse for a maid could be bothered to get Dr. Upton's tea up here. Though I need out of this bed more than I need that tea. Anthony's probably keeping her busy with his prattle,

though I've told him a hundred times to stop talking to
her. He's hopeless.

    Oh, please let Kate come tonight. I need the distraction.
I've coughed more blood today than all last week.

Silas wiped the crate with his shirt before setting it on the bed.
He stared at the journals. Her entries might answer questions
that had plagued him for a decade. Not long ago, he'd finally
forgiven himself for the dark days of his alcoholism. Each day
he abstained from drink and offered his broken self to God,
he'd slowly found peace, despite becoming increasingly certain
Lucy had left him for good.

Was he ready to discover why she'd abandoned him? Would
he have to fight for peace all over again?

What if he discovered Anthony wasn't his . . . Silas wiped
his sweaty palms down his shirt to press against his stomach
where his heartbeat had suddenly sunk.

"What are you doing?"

Miss Dawson stood in the open doorway looking down her
nose at him, hands on hips, lips puckered. Did her students have
difficulty suppressing smiles at that seriously stern look? Mrs.
Grindall would certainly look scary sporting such an expression,
but Kate was too petite and youthful to pull it off effectively.

"Going through Lucy's things. Found her journals, our best
bet to find anything." He picked up the crate. "There's plenty
to keep me reading for a while."

Anthony walked in, carrying two carpetbags, which he
dropped at the end of the bed with a thud.

Silas raised his eyebrows. "What's all this?"

"I'm moving in with Anthony."

"I thought you lived with a student's family."

"With Richard taking a room down the hallway, I figured
it'd be best I stay with Anthony."

He shrugged. He'd kept his door open all night listening, but it wouldn't hurt for someone to be in the room with the boy, and since Anthony still didn't want much to do with him, Kate sleeping here would be better than forcing the boy to his room.

She looked at the stack of journals. "How many are there?"

"Ten."

"Not so bad. If I took a few, we could have them done before the weekend."

He swallowed. He'd not thought she'd be reading them. There were certainly things in his past he'd not want her or anybody to know. "I'll handle them."

She gave him a look that proved he didn't want her to think of him any worse than she already did.

Kate woke with a start, the sun hitting her directly in the eyes. She blinked toward the window. That's why—no curtains. She yawned and looked over at Anthony, who was sitting on his cot, staring out the window. Dressed.

Wait.

"What time is it?"

"A quarter 'til seven."

"A quarter 'til?" She flung off the inadequate bedspread and shivered. The board expected teachers to be prim, proper, and punctual, but her hair never behaved, even after half an hour of arranging. "Why didn't you wake me?"

"I didn't think my teacher needed me to wake her."

She scrambled to her bag and pulled out her stockings and other underthings. "Have you eaten breakfast?"

"Didn't feel like it."

Taking a quick look around, she was confronted with the same reality as last night. "I guess you'll need to sit in the hall."

46

At least it was likely warmer out there. "How did this room get so cold?"

He shrugged. "There's a gap under the window. Mother doesn't want me to leave the door cracked open at night like we do during the day, so it gets cold." He hopped off his cot and grabbed his coat. "Guess I'll start walking to school since I hafta go."

"Yes, you have to." She grabbed him and kissed his forehead. "One day at a time, Anthony."

The moment he left, she shed her dressing robe and unbuttoned her nightgown. Did this boardinghouse have any suites? Could she afford two rooms? Not if she was going to clothe the boy and maintain her wardrobe.

Brushing her hair as quickly as possible, she debated over arriving at school late or spending the time to put up her hair. Neither tardiness nor a messy updo would make the board happy. Not that they ever dropped by, but Miss Jennings, the teacher across the hallway, seemed to make it her personal duty to tattle on the "pretty young thing" who hadn't taken the state's teacher exam but rather passed the one the local school board had created on the spot.

And she didn't need the extra scrutiny—a natural teacher she was not. Especially when she sympathized with the children whose focus waned because they had to work at home instead of play. How many times had her own teachers pegged her hair to the wall, forcing her to stand on tiptoe in front of the whole class because all she wanted to do was sleep or go outside and run the hills like she had before her mother died?

Kate's much-older sister's husband had treated his ward more like an acquired maid than a child in need of love—so whenever she'd been allowed to go to school, studying had been difficult.

Though, thankfully, she'd learned enough to pass that teacher test.

She batted at her wrinkled skirt and splashed cold water onto her puffy eyelids. If only she hadn't stayed up late looking through Lucinda's things. She twisted her hair up tight and poked in pins haphazardly.

After grabbing her schoolbooks, she raced down the hallway and tromped down the stairs, silently apologizing to the people still trying to sleep. Once she made the alleyway, she sprinted toward the schoolhouse, cringing at the way the pins pulled against her hair and the loosened tendrils tickled her neck.

She ignored people's stares as she ran faster. Even if the board overlooked her being late—which they likely wouldn't if they heard of it—she shouldn't leave her pupils unsupervised for long. Hopefully she'd arrive before any of them alerted another teacher. Surely Anthony would tell them she was coming.

She slowed when she hit the block before the school and took in deep draughts of air to cool her face and settle her lungs. At the school's front door, she used the glass's reflection to repin her wild tresses as best she could. If she gained her room without the other teachers seeing her, she could rearrange her hair before first recess. Oh, why hadn't she brought along a brush?

Releasing one long, steady exhale, she pushed on the door and walked into the foyer, through the quiet hall, and toward her silent room. Considering the lack of noise, her students were evidently behaving themselves. How lovely. Her hard work at disciplining had gained her something. Not only could they behave when necessary, but today, they didn't call attention to her absence.

She opened her classroom door and smiled at the back of their bent heads. "Good morning, class."

"Good morning, Miss—"

"Where've you been, Miss Dawson?" Mr. Kingfisher stood behind her desk.

Kate's heart skipped two and a half beats. "What—" She pressed her mouth closed. Questioning the superintendent's presence would not be wise. "I mean . . . I . . . I'm late."

"Obviously, but why?"

She darted a glance at Anthony, who gave her a wide-eyed look. Had he not given her excuses? But what would he have said? *"My teacher's a slug-a-bed?"*

"I fear I was unaccustomed to . . ." At the quiet snicker of her biggest troublemaker, she straightened. "If you would join me in the hallway, Mr. Kingfisher, I'll give you an explanation." She turned on her heel and strode out.

Why, oh why, had the superintendent chosen to visit her classroom today? He'd never checked on her before. Maybe if she returned his attention to his original purpose, he'd forget her tardiness.

When he stepped into the hallway, she shut the door behind them. "What brought you here today, Mr. Kingfisher?"

"The Logans informed me you've moved out." He crossed his arms. Since he was at least a foot taller than she was, his gesture made her feel smaller than usual.

"Yes, I settled into the boardinghouse last night." She smiled as wide as her lips would allow, trying to keep anxiety from showing in her eyes. "I didn't know I had to inform you, but—"

"Do you make a habit of being late, looking as disheveled as you do?"

She clasped her hands together tightly to keep from spinning a finger into the untidy locks of hair tickling her shoulders. "This is the first time I've been late. I suppose I didn't adjust well to sleeping at the boardinghouse. I didn't have—"

"I'd hoped our talk at the funeral would've settled this, Miss Dawson. I suppose this boardinghouse is the one that houses Anthony Riverton?"

"Yes."

49

"You told me taking on a child would not hinder your teaching."

"It hasn't—"

"I know you're softhearted and don't discipline the students as much as I'd like, but this is too much. You cannot take him on."

"The first day of adjustment doesn't mean I'll continue having difficulty. Check on me every day if you must, and I assure you, I'll be punctual."

"You better be, Miss Dawson, or you'll find yourself being asked to give up the position instead of the boy."

She attempted to swallow, but her throat refused to work. She couldn't lose this job. If Anthony ended up going with Silas, she couldn't put herself in the same position as she'd been in Hartfield, so desperate for security she'd almost married a drunk. "I promise, I'll give you no reason to chastise me from here on out."

Chapter 5

"Thank you." Silas smiled at young Myrtle as she set his plate in front of him.

She gave him the same wide-eyed stare she gave him every morning when he thanked her—which was precisely what he should do since she was highly efficient. The moment he sat at one of the three rickety tables in the boardinghouse's dining area, she placed a plate in front of him. Even arriving earlier than normal this morning, she'd gotten him breakfast immediately.

He wasn't hungry yet, but yesterday he'd slept in after reading late and missed Anthony and Kate before they headed to school. And evidently, they'd skipped breakfast the day before, perhaps because of Richard.

He'd stay the whole three hours of breakfast if necessary to make sure Richard didn't keep them from eating.

He yawned a greeting to a man walking past him and leaned back to wait. He'd learned a lot about Anthony's teacher, Richard, and Lucy from her journals. Her embittered words and complaint-filled pages made him wonder why Kate had befriended her. Lucy might not have admired Kate, but she hadn't slandered her either—which was high praise coming from Lucy's pen.

Richard walked in the door, face scruffy, eyes dark-rimmed, a slight off-color tone to his skin. The man frowned at the lack of places to sit that weren't at Silas's table.

As much as he wished to tell the man not to sit with him, he hadn't the right to tell another lodger he couldn't eat breakfast.

The man plunked down to his left, the smell of bay rum and body odor overwhelming. "You still here? I'd thought you'd wise up and realize you're wasting your time."

"There's a bathhouse down the street on Pine and Fourth, in case you didn't know. Might not want to offend the judge's nose if you're looking for a favorable ruling."

The man scratched at his stomach and stretched. Silas tried not to gag at the smell wafting from his shirt's now-exposed underarms. "I'll probably go tomorrow—need a shave."

So would he just douse himself with cologne again today?

Silas set down his fork. The smell of this man made his entire plate unappetizing.

Unfortunately, there were no journal entries on how Richard treated Anthony, but there were plenty on how Richard had treated Lucy—damning stuff.

But there were scathing things about himself in the journals as well. Were Lucy's stories about Richard as exaggerated as her stories about her Kansas hardships?

Given that she referred to Richard as Anthony's pa though, he could only hope some page clearly stated Anthony was his; for as it was, the journals would be enough for Richard to make his case the upcoming Monday.

If he knew they existed.

Lord, if Anthony truly is mine, let her have written something.

52

Of course, if Anthony was Richard's son, should he not be praying *for* Anthony's father rather than against him?

Myrtle scuttled over and handed Richard a plate of bacon and corn mush. "Here you are, sir."

"'Bout time." He wrinkled his large-pored nose and yanked his plate from her, as if her touching the dish's edge tainted his food.

Silas's arms itched to stretch out and accidentally whack him in the face, but that'd not help his case come Monday.

"Could I bother you for salt and pepper, Myrtle?" Maybe if he could doctor his mush so it wasn't tasteless, he could get it down before it got cold—now that Richard had put his arms down. Though at the rate the man was shoveling in his food, perhaps he'd leave before he had to worry about his breakfast cooling.

"No problem, sir." Myrtle bustled toward the door as Anthony entered. She quickly sidestepped to the serving table, prepared a plate of food, set it across from Silas, and smiled at Anthony. "There you are, Mr. Riverton." She gave Silas a wink. "Now I get the salt."

Richard called Myrtle a derogatory name under his breath, and Silas clenched his fists to keep from punching the foul-smelling brute.

Anthony sat warily, choosing the chair directly across from Silas instead of Richard. At least he favored him a bit.

Kate's pretty form swept into the dining area and stopped. Her face looked as if she could smell Richard across the room.

Silas wiped his greasy fingers on his stained linen napkin and waved. "Good morning."

Anthony dug into his mush, swallowing the tasteless concoction as quickly as Richard did.

Myrtle skirted around Kate, set the shakers down, and then moved to answer another man's bellow.

Silas stood and dragged an empty chair over for Kate, squeezing her into the small spot next to him. "Did you sleep well last night, Anthony?"

Anthony shrugged.

"Answer him, boy." Richard's bark made them all jump.

"Fine," Anthony mumbled.

"I didn't—too hot." He'd not let Richard know he'd been up reading Lucy's journals.

His eyes dreaded reading any more of her cramped, frilly handwriting, growing illegible with fading ink—his hope of finding anything barely intact.

He had to spend time outside today. He had three more days until the hearing— plenty of time to read the rest, so he could take a break to work on his relationship with a boy he prayed would be returning to Salt Flatts with him next week. "What're your plans for today?"

"Hoping another cup of coffee will stop this headache," Richard mumbled, then swallowed his last spoonful of mush. "Then I'm going to take a nap before I head back to Lucky's."

"Sounds like a plan." He hadn't been asking Richard, but at least he'd be busy and out of the way.

But how to arrange an outing with Anthony after school when Richard might be opposed, or worse, decide to come along?

Myrtle filled the cup Richard tapped as he growled, "Have you packed, boy?"

Anthony shook his head. "I only have two outfits."

"My wife won't be happy with those rags of yours." He glared at Anthony. "We'll get some ready-made clothes while we're in the big city before heading home."

Anthony lifted his eyes to look at Silas.

He nodded a bit to encourage him to answer civilly.

"All right."

Richard appeared rooted to the seat, sipping and staring.

He'd ignore him. "Know a good place to fish around here?"

No interested gleam lit the boy's eye, though Kate turned an accusatory glare on him. "You're going fishing?"

"Or I might play chess." Silas tried to cut through his rubbery bacon with the edge of his fork.

Not even a fidget from Anthony. Too bad—he liked chess. "Maybe I'll find a place to shoot targets . . ." Could the boy truly not be interested in any of those things? "The library perhaps? Maybe I could learn to draw or paint."

"Paint?" Anthony's spoon hovered in front of his mouth, his left eyebrow raised.

Richard huffed. "Sounds like a waste of time to me."

"Well sure." Silas blinked against the thought of actually having to go through with painting lessons. He couldn't even draw a recognizable map.

"Miss Dawson paints." Anthony shrugged.

"Not you?" He grabbed the salt shaker for the second time to doctor his mush.

"Only when she wants me to."

Silas blew out a breath. At least he didn't have to pretend to like art for the boy's sake.

Myrtle set a plate in front of Kate, and she bowed her head over her food. Too bad he hadn't thought to ask Lucy about her relationship with God before the wedding. Maybe if she'd been like Kate, things would've gone more smoothly.

He now told people he liked living alone; it was quiet, gave a man time to think. But maybe his life would've turned out better if he hadn't written for a wife but waited on a praying woman to show up in his little town in Kansas.

One who smelled like flowers and soft soap like Kate.

He blinked. Wait, what was he thinking?

Once Kate took up her spoon, he tried again with Anthony. "So what do you do when you're not in school?"

The boy shrugged again.

Silas swallowed a sigh. Was he simply not much of a talker? Or was Richard the problem? "Are you a good runner? I used to outrun all the boys. Bet you're fast."

"Not as fast as Miss Dawson."

He looked to Kate, who was now the one afflicted with shrugging.

She *had* flown past him rather quickly that first day. Why had he brought that up anyway? It'd been an age since he'd run. He'd probably hurt himself if he challenged anyone to a race.

"Boy, you don't admit that a girl can outrun you. If you can't outrun her, you practice until you can." Richard snapped his fingers at Myrtle and pointed at his coffee.

If only Myrtle could slip some of that soft soap Kate smelled like into his cup. Of course washing out his mouth wouldn't clean his heart.

"Well, I'm thinking of taking a walk this afternoon. Where would you suggest I go?" He tensed, waiting for Richard to spout off a recommendation for him to go home.

"You can find snakes at the river sometimes."

"Snakes?" He couldn't stand the creatures anymore, not after waking to one falling from his ceiling smack onto his chest, then wriggling into his nightshirt.

If he wasn't mistaken, that was just a few days before Lucy left him. He'd not been particularly fond of remaining in his soddy after that incident either.

Silas stuck his spoon into the bland mush that remained in his bowl and left it there. Hunger pains weren't the worst thing a man could face. "Do you look for anything else at the river?"

"Frogs and crawfish, but since it's getting cold, you can't find much."

Creepy crawlies had yet to terrorize him. "What about bugs?

They're great for science lessons, I'd bet. Maybe Miss Dawson wouldn't mind you collecting some for school."

Kate hummed negatively. "We don't need more pests in my room. We've got plenty of mice." She went back to stirring her mush. Had she taken a bite? Not that he'd blame her if she passed on the morning's vittles.

"Snakes eat mice. Maybe she'd appreciate you bringing in one of those." Silas winked at Anthony, who actually let a grin slip onto his determinedly blank face.

"I'm afraid the boys would find a snake too useful for scaring the girls." Miss Dawson's greenish eyes brightened and she turned to Anthony. "Though, if you found a small snake, we could keep him upstairs for a while."

Anthony's face lit. "Really? Mother never let me keep anything I caught."

Silas frowned. Was there really a woman who wasn't against living with a snake in her room?

Tenacious, spirited, hardworking. Kate was the kind of woman who'd make it on the Kansas prairie, one who wouldn't run away . . .

Silas blinked. Where had his thoughts gone off to again? He grabbed his coffee.

"Don't get your hopes up, boy." Richard set down his empty cup. "Did you see Mr. Jonesey shiver when you mentioned snakes? He's not about to let you keep one. And Miss Dawson here ain't going to get the boardinghouse woman to agree to let you keep varmints in her place either."

"Now, hold on—"

"Kid, they're just buttering you up, making you think they're going to take time out for you, but they won't. Since you left, did your mother and Miss Dawson have time for anything like that?"

Kate drew up. "Lucinda was sick!"

"Let's all stop lying." Richard stood. "The boy'll be coming home with me on Monday after you all have your fun getting him to dream big. Boy, they're not doing you any favors. You'll be faced with reality next week."

Richard stomped off, and Anthony stared at his plate.

"Don't listen to him." Kate put her hand on his shoulder. "We—"

"Can you promise the judge won't make me go with him?" Anthony looked at Kate with sad eyes.

Kate took back her hand and swallowed. "Well, no."

Anthony wadded his napkin and stood. "I'm not hungry anymore."

Kate winced, then looked to Silas. "We better head to school anyway." She stood and went after Anthony.

Frowning at the dirty dishes left around him, Silas sighed. His stomach churned. He wouldn't have to deal with Richard much longer, but Anthony possibly would—without Silas or Kate nearby.

"Are you all right?" Myrtle gathered silverware and piled them on a plate.

He pressed his eyes closed for a second, wishing he could answer affirmatively. "Unfortunately, no."

A man called to Myrtle from across the dining area.

Silas cleared his throat. "You've got people to attend. I can see to our dirty dishes."

She left to go serve more tasteless corn mush.

Besides, I've got more journals to read, he thought. Though considering he'd gone through seven with nothing pointing to him as the father, Richard was likely right. Maybe they were dreaming to believe the world held anything better for the boy than it had for him.

Was there anything he could do if the journals came up empty?

Walking out of the schoolhouse behind Anthony on Friday, Kate spied Silas on the street, pacing in front of a wagon.

Had he finished reading all of Lucy's journals? Did he have good news or bad?

"I smell fried chicken." Anthony tipped his nose into the air and sniffed.

Catching sight of them, Silas smiled as they approached.

"Did you find out something?" Would he tell her now, in front of Anthony?

He shook his head. "I only have one journal left, but I'm not holding out much hope. But as I said yesterday morning, I need to get outside. So, I'm taking you both to Dry Creek."

"Dry Creek?" Anthony's eyes lit.

"Yes, see here?" He leaned over what must have been a rented wagon and hauled up a crate. "If you find a snake, we have something to put him in."

She glanced at the box, thankful he'd chosen something with tight slats. "Is the chicken to lure the snake?"

"No, it's our dinner." Silas held out his arms for her books.

How long would they be gone? "Shouldn't you be reading?"

"I can finish tomorrow. I wanted to make sure we spend time with Anthony. Richard made me realize our pursuits shouldn't keep Anthony from enjoying the bit of growing up he's got left to do. I rarely had time for fun at his age, not sure I have enough of it now."

Relaxing was necessary once in a while, but right now? "What if you find nothing in that last journal?" She stepped closer and lowered her voice. "What if you can't keep him?"

"Then he'll have a great memory." His face was solemn.

"Is that all you're going to do for him—give him a memory?"

Silas glanced over his shoulder to where Anthony had climbed onto the bench seat before leaning closer to her, lowering his voice. "Almost every diary refers to Richard as Anthony's pa. That's a lot of evidence against the one sentence that says, 'Silas doesn't deserve to know.' I don't think that's going to get us anywhere."

"But I know Richard isn't his father. She told me."

"Did she tell you I'm his father?"

"No, but surely if the judge knew Anthony would rather be with you—"

"Does he?"

She bit her lip and took in Anthony's serene face. "I think your afternoon plans might move things in your favor."

"And what about you?" He held out his hand.

She blinked at his open hand. He was only offering to help her into the wagon, of course, so why had her brain jumped to make that question mean something more?

"What do you mean?" She swallowed and let him guide her up into the wagon, the touch of his hand on her elbow strangely intensified. "Why do you care what I think?"

"When I first arrived, you lumped me into the same category as Richard. I'm hoping you'll see I'm not like him."

"Then no. If that's what this afternoon is about, it won't make me change my mind about you."

He stopped and frowned up at her.

She shrugged. "I've already realized you're not how Lucinda painted you. At least not anymore."

He let out a steady exhale. "Thank you." He went around the other side of the wagon and climbed up. Calling to the team of bay horses, he drove them out of town.

She stared at her hands in her lap. Should she even go with Anthony and Silas this afternoon? She needed to plan for possible bad news at the hearing, not stroll along the creek and . . . and daydream about the judge deciding to give her Anthony.

Having him with her at school all week had made the up-coming court case feel so far away, but now that the weekend had come, dread swelled her throat.

Despite what Richard thought, she'd run with Anthony if the judge decided in Richard's favor . . . she'd only promised not to do so before the court date.

Anthony needed to be safe more than he needed to be with a blood relative.

But without this teaching job or anything more to sell . . . If it was just the two of them, they'd likely turn into beggars and need Anthony's pickpocketing skills to stay alive.

No, she had to trust God would take care of them. But then, He'd not kept either of them out of hard situations before. . . .

Maybe the best she could hope for was that Silas was the nice man he seemed to be and the judge decided on him.

She swiped at her eyes, determined not to lose a single tear. She'd not ruin this happy memory Silas was creating.

The wind tugged at her bun, so she pulled it free and made a looser one at the nape of her neck while Anthony bounced on the well-sprung seat.

At the creek, as Silas helped her from the wagon, Anthony tore off, calling for her to run after him. She looked in the back of the wagon for something to carry.

Silas lifted an eyebrow. "You're not going to chase him?"

"I'm not sure leaving you in the dust is a ladylike thing to do."

"Oh, I thought you weren't giving chase because you can't actually beat him."

Well, she'd show him. After one quick glance back to let him know she'd taken the dare, she picked up her skirts and took off.

Anthony had skidded to a stop on the rocky bank before she caught up, but she'd gotten close. She ruffled his hair and looked over her shoulder expecting Silas to be making his way toward the water, but he was still at the wagon, lifting out what must have been their supper in a basket.

"Do we have to eat now or can I start looking for snakes?" Anthony danced around as if he couldn't possibly sit.

"I'm not sure what Mr. Jonesey wants to do, but I'm sure you can stop playing the moment we tell you to, right?" She gave him her teacher glare, the one that said she expected immediate obedience.

"Sure." He dropped onto the rocks and reached for his laces.

She frowned at the state of his shoes. The leather and sole at his right heel had separated, and both toes were so scuffed that a hole would appear any day.

"What do you think about setting up here?" Silas stood under a tree just starting to turn light yellow, the basket in one hand and a blanket draped over his arm. The sun filtering through the leaves played across his face. Scruff along his jaw had turned from a thick shadow into a full beard this past week.

Though he'd asked her a question, his eyes were fastened behind her on Anthony, who was hooting after plunging his bare feet into the cold water.

The half smile on Silas's face made her heart trip. He might not have known the boy long enough to truly love him, but that expression was miles closer to love than the way Richard looked at him.

Or even how Lucinda had looked at him.

How would it feel if Silas looked at her like that?

No, a man as handsome as Silas wouldn't waste his time on her. Though quite a few years older than her, with a face like his, he could scoop up any young woman he desired. Certainly a woman with a fresher face and a more compliant disposition would snag his attention. He needn't turn such a gaze onto a twenty-five-year-old spinster.

Why did she care anyway? He'd not be around much longer to look at her in any manner.

"I think that's fine." She picked her way over to the spot he'd chosen. "Do you want to eat now? I thought we could let Anthony play awhile."

"Aren't you going to get in with him?"

"Me?" She frowned. "It's not exactly appropriate for me to wade."

"Didn't stop you from running just now . . . and losing."

She scrunched up her face. If she'd known him better, she'd probably have picked up something soft to throw at him. "He had a huge lead."

"It put a flush in your cheeks."

She brushed away the hair that had fallen from her sloppy bun. "Red faced and sweaty. My sister always did tell me running made me look terrible."

Silas's mouth twitched. "I wouldn't say that."

What would you say? She pressed her lips together to keep from asking, and he turned to flick out the blanket.

"He's not going to be around much longer. He won't remember you took your stockings off, but he will remember you played with him in the water." Silas set the basket of food on top of the smoothed-down blanket.

She hadn't so much been put off by the idea of being stockingless, but more so by the hooting Anthony was doing because of the cold water. Of course, that didn't sound like a good excuse now.

And where did all this child-rearing wisdom come from? "I suppose you had good memories like this from your childhood?"

"No."

His dejected tone made her look back at him. Once again, he wasn't looking at her but rather at something distant.

"No good memories at all?"

"I'm an orphan."

"Well, so am I." And she certainly had her share of bad memories because of it. "But I still remember a few things about my parents. Father letting me play with his hunting dog's pups. Mother singing with me while I attempted to help her wash dishes."

"My only memory of my mother is of her sending me into the orphanage."

Wait. "Your mother is still alive?"

"Maybe." He shrugged and rolled up his sleeves. "But sending me away without a tear on her face was enough for me to know she didn't want me."

"How old were you?"

"Five, I think."

"That's pretty young. Why didn't someone adopt you?"

He nodded his head, but the look on his face definitely wasn't good. "The first couple, the Lewards, were impossible to please. They returned me as if I were nothing more than a rotten piece of meat they'd mistakenly purchased from the marketplace. The second couple, the Miltons, never took me back to the orphanage, though I couldn't please them either. They were content to take strips from my hide."

What was she supposed to say to that? "I'm sorry."

He shrugged and then unlaced his boots. "Richard was right. A childhood without good memories is a terrible thing. So maybe I want to splash in the water as much as I want Anthony to do so. Might be the last good memory for the both of us."

"How could it be your last one?"

"Lucy was my wife for only seven months. She left me without any way of knowing whether I was a widower or not, and so I was stuck without a family." He pried off a boot and placed it beside the other. "I'd like to believe Anthony's mine, but considering Lucy's journals and the way she's lied to us all about different things . . ."

64

"But even without Anthony, you know for certain she's dead now." Probably not entirely couth to bring up how someone's death was a good thing. "You can get married again."

He stopped pulling off his sock and blinked out over the water. "You'd think I'd have thought of that already. After years of believing I'd forever be alone, I guess I'd just accepted that as my fate." He looked at her, and all of a sudden the intensity in his gaze made her drop hers.

She swallowed. She was imagining the intensity—she had to be. Lowering herself as primly as possible, she stuck her boots out just past her skirts and stared at the row of buttons.

"Come on—off with them. You won't see us after Monday, so you won't be embarrassed in our presence, knowing we've seen your toes."

"I'd rather be embarrassed than have Anthony leave so soon." She sniffed and worked on her boots. "You really think the judge will side against you?"

"I have no idea."

He seemed too cavalier. "But don't you want Anthony?"

"That's all I've been praying for, but . . . maybe I'm not praying hard enough. I'm afraid to want him too much. I wanted a family so badly once I . . . well, I married in haste and was left lonelier than ever." He stood. "Anthony coming home with me could cure that loneliness, but if he doesn't, and I'd hoped for it, I'm not sure I could stand the quiet again." He rolled up his trousers. "No, sometimes it's better to be surprised than face such disappointment."

His open palm appeared beside her. She couldn't help but squeeze his hand as she moved to stand. How could she insist he fight harder for Anthony, knowing the law might not see what she saw?

"Did no one ever . . . care for you?" Somehow she doubted Lucinda had been the most loving wife during their short marriage.

"Like you do Anthony?" He let go of her hand and smiled out at the boy, who was creating a round well with a wall of rocks in the middle of the water. "No, but a janitor at the orphanage was kind to me. He didn't offer to take me home and call me *son* or anything. . . . A black man adopting a white child would've caused too many problems. But he was the closest thing to a father I ever knew."

"Hey! Come look what I found!" Anthony waved at them. He headed for the water. "Let's not keep him waiting."

Gingerly she crept across the sun-bleached rocks to the water's edge. How was Silas walking across the stones so quickly?

Hissing the second the water hit her toes, she was about to use her skirts as an excuse to stay on the bank when Anthony looked up, eyes alight. "Come on, Miss Dawson!"

Steeling herself, she gathered her skirts and stepped out onto the brown, rounded rocks in the water. After submerging her feet to her ankles, she stopped to get used to the cold.

"Anthony, it looks like all you have to do to win a race against Miss Dawson is throw cold water on her feet." Silas laughed, already standing beside Anthony, who stood waiting with his hands against his scrawny hips.

"You also aren't dealing with a dress." She slid a foot across a slimy rock. "Not sure how I'm going to keep my balance when my hands are needed to keep my dress dry."

"Can't you tie your skirt around you or something?"

She gave Anthony a look to let him know he was crazy.

"Don't girls climb trees?"

"Well, yes, but—"

At Silas's raised eyebrows and Anthony's frown, she quit making excuses. "All right," she grumbled. She turned around, pulled her skirts between her legs, and wrapped them around the way she'd done when she was a little girl—and hadn't done since. Thicker winter clothing was not at all good for this.

Once she had a good knot about her waist, she exhaled until her cheeks had cooled enough she wouldn't need to dunk her face in the water to approach the two of them without a face-staining blush.

Anthony giggled the second she turned around. "It looks like you're wearing a diaper."

And now she really wished she could stick her head in the ice-cold water. "I don't believe you could've said anything more mortifying to me."

"Hush now, Anthony. Don't make her feel any sillier than she looks." Silas's shoulders shook with silent laughter. "She won't come and see what you caught if you embarrass her."

"Come on, Miss Dawson—before he gets away!"

She closed her eyes and slipped her feet across the rocks. "Why are the stones so slick?"

"I don't think you want to know that." Silas really did laugh this time. "Don't think about it."

Don't think about it, don't think about it. Ugh. "Too late. I figured it out."

"Don't let that keep you from coming." Silas's voice held a note of concern.

No, she wouldn't keep from giving Anthony this memory because of slime. On her bare feet. Waddling through ice-cold water with her skirts gathered up like a diaper.

"Why couldn't he have chosen to take the boy fishing?" she muttered under her breath.

Forcing herself to look up, she picked her way out to Anthony's little stone circle in the water.

He stooped down the second she reached him. "He's under this rock. Watch." When he lifted a rock from inside his haphazard wall, a flash of brown flickered in the water and disappeared.

"I didn't see it." She moved closer, slipping a little.

"It's a huge crawdad." Anthony swished his hand around, and the creature moved.

She leaned down trying to see where it'd gone, but it blended in with the rocks somewhere.

"Maybe I can catch it." Anthony plunged his hands in, and the creature scurried between the rock wall and straight for her foot.

She hopped to the side, and a rock teetered. "It has huge pincers!"

Silas grabbed her arm. "Careful, he's not worth a tumble in the water. He won't hurt you."

"How do you know? Have you ever been pinched by one?"

"No, but they're awfully small."

"Not so sure size matters—snake fangs are awfully small."

He chuckled. "Point taken. But I still don't think it'd be that bad."

"Well, I don't want to find out." The crawdad scurried under a rock.

"Come over here and look!" Anthony called.

How had he gotten three feet away in a blink of an eye?

"What do you see?" She grimaced at the thought of clambering after him, especially since he'd gone through a deeper section to get to whatever he was pointing at.

"A ton of fish!"

Well, she'd seen fish before. Surely she didn't need to see them again.

"You're thinking of not going, aren't you?" Silas held out his hands. "I could carry you."

"On slippery rocks? We'd both end up in the water."

"A hand?" He held out one of his.

And she wanted to put her hand there. And not exactly because she was afraid of slipping. "All right."

She shook her head. What was she doing?

He enfolded her hand and the tension in his arm did indeed make her feel steadier than she had since she first stepped off the bank. Together they made it to the edge of a drop-off in the water where myriad fish swam in darting lines. "What are they?"

"Not sure." Silas shrugged.

Did he realize he was still holding her hand?

Anthony grabbed up a rock and threw it into the pool, making the fish rapidly change course. "Hey, come look at this."

Without bothering to protest, Kate let Silas walk her closer to the edge. "What am I supposed to be looking at? Please don't tell me a snake. I don't mind one in a box, but darting between my feet on slippery rocks . . ." A shudder took over her body and seemed to find its way over to Silas.

"No, look at all the babies."

She pressed forward, teetering on an uneven rock. A mass of minnows flickered right below the ledge where Anthony was systematically kicking rocks off with his toes.

"Why don't you stop destroying the wall we're standing on?" She put her foot on another rock that looked more stable, but it teetered as well.

Anthony picked up a flat rock the size of her hand. "I wonder if I can skip this one?" He chucked it, but it only made a resounding *glug* in the water, sending the fish back out in rays.

"Whoops!" She slid a bit but finally got planted.

They selected rocks from around their feet and competed against each other, Silas winning with five skips before her feet grew numb. "I'm getting hungry now."

"Oh, all right." Anthony whimpered, turned, and just about went face-first into the water.

Silas caught him. "Be careful there, kid. We don't have dry clothes for you if you take a dive."

Anthony stuck out his arms and walked through the deeper trench.

Silas turned back for her. "Let me help you."

"Thanks." She grabbed his hand but forgot about the teetering rock and almost plunged in herself.

Silas's arm clamped across her torso and righted her. "I don't have any dry clothes for you either."

Just the thought of him bringing her a set of dry clothing made her blush. "I shouldn't have come out here."

"Oh no, don't think that way. He had a better time with you here than if you'd sat on the bank." He kept ahold of her hand to keep her in her place and navigated the dip himself before turning. "Let me lift you across."

She glanced at his feet buried in the rocks. "Are you sure?"

"Yes." He pivoted his feet down deeper. "I'm not going to fall."

She put out her hands, but instead of taking them, he grabbed her under her shoulders and lifted her as if she weighed as little as one of the fish that had nipped at her toes. He set her down next to him, but his hands didn't drop.

Inches from his chest, she stared up at him.

"Thank you." Silas's voice sounded shakier than normal, or maybe it was the sound of the rushing water around them.

"For what?"

"I know you weren't exactly thrilled, but if you'd chosen to come out for me despite the slimy rocks, you'd have made my day, so I'm sure you made Anthony's."

Did he mean she'd have made his day when he was younger . . . or now? "I wish we had time to come with him again."

Silas smiled and let go of her with one hand to tuck a strand of hair behind her ear. A clatter of rocks drew their attention across the creek.

Up on the embankment, Richard's menacing glare stayed

intact despite his needing to grab a tree limb to keep him from slipping farther down the earthen wall.

The cold water around her ankles did little to cool the flushing heat spreading through her body. They weren't doing anything wrong, but for some reason, she wasn't sure Richard would agree.

Chapter 6

Kate glanced about the crowded sanctuary. Would Mr. Kingfisher fire her right now in front of everyone? She'd approached him to ask for time off tomorrow to go to court with Anthony, but now . . .

"Mr. Fitzgerald's accusations are more than enough to merit your suspension at the very least." Mr. Kingfisher shook his head, his brows heavy with irritation. "There's no good reason for you to have been in Mr. Jonesey's arms, improperly dressed."

She wouldn't let Richard get her fired. "Mr. Fitzgerald has skewed the entire incident. He's intent on taking Anthony, so he's trying to make the situation sound as bad as possible in an attempt to make Silas seem unfit. I told you, I was wading in the creek with Anthony, and Silas was helping me cross a trench."

Mr. Zahn, a board member standing next to Mr. Kingfisher, shrugged. "She did meet expectations before this orphan stuff came up, Bob. One tumble in the creek doesn't negate that."

She gritted her teeth. *Orphan stuff.* To them, Anthony was nothing but a bothersome detail. She glanced at the rows of chairs where the congregants mingled before heading home. Anthony was talking to a friend in the corner by the organ.

Both Silas and Richard hovered not far from him.

"This year's already started." The voice of one of the ladies on the board quietly broke into the men's debate. "Is letting her go worth the time we'd waste locating a replacement?"

"But she's been late once already this past week, Mrs. Monteclaire." Mr. Kingfisher's hand swooped out and almost hit her. "Now she's dallying with a stranger—inappropriately dressed, no less!"

Kate winced and glanced around hoping no one else heard his heated announcement. "I took my stockings off to wade with Anthony, yes, but I'll likely never see him again, and I . . ." Her throat constricted. She would not cry in front of these men. She sniffed and tightened her facial muscles to ward off the flow.

Within a minute or two, she might be back in the same position Jasper Goldwater had put her in two years ago when she'd arrived in Missouri as a mail-order bride and found him to be so much worse than he'd painted himself in his letters—or rather the letters his brother had written for him.

She'd not be penniless and without a job again if she could help it.

"No need to fire her. She's only had trouble with punctuality while keeping the boy, and he'll be gone next week." Mr. Zahn looked at the woman next to him. "Mrs. Monteclaire's right—we'd be in a terrible lurch if she leaves."

"Then fine." Mr. Kingfisher pulled at his tie.

That was it, no apology? No asking Silas for his take on the events Richard had blown out of proportion?

If the superintendent was willing to fire her because of one random man's testimony, would the judge believe her accusations about Richard's misconduct? Richard would surely call her a liar, and since Mr. Kingfisher hadn't even bothered to ask her if the story was true before accusing her of wrongdoing . . .

Would Richard mention seeing her in Silas's arms at the

hearing to discredit him? Surely that wouldn't matter between men—they'd not consider misconduct with a woman as detrimental to a man's ability to parent.

She wrung her hands. "Do I still have my job?"

"Yes, but I don't want you dillydallying with any more men."

"With all due respect, Mr. Kingfisher, I wasn't."

"She's always been upstanding before," Mr. Zahn said with a sigh and a glance at his watch. "Let's give her the benefit of the doubt."

"Thank you." She smiled at the more reasonable of the two men before spearing Richard with a glare from across the church.

Did amusement light his eyes? She clenched her fists. It would do her no good to go over and slap the smirk off him.

Well, besides feeling good. Real good.

"We'll see you at school at seven o'clock sharp on Monday morning, Miss Dawson." Mr. Kingfisher's smile was lackluster. "No hard feelings?"

No hard feelings? He'd never have to worry about his safety should he find himself without a job.

She pressed the heel of her hand into her left eye socket, hoping to squelch the stab of pain caused by her taut hairdo. "Of course not, Mr. Kingfisher." What good would hard feelings do for her predicament anyway? She still had to work for the man.

Once Mr. Kingfisher tromped away, Mrs. Monteclaire gripped Kate's arm. "Be careful." She turned to look at Silas, a small smile on her face. "I'd tell you to be careful with your heart too, but since they'll be gone soon . . ."

Richard strode straight for them.

She had no intention of talking to that man. Nothing she wanted to say to him was appropriate in the house of the Lord. "Thank you for helping me, Mrs. Monteclaire, but I need to excuse myself." She wove her way through the crowd, keeping her eye on the church's front door until she found herself on the other side of it.

The bright sunlight was not enough to chase away the storm clouds swelling inside her.

Clenching her fists, she forced herself not to run past Mr. Kingfisher on the crowded sidewalk. Because she needed to keep every stupid school-board rule until their concern about her conduct dissipated.

But they had no rule against walking very, very quickly. Thankfully Mr. Kingfisher was getting into his carriage and would soon be out of sight.

"Miss Dawson!" Silas's low rumble sounded from behind her.

Could he not see she didn't want company right now? And what if he ran after her in front of Mr. Kingfisher?

She refused to look back and walked even faster to put distance between her and the superintendent. All she wanted to do was hit someone, and Silas didn't deserve to be the scapegoat for her pent-up anger. And hitting a man in public surely wasn't on the list of things a teacher was allowed to do.

Half a block farther, Silas's hand touched her shoulder, and it fairly tingled with the contact.

"What were you talking to the superintendent about?" His breath puffed faster than normal.

She clamped her hands together behind her back and forced her clenched jaw to open. "Richard told Mr. Kingfisher he saw me acting like a wanton, half-dressed in your arms in the middle of the creek."

"What's a wanton?" Anthony's youthful voice made her wince.

Why hadn't she looked to see if he'd come with Silas before spouting off so carelessly?

Silas put a hand on Anthony's shoulder. "That just means

they don't think Kate should've been in the creek without her shoes."

The boy screwed up his face. "But then her shoes would've gotten wet."

Silas ruffled his hair a bit. "Silly, right?"

Richard leaned against the wall of the haberdashery several buildings back, his arms crossed as he watched them through the milling people.

She glared right at him. "That man thrives on stirring up conflict."

"Or the thrill of raising stakes." Silas pulled her out of the way of an oncoming cart. "He's a gambler, after all, and he's been dealt as many useless cards as we have. He's got as little proof of his fatherhood as I do, so he's attempting to rattle us, hoping we do something crazy."

"Proof of what?" Anthony swallowed and grabbed her sleeve. "You're not going to let him take me, are you?"

She looked to Silas. Though she already knew the answer by his cheerless eyes, she had to ask. "Anything in that last journal?"

He shook his head slightly. "The journals only covered the years since she left me. I went through the room again, but there weren't any more. I'm guessing she got rid of the ones she kept in Kansas when she moved in with Richard. I found nothing worthwhile."

"Found nothing what?" Anthony's voice held a whine of impatience.

Her throat felt dry, as if she'd spent an hour sitting atop a factory's chuffing coal chimney. How could she tell him he might be going home with Richard tomorrow?

Silas got down on his knee to look Anthony in the eye. "I'm afraid we're not certain who your father is."

Kate forced the lump down in her throat. "Tonight we need

to pray very hard that the judge says you can go home with Mr. Jonesey."

Anthony moved away from Silas and stepped so close to her he had to look up. "But I don't want to go home with him. I want to stay with you."

A whimper from deep in her chest escaped. "Oh, honey, I can't keep you."

"You told me God could give me what I asked for, and I prayed that you get to keep me."

She grabbed his cold hands. "It'd be better to pray for Mr. Jonesey to—"

"No." Anthony pulled his hands from hers. "I mean, he's nicer than I thought, but—" He threw a side glance at Silas. "Mother didn't like him. And I don't love him. I love you."

The notion of running away with him came back full force. If Mr. Kingfisher thought to get rid of her over one accusation, how much security did her job actually give her?

She tucked a lock of hair behind his ear. "I wish I could keep you. I so wish I could."

She wanted to tell Anthony she'd do anything to keep him, but what if he gave away her plans tomorrow? If the judge ruled for Richard, would he let her and Anthony out of his sight long enough for them to get away? It'd be harder to disappear if Richard had even the smallest hint of her intentions.

She slanted a glance at Silas. Would he help?

But would running away with Anthony provide him with a better life, or was her heart just too entangled to be objective? Richard's wife, with no kids of her own, might actually do well by Anthony.

Or she could be a wicked stepmother of fairy-tale proportions.

"What if the judge tells me I have to go with Pa? You told me never to steal again. He'll make me steal—I know it."

"I . . ." What to tell the boy? "If it's between him beating you or stealing . . ." What was the lesser of two evils? Could she tell him to break the law to save his skin?

"You could beg." Silas turned Anthony around by the shoulders so the boy would look at him. "Instead of pickpocketing, you could ask for handouts, give Richard whatever you get that way."

"That won't be enough. He'll know I could get more."

Silas ran a hand through his hair. "Tell him you're not as good as you once were."

"Oh, this just can't happen." She pressed the heels of her hands against the throbbing under her eyelids. "We have to think of a way to keep Anthony away from Richard no matter what happens tomorrow."

"Keep praying. We'll trust God to do what needs to be done."

"But if Richard wins?"

"Then we'll trust that God knows what Anthony needs better than we do. He knows who Anthony belongs with." Silas spoke as if he believed his words, but his quick breathing and erratic movements reflected the same panic that raced through her body.

Surely there was something more they could do on their own. And if Silas's words were true, then why hadn't God rescued her from her brother-in-law? Being her only living relatives, she'd belonged with her sister and her husband, but nothing good had come of it.

Maybe she could take off with Anthony for a little while, hiding until Richard gave up searching for them. Since he didn't love the boy, he'd give up eventually, wouldn't he?

But then her teaching job would be gone. How could she provide for Anthony after they came out of hiding?

His knock on Anthony's door went unanswered, so Silas tried again. "Anthony? I know you're in there."

The boy had been alone all morning. He'd begged not to be sent to school, and since he'd not be returning next week, Silas hadn't the heart to make him go. He couldn't keep the boy from one last day in his mother's rooms. If only he could have spent today with Kate. But after her conversation with Mr. Kingfisher yesterday, she hadn't felt as if she could ask the other teachers to take her students and had gone to school alone.

Silas looked down the hallway at Richard's door and worked hard not to think of the unpleasant things he wanted to say to that man. To have any hope of persuading the judge to send Anthony to Kansas with him, he couldn't act like Richard.

Silas turned his attention back to Anthony's closed door. "Why don't you come have lunch with me?"

"I'm not hungry."

"Anthony . . ." Silas tried the door.

Open.

Anthony lay on his cot, arms crossed behind his head, focused on the ceiling as if he could burn it down with intense staring.

"You can't hide in this room forever." Though if he were him, he'd have certainly wanted to. "Staying hungry won't keep the clock from ticking."

He settled onto the end of Lucy's empty bed, taking in every inch of Anthony, a long, thin rail of a boy. His feet hung off the cot as he stared at the ceiling, not once deigning to glance at him. "We're expected at the courthouse at two. We've got plenty of time to eat, and you can stare at the ceiling later."

The boy's face remained rigid.

"Well, if you're not going to eat, you should pack." Nothing in the room looked as if it had moved since morning. "Since neither Richard nor I have need of a woman's things, maybe you should go through your mother's stuff before we leave and

79

see if you want to keep anything. Perhaps give something to Miss Dawson?"

"What're you going to do with the rest of Mother's stuff? Throw it away?"

Silas flinched at the boy's anger but sympathized.

Twenty years ago, he'd seethed while at the mercy of adults who cared nothing for him. Though that wasn't Anthony's problem—both Silas and Kate certainly cared. Would the judge recognize that a caring stranger would be better for Anthony than a hardhearted gambler? "I thought we'd give the rest to Myrtle. Hopefully, she can alter the dresses to fit."

Anthony looked at him out of the side of his eye. "All right."

Good, he'd softened the boy a little. "I'll bring in the crates I found for your mother's things."

Anthony remained motionless, staring at the ceiling again.

The desire to touch him fought against his earlier decision not to get too close . . . but the boy looked so forlorn.

He swallowed and reached out to squeeze his hand. Anthony didn't seem to mind, and Silas couldn't help but clasp him harder, as if permanently attaching himself to the boy would prove to the judge Anthony needed him.

"I know this is going to be tough." Silas choked as the feeling of the boy's warm skin burrowed into his heart. "But I understand the uncertainty you're going through. You'll survive. I promise."

Anthony didn't so much as twitch.

It took a moment, but Silas finally forced himself to let go. With a deep breath, he went out into the hallway to carry in the crates he'd scrounged from a nearby mercantile. After he thumped down the last box, Anthony still hadn't moved.

He ran a hand through his hair. "Do you want me to come in after lunch and help you pack?"

"No."

"You've only a few hours . . ."

The boy blinked and stared out the window. Was he crying? Silas walked over, crouched beside him, and put a hand on his shoulder, which immediately stiffened.

"Why don't you come eat?"

"Will Pa be there?" The boy scooted far enough away that Silas's hand slipped off onto the cot.

So the boy had as little hope as he did about what would happen today in court. "I'm sure he will be." After a minute of silence, Silas sighed. "I'll come see you after lunch, then."

He left, shutting the door softly behind him. "I love you," he whispered. "Son or not."

Sharing his budding feelings would not help Anthony through this rough time, would it? Knowing someone else loved him wouldn't help him adjust to life with Richard.

No, better to hang on to that thought and pray he'd get to tell him after he was awarded custody.

Back in his room, Silas picked up the journal on top of the pile and flipped through it again, hoping somehow he'd missed a line that would be the miracle he'd prayed for.

Of course, maybe he didn't need to find a miracle in these pages. Maybe God would provide one in the form of a concerned and discriminating judge.

But he forced himself to scan through Lucy's entries again anyway—the depression, self-loathing, and unflattering descriptions of Anthony and every other man Lucy had harped on hadn't changed. The few wickedly biting descriptions of him made the hollowness in his chest rise to choke him.

She'd not written one thing about wishing for forgiveness, nothing about loving her son, nothing worth passing on to Anthony.

Nothing.

He shut the journal and closed his eyes.

81

Oh, Lord, I've sought your forgiveness for our past together, but now I ask you to forgive me for not praying more for her well-being. If I'd prayed for more than her to come back, maybe Anthony would've been treated better—not that I knew there was a boy who needed my prayers, but still, she was my wife, and I prayed more for me than her.

He dropped the journal back onto the pile and headed downstairs, his stomach revolting against the idea of eating but grumbling just the same.

Should he bother to pack the journals or throw them into the fire?

If someone handed him his own mother's journals, would he want to read them? What if they confirmed the hardheartedness he'd come to believe defined her? Would it make him feel better? What if she was a really nice woman and he a victim of terrible luck? Would he mourn the years of his life spent reacting to a lie of his own making?

Despite his dreary thoughts, he forced himself to smile at Myrtle as he passed her, but he couldn't keep his lips curved up when Richard's bellow for more salt rang across the room.

Did he really want to eat with him today?

"The meat's overdone." Myrtle brushed past him, heading back to Richard. "But it's more tender than Mr. Fitzgerald—that's for sure and for certain."

Seems it was possible to smile a bit despite the man's presence. "Thanks for the warning."

Myrtle slapped down the salt, pivoted, and rushed past him again, talking as she went. "But the pumpkin pie's good. Had a slice this afternoon."

Richard's hair looked damp, so he likely smelled better than usual. However, Silas chose a chair next to a man reading his paper at the far table.

Stretching his arms, Richard groaned loudly, as if everyone

needed to hear his protest. "So the day's finally come to quit playing and get back home, eh, Mr. Jonesey?"

Evidently sitting at a different table didn't mean he could avoid talking to Richard. Unfortunate.

Silas gritted his teeth, but the urge to say something nice to the man overwhelmed him. Had to be the Holy Spirit, considering last night he hadn't even been able to look at Richard when they'd passed in the hallway.

Could he even come up with anything nice to say?

"Thank you for . . . allowing Kate and Anthony so much unhindered time this week."

Richard shrugged. "I'm not a complete monster. I know the boy likes her."

He wanted Richard to be a monster. He wanted to believe Kate's awful stories because it gave him hope that the judge would see the man as pure evil and award Silas a son.

Though maybe Anthony would be all right no matter who took him home today.

"A boy who's happy is compliant." Richard stuffed a piece of beef in his mouth.

A happy boy would be more willing to steal. Always a silver lining.

"Had a good run at Lucky's this week. Going home with my pockets twice as heavy, so no problem, regardless of the decision."

Staring at his charred beef flank, Silas urged himself to ignore Richard for the rest of the meal.

But the prodding to talk to the man was still there. Maybe Richard would be his miraculous answer to prayer?

What would it hurt to try to talk him out of taking the boy? "I'm glad you're concerned about Anthony's happiness. I'm sure you can see he's attached to Miss Dawson and would rather—"

"Who cares about her? He's going home with you or me."

"Right, but I happen to know why you want Anthony." He gave the man a penetrating look.

Richard didn't so much as shrug or look apologetic. "You mean, because he's my son? You're not planning to accuse me of something crazy at the hearing just for your gain, are you?"

"My gain would only be to have a boy to care for. I've never had family of my own."

"Children don't turn your life into some happy land filled with roses."

"So, then, if children mean so little to you, what would encourage you to turn him over to me?"

Myrtle sidled in between them replacing Richard's dirty dinner plate with dessert. Her big brown eyes were alert, looking between them both as if leery of a fight.

But there'd be no fight; hopefully the only thing that took a hit was his pocketbook.

Richard stared at him for a few seconds before stabbing his fork into his pie. "I think the judge will find it mighty interesting you're trying to buy the boy as if he was some slave. What do you think, missy?"

Myrtle startled, a fork slipping off the plate she'd picked up. "That it ain't none of my business—that's what I think." She scurried off and Richard huffed.

"I'd not be wasting any more of your breath on that bloke." The man next to Silas, his head tucked behind a newspaper, had a deep roll of a Scottish accent. He glanced at Silas with tired eyes as he turned the page of his paper. "He'll only turn your words against ya."

Silas sighed, a hint of a headache coming on. Ignoring Richard's lip-smacking proved harder than ignoring the late-night skitter of rodents within the flimsy walls of Mrs. Grindall's lovely establishment.

Thankfully, within a space of a few minutes, Richard finished his food and wadded his napkin. "See you in an hour."

A dull thudding throbbed against his temples as Silas forced himself to respond. "Do you want to take Anthony to the courthouse or shall I?"

"You'll want to since it'll be the last time you see him."

Was Richard trying to be kind or just taking advantage of someone else getting the boy ready? "Thanks."

Once Richard left, Silas picked up his fork and poked at his now cold meat. Maybe he could have Myrtle warm it. He glanced around the dining room but didn't see her.

A man called for tea, but the swish of skirts and approaching footsteps barreling through the hallway didn't sound like Myrtle.

"What's with the hollering?" Mrs. Grindall came in, a severe frown weighing down her cheeks. "Where is that girl?" She stomped to the sideboard then thumped the pitcher down on the man's table. "There."

"I could've gotten the pitcher myself if that's all you was going to do."

"Then why didn't you?" Mrs. Grindall glared at the man, then turned heel.

How did Lucy and Anthony last so long in this establishment? Pushing away his half-eaten meal, Silas blew out his breath and left.

At the top of the stairs, he knocked on Anthony's door. "I'll be back for you in an hour."

After no answer, he glanced inside. The crates were haphazardly filled with lady's clothing. Evidently the boy hadn't been taught to fold. He glanced at Anthony curled under the covers and backed out quietly. Might as well let the boy sleep.

In his room, he ignored his growing headache and picked up the journals, carrying them downstairs to the vacated kitchen. Though

Mrs. Grindall would surely chastise him if she found him in here, he opened the grate and fed the fire handfuls of ripped pages.

"Anthony it's time." After no answer, Silas pushed inside Lucy's room. Her clothing was strewn about the place as before, but Anthony was no longer curled up on the bed.

Silas sat down and began folding the items they'd give to Myrtle. By the time the boy returned from the necessary, they'd have to leave.

Checking through all the drawers and under the furniture, he found another of Anthony's stockings.

Wait. Where was Anthony's traveling bag? His heartbeat accelerated.

He tossed aside the one dress still sprawled across the floor. The brown bag he'd bought Anthony yesterday was not there. He checked behind Kate's things, under the bed, cot, and ward-robe—nothing. He ran across the hall to his room to see if Anthony was there.

No.

The boy couldn't be as foolhardy as his mother.

He flew down the stairs. A muffled "Quit your stomping!" didn't slow him. He slammed out the side door. Running to the necessary, he pounded hard enough the door bounced. The man inside assured him with colorful language that he was not Anthony.

Silas ran down one alley, looked both ways on Morning Glory, saw no hint of a child walking among the sparse street traffic, and then ran down the other alley. Back at the side door, he hollered, "Anthony!"

Nothing.

He called for the boy through the building on his way to the dining area. Deserted.

He poked his head into the kitchen, where Mrs. Grindall sat peeling potatoes. "Have you seen my boy?"

The proprietress only had time to shake her head before he raced back up the stairs.

Maybe Richard had changed his mind about taking the boy to the hearing without telling him.

Silas worked at calming his erratic breathing. He thumped on Richard's door, and it swung inward with the force.

"Wha—!" The man frowned at him from where he was stuffing something into a trunk atop his bed.

"Where's Anthony?"

"How am I supposed to know? You said you were taking him."

He rubbed a hand down his face and turned back into the hallway. Perhaps he'd missed the boy returning from the necessary or saying good-bye to Myrtle or swiping a cookie . . .

In the hallway, something white lay wedged in a floorboard under his door, shivering in a draft. He snatched it up, hoping somehow a torn bit of Lucy's journals had clung to his clothing earlier and dropped.

But the writing was definitely not her swirling, cramped penmanship—but a child's.

Tell Miss Dawson not to worry about me and not to come after me. I can do just fine by myself.

Silas crumpled the note and groaned.

He slammed his fist against the wall, wincing at the splintering crack of wood and the pain shooting up his elbow. The boy couldn't have gotten far. Silas ran to Richard's room and thrust the note at the man. "Seems Anthony decided he didn't want to attend the hearing."

"What?" Richard took the paper from his hand and stared at it.

"I'm going to the school to make sure he isn't with Miss Dawson. Then I'll . . . I don't know. I'll rent a horse and go up and down the streets."

"I'll go to the courthouse to explain." Richard stuffed the note into his pocket.

"Let's meet at the schoolhouse after Miss Dawson dismisses class at three twenty. Hopefully one of us will have found him by then."

At Richard's nod, Silas raced down the hall, his heart thumping so hard it felt close to breaking his rib cage.

Lord, help me find him. You and I both know what dangers lie out there for a young boy alone.

Chapter 7

"Let's erase that." Kate picked up her student's slate. "You can't forget to carry the one, no matter how many numbers are in your problem . . ."

The door behind Kate opened. Was the hearing already over? Was Anthony . . . ? Her heart crawled into her throat as she turned around.

Silas stood in the doorway—alone. A few of her students began whispering, and his appearance certainly warranted whispers. His shirt was barely tucked, the laces of one boot undone, his hair mussed to the side.

His gaze razed the room. "Has Anthony been here?"

"No." Her throat went dry. She touched Arvilla's poofy-sleeved shoulder and handed the little girl her chalk. "Try again, dear. I've got to talk to Mr. Jonesey." She gave the children her teacher glare. "Back to work, boys and girls."

Once half of them seemed to obey, she shooed Silas into the hall.

Outside the classroom, he leaned against the wall, letting his head tip back against the hard plaster. "He ran away."

Her breathing quickened. "What do you mean, 'ran away'?"

She glanced at her timepiece. "The hearing can't be over already. How could he have run away?"

"He ran before the hearing. I checked on him after lunch, and he'd started packing his mother's things, but when I went back to take him to the judge . . ." Silas ran his hands through his hair, then huffed. "Surely he'd say good-bye to you first, right?"

Kate bit her lip, her insides as heavy as the weight bowing Silas's shoulders. Anthony couldn't be gone—not without her.

"Don't play with me, Miss Dawson. If you're hiding him—"

"I'm not." Though she had thought of different ways to sneak off with him after the hearing, those plans involved an adult being with him, not him being alone. "I wouldn't hide him from you."

The pinched lines surrounding Silas's mouth deepened.

"What about Richard? Do you know where he is?"

"He went to tell the judge Anthony's missing."

She hesitantly placed a hand on Silas's arm. If only she could smooth away the furrows in his brow, but she felt her own worry lines pinching in around her eyes. "It'll be all right. We'll find him."

He gazed up at her from his slumped posture, his green-hazel eyes drawing her into his worry. "So he didn't come by?"

She swallowed and shook her head.

Silas pushed off the wall and paced. "But *I* wouldn't have left without seeing you first."

He wouldn't have? Her hand crept up to her throat, where a sudden lump had stuck. He wouldn't have left Missouri without saying good-bye *to her*?

Silas pivoted and walked back toward her, gesticulating. "I didn't leave the orphanage without saying good-bye to Jonesey . . . of course I didn't say anything he'd have interpreted as me running away either, just a good-bye of sorts." He about-faced. "And you mean more to Anthony than Jonesey meant to me. . . ."

"I'm lost." Who was this Jonesey, again? And why did it matter? "What does this have to do with anything?"

Silas stopped pacing and walked toward her. "You're the person who matters most to Anthony—he'd not leave you in the dark."

So Silas hadn't meant he personally would miss her—just if he were in Anthony's position, he would've stopped by. Her stomach sank lower, if that was even possible. And why did she even care about Silas missing her—or rather that he wouldn't— when Anthony was in trouble?

"When I was in his place, I would've made sure I'd seen you at least once before I left for good. Surely he'd do the same."

Left for good? She'd been girding herself for the last day she'd see Anthony, but to never know what became of him? Her knees grew weak. "But he hasn't, so—"

"If he told you he was running away, you'd have stopped him, right?"

"Of course. He's only a boy." She looked at the wall clock at the end of the hallway. "When did you say you found him gone?"

"Right before we were to leave for the hearing. Last I saw him was lunchtime."

How far could a boy have gotten in less than an hour? But if he'd hopped the train . . .

She glanced past Miss Jennings's room. Mr. Tanner and Miss Leeright shouldn't mind taking her students too much. "Let me get the children switched over so I can help—"

He caught her by the wrist. "No, don't jeopardize your job. It's not long until school's over."

She looked at her hand caught in Silas's grasp. How could she continue teaching knowing Anthony had disappeared? "I could help you find him."

"I'm hiring a horse so I can look around town." He blew out a breath. "You stay here, and I'll go wherever you think I should look first."

"It'd be easier to show you." She opened the door. "Class—"

"No." He placed his hand on top of hers on the doorknob.

The heat of him trapped her against the door, and her breath momentarily disappeared. If it hadn't been for the nightmarish information he'd just told her, she might let herself dream about him inching closer, his mouth descending—

Wait. She glanced to the side, and her whole body flushed. The eyes of half her students focused on them. "You need to step away from me," she whispered.

His hand dropped, and he used it to rub his left eye. He blinked hard, shook his head a little, and backed up. He looked pained, maybe distracted. Hopefully distracted enough to miss that her face was likely bright pink. "I don't want you to lose your job, Kate. You were close enough to that before Anthony did this."

She stared at him, his face full of concern . . . and handsomer close up. Did he truly care what happened to her since it wouldn't affect him or Anthony? "You're right, I might get in trouble, but surely a boy's life is more important than a job."

Silas shook his head. "Please don't get fired. Give me places to look, and if I haven't found him by the time school's over, you can give me more suggestions."

Did he think she'd only give him suggestions? She'd be out looking the second her last student left. Staying now went against her every inclination, though Anthony's well-being was soon going to be none of her concern.

No, Anthony would always be her concern, even if only in prayer.

"All right." She closed her eyes to think since Silas was still close enough for her to see the dark green rim around his golden irises. "Check the shacks at the end of Fifth Street—they used to live in the one with the peeling green paint. And maybe the shops on Main? He likes to look in the windows, especially at the toy store, but I can't imagine he'd just sit there waiting . . ."

"That's enough to start." Silas turned and left without even a wave.

A small hand wriggled into hers. Arvilla blinked her doll eyes up at her. "Can we pray for Anthony before school lets out?"

The sounds of children fidgeting in their seats reminded her how far away that was.

"Momma says we can always pray, even when we can't do anything else."

Kate nodded. "Your momma's right." As much as she wanted to look for Anthony right now, she had children to tend, a job to keep.

Oh, God, please let us find Anthony. I'm sorry I railed at you last night about taking him away from me. And I thought I knew where he was going then. This could be so much worse.

Silas rubbed at the ache behind his eyebrows. He threaded his way toward the school steps amidst a sea of exiting children, grabbed the swinging door, and turned down the hallway.

Kate flew out of her classroom, hat and umbrella in hand. She gave him a once-over, and her frown deepened. "You didn't find him." She barreled past him, pinning her hat on as she walked. "We've got no time to lose. The sun'll be down before we know it."

He reeled a bit, then gave chase. "We need to wait for Richard. He could've found him."

Please, God, let him have Anthony. Even if I don't get to

*keep him, at least he'd be safer with Richard than on his own,
where who knows what kind of slimy men could take advantage of him.*

Not that Richard isn't slimy . . .

Kate's heels tapped faster against the tile floor. "We can't
wait around and twiddle our thumbs. Every minute, he gets
farther away—"

"You don't even know where I've checked yet."

"Doesn't matter. Anthony might have hid from you both.
He'd come out for me." Her skirts swished against his shin
when he caught up. "But go ahead and tell me where you've
been, who you've talked to, where you're planning to look
now."

"We need to see what Richard knows first—"

"I can look while you wait for him."

She shouldn't go looking alone. He'd tried to find the house
she'd mentioned, which had been in a rather rough neighborhood. "You don't like listening to reason, do you?"

"Reason?" She flung out her hands, her umbrella hitting the
wastebasket beside her. "What does this have to do with reason?
Anthony's out there alone."

"Your job—" He shook his head. "Don't you think Mr. Kingfisher will care where you go without a—"

"I go where I please." She planted the umbrella's point in a
crack of the tile and straightened.

"All right." He hadn't the time or brain power to fight with
her. And who was he to tell her what to do anyway? "I couldn't
find the shack on Fifth you mentioned. Maybe they painted it?
But I looked around that area, from First to Seventh and from
Main to Cypress."

"I'll go to the house first, then." She turned. And with that
she was gone. Reckless woman.

He trudged out behind her into the cool fall air.

Richard moseyed up the road from the east, whereas Kate had turned to the west.

"Kate!" Silas hollered after her.

She kept going.

He whistled loudly.

She turned and glared at him, but at least she spotted Richard and came barreling back.

If only the man had Anthony in tow. Did the boy have enough know-how to survive on the streets? The pickpocketing skill might indicate he did, but still . . .

"I take it you know nothing more about Anthony's whereabouts than we do?" Kate said as she marched toward Richard.

He shook his head. "He wasn't at the courthouse."

"Where else did you look?" Silas rubbed the pinched spot between his eyes.

"I didn't have time to look anywhere else."

No time? What else had he done since they parted? Buy a drink?

He knew how dependent one could be on alcohol, but a boy's life was at stake. "You do realize that every second he's gone, the farther he gets?"

Kate stopped in front of Richard and crossed her arms. "No more dillydallying. I'm checking the southwest corner of town where Lucinda and Anthony used to live. Where will you two be going?"

"I figured the creek." But that's not where he'd go if Kate was headed to the house on Fifth.

Richard licked his lips. "I'll ask around the railroad. See if anyone saw him get on."

Silas closed his eyes. If the boy had jumped a train, did they stand any chance of finding him?

"And if either of you catch him, you bring him straight to me." Richard's ugly mug turned sly.

95

"Why would we bother to bring him to you?" Kate huffed. "We can meet at Mrs. Grindall's for dinner if we haven't found him before then and discuss where to go next."

"As long as you go with one of us." Silas held out his hand as if his gesture would stop her. "It'll be dusk soon. You shouldn't wander the streets alone after dark."

"You can take her." Richard pulled a piece of paper from his chest pocket. "But as I said, you bring him to me at the railroad if you find him before dinner. I have a ruling stating he's mine." He unfolded a piece of official-looking paper and dangled it between them.

Silas blinked. Was he hallucinating? "Did . . . didn't you inform the judge Anthony was missing?"

"Sure I did, but I'm done lollygagging. You've had your week to say good-bye. Once we find him, I don't want to sit around twiddling my thumbs again waiting for another hearing."

"I can't believe it." Kate stared at the ruling as if she'd never seen paper before.

Richard thrust it at her. "Here, read it. I had them make two copies."

Silas forced his mouth to move rather than just hang open. "Why did you go through with the hearing without me there? Or Anthony?"

"What did it matter, you've got no proof of being his father—"

"But the boy should've had his say," Kate sputtered.

"He evidently didn't want to go home with either one of us. A young'un shouldn't have much say anyway. He obviously doesn't know what's good for him, considering how he's run off."

Kate read the paper in silence, then handed it to Silas. But he didn't need to read it to know it contained exactly what Richard said it did. Her ashen face and limp expression told him the truth of it.

Why did his heart slow so much at this news? Hadn't he been preparing himself for this likely outcome? "This doesn't change the fact that Anthony needs to be found and minutes are being lost."

But if they did find him, would the boy not do this again sometime later if he had to go home with Richard?

"Let's go, then." Kate shoved the paper at Richard's chest and gave him a cold, hard look. "We'll meet at dinnertime."

What if she found the boy first?

Another reason to follow her. She'd mentioned Anthony would come out for her if not for him.

And somehow he doubted she'd simply hand the boy over to Richard.

Twenty minutes before Mrs. Grindall and Myrtle would have dinner ready, Silas had followed Kate far enough to know she was heading to the house where she'd been boarding. After leaving the school, he'd trailed her as she swept through neighborhoods she shouldn't have tromped through alone. Though she hadn't found Anthony, he'd made the right decision by following her instead of going to the creek.

Now standing in front of Mrs. Grindall's unimpressive boardinghouse, his gaze landed on Lucy's window. What if the boy had left a clue in the room he'd overlooked? What if the note Anthony had shoved under his door hadn't been the only thing he'd written?

Silas entered the sweltering back stairwell and trudged upstairs. Pushing the door open across the uneven pine flooring, he let out a breath. Nothing seemed disturbed. The crates for Myrtle still lay where he'd left them. Kate's things were still neatly arranged in the corner.

Silas crossed to the table, looking for an envelope or a slip of paper. He'd leave Kate's things for her to look through. Where else might Anthony have left something for Kate?

The cot was stripped bare. The trunk at the end of the bed was empty. He couldn't help himself and peeked inside Kate's things. No notes anywhere unless they were buried in Kate's clothing—hopefully she'd find something there when she returned.

Silas slumped onto the bed and rubbed his hand against Lucy's fraying quilt.

After a week of taking in Anthony's features—his dark, hurting eyes, the thick hair that failed to play nice with his two cowlicks, the one subtle dimple Myrtle had pointed out—how could he go home and live life, knowing Anthony could be out there hurting or taken advantage of? Despite trying not to, he'd dreamt about Anthony coming home with him—having a son.

Several large bottles of tonic sat untouched on the end table. He moved closer, reading the labels. Horn's Cough Syrup, Colonel Muggin's Bitter Elixir, Holcomb's Nerve Tonic, Mr. Miracle's Elixir . . . He knew that last one. His shaky hand closed around the blue bottle . . . heavy. Barely used.

He swallowed against the dryness taking over his throat.

The elixir would keep his thoughts from wandering to their inevitable conclusion—God never intended for him to have a family. God didn't . . . love him. Didn't love Anthony.

He clinked the bottle back down, closed his eyes, and forced himself not to pick up the smooth glass container he could still feel in his hand again. He shouldn't have touched it in the first place.

One day at a time. Just one more day to get through without swishing the contents of the bottle, one more day without popping the cork with his thumb, one more day without pouring it in a glass with a flourish—

He left Anthony's room, chased by the images of his old routine, the memory of liquor's burn calling him.

He fled down the stairs and straight for the kitchen, where Myrtle gave him a side glance before going back to slopping what looked like beef stew into bowls littering the counter beside the stove.

Without bothering to ask, he took the pot of coffee sitting on a burner and poured himself a drink. It was weaker than he preferred, but it was something to keep his tongue busy.

"Are you all right, Mr. Jonesey?" She stopped to look at him as he sputtered.

"No." He trudged out toward the dining hall and sat at the table closest to the door. A few men were already sitting at the tables, laughing loudly.

He held the warm mug in his hands, attempting to anchor himself to the table with the weak brew, even though a whole line of spirits on Lucy's bedside table called to him. He'd not move until Kate and Richard returned. Hopefully Richard had Anthony in tow. He could at least say good-bye, tell him he'd be praying for him.

The smell of roses grew stronger as Kate pulled out the chair beside him. "Richard hasn't returned?"

"No, I'm praying it's because he has Anthony, because he's usually the first one in here." He took a sip of his coffee. "You should go up to the room and check through your things, maybe he left—"

"I just did." She sat quietly beside him as the room filled with more men and Myrtle carted in food.

She leaned toward him. "If Richard hasn't found him . . ." She lowered her voice. "What if we find him first?"

"What does it matter who finds him? Just as long as he's found."

"You and I both know Richard doesn't love him. He only wants him in case he needs his pockets replenished."

He had to hope the man wanted him for something more than that. "Maybe his wife wants a child to care for. Lucy's journal mentioned his wife was barren and that's why he favored Lucy. Anthony proved his virility wasn't in question."

"But Lucy had no other children."

He rubbed his hand down the back of his neck. "Even if that does sound like pretty good proof I'm the father, he's got a ruling."

"You can contest it."

"What good does it do if we can't find Anthony? And even if we did find him, Richard isn't about to wait for another trial before taking off with the boy."

"Then go to Hartfield to contest it."

He rubbed at the dull ache at his temples. "When do you know God is saying 'no'?"

She leaned back against her chair as if she were trying to get as far away from him as possible. "You're not going to fight this?"

"I want to, but I have my farm to think about, and—"

"If we find him first"—she leaned forward again—"you should just take him."

"We also have the law to obey." Wasn't she the one who told Anthony he should never pickpocket again?

"Challenge the court."

"I'm not sure it would do any good."

She leaned closer, her voice just above a whisper. "Then what if I took off with him and brought him to you later, after Richard tires of looking for him?"

"Oh, Kate. I know this seems unfair—and I would say it

is—but I can't go against what God seems to be orchestrating, no matter how much I dislike the outcome. How could I live with myself? Would I be any better than Richard as a parent if I refuse to follow the law?"

"But—"

"Here you go, sir." Myrtle placed a bowl in front of Silas and looked between them.

Richard stomped into the dining hall.

"Is Anthony not eating?" Myrtle widened her eyes. "I hope he's not ill. I could take him something."

"He's not here. He's run away." Richard plopped into his chair. "If you see him, bring him straight to me."

She glanced at Silas, so he nodded. What else should she do? "Keep your eyes open for him if you would. Mr. Fitzgerald needs to take him home."

"Yes, sirs." Myrtle moved off.

"Where'd you two look?" Richard grumbled.

"I searched his old neighborhood, visited some of his school friends, and then checked at the Logans'."

"About the same area she did." Silas shrugged and kept his eyes off Kate to avoid the glare he expected if she realized he'd kept watch over her. "Figured the creek could wait since he'd be looking for shelter this late in the day."

"Well, he's not been seen at the railroad. The manager let me look through the yard and outbuildings in case he was waiting there to jump the next train. I started walking Locust Street, too, but came back here before I got too far."

Myrtle set bowls in front of both Kate and Richard.

"When that boy comes back, I'm going to thrash him." Richard stabbed something floating in his stew with a fork.

Kate widened her eyes at Silas as if she expected he'd take Richard to task over such a proclamation. But hadn't the orphanage directors given him plenty of lickings for much less?

101

He kept his gaze on Kate's. "We can pray." That was indeed the best thing they could do. Even if they never saw him again, maybe God would hear and guide Anthony to someone who'd treat him better than Richard.

But if that's what God was doing, why hadn't He given the boy to him?

Chapter 8

Kate wiped her chalky hands on a wet rag and gave the blackboard a good scrubbing.

The end of the week had come—a week without any clue to where Anthony went. It'd been tough to teach every day, knowing she could only search for a few hours before night fell. Even if she weren't tied to this job, what more could she do? There wasn't an inch of Breton she hadn't walked or a person who knew Anthony that she hadn't questioned.

Silas knocked on the door to her classroom despite it being open and him having no reason to believe he wasn't welcome. He'd come by every day to escort her around town.

Of course, she'd met Silas at the front door the last several days, impatiently tapping her toes. They could've covered more ground separately, but he'd insisted he couldn't live with himself if anything bad happened to her.

"Do you need help?"

She dipped her rag into the pail and wrung the murky water out. "Unfortunately, the school board won't let me leave without doing my weekend chores since they don't think an extra fifteen minutes of searching is important. . . ." But after a week, was every second as important as it once was? She sloshed her wet rag against the stubborn marks the wool eraser hadn't eradicated. "You could sweep if you're willing."

"Of course." He grabbed the broom from the corner and swept without even a groan. Had her brother-in-law ever cleaned anything besides his plate?

Making quick work of the room, Silas tossed the dirt out the window. "Where do you plan to look today?"

A sad smile wriggled her lips. How many times had this man asked for her opinion as if he truly believed she could make good decisions as well as he?

Oh, why couldn't she have seen what a nice man he was the day Lucinda died and shoved him and Anthony onto a Kansas-bound train before the funeral? "Do we have time to go to Burrow?"

"The town north of here?" At her nod, he stroked his beard, which had grown thicker every day.

She'd never found beards attractive before, but on him . . . Or maybe she was starting to find everything about Silas attractive.

"I think we could, but we'd only have enough time to go to the sheriff. Maybe one or two other places before we had to return."

She shrugged and looked out the window to where someone was passing through the alleyway. For some reason, she couldn't keep from hoping every slight flicker at her window was Anthony come to tell her he'd been hiding somewhere and feeling guilty for not letting her know where he went. "I suppose our time would be better spent around here today. Maybe we can go tomorrow."

Silas went back to the window and leaned to see the person who'd walked by.

Knowing the moment they found him, Silas intended to hand

him over to Richard, trusting God to know what was best was endearing . . . and annoying at the same time.

Was the man the judge awarded a son doing anything nearly as worthwhile as this one? "Where's Richard looking?"

Silas's face grew dark, but he rubbed his hands over his fore-head as if he were trying to erase the answer he was about to give. "I think he spent most of today at Lucky's."

"What?" She hefted her water bucket. If Richard had been anywhere nearby, he'd have found himself drenched. "Is he waiting for us to find Anthony for him?"

"He says it's the law's job, but of course . . ." Silas strangled the broom handle. "If we find him, we're to drag him directly to his poker table."

"Well then, he doesn't deserve him." Kate sloshed water on her way across the hall to the Widow Larson's room.

"We don't get to decide, unfortunately." He rushed past her to open the door.

"Why not? If we find him, I still say we run with him."

"We?"

She cleared her throat while wringing the water from her rag. "I mean *you*, of course." Unless he wanted it to be *we* . . .

"I can't run with him."

"Why not?" She kept her face turned toward the board, afraid he might notice how distracted she was by trying not to think how the *we* possibility might play out. Of course, he'd only think she was frustrated by Richard's lack of concern over An-thony's well-being—and she certainly was that.

"Lucy."

She stopped washing the board and turned. "What about her?" What had she asked him again?

"She ran from me."

"Why does that matter?" She scrubbed with a vengeance. Silas hadn't deserved being shackled to the bitter Lucinda she'd known, but at the same time, he hadn't deserved being abandoned for ten years without knowing what had happened to his wife either. That first day she'd seen him, that grieving she'd flippantly assumed was acting, had likely been real. Had he truly mourned for ten years over a woman who couldn't be satisfied?

She winced at her unkind thought. *Lord, forgive me for thinking ill of the dead.*

"Lucy was the only family I had, and she ran away. Though Richard has a wife, he believes Anthony's his son, and if I had a son, the devastation of not knowing where he was, if I'd ever see him again . . . I'm too well acquainted with that kind of heartache."

He'd mourn Anthony far longer than Richard would.

How could you have made the judge give Anthony to this man? Even if he truly is Richard's son. . . .

No, Silas was right. Who was she to judge who got to keep their children and who didn't? She sighed. Maybe they should stop looking for Anthony. Maybe if they quit, Richard would go home and Anthony would find out and return.

She marched to the other room to clean the blackboard, trying not to let her brain talk her out of hoping that Anthony was simply hiding. Otherwise she'd have to admit nothing they did could save him.

Oh, God, what can we do?

"Are you all right?"

She hadn't meant to let that hiccup of a sob escape. She dumped her rag into the bucket and marched back to her room. Dirty corners be hanged. "Let's talk to the sheriff. If he's heard from any of the towns he contacted, maybe we might need to go somewhere else tomorrow instead of Burrow." She gathered the primers she needed to take home, and Silas opened the door for her.

"Sounds good." He walked out in front of her, opening every

door and then, at his hired buggy, took her books and held out his free hand.

She knew it was only to help her up onto the seat, but for a second, she wanted to hold on to his hand just because it was there . . . because it belonged to him. Because he might pull her closer and let her cry.

Stupid desire. She needed to get ahold of herself before she fell for a man who was going to leave as sure as chalk breaks.

Of course, lecturing herself right now would probably do little good.

Her heart already ached at the thought of him leaving, maybe not as much as it ached the day Anthony had disappeared, but it was certainly a portion of the pain constricting her rib cage whenever she let herself dwell on the past two weeks—and the future she didn't want to think about.

"Are you settled?"

A blush swept up behind her ears, and she quickly let go of the hand she'd held on to for too long. "Yes." She was settled on the seat, but her insides were a complete jumble.

He crossed to his side of the wagon, and she tried to imagine him staying in Breton and picking her up from school every day.

Of course, once he realized searching for Anthony was as futile as Richard did, he'd not stay around for her. What man ignored his livelihood for a sassy, independent spinster when he'd been away from home for two weeks already?

He could find a woman past marriageable age in Kansas to court just as well as he could in Missouri. He didn't need to get to know her any better.

"Here." He handed her a lap blanket after climbing onto his seat. "There's a chill in the wind, gets worse with the speed of a horse."

"Thank you." When had she ever had such solicitous attention from a man before? Certainly not from her two betrotheds, and this man wasn't even courting her.

On the ride across town, Silas seemed transfixed by the clouds sitting heavy and low above the ramble of businesses and houses crowding the downtown streets.

Were they both staying silent to keep from voicing the same question?

How would they know when to give up?

Luckily, she never had to give up. She could search Breton in her free time for as long as she had a glimmer of hope. But unless Silas gave up his farm, he'd have to return home, leaving her behind to do the searching without him.

She needed to make sure her heart understood that before it got stuck on him more than it already was.

Chapter 9

Silas knocked on the Logans' door. The pale morning light wasn't yet bright enough to warm the autumn air.

After a week of searching with no results, the sheriff being of absolutely no help yesterday, and knowing that if he found Anthony, Richard would be taking him home . . . when would his thinning pocketbook override his heart?

Random strangers in Breton had about the same odds of locating the boy as he did, and they could turn him over to Richard with less heartache.

Last night, he'd imagined talking to his best friend, Will Stanton, trying to explain why he was still scouring the same square footage. There weren't words sane enough to explain why he felt so compelled to find a boy that wasn't his.

Mr. Logan opened the door and narrowed his eyes. "You here for Miss Dawson again?"

"Yes." Why was Mr. Logan looking at him like that? He'd cooperated with them when they'd searched the property last week hoping Anthony had left Kate a note or was hiding nearby.

"She's not here."

Silas scratched his head. It couldn't be much past seven. Being Saturday, he'd figured they'd search town for a few hours before getting on the train to Burrow. "Where has she gone?"

Had Kate figured out somewhere to look and couldn't wait? He'd visited every decent hiding place around town more than once. Knocked on every door he passed. Asked anyone who'd talk if they'd seen anything that might lead to Anthony.

Mrs. Logan poked her head around her husband's shoulder where she stood behind him in the doorway. "I believe Miss Dawson is painting."

Painting? The sheriff's hopeless outlook yesterday had surely deflated her, but she couldn't have given up entirely. "I'm sorry. Did you say Miss Dawson was painting?" Why did it rankle that she'd not discussed her change of plans with him?

"I believe she usually paints at Plum's Rock on Saturday mornings. Do you know where that is?"

"On Dry Creek behind the flour mill." Silas had gathered that information from a random man who'd grown up in Breton when he'd asked him about places boys might hide.

"Are you intending to go after her?" Mrs. Logan stepped around her husband. "We've been concerned about her wandering around with you lately. I mean, I know the boy is missing, but he's not even yours, and we think she's . . . Well, not that we aren't worried about Anthony too, but the unseemliness of things—"

"Nothing against you, Mr. Jonesey." Mr. Logan held out his hand, sending his wife a silencing look. "We only want to be assured her reputation and morals remain impeccable, since she's under our roof and teaches our girls."

"We've been nothing but upright. We've . . ." He glanced at the children behind their mother's skirts. Were the Logans truly accusing him of impropriety in front of their daughters? "I don't see how a teacher searching for a runaway student during her free time is something to frown upon." Though he was finding it hard not to frown himself. Why did manners matter when a boy might be huddled in a ditch somewhere trying to stay warm at night . . . or worse.

"Oh, not that, but . . ." Mrs. Logan tucked a white-blond strand of hair behind her ear. "Well, some might think the amount of time she's without a chaperone, or with you without a chaperone . . . perhaps it's not wise for you to search along *with* Miss Dawson."

They'd rather she wander about alone? Silas pressed his lips together to keep from saying something unkind.

Mr. Logan held his gaze as if expecting a response.

"If you're concerned about Kate's reputation, why don't you and your wife search with us?" He glanced at Mrs. Logan, whose eyes held a condemning glint. She'd be one mean chaperone.

"We've got our own children to attend to."

Silas swallowed, then glanced at the children. He'd have to watch his tongue. "Well then, be assured the amount of time she's spending with me will soon come to an end. Either we'll find Anthony or . . ." Or they wouldn't.

How long until the logical part of him demanded he return to Kansas and care for his property instead of searching for a boy who may never be found?

Silas tipped his hat. Nothing good would come from saying anything more. "Good day, Mr. and Mrs. Logan."

Heading east, Silas kept the high cylindrical towers of the mill in view as he wove through alleyways. Behind the mill, he crossed over to the ditch containing the meandering creek and slid down through the prairie grasses onto the wide bank below.

A little past the bridge outside of town, he scanned the thick tree growth hiding the little rivulet of water that was Dry Creek.

111

The big stone jutting from the dirt bank wasn't too much farther, but he was more concerned about catching a glimpse of a woman's form than the exact location of a rock.

About fifty yards behind a tree hanging low over the water, a brown flurry caught his eye. Not an uncommon movement with the trees losing leaves, but something . . . yes, a sideways motion and a glimpse of auburn hair.

On the pebbly bank, Kate stood beside a blank canvas propped up against two large rocks. She held a thin paintbrush flat against her lips as she stared out across the creek to where the trees' leafy castoffs raced atop the cascading water.

A beautiful picture—the water, the sunlight, and Kate. Her hair was sort of on top of her head, but the tendrils framing her face danced in the breeze. Her lips, pursed against the paintbrush handle, looked fuller than usual. He couldn't see her freckles, but he could imagine them disappearing under the lovely blush that often tinted her cheeks without much provocation. All she needed was a fashionable gown and she'd catch any man's eye.

Why was she still single? She'd given him the impression she taught to support herself, not because of a high calling or insatiable desire.

She startled and turned in his direction, shoulders stiffened and head cocked.

Hmm. What noise had he made? He'd quit walking for some reason. "Hello, Miss Dawson!"

She waved her hands in front of her as if attempting to get him to go back.

He stopped. "I didn't expect—"

"You shouldn't have come!" Those plump lips had compressed into a tight, thin line. She glanced behind herself.

"Why?" What was she looking for?

She stomped her foot, but then her shoulders went slack,

and she let out a perturbed exhale. "Doesn't matter now, if he was here, he would've already seen you."

Did she still hope Anthony was waiting to catch her alone? He sighed. Seemed he wasn't the only one too fixated on finding the boy to realize the likelihood of it happening had expired days ago.

Her shoulders rolled forward in a slump. "I figured he might come to our spot if I separated from you."

He looked upstream. Nothing out of the ordinary lay along either bank. No flicker of color in the brush.

"What are you thinking?" she asked, lifting her eyes to look at him.

What good was it to deny it anymore? He turned his gaze up to the clouds so he didn't have to look at her when he spoke. "That my staying is as hopeless as the sheriff said it was."

Kate walked across the crackly leaves and clasped Silas's tense arm. She almost let go when she realized how muscular he was, but she couldn't tear her hand away. He needed comfort, did he not? "Don't say hopeless. We can't give up."

What would be left of her heart if they did?

Silas's Adam's apple bobbed as he looked down at her.

She dropped his arm and her gaze, not realizing she'd been staring up at him with . . . with some kind of hope.

Hope that he could do something to make Anthony return?

Hope he'd stay for her?

Why was she even thinking about a man when Anthony's life was likely in danger?

And even if Silas stayed for a few more weeks, she wouldn't quit her job for him. She'd not engage herself to anyone again after so short a time—just like he'd not give up his farm for a woman he'd just met.

A passing infatuation wasn't going to turn her into a fool.

Silas glanced at her empty canvas. "Did you just get here?"

She'd brought everything she needed to paint but hadn't been able to start. The bright yellow sunbeams dancing across the water's rapids should have inspired her, but all she'd done was scrutinize every tiny movement in the brush hoping to catch a glimpse of a hiding boy.

"No." Something downstream flickered. Nothing but a robin. "I was hoping Anthony would show up, since we often came here on Saturday mornings."

But now that Silas had arrived, should she stay any longer, considering the lecture Mrs. Logan gave her this morning? How could the woman chastise her for searching for the son of her heart even if she couldn't keep him? Mrs. Logan wouldn't be complaining if it were her daughters missing. "I might as well pack up. The Logans wouldn't find you being here alone with me fitting. They're concerned—"

"About themselves, I know." He scanned their surroundings. "Surely the Logans wouldn't chastise you for being out in the open?"

"I wouldn't be so sure." It wouldn't hurt Silas's reputation if people believed them attached, just hers.

He glanced away from her toward the empty canvas. "Do you have any finished paintings you could show me?"

She'd rather have the whole town talk ill of her than show him her sorry attempts at landscapes. "I don't let anyone see my work." And none could, since she threw them in the trash bin as soon as she finished.

"Now it makes sense." He gestured toward her blank canvas. "Invisible paint."

She chuffed.

"You know, you're rather pretty when you smile."

She frowned, and her arms prickled with gooseflesh.

"Oh, well now, a scowl is definitely the more pleasing option."

She held her breath and tried to get her face to settle somewhere between a smile and a frown. Though why was she shying away from letting him think her pretty? Did he really believe she was, or was he just teasing?

She didn't want to know the answer.

She was being ridiculous, expecting a man with a home a state away to stay and twiddle his thumbs hoping to find a boy who was likely never returning so he'd realize she'd be interested in his suit. Was this what people meant by being smitten?

"You're not at all like Lucy."

"What?" She sucked her lips in. Would he compare her looks to Lucinda's? His late wife had been far more attractive than she. Or would he tell her he found her more agreeable?

Why did her heart flutter so badly waiting to hear his thoughts?

But instead of saying more, he stooped to pick up a flat rock. He threw the stone across the water. It skipped once, then hit the rocks in the middle of the rapids. "After we go to Burrow, do you have other places you want to look for Anthony?"

Was she fooling herself—and him—holding on to hope? "After what the sheriff said yesterday, I wonder if going anywhere is worth our time, but I can't bear to stop looking yet."

He swallowed hard and stared out over the water. "I've paid Mrs. Grindall for next week, but I don't think I'll pay for another after that. I need to head back to Salt Flatts, to my homestead." His voice hitched. "You'll write me if he turns up? Tell me he's safe?"

Were they truly at the end of a fruitless search?

"I promise, Silas." She walked over to her painting stuff and

115

packed her brushes, trying not to let the ache inside keep her from her task.

He took the box she'd snapped shut and turned to walk back the way he came.

"Why don't we go this way?" She pointed to several stones lodged into the steep bank walls.

He raised his eyebrows at the makeshift stairs. "That seems a lot easier than the way I came in." He gestured for her to go first.

At the top, she stood waiting for him to finish climbing. "Did you bring a wagon?"

"It's at the Logans'."

She'd rather hoped not to see them again today.

"Let's stop at the telegraph office on the way back. I'm expecting to hear from the guy watching my homestead." He insisted on carrying her things and strode toward town, but they made slow progress toward the telegraph office since they meandered up and down every street where they heard children playing.

Thankfully there wasn't a line at the office, and Kate took a seat in one of the room's two chairs while Silas approached the operator behind the counter and waited for him to finish taking a message.

She stared out the window. Was there anywhere else in town where children gathered that they could get to before the train left? There was a patch of land by the cemetery where some of her students pretended to chase ghosts, but that was in the opposite direction of the Logans' and the train depot.

"Are you all right, sir?" The operator's voice held concern.

She glanced back to see Silas holding two pieces of paper with one hand and the other hand gripping the counter as if he needed it to keep from collapsing.

"What's wrong?" Kate dumped her painting things onto the

116

chair and went to put a hand on his shoulder. He looked as if he was having difficulty breathing.

He handed her one of the telegrams. She took it, bracing herself for terrible news.

HAVE PROOF ANTHONY'S YOUR SON LUCY SENT HER SISTER LETTERS SHE'LL FIND THEM AND SEND THEM TO YOU SHORTLY

IDA RIVERTON

"Why, this is good news. Wonderful, actually!" She lifted her eyebrows and tried to get him to smile with her, but he handed her the other telegram.

YOUR FARM'S BEEN ABANDONED I'M DOING WHAT I CAN BUT IT'S NOT GOOD

WILL STANTON

"What does this mean?"

"I don't know. I hired a man to watch my farm until Friday. I sent him a letter when I first found out about Anthony asking if he'd extend his stay, but he never got back to me." Silas swallowed. "I know Will will do what he can for my place, but he's mighty busy with his doctoring. I'm not sure he'll have the time to keep things going."

She tugged on his shirt sleeve. "But Anthony's yours."

He nodded, rubbing his head as if that information was still trying to make its way through his skull and into his brain. "That's great news, of course—though I'm not sure it makes me feel any better."

Was the shock of the unexpected telegrams messing with his mind? "How's that?"

"I finally have a flesh-and-blood relative—a son . . ." He

117

closed his eyes and shook his head. "And I may never see him again."

"Oh no, Silas. We can't give up now. We'll find him."

But the wounded look in Silas's deep green eyes made her feel as if she'd lied to him.

Please, God, let it be true.

Chapter 10

Kate walked amidst the exiting church crowd, hoping Mr. King-fisher wasn't glaring at her again, but he seemed to be watching her every step from where he stood on the church lawn. What had she done now? She should keep walking, pretend she hadn't seen him—

"Miss Dawson." He smiled, but it appeared obligatory rather than genuine.

Mrs. Logan shot a glance at them from under the church awning where she conversed with the minister's wife.

"Yes, Mr. Kingfisher?" She forced herself not to stare at the drying grass crushed beneath his ugly brown, pointy-toed shoes. "What would you like me to reassure you of today?"

He blinked innocently but scratched his chin. "Mrs. Logan has informed me you're still traipsing about town with Mr. Jonesey."

"I'm not frolicking down sidewalks, fluttering my eyelashes, and hoping for him to sweep me up into his arms!" *Wait*. Heat poured into her face. Hadn't she almost wished that at the creek?

The two ladies who'd been conversing under the catalpa tree beside them turned to stare.

119

She shook her head, hoping he'd believe her red face and shaky voice resulted from anger instead of embarrassment. "I'm searching for a lost student."

"Come now, Miss Dawson." Mr. Kingfisher's frown creased his brows, and he beckoned her away from the crowd to the church's side yard where the carriages were parked in neat rows. "Many of us have looked and made inquiries too. There's nothing more anybody can do but pray. Mr. Fitzgerald has our prayers. Why Mr. Jonesey bothers—"

"Anthony is Mr. Jonesey's son."

He glanced across the churchyard toward Silas. "That's not what I heard."

"He has proof now, so he's not going to stop looking for him."

Mr. Kingfisher straightened and cleared his throat. "Even so, he can certainly look on his own. The urgency has dwindled enough that you should start worrying about yourself."

"Dwindled?" When would concern about a nine-year-old needing to be saved from facing the world alone ever dwindle?

The Logans and her boss would likely dance a jig if she gave in and relinquished the task of finding Anthony to Silas alone, but she wouldn't. Couldn't. "I'm sure Mr. Jonesey and Anthony appreciate your prayers, but I'm not going to rely on prayer alone."

At least Silas had rallied after his bad news at the telegram office yesterday and returned to searching for Anthony with vigor.

Mr. Kingfisher sighed. "I know you think people daft for focusing on your whereabouts. It's starting to annoy *me* how many parents worry about your free time, but I must remind you how concerned some of the board members can be about propriety when it comes to our teachers. Perhaps prayer would be a better way to channel your efforts."

"I already pray." God said He heard everyone's prayers, but

He never seemed to care enough to listen to hers, let alone answer any.

I'm sorry, God. That's probably blasphemy or something, but I'm frustrated with you. Why aren't you helping us find Anthony?

She opened her mouth to tell Mr. Kingfisher he could offer more than just a bended knee but stopped. His searching would likely end up as unproductive as hers. "No need to worry about me running around town much anymore." At least not in Breton. "I haven't the foggiest notion where else to look."

A male sighed behind her. "How I wish that wasn't the truth."

Her skin prickled. How long had Silas been standing behind her?

Mr. Kingfisher pulled himself up to his full height, his shadow falling across both of them. "Mr. Jonesey, please have a care with Miss Dawson's reputation."

Silas's eyebrows puckered almost as much as his lips. "Would you join us this afternoon when we look for Anthony, then? Your presence would certainly keep Miss Dawson's reputation from being sullied by my lonesome escort."

"Do be reasonable." Mr. Kingfisher tugged at his tie. "It's been a week. You've alerted the proper authorities, have you not?" At Silas's nod, he turned a twitchy smile toward her. "My wife and I'll continue to pray you find him soon . . . or find the peace to go on without him."

Kate's hands trembled at his lack of true concern, her fingers clenched involuntarily. She took a step forward—

Silas's hand gripped her shoulder. "It's all right."

"I must be going, Miss Dawson. I'm warning you though— people are watching." Her boss's gaze lingered on the hold Silas had on her shoulder. He opened his mouth as if to say something more, but he simply nodded before turning to leave.

"I can't believe they're worried about my behavior when a

student is missing." If she were younger, she'd have stomped her foot.

Silas lowered his voice. "The world continues to revolve, Kate. Even when you're stuck in grief or pain or anger or sin—it's how it is. Bad things happen every day. If everyone quit to mourn every tragedy, society would fall apart."

She whirled on him. She knew how little the world cared for the trials of widows, orphans, spinsters . . . "So you think we should give up? Just yesterday—"

"I don't want to."

Doesn't want to? He considered it a possibility? He'd just learned Anthony was truly his son!

Well, she wouldn't give up. Not ever. The pain of simply contemplating defeat had her falling asleep at night with tears in her eyes.

Silas's hand on her shoulder tightened. Was she imagining him pulling her closer? Would he dare hug her in front of people who were so set on finding fault with two people grieving over the loss of a boy? The memory of the strength of his arms when he'd kept her from falling into the stream called to her as much as the musky smell of man and—

Over Silas's shoulder, Richard's narrow-eyed glare was almost palpable. What was he doing at church?

She stiffened and took a step back.

Silas grabbed her, preventing her escape. "Where're you going?"

"Richard's watching."

Silas stepped in front of her, his eyes probing hers. "I told him about the telegram. He doesn't believe me."

"So he's going to start trailing us now?"

"He'll probably be watching us more than ever. He seems to think his court ruling supersedes any information I have."

If Richard found Anthony first, now that Silas would soon

have proof he was Anthony's father . . . how much trouble was Richard willing to go through to procure the boy's talents?

Probably quite a bit, considering he'd stuck around Breton for two weeks.

Though, if his bragging to Silas was true, he was having a stroke of luck at the gaming tables. Maybe that's more of what held him in town.

Silas blew out a breath. "Did you mean what you said to Mr. Kingfisher just now? Have you thought of no new places to look?"

"I'm out of ideas—other than going to more neighboring towns. I'm worried that with so much time gone by . . ." She clamped her teeth—she would not cry. Too many parishioners milled about.

Anthony was either well hidden or gone . . . Hopefully not into eternity. She pinched the bridge of her nose to keep from thinking in that direction.

"I know you want to help me find Anthony, but after a week . . ." He took her hand. "Maybe you *should* worry more about maintaining your teaching position since they've brought it up again."

She stared at his rough fingers encasing hers. He probably shouldn't be holding her hand with so many people around, people who might imagine improprieties when there were none, but she didn't want to treat his gesture as anything but kind.

"With the possibility that . . . well, Anthony's life may be ruined or . . ." He stared off into the distance.

She closed her eyes and concentrated on his thumb absent-mindedly causing flickers of sensation across the back of her hand, taunting her with what was likely the last touch he'd give her.

"His life might be over . . . but yours . . ." He looked at her again, his eyes containing far more compassion than she'd mustered for him when he'd lost his wife. "I don't want your life ruined because of me."

At present, she was an old maid in a town with no family and no marriage prospects. If she lost her job, her situation would be worse than when she'd gotten off the train in Missouri two years ago.

Her life wasn't all that grand. Especially since the man holding her hand was going to leave soon, with or without Anthony. She'd ruined her life well enough on her own.

·—◦—·

Silas slid off his hired horse and stared at the dark, dilapidated building that often haunted his nightmares. Yesterday, he'd gone to the courthouse as soon as it had opened and informed the judge of the expected proof of his fatherhood coming in the mail. The judge had assured him he'd change the ruling if the letters were convincing. Silas rubbed the back of his neck. What if things still didn't turn out the way he hoped? What if Lucy's sister's proof was as flimsy as the sentence he'd found in Lucy's journal?

Even so, he was going to check out every possibility he could possibly dream up. Which was why he'd traveled most of the day to get to this building full of terrible memories.

Surely Anthony wouldn't be here, but Silas couldn't return to Kansas without looking. If someone had found him, they might have taken him to an orphanage.

He'd first checked the one the judge had told him about. It was closer to Breton, in Hightree, but Hall's Home for Boys was one of the larger ones in the region. And he well recalled the long wagon ride he'd endured before being dropped off here.

The clapboard building looked smaller than he remembered. The roof was missing shingles and the windows were cracked. Angry starlings fought over a nest in the eaves, but no sounds of children playing, laughing, crying, or screaming emanated from within. Was that a good thing? The place seemed far too silent for an orphanage. But boys' pants and shirts hung on the clotheslines in the side yard, so there were children there somewhere.

Did Anthony realize if he ended up in an orphanage, he'd likely be given to a family who wanted a servant more than a son? Richard would likely have been a better alternative.

Silas marched up the front stairs and pushed against the door to the one place he'd vowed he'd never return.

The heavy smell of turpentine and the acrid scent of burning food made his eyes water. He stared down both empty hallways flanking the wide staircase to the second floor. Should he talk to the directors first? If the Oldsteins still ran the place, could he be civil? Down the right hallway and past the office, he treaded softly, then ducked his head into the dining area. The burnt smell was definitely beans. Three redheaded boys, stair-stepped in size, ate from tin bowls on the left side of the scarred table. A larger blond boy sat across from them, hair hanging in his eyes, absently staring out the back wall's window.

No adults, but the clanging of pots indicated the cook was busy.

So few children. Did more people open their homes to orphans now, or had the demand for cheap servants after the war surpassed the number of abandoned children?

He ducked back out. Adult voices sounded somewhere down the hall, likely from the office. Anthony might not be in the dining room, but he could still be here somewhere. Slipping back into the main foyer, he looked up the staircase. The only other adults who'd worked in the orphanage when he'd lived here were a janitor and a preacher, whose sermons had always been the same: obey the directors, and when the time came, their new parents. He never seemed to realize that some children, like Silas, had resided there long enough to quote his lectures verbatim.

Padding quietly upstairs, he shot past the first landing, up the next flight, and then headed straight for the small square door next to the first bedroom.

His throat tightened, and he forced himself to breathe normally. No one would be shoving his now-five-foot-ten frame under that two-foot door, but his palms still turned clammy. Kneeling, he grasped the brass bolt that slid so easily for him now. How many times had he tried to kick against the sturdy latch from the other side or attempted to jiggle it open with whatever utensil he'd hidden in his sock for when he was thrown back in?

Grasping the little doorknob, he braced himself for the sour smell of unwashed bodies or worse, but strangely, cleaning supplies lined one side, cloths on the other. He couldn't see the back wall without a lantern, but nothing smelled as if a child had been jailed there for days. He let his eyes adjust to the dimness, trying to erase the nightmarish details with the vision of everyday cleaners and rags.

"Can I help you?" The wizened voice made Silas's heart pound.

He hit the back of his head on the doorframe's top. He groaned and rubbed what would surely become a bruise as he turned to face the one man he'd hoped to see even if Anthony wasn't there. "Jonesey." He smiled at the beloved janitor dragging a wet mop behind him.

Jonesey's freckled, light-chocolate skin sagged under his now foggy brown eyes. A pair of cockeyed, wire-rimmed spectacles sat on his large, flat nose, his five o'clock shadow now mostly white. Jonesey tilted his head to look over his glasses. "Do you know me?"

"I'm Silas."

The man stared at him with a raised eyebrow.

Silas pointed to the closet. "You used to let me out of there to stretch my legs when Mr. and Mrs. Oldstein left the building, used to sneak me food."

"I did that for countless young men when they was running the place." He propped the mop up and leaned on it heavily.

Silas's smile wavered. "Do you remember a Silas? I was here between '59 and '66 off and on."

The old man scratched his head. "I came in '64."

No wonder those first years had been so dark in his memory. He'd not had a hug before 1864. He pointed at the cleaning nook. "One night I'd been in there two days I think, screaming and kicking, not caring how many more beatings I'd get if I didn't calm down. You whispered through the closet door, told me God thought you and I were worth something even if nobody else did."

"The Oldsteins treated you children like dogs." The man's hazy eyes hadn't cleared.

Silas pushed around his sticky tongue until he was able to shove out more words. "You don't remember me, then?" He hadn't been anything special to the man? Just one of many?

"My memory ain't what it used to be." Jonesey shook his head and put down his bucket, the dirty white foam sloshing over its battered rim. "I'm surprised you remember me though. I'm nothing no white child would care to remember."

Silas stepped toward him and gripped the man's arm.

Old Jonesey looked down at his hand as if alarmed.

"You were the only adult I remember who cared a whit for me, Mr. Jonesey. After I left, I . . . I even took your last name since I didn't know my own." He let go of the janitor's arm and offered him his hand. "I'm pleased to see you again—name's Silas Jonesey."

The old man didn't take his hand. His eyes didn't quite look straight at him either. Maybe he couldn't see well enough to recognize him or see his hand. "I'm Ezekiel Jones."

Not Jonesey? He blinked. "I guess I should've realized Jonesey was a nickname."

The man's face split with a grin. He had far fewer teeth than twenty years ago. "Never heard of no white child naming himself after a black man. Jones was my old master's name, though. Don't rightly know my family name either."

Silas let his hand drop. "I want to thank you for everything you did for me."

The man nodded slightly, but his face still looked blank. Was he going blind?

Silas waited for light to fill the man's foggy eyes, but the janitor only stood politely, patiently. "You wouldn't know if a dark-headed boy named Anthony came here sometime in the last few weeks?"

"Naw, just got five boys right now, and they've been here awhile. None of them dark headed."

Silas sniffed and glanced down at the little torture chamber. "Glad to know they don't use the closet like they used to."

"Yes, sir. My mop bucket and rags are much happier occupants."

Silas rubbed a hand across his face. "You wouldn't happen to know what my real last name is?"

"What's your name again?"

Silas's shoulders slumped. "Silas."

The man rubbed his stubble. "Was your hair the color it is now?"

Silas nodded and closed his eyes. *Please remember.*

"Hmm, there were so many of you after the war. But I hear the new directors are sticklers for paperwork. Might ask them if they have a file on you."

"Yes, I suppose I should talk to them before I leave." He

shoved his hands deep into his pockets. The whole way to the orphanage he'd imagined giving his namesake a hug, but now? Had old age fuzzed his memory? Or had no one—not even this cherished memory of a man—ever had a lasting care for him?

God . . . oh, God, why does this hurt so much?

The hole he carried around inside him widened, felt emptier, bore deeper.

No one had ever cared for him enough to miss him, to want to stay with him.

The Bible said Jesus offered to love everyone, and he'd begged for that love years ago, clung to that promise as he'd clawed his way out of a life of despair. But if God couldn't arrange for one person on this earth to trouble themselves with him . . .

Silas tipped his head toward the janitor, who'd at least made him feel loved once. "It was. . . . nice to see you again."

The man nodded, his eyes foggy but concerned. "I wish I could help you, son."

He swallowed at the man's choice of words, wondering if they were as intentional as they sounded, despite the man claiming he didn't recall him. He nodded before turning to tromp down the stairs to meet the new directors and see if he could find out his real last name.

Though with Anthony gone, what did it matter?

Chapter 11

Silas stood outside Red's Tavern, one hand strangling the brown paper-wrapped bottle hidden inside his coat pocket. Troubled by his visit to the orphanage and the telegram he'd picked up after returning to town an hour ago, he'd wandered around Breton in the spitting rain . . . and gotten himself into trouble.

How long had he grasped on to that thread of love he'd believed Jonesey held for him?

Now he had nobody, and nobody cared what he did.

A flash of navy blue and auburn hair flounced in his peripheral. He groaned. Was Kate looking for Anthony by herself in this weather?

Would Kate still believe he'd become a better man if she saw him now? She'd told him she no longer believed him to be the man Lucy described, but he'd read enough of his wife's journaling rants to know he'd been a short-tempered drunk. And what did it matter if he became one again? It wasn't as if he had a son to care for. It wasn't as if anyone needed him. Least of all her. But she was the only person who might care enough to wrestle the demon from his hand.

Maybe, maybe not.

He caressed the curve of the heavy bottle. At one time, he'd thought a fine whiskey could help solve his problems. It had at least dulled the pain for a while. And he certainly had plenty of worries to bury right now. He crumpled the telegram in his pocket more compactly.

The thumb of his other hand ran across the whiskey bottle's firmly seated cork, and he pressed against it. He could pop it off if he pushed with a little more oomph. The aroma, the wet glass against his lips, the fire down his throat, all those tempting sensations were seconds away. Only a few ticks on the clock separated him from relief—and being as hooked as ever.

One drink would free him to ignore the rules, ignore the despair, ignore the need to care. The indigestion and next day's headache? Minor things to overcome. All he had to do was drink again, and again, and again . . .

He tried to pull out the bottle so he could throw it away before Kate noticed him, but his fingers wouldn't cooperate. He stepped out of the shadows before his brain insisted he flee and flagged her with his free hand.

When she caught sight of him, she hurried his way, a slight smile on her face.

The whiskey in his pocket would give her good reason to scowl at him like she used to.

He'd known better than to buy it, but his fingers only clenched the bottle neck harder.

Kate stopped in front of him, her dark auburn hair covered with a shawl glistening with drizzle.

Would she help him? If he didn't get help now . . .

She looked up and snatched her shawl before it slid off her head. "When did you get back?"

His jaw refused to unclench. He could keep the bottle hidden.

"The weather's gotten nasty." She rubbed her hands together. "I was thinking—"

"Take this"—Silas forced his hand to pull out the whiskey—"from me."

Her lips puckered. She reached for the bottle but stopped. "Carrying that around town won't help my reputation any."

"If you don't, I'll drink it."

She glanced over both shoulders, then grabbed him by the wrist and pulled him into the alley. Not a good place for any passersby to see them go, but she was right, liquor in her hand would look worse than in his. He gripped the paper-wrapped bottle tighter. "Maybe you shouldn't take it. Don't want you getting in trouble."

"Why are you shaking?" She stopped and eyed his white knuckles.

"I shouldn't have bought it." His fingers wouldn't yield. "I need you to take it from me."

She pried the whiskey from his hand.

His empty fist clenched, driving fingernails into his palm. "Pour it out, please."

"On the ground? Right here?" Her pretty hazel eyes blinked in confusion.

His lips were as dry as the tongue he poked through them to unseal the word, "Yes."

No one was in the alley, but she glanced toward the street. "I'm not sure I should, but—"

She looked into his eyes, and he tried to let her see inside them. The misery he'd almost inflicted on himself, the desire to stop her from doing what he'd asked, the desperate need for her to do what he couldn't.

She pulled down the paper and twisted the cork. She'd obviously never opened whiskey before. "I can't get it out." She pointed the bottle neck at him. "Could you open it for me?"

"No." He stepped back and knocked into some discarded boxes. "No." He couldn't touch it again. "If you can't open

132

it, maybe Mr. Logan can when you get home, or maybe he'd want to keep it."

"As if letting Mr. Logan open a bottle of . . ."

"Whiskey. Good whiskey."

She hiked her other eyebrow. "Having him open your whiskey wouldn't make the Logans any happier about the time I'm spending with you."

"Please."

She scrunched her lips sideways and looked deep into his eyes. He held her gaze, not hiding the desperation.

Pulling the bottle close, she wriggled on the cork until it finally popped. She watched him as she tipped the bottle over beside her. He tried to hold her gaze, but . . .

The amber liquid ran straight into the grooves between the alleyway's red brick. Each glug turned his stomach.

"Kansas prohibition has been good to me. I haven't been tempted to enter a tavern for years now since there aren't many and I don't like to go against the law."

Halfway through the bottle, his drinking hand started to lift of its own accord. If he stopped her now, there'd be a glass or two left to consume. . . . That wasn't too much.

He closed his eyes, dreading the last glug. "But I've crossed the threshold of too many bars looking for Anthony the past few weeks. I've been asked what I planned to drink, offered a swig . . ."

The terrible, wasteful glugging ceased.

Kate shook the last drops of whiskey onto the ground.

No more quandary over whether to taste or not, whether to sip, to consume, to binge.

Over.

His heart fluttered free. "Thank you."

She handed him the empty bottle, her head tilting a bit as she took in his face. "You couldn't do that yourself?"

Surprised her voice held concern rather than the disdain he'd expected, he met her eyes. "I tried, but then someone poured me a glass on the house this afternoon. After my visit to the orphanage yesterday, and the message I just received . . ."

He stared off into space, the vision of that glass full of golden liquid taunted him. "I left the drink behind. I didn't pick it up, didn't touch it, but at the next place I wanted a drink something fierce. The bartender would surely see it in my eyes, so before he offered, I asked for a whole bottle—I could pick that up without drinking it, as long as I didn't uncork it. Figured I could . . . Well, I don't know what I figured I could do with it besides the inevitable."

"An expensive drink to give the pavement."

"It would've cost more if I'd consumed it." He threw the bottle in a heap of trash next to a side-door stoop. "I'm sorry I made you do that."

"It's all right." She patted his arm, then snatched her hand back to catch her slipping shawl. "If only my brother-in-law had the strength to hand over his liquor to my sister years ago."

"Strength? I caved and bought a bottle." He shook his head. "I picked it up."

"Once you did, it was a hundred times harder to put down, yes?"

He searched her eyes. Understanding mingled in the golden flecks sparkling in her hazel irises. Did she have a similar problem? "Yes."

"Testing yourself with no one around is a dangerous game, Silas."

"How do you know?"

She shrugged. "My sister drinks too. She struggles with the same problem . . . or did." Kate looked toward the busy road, her mouth puckered. "We ought to leave the alley."

He blew out a breath and followed her onto Cedar Street.

He figured she'd look down on him for his weakness, figured her opinion of him would sink. But she didn't seem to look at him any worse.

He ran his hands through his hair. He wasn't strong. No one should admire anything about an addicted, God-disappointing man. But no condescending pity filled her eyes, which eased the pain of wasting an entire bottle of good whiskey. They walked a half a block in silence before he found his voice. "So you still have family?" Hadn't she said she was an orphan?

"A much-older sister and a drunk brother-in-law. I went to live with them after my parents died when I was twelve. My sister tried to help me, but she drank too. She quit . . . many times . . ." She looked up at him. "How many times have you quit again?"

"Three. The last time was four years ago. The first time was after I left Hall's Home for Boys—about a day's ride from here." He pointed in the general direction.

"Do you know why your mother gave you up? Was it during the war?"

"I was at the boys' home then, yes, but I wasn't an only child—just the only one she gave away." His one memory prior to the orphanage was climbing high in a tree with a brother, and a voice calling them to supper. How many other siblings might he have that he'd never meet?

"I wonder why."

Yes. Why? What could he possibly have done as a four-year-old to lose his mother's love? He closed his eyes and fought against the hollowness begging for the whiskey she'd dumped on the ground back in the alley. He'd promised God he'd never go down that rat hole again . . . but did it matter?

He drew a hand across his face. Of course it mattered. But now with Anthony gone, and Jonesey not remembering him, and the telegram forcing him to decide between staying in Breton to look for Anthony or keeping everything he'd ever worked for, the hole was calling to him.

He was weak. Kate might be sympathetic, but how could she possibly think well of him now? Everything Lucy had said about him must be playing through her mind, reminding her of how terrible he really was.

Her hand patted his arm lightly. "I'm sorry, I shouldn't have asked."

He forced his eyes open, letting in the light. "I don't know why she left me." He shook away the image of his mother pinning his name to his coat before sending him inside the orphanage. "I was offered alcohol for the first time not long after I ran away from my second set of foster parents. Sobered up when I met God. Then after Lucy came, I went back to the bottle."

"Did you say you visited the orphanage? Did you learn anything about Anthony?"

He let a smile slip onto his lips at her change of subject. Whether she could tell he was uncomfortable with talking about his past or he was making her so, her focus on finding Anthony was endearing—even though it became more hopeless every day. "Yes, I visited the orphanage. Anthony hasn't been there." And the new owners hadn't found a single piece of paperwork on any boys named Silas.

"So what do we do now?"

He heaved a sigh and stopped in the middle of the sidewalk. Where were they going anyway? He pulled out the crumpled telegram. "Not much. I got another telegram. My friend says the man I had watch the place ransacked it before he left."

"Can't somebody else watch it for you—fix it up while you're gone?"

He shrugged. "Will won't let my animals die—the ones left, that is. But he's busy with his doctoring. I can't ask him to do more than that. The real question is, should I bother to stay?"

"Of course you should."

"What can I do here that you can't?"

She pressed her lips together and stared off into space. "What you're really asking is when do we give up?"

"I'll never give up wanting him back, never give up praying. If someone said they saw him somewhere, I'd be off in a heartbeat, but what's a man to do when his livestock needs feed and the last of his garden needs tending? When the ability to eat this winter's at stake?"

Silas joined her in looking out at nothing. So much easier to keep his voice in check if he wasn't looking into her eyes. "There're too many places he could be. He could've hopped a train to New York, hid in a wagon traveling to Arkansas, found work in a mill under an assumed name. He could be . . ." He didn't want to say the word, but he'd known for years Lucy could've died and he'd never have found out.

The black hole in his chest was roughly the size of the puddle of booze Kate had poured between their feet. How long until he fell back in?

Standing still on the sidewalk with Silas, Kate rubbed her numbed hands together, the frosty gray air promising more cold rain. She nodded to a few people, hoping her casual smile would ward off their curiosity. With Silas's face so haggard, so broken, so lost, she couldn't imagine him being able to answer anyone who might ask what bothered him.

Would anybody in town care to keep him out of the taverns? She didn't have the right to order a grown man not to drink, but if he didn't want to, who else would care enough about him to help?

Strange that the man she'd once wished had never come to Breton was the only one who didn't seem to think poorly of her.

If only he thought more of her.

Though she'd known from the beginning her attraction was impractical, she wanted to grab his crumpled telegram and burn it—as if that would allow him to stay.

But if she hadn't captured his interest already, it didn't matter if he stuck around any longer. At least she'd be useful to him here, waiting for word of Anthony. She hadn't the strength to convince him to stay when her own hope was dwindling, when everything seemed to point to them never knowing what happened. How could she tell him what to do when he'd already gone through something like this before?

"I'm sorry, Kate. I shouldn't keep you out in the cold." He glanced at his pocket watch. "I doubt there's anything left for me to eat at the boardinghouse, so maybe we could—" He shrugged. "Never mind."

"What?" Had he about asked her to eat at the hotel? Could she invite him to the Logans'? They were already put out with her, so what was one more thing to add to their list of grievances?

Silas stood as if someone had beaten him. "I was going to ask if you'd eat with me, but maybe that wouldn't be a good idea, considering what people think."

She tried not to frown. "It's all right. Thank you anyway." Probably best.

Silas sighed and wiped a hand down his jaw. His newly clipped beard and mustache might be more attractive if he'd smile again.

Why did Lucinda leave you?

"Why? I thought I'd told you."

She slapped a hand to her mouth. "I'm sorry. I didn't realize I said that aloud."

A small flutter of a smile kindled a spark she hadn't seen in his eyes for a while, but the glimmer died quickly. "She came to Kansas at harvest time, and I expected her to work as hard as any other woman in Salt Flatts. She wasn't thrilled, and well, whiskey dulled the pain of hearing how my farm and I did not live up to her expectations. And who wants to live with a drunkard?" He seemed to wilt in place. "Nobody— that's who."

"But you don't drink now." She'd broken off her engagement to Jasper Goldwater because of his addiction to alcohol, so why was she still so drawn to Silas after seeing him struggling to let go of a whiskey bottle?

"You can't have forgotten what I just asked you to do. Just one bad day and I could . . ." He snapped his fingers.

"Would you drink with Anthony around?"

"No," he spit. "Or rather, I'd do everything possible to avoid even the smell of liquor. I've lived with a drunk, I've been a drunk, and no child of mine will endure that. I'd chop my hands off first. But then, Anthony's gone and I'll go back home—" He pulled up short and blinked at her. "You're probably glad I can't take him home knowing what you know about . . ." He held out his empty hand in front of him—the one she'd had to pry a bottle out of.

And that was the difference, he knew just as well as she what liquor could do to a person and didn't want to live with or be a drunk.

She reached for his hand to give him a reassuring squeeze but stopped short when Richard turned the corner and walked toward them on the sidewalk. "You've got a good reason to keep away from drink now. Whether Anthony shows up today or next year, he needs a sober father waiting for him."

Silas nodded and opened his mouth to say something when Richard called from behind him. "What are you doing over this way?" He stopped next to them and took stock of Silas. "You finally going to join me for a round of cards?"

She looked around and realized they'd stopped between two taverns. The sign on the left dangling by one hook read *Lucky's*.

"No. I told you I don't play."

"Seems as if you like to play with a certain woman's affections." He sneered at her. "While you're parading Miss Dawson through the seedy part of town without an escort, she's looking up at you like you're the doggone moon. And you pretend you'd be the best father for the boy."

"I told you, he's my son."

"You can say whatever you want to say—I'm the one with the paper proving he belongs to me." He eyed Kate. "And don't you forget it. I told the sheriff to watch you. The second that boy shows up, you're to turn him in. I can't stay here much longer, and I'm assuming Mr. Jonesey can't either, so if I were you, little lady, I'd send this dallier home before he ruins you."

"He's not ruining me."

"Oh yeah?" He pointed at Silas's face. "You and I both know what people think of you two running around. You going to make an honest woman out of her?"

"An honest woman?" she sputtered. "There's no reason to make me an honest anything."

"So you're marrying her, then?"

Her insides quaked too much to retort. Of course Silas wasn't, but then why did she all of a sudden wish he'd answer Richard with something other than a vehement "No!"

Of course, there was no reason to answer Richard at all. Silas had been searching with her to keep her safe. It was Richard who wanted to make that into something more than it was.

Silas gave Richard a scrutinizing look. "There's no reason to push her toward marriage just because you gossip like an old woman."

"It's not gossip when it's what I've seen with my own two eyes."

Silas raised his hand in disbelief. "Can't you find something more productive to do than follow us around? Look for Anthony, perhaps. Or at least learn how to play a hand of cards decently enough you don't need a boy's nimble fingers to make up for your lack of skill."

Kate took a step toward Richard, making sure she captured his attention. This conversation needed to stop before one of them threw a punch. "Let's not fight."

"The little lady's standing up for you now." The smell of alcohol wafted off of Richard in waves. "She's besotted, and you tell me I don't know what's going on."

"Come on." Kate stopped short of taking Silas's hand and pulling. "All he wants to do is pick a fight. Don't give it to him."

She didn't bother to tell Richard good-bye as she strode away, praying Silas would indeed leave without an altercation.

After a bit, Silas caught up to her, and she let out the breath she'd been holding since she'd smelled Richard's.

They walked back toward the boardinghouse in silence but stopped at Fifth, where she'd need to turn to head back to the Logans'.

The misty rain started to pick up again, and she repositioned her shawl to keep the droplets from her eyes. Silas stared at the rain clouds, hands in his pockets, drizzle collecting on his hat's brim and slowly rolling off the back.

He didn't say anything, even after his gaze dropped down to meet hers. How long would she have to stand here in silence for him to say something?

And she wanted him to say something.

Something that would cut the tangles overtaking her heart so she could get back to the life of a spinster who knew better than to let an attraction beget daydreams.

Silas swiped a hand along the shawl she'd tossed over her hair, flicking off the mist-formed droplets on her head.

She stilled under his hand. Had Richard been wrong? Did he feel something for her?

His lips twitched and he swallowed twice. "You'll likely catch a cold after all this talking we've done in the rain—no need to waste any more of your time on me today."

Then he didn't want to spend time with her unless they were looking for Anthony? As it should be. She swallowed. "In light of what Richard said, maybe you shouldn't walk me home."

He squared his shoulders. "Richard's right, I can't stay in town much longer. I'll be heading back to Salt Flatts as soon as I get the letters from Lucy's sister and the judge changes the ruling. But I'll pray I hear from you sometime soon, when you write to tell me Anthony's back and I can come get him. You would tell me, wouldn't you?"

"Yes," she whispered. Though it'd break her heart, she wanted Anthony to be with Silas more than she wanted Anthony to be with her.

"Thanks for your help, Kate." His mouth seemed unsettled, like he wanted to say more, but suddenly he jerked his hand up to his hat in farewell, then turned and left her behind.

And she'd gotten her wish. He'd said something that obliterated her hope. Soon he'd be gone and he only wanted to hear from her if she found Anthony.

So why didn't the knots around her heart loosen?

Chapter 12

Stirring more cream into his coffee, Silas felt Myrtle watching him as she cleaned the last of the dinner dishes. She probably wanted him to leave so she could clean his table. But he couldn't leave quite yet, not when he needed more coffee.

Or did he? What would it matter if he hadn't the energy to go looking around Breton for a few more hours in the rain?

He flipped over the letters he'd picked up at the post office yesterday after leaving Kate and read the most important paragraph again.

If I can get Richard to believe this baby's his, then I won't have to crawl back home to Father. If Silas ever writes, don't let him know where I am. It'd be best not to answer him at all. If he ever found out, he'd be the kind to actually want a brat, and I'm not about to go back to that soddy because of his kid.

Rubbing his brow, he shook his head. How had he not seen what kind of woman he'd sent for before he'd married her?

Sure, she'd been contentious and grumpy, but had he been so desperate for family he'd willingly ruined himself?

Lord, I want you to be enough, but I still have this ache for someone to care for and to care for me . . . someone I can touch. I fear for Anthony something fierce, and I can't do anything.

He thumped his fist against the table. He might as well admit he was powerless to help Anthony and leave. His son was lost—quite possibly forever—and there was nothing he could do to save his only family member.

Again.

He couldn't help Anthony any more here in Missouri than he could in Kansas. The judge had changed his ruling this afternoon, so if Anthony ever showed up, Kate could write and let him know.

He'd already inconvenienced Will enough by asking him to watch his place—and knowing Will, his friend was probably wearing himself out trying to doctor and fix up his homestead at the same time.

Silas sighed. And he'd thought Lucy deserting him was the most hopeless he'd ever been.

Myrtle's skirts brushed against his leg, and he looked up at her. Her pupils were large and sorrowful-looking under her heavy lashes. "Mr. Jonesey, are you going home anytime soon?"

He grabbed his spoon again and swirled his cream. "You think I should?" Was he that much of a bother? He treated her better than most of the tenants.

She took a step back and laid a hand against her chest. "You actually asking me?"

"Why not?"

"Well . . . because I'm . . ." She shook her head. "You're too nice. Not at all like Miss Lucinda."

"I didn't know Lucy all that well, but I suspect I'm not much better than her, as none of my family ever cared enough to stay

144

with me for long." He sucked in a steadying breath, letting his chest fill with onion-laden air.

"Why's that? What'd you ever do to anybody?"

She flinched when he looked her in the eye.

"I'm sorry, not my place—"

"I don't mind you asking." He shrugged. "The honest answer is I don't know. Though I wish I did."

"Did I hear Mr. Fitzgerald right?" Myrtle looked behind her before lowering her voice. "A while ago, he was hollering about you getting the court to take Anthony from him."

"Yeah, Lucinda's sister sent me this letter." He toyed with it again. "Confirms I'm Anthony's father."

She shifted her weight. "I'm real sorry he left you, Mr. Jonesey. You thinking of giving up?"

He pushed his coffee away. "I won't ever stop praying, but I can't stay any longer. Anthony could be a hundred miles away, and I've got a farm with problems. I'll just have to pray in Kansas. It's all I can do."

Myrtle stared at him as if he had something on his face.

Rubbing a hand across his beard, he didn't dislodge anything. "Do I have food stuck in my teeth?"

"No." She chewed a bit on her lower lip. "I'm just trying to reason out why Anthony didn't want to go with you. You seem plenty nice."

"I'm nothing special." He snatched the towel from her hand and wiped up his spilled cream, which earned him another wide-eyed stare. "I've got two crates full of Lucy's things upstairs I meant to give you the day Anthony ran. Don't know if you could stand wearing a dead woman's dresses, but I'd want you to have them. Remake them to fit you or your siblings or use them for rags—whatever would help you most."

Myrtle pursed her lips, angry-like. "Anthony's got his head all screwed up the wrong way, that's what."

Silas raised an eyebrow.

"No white man's ever given me dresses unless he wants—"

"Oh no." The back of Silas's neck flamed. How could a girl barely older than Anthony insinuate such a thing . . . even know to insinuate such a thing? The cream in his stomach curdled. "I didn't mean—"

"I know that's not what you mean." She stole the wet towel from him. "I'll be done here in about an hour, then you come with me to my house."

"I thought you realized that's not what I meant." He cupped a cold hand against his neck, trying not to look disgusted. He didn't want her to think poorly of herself, but—

"Oh stop. I know where Anthony is."

The heat in his neck drained, and his legs turned into soft lead. He stood and had to catch himself before he fell over. "What did you say?"

Mrs. Grindall poked her head into the dining room. "Aren't you done in here yet? You got another tub of laundry to do before you go. I don't have time for your dillydallying." She glared at Myrtle, and then at him.

He handed Myrtle his coffee cup, his hand shaking so badly he was afraid the dregs might actually slosh enough to make it over the brim. "Here."

He couldn't say any more with Mrs. Grindall staring at him like that. After walking past them both, he stopped outside the dining room and stared at the lopsided pictures hanging on the hallway wall. Had he imagined it, or had Myrtle said she knew where Anthony was? His muscles bunched tight.

He tried to relax, but how could he until he saw his son again with his own eyes?

* * *

Moving silently behind Myrtle, Silas followed her down a street he'd visited twice this past month. The only things he'd unearthed during those visits were suspicious glances and tight-lipped responses. He'd figured a white man knocking on doors in a black neighborhood was so unusual they assumed he had ill intentions.

Myrtle stopped in front of a leaning shack, one similar in size and shape to the structure Kate showed him where his wife and Anthony had lived before Lucy got sick. No bigger than the cramped soddy he used to live in—the one Lucy'd complained about every day. "Didn't you say you have four siblings?"

"And a father who left us. Mother's dead." Myrtle's eyes darted off to the right.

He looked over his shoulder. Three shacks away, two men stared at him. Another man across the street had stopped walking, a large load of firewood in his arms. The flour-sack curtain in his shack's solitary window dropped back into place.

Myrtle pushed a stray lock of hair off her forehead. "Maybe I shouldn't have brought you."

"This isn't the first time I've been here."

With a quick glance at him, she inhaled sharply, then turned the knob. A little girl with short curly hair scurried out and clamped herself to Myrtle's knees. "MeeMee!"

Myrtle placed a hand on what must be her little sister's back and stepped into the shack. "George, I've brought—"

A large mountain of a young man shoved Myrtle behind him and filled up the doorway. His eyes raked Silas. "What're you doing with Myrtle?"

Silas held out his palms and swallowed hard.

Myrtle popped out from beneath the man's outspread arms. "I brought him here, George."

The man blinked, then his face grew harder.

Silas took a step back. "I'm only here looking for my son." He recalled this man. A few weeks ago, George had given him a glare as chilly as the one icing his forehead now, but from the yard of a different house.

George glowered at his sister, his rage barely hidden. "Why didn't you just bring along the lynch mob?"

Silas pulled off his hat and assumed what he hoped was a nonthreatening posture. "I'm not looking to blame anyone for anything. All I want is information about Anthony Riverton."

The chubby girl who'd buried herself in Myrtle's skirts peeped up at him as if she'd never seen a stranger before. Myrtle stepped in front of her brother and pushed back against him. "Mr. Jonesey's all right. He ain't meaning to harm us none."

George didn't take his eyes off Silas. "Doesn't matter if he don't want to harm us none. If word gets out we're housing a white boy—"

Silas's chest inflated with weightlessness. Here! Anthony was here! "I could come inside and wait until dark to take him home."

George's large round eyes found a way to get larger.

"I don't care why you have him as long as he's healthy and whole." He stepped forward. "If you'd like to question me—if you're worried I'm unfit to be a father—I'm willing to talk, to set your mind at ease."

The big man's mouth unhinged. He moved his lips as if he wanted to say something, but no words came out.

Silas tentatively held out a shaky hand. "Please."

George glanced at his open palm but made no move to touch him. He fastened his gaze back on Silas's and talked out of the side of his mouth. "Get Anthony."

Myrtle gave Silas an apologetic look and ducked back under her brother and into the house. A moment later, Anthony came out, arms crossed.

How he wanted to sweep his son into his arms and hug the stubbornness out of him. But he wasn't about to shout and alert the neighborhood that George had been keeping a white boy in his home.

Myrtle appeared with the bag he'd bought Anthony weeks ago. "I'm real sorry I didn't tell you where he was, Mr. Jonesey. I thought I was helping."

"Don't apologize. You did help." He'd have offered his hand to George again, but the man still looked immovable, though his glare had softened. "Thank you for taking care of him."

"I help those who need it." George straightened and then slammed the door.

A knock sounded on Kate's bedroom door. "There's someone here to see you," Mrs. Logan's voice called.

"I'll be right down." Kate put the primer she was reviewing on her desk and glanced at Leonora, who'd just put on her long flannel nightgown. The sun's darkening orange light bled through the cotton eyelet curtains and suffused the oldest Logan girl's tiny attic room. "Good thing I put off retiring."

She frowned at her boots at the end of her trundle and then toward her house slippers. Crossing over to the little window, she tried to see down to the front door below, but the eaves obscured the drive, like they always did. Who'd come to see her at this hour?

It wouldn't be Silas. Mrs. Logan definitely wouldn't have let him call on her at this hour without having a conniption. Kate sighed and repinned her hair until it appeared presentable.

What if her visitor was Mr. Kingfisher? Would it matter if he saw her in house slippers?

Of course it would. She grabbed her boots.

After making her way down the steep, narrow stairs, she slowed and peeped around the angled wall to the foyer area, but no one stood there. She took the last of the stairs as quietly as possible and found Mr. Logan smoking a pipe beside his wife in the parlor—no one else. Kate cleared her throat, and Mrs. Logan indicated the front door with a tip of her head rather than putting down her embroidery hoop. "He's out front."

Kate's throat tightened. She should just ask who awaited her, but the fact that the woman hadn't told her didn't bode well. Why hadn't the Logans invited him inside? Wouldn't that have been more proper than sending her out alone at dusk? Kate smoothed her hands along the planes of her simple dress and grabbed her shawl off the foyer hook.

She opened the door and fell on her knees. "Anthony!"

The boy stood on the bottom step, his hands behind his back, one foot crossed behind the other, his head hung low. A slight movement a few yards away by the poplar caught her eye. Silas had found him!

She held her arms wide, and when Anthony didn't come, she reached for him and smashed him against her. "I'm so glad you're back." She sniffed against the wetness taking over her eyes, nose, and throat.

If her heart were a cage equipped with a strong padlock and chains to keep him there, she'd never let him escape again. She glanced over Anthony's head toward his father, who sported a charming, albeit sad smile. She forced the boy out in front of her at arms' length and attempted not to shake him. "What were you thinking?"

Anthony at least looked remorseful, though he wouldn't meet her eyes.

"Do you know how much you worried your father and me?" A flush crawled across her cheeks. Her question sounded like what Anthony's mother—Silas's wife—might say rather than a teacher.

But she felt like this boy's mother. That's why her heart hurt so much to see him again, knowing he was safe . . . knowing he'd soon be as far out of reach as he'd been yesterday. She looked at Silas, whose smile had faded. His eyes seemed even more beseeching than when he'd begged her to dump his liquor for him. What could he want from her? He had what he wanted. She pulled Anthony closer, hoping he'd soften a little. "Where have you been?"

"He was at Myrtle's." Silas's rough voice answered for the mute boy.

Myrtle? "Who?"

"The young black maid who serves at the boardinghouse."

She turned back to Anthony, her fingers digging into his arms more than they should. "You were there this whole time?" At his nod, she did shake him a little to make him look at her. "Do you know how much trouble you'd bring her family if certain people discovered they'd been hiding you? Especially if Richard found you!"

The boy shook his head, his Adam's apple bobbing a few times, protesting his attempts at swallowing. "I didn't want to get them in trouble."

Kate looked over the top of Anthony's head at Silas. "I thought you checked every neighborhood."

"I did, but no one near Myrtle's gave me more than a shake of their head. They might not have known, or if they did, they feared what would happen. I'd knocked on Myrtle's door, but no one answered."

Anthony shifted away from her. "They told me no one could know where I was. They were trying to figure out where I should go and how to take me there without anyone knowing, but I didn't want to go anywhere, not until Pa and Mr. Jonesey left. I wanted to come back to you." His big eyes dripped with more heartache and sorrow than a boy of nine should know.

Silas pushed off the tree and walked toward them. "They should be all right. No one knows where he was but us, Myrtle's family, and some neighbors." He put his hands on Anthony's shoulders. The two of them standing together made her throat ache. Silas had found his family, but what about her? She'd soon trudge back up a tiny staircase to sleep on a sliver of a bed for the rest of the school term before trundling off to another student's house next year.

Pressing a hand against Anthony's slightly wavy hair, she smoothed it away from his face. "Don't you ever run away from your father again. He told you he's your real pa, right? The court even says so."

Confusion flashed in his eyes. "But I was coming back to you. Don't you want me?"

She blinked against the tears welling up. "I'll always want you, but . . ." Her throat closed off for a second, and while keeping her hand tight on his shoulder, she stood and looked into Silas's worried eyes. "Do you mind if I talk to him alone?"

The right side of Silas's mouth turned up. Oh, he was handsome. And not just because of the way his eyes looked just now, but because she didn't have to worry whether he'd love this boy he barely knew or give him a better life than she could.

"Just keep him in sight, if you would." He gave Anthony's shoulder a squeeze, then walked back to the poplar.

"Let's go to the swing." She took Anthony's cold hand and led him to the tilted oak. She gestured to the rough wood plank tied at the end of the knotted ropes, but Anthony didn't sit.

She smashed her skirts to sit between the ropes and took both of his hands in hers, hoping to warm his ice-cold fingers. The sun's fiery glow warmed his hair. "I'm so glad your father found you. He's been worried you were gone forever. You're his only family, and he's the only family you have now too."

He took a tentative step forward, his chest puffed as if he were filling his lungs for a good cry. "You don't want me anymore?"

152

"Oh, Anthony, I want you more than ever." She pulled him in for a hug, but his bony little shoulders stayed stiff. "I'm a lot like you, you know. I've never been good at obeying authority or doing what I ought." She pulled back and gave him a grin. "My parents were good people, but I often ignored my chores to run in the pastures with the puppies or anything else I thought sounded fun. But when I was a little older than you, they died and I went to live with my older sister and her husband. Do you remember the story of Cinderella?"

He nodded.

"They treated me more like a maid than a sister, but I wasn't as good as Cinderella. I argued and hid and did as little as possible. My brother-in-law wasn't nice to me or my sister because of how I behaved, and no Prince Charming came to rescue me." Probably because she chose to steer her own pumpkin and never ended up in front of the right castle.

"But Mr. Jonesey is not like my brother-in-law. He cares so much about you, though he's only just met you—before he even knew he was your father. He spent hours knocking on doors trying to find you; he went to the orphanage he grew up in to look for you, even though it wasn't—"

"But Mother didn't like him. How do you know he won't be awful to me after we leave?"

"I think your mother and Mr. Jonesey had a hard time getting along, but he seems to have learned from it. It's good to learn from your mistakes." Was that why she was always in a bind? Because she needed to start learning from her mistakes—pay attention to propriety, stop shirking authority, quit agreeing to hasty marriages?

She smoothed Anthony's hair. "He used to drink, but he doesn't anymore. He knows that got him into trouble with your mother, and he doesn't want to hurt you like he did her."

"You said he only wanted me for chores."

"Did I say that?" What kind of parent would she have been, telling him such things with no more proof than one person's word against another's? "I don't think that way anymore. I think he'll expect you to help around his farm, as you should, but not to the point he'll be unfair. He'll want you to learn how to homestead so when you leave—when you're much, much older . . ." She poked him in the chest and tried to smile big enough he'd give her one back, but he refused. "You'll be a wonderful, hardworking, knowledgeable man. You'll grow to love Silas. I'm sure of it."

Who wouldn't love Silas after being with him for a while? She swallowed. Had she grown to love him? She hadn't lied to Anthony. She believed Silas to be all she'd described. If only she could find a happy ending like Anthony would.

"I want you to go with him, not because I don't wish to keep you, but because he'll give you a better life than I could, a better one than I had myself."

Anthony nodded slightly, then sighed, his little chest caving in on itself as he slumped into submission. She pulled him into an embrace and talked against his hair. "I'll miss you more than anything, so we need to enjoy the rest of the time we have together—"

"We're leaving tomorrow," he mumbled against her shoulder.

She stopped rubbing Anthony's arm. Her lips twitched. "Tomorrow?" She shouldn't have said that aloud. It sounded so . . . whiny.

But tomorrow? She'd just gotten him back! "Oh, Anthony. If you hadn't run, we could have had more time." She swallowed against the lump in her throat.

"I'm sorry, Miss Dawson. I thought . . . I didn't want to go with Pa or Mr. Jonesey."

"Silas is your pa, Anthony, and he's a good man. In time, he'll show you."

Still leaning against the poplar, Silas watched them. A kind, wistful look on his face.

She stood and turned Anthony by the shoulder and gently pushed him toward his father. She couldn't look into either of their faces or she might cry. "We'll write to each other every week. It'll force you to practice your penmanship."

The boy groaned, and she ruffled his hair. She left her fingers curled into his thick locks at the base of his neck, unable to take her hand away from him. Would this be the last time she touched him?

"Are we better?" Silas cleared his throat, love and concern nearly dripping from his eyes as he looked at his son.

"Is there any way you might . . ." She frowned down at Anthony. She didn't want him to argue with his father, so she shouldn't model the behavior. "Anthony, why don't you go inside and get yourself a cup of tea? Mrs. Logan always has some brewing. It'll warm you up."

The boy nodded and scuffed his way inside.

The second the door closed behind him, she turned to Silas, her right hand wringing her left. "There wouldn't be any way you could stay longer?"

"I shouldn't, not with my farm being in the condition Will says it is. Plus, if Anthony wanted to run, he knows Breton, knows people here willing to help him, but he won't in Kansas. He'll have to rely on me there."

She held on to his gaze. "Just one more day?"

He stared back. She'd never noticed the dark flecks in his hazel-green irises, the smell of sandalwood coming from somewhere around his square jawline, something dark and warm dilating his pupils.

Her heart suddenly kicked up a notch, and she cut eye contact. Her body's reaction was one of attraction. She definitely did not need that happening.

"Would another day help?" His voice sounded rough against the falling twilight.

"Yes." She didn't dare look at him. Another day would be torture, but she could handle it.

"All right, Kate. We'll stay for the weekend. Make it good."

Good? Only the day her parents had died would be worse than next Monday. Because then, this potential Prince Charming and the little boy she loved would leave when the depot's bells announced the next Kansas train's departure.

But she'd try to give Anthony the best memories possible before then.

Chapter 13

Following Silas out of the general store, Kate tried not to squeeze Anthony's hand too hard, but she wanted to memorize the fragile little grip she held. About a year ago, he'd told her he was too old to hold her hand, yet today he'd slipped his long, thin fingers against hers as they walked down Main Street.

Two more days and she'd never hold his hand again. How would she get through teaching the rest of the year with his third-row seat empty?

Silas slid the two boxes of clothing he'd bought for Anthony into his rented buggy, one of which contained a band-collared shirt for himself, one with a golden line running through its checked pattern that would highlight the hazel in Silas's green eyes. Not that she'd told him she knew his eye color well enough to know the fabric would play up the flecks of morning sun in his irises—she'd simply handed it to him and told him he deserved a new shirt too.

And she'd likely never see him wear it since he'd tucked it away with Anthony's purchases. Helping them pick out new wardrobes and watching Silas buy things for his cupboards reminded her that she should start detaching her heart from them both.

She needed to let them go, physically and emotionally. She had to. No choice.

And how her heart balked.

"Are you all right, Miss Dawson?"

She looked down at Anthony tugging on her hand. She'd stopped in the middle of the sidewalk evidently. "Would you like to call me Kate since I'm no longer your—" she swallowed and had to clear her throat to continue—"teacher?"

"But you said you'd force me to practice my penmanship by writing too many letters. Shouldn't I call you Miss Dawson in those?"

"Kate would be fine, if you'd like. And there's no way you could write me too many letters. You could write me every day and it would never be enough."

"Ugh." The boy dropped his shoulders and lolled his head back exaggeratedly. "That's too much. Maybe Mr. Jonesey can write you some of those days."

Silas cocked his head. "What am I writing about?"

"Miss Dawson wants to know all about your farm and what your house looks like and what you do every day." Anthony shrugged.

"You do?" Silas lifted an eyebrow.

Kate closed her eyes against his inquisitive expression. Anthony had made her sound like a busybody. "Well, he said he couldn't possibly think of enough things to write me about, so I gave him a list of possibilities. I don't actually need to know all that."

Though she did want to.

What would Anthony's life be like with Silas on a huge homestead with blooming pear trees and rust-red cows? She'd soaked up the descriptions he'd told Anthony before he'd run away, and they'd invaded her dreams last night, complete with dandelion fields, a quaint little house, and a whitewashed fence.

Surely it wasn't as welcoming as she'd pictured, considering Lucy ran from the place after a snake fell from the ceiling of his home.

But that hadn't stopped her imagination from taking over. Perhaps she should paint the visions her dreams had conjured, since she'd never see the place any other way. She had a teaching course scheduled for the upcoming summer to earn her a proper certificate, and by the time the next year rolled around, Anthony would likely not write her anymore.

He tugged her toward a display window. "Can we get that for Myrtle?" Anthony pointed at a green, feather-covered hat.

Silas looked at the millinery's display. "That's too fancy."

"She'd like it. Or that one!" He pointed at a more elaborate white hat with long plumes and netting.

Silas cringed and looked at Kate. "We were discussing what to get Myrtle's family last night. A doll for Frances, a sharpening stone for George, and the two other boys are Anthony's age so he'll pick toys for them, but we're stumped with Myrtle. She's not much older than Anthony, but I figured a doll was too childish, especially for how mature she acts, but neither of us have any ideas. What would you get a young lady who's not quite grown up?"

"All girls like pretty things." Anthony pointed at a pair of silk gloves. "What about those?"

"I don't think so." He looked at Kate again, and . . . was he flushing? He rubbed the back of his neck and didn't look her in the eye. "I already kinda got in trouble by offering her fancy stuff. She thought when I gave her Lucy's clothes that . . . that meant . . ."

Kate laid a hand on Anthony's shoulder and tried not to smile at Silas's fidgeting, considering the uncomfortable scenario he was insinuating. "Silas is right. If she already has your mother's things, she's got enough pretty clothes."

Anthony scrunched up his lips, then his eyes flit toward something else. "A necklace."

"Ah . . ." Silas shook his head. "Maybe sewing stuff, so she can fix the dresses she already has?"

"But that's work." Anthony shook his head. "She already does enough of that."

"For some reason, some girls think sewing's fun." Kate widened her eyes, and poked out her tongue as if the mere thought was horrendous.

"So you don't like sewing?" Silas sounded curious.

She dropped the exaggerated expression. "Not really, but one does what one must."

"She'll have to fix every one of Lucy's dresses if she's going to get any use from them."

"So you're going to get her sewing stuff?" Anthony looked as if they'd decided to buy her liver.

At Silas's nod, Anthony slumped and looked over his shoulder. "Can I go decide on what to get Jeremiah and Noah, then?"

"Sure." Once he ran off, Silas stroked his beard. "Since I'm getting the others something fun, won't she be disappointed?"

"From what you tell me of their house, I doubt anything you give them would be a disappointment."

"Myrtle's the reason I have Anthony." Silas's voice clogged. "If it hadn't been for her, Richard would've gotten his ruling, Anthony might never have returned, and I would've left before I received that telegram from Ida." He stopped to compose himself since his voice had cracked. "It was a terrible two weeks, but I wouldn't trade the heartache for anything. Myrtle needs more than needles and thread for the gift she preserved for me."

"You're right." She laid a hand on his tense arm. "Anthony is quite the gift." She prayed Anthony would quickly see how lucky he was to have such a grateful father. Considering Myrtle's actions hadn't exactly been legal, if Richard had found Anthony, he'd not be buying the family presents.

"I'm sorry." Silas squeezed her hand. "Here I am telling you what you already know while planning to take him away from you."

"Well . . ." What could she say? Though Silas was indeed Anthony's father and he deserved his son, a bit of her felt cheated that he got to keep him after only knowing him for three weeks, when she'd cared for him and his mother for two years.

And now all she had was two days.

"Who's that?" Silas dropped her hand, his voice suddenly steady and cold.

"Who's who?" She looked up and saw Anthony walking toward a man near the toy store. The stranger was leaning nonchalantly against the side of a carriage, stroking his mustache, looking like a *Pinocchio* illustration of one of the cigar-smoking boys luring the puppet to Pleasure Island. "I don't know him."

"Anthony!" Silas barked, but the boy must not have heard, because he kept walking.

"Maybe he knows him from the boardinghouse?"

Silas strode toward the carriage. "Anthony?"

This time the man heard Silas and narrowed his eyes. When Silas hollered again, Anthony turned to look, but the man grabbed the boy's arm and yanked him toward the carriage's open door.

The boy caught the window frame behind the door, and the stranger struggled to pull him in.

Kate's heart stopped and a rush of cold moved though her

limbs. She forced herself to take in a breath and hollered, "Stop him!"

Silas broke off in a run. Picking up her skirts, Kate ran after him, stumbling around a man Silas dodged.

With a hand clamped over Anthony's mouth, the mustached stranger yanked the boy's head backward at a terrible angle. Anthony's foot hooked under the bottom edge of the buggy, thwarting the man's attempt to slam the door closed.

The carriage driver yanked on his reins, maneuvering his team around a wagon parked in front of him.

A woman screeched as she tried to jump out of the horses' way.

Silas outdistanced Kate by a few feet, and with three more strides, he leapt toward the carriage and caught the swinging door.

Gesticulating wildly, Kate screamed at the men in front of them. "Stop that carriage!"

A few pedestrians blinked, but in the time it took for them to figure out where she was pointing, Silas had hooked Anthony around the torso, his other hand gripping the door, and the bottom half of his left leg scraped along the ground as the carriage picked up speed.

She ran faster, reaching for the strap flapping loose at the back of the carriage, angry at her inability to speed up. She growled as the gap grew wider between her outstretched fingers and the strap she'd almost caught.

She raced into the street, waving her arms above her head. "Someone please help! Somebody's taking my boy!"

One solitary man in the street held out his arms, but the driver kept beating the team, and the brave pedestrian barely jumped out of the way in time.

All of a sudden, Silas and Anthony fell. The door smacked Silas in the back of the head, yet he somehow managed to keep his body under the boy as they hit dirt. The wheel of the carriage missed Anthony's flailing hand by a fraction as he and Silas rolled to a stop in the middle of the street.

Kate couldn't stop fast enough and tumbled over Silas's outstretched leg. She sailed through the air for a split moment before her palms plowed into the road, scraping her to a stop.

A man's big hands grasped her upper arms and pulled her upright. "Are you all right, miss?"

"Anthony!" She looked over at the huddle of people beside her and pushed the man away before worming her way through the crowd, her every nerve taut and shaking.

With a relieved rush of air, she threw her arms around Anthony, who was sitting up. "Oh, Anthony!"

"Pa?" The boy widened his eyes, and Kate's hackles raised. She turned to scan the crowd.

Anthony wrestled his way from her embrace and crawled to the group of men kneeling around a sprawled-out Silas, his head covered in blood.

Her heart seized, and for a second, she couldn't move.

But Silas groaned and pushed himself up onto an elbow.

"I don't think you should move, mister." Some man next to him grasped his shoulder.

Silas caught sight of Anthony and then closed his eyes. "I'm all right." He winced and pressed a hand to his temple. "That door got me good though."

Scrambling over on wobbly knees, she joined Anthony kneeling beside him. "I think the man's right. We should get you onto the sidewalk and have a doctor to look at you."

"Are you all right?" Thankfully Silas's eyes weren't hazy.

"Fine."

"You're bloody too."

She looked down and winced at her palms. "Scraped my hands good, nothing more. No hit to the head like you."

Anthony hiccupped. His face streaked with dust and tears.

"Did you see me, Anthony?" Silas staggered to stand. "I beat Kate."

"What?" Kate narrowed her eyes at him. Had he hit his head too hard?

Silas winked at Anthony, though it looked more like a painful wince. "I outran the fastest woman in Missouri. I should earn extra points for that, don't you think?"

Anthony smiled a little, but then tears started to flow.

Kate reached out for him, but Silas pulled the boy up with the hand he wasn't pressing against the gash in his brow. "It's all right." He tugged him close, and the boy wept. "He didn't get you."

"We'll get him a doctor." The same man who'd tried to lift her from the road was at her side again. "But if we don't get out of the street, we're all going to need one."

She winced when he took her elbow, which must have gotten scraped as well, and hobbled over to the sidewalk with Silas and Anthony as the crowd dispersed.

All three of them sat on a nearby bench, though Anthony had yet to quit crying. Silas caressed the boy's tousled locks and shushed him as if he'd had years of practice comforting children. "Are you hurt anywhere, buddy?"

The boy shook his head against Silas's chest and started trying to hold his breath in an attempt to stop his tears.

Silas glanced at her bloody palms. "Did you see Richard?"

Of course. Richard. She fisted her hands and let out a hissing breath at the pain the action caused. "No. But how could he . . . in front of everybody!"

Silas shook his head. "We'll need to leave on the next train out."

So instead of two days, she might have two hours. Despite

the scrapes and bruises, she reached over and gripped Anthony's hand as tightly as she could.

• ◦ •

The hands on the train depot's clock raced toward six. Silas blew out his breath and dropped their hastily packed bags for the porter to load when the train rolled in. He pressed a hand against the knot on his head and glanced at the train schedule again.

Fifteen minutes and they'd be gone. Safe.

Silas scanned the crowd milling about the depot and walking along the street. After the bad weather they'd had this past week, the town was taking advantage of the sun. More men and women strolled the roads than he'd seen for a month.

No sign of Richard.

He checked a second time, taking a closer look at anyone watching Kate and Anthony, who were sitting on one of two benches on the depot platform. On the other bench an elderly man destroyed a loaf of bread to feed the birds hopping around his feet, but he'd been there before they'd arrived. The gentleman kept looking between Silas and Kate as if wondering why Silas couldn't keep his eyes off her and the boy. But no one else seemed interested in the heartbreaking embrace of a woman saying good-bye to a beloved boy in the space of an hour after being promised a weekend.

If he could only find Richard, he'd strangle him.

But the man had checked out of the boardinghouse, and Lucky's owner claimed he hadn't seen Richard since he'd lost everything in a game yesterday.

When they'd gone to the sheriff, the lawman tried to look as if he believed Richard was behind the attempted kidnapping. But since Silas had no proof Richard had anything to do with

165

the incident and the boy was safe, the sheriff wasn't going to do anything about it.

Thankfully his son and his heart were intact, but Kate's emotions were being obliterated right now. But what could he do? He'd promised her days, but he couldn't chance Anthony being taken.

Rubbing the bump on the side of his head, Silas tried to tamp down his murderous thoughts.

Had Richard really thought he could get away with kidnapping his son? Had he truly believed Silas had played with Kate's affections and ought to propose to the woman? All anybody had to do was look at her sitting with her arms encircling Anthony to know her affections were completely wrapped up around the boy—not him.

But why, then, did she keep looking over at him?

What if it were possible for her to move to Kansas? She'd surely do so for Anthony, but the only way that would happen was if . . .

No, a man did not propose to a woman he'd known for barely four weeks because people thought they spent too much time together and someone accused her of looking at him like he was "the doggone moon."

Of course, he'd asked Lucinda to marry him without even meeting her.

And a month with Kate was long enough to know they'd not have the same problems as he and Lucy.

Why was he thinking about this?

Because he was leaving today.

He could write her letters along with Anthony, but what could he learn in letters that he didn't already know?

Sure, she might tell him her favorite color or more stories about her family and growing up, but nothing that would negate what he already knew: She was smart, feisty, a good runner, bent on doing things her way, not exactly submissive, beautiful . . .

Across the way, she chuckled and pulled his son tighter into her embrace, kissing his temple. The boy's expression was a mixture of love and sorrow.

Had he ever been loved the way she loved Anthony? His son needed to be loved fiercely and unconditionally, and he would certainly try to provide that kind of affection, but she already did so.

The man on the bench looked at him again, one bushy gray eyebrow raised as if asking a question.

Yes, why indeed had he not thought about marrying Kate until now? His breathing quickened as he tightened his hold on the railing.

Surely he ought to provide a mother for his son, but who would he marry back home? Though Lucy had left him in limbo—not knowing if he was a widower or not—he'd not allowed himself to become attracted to any of the single women in Salt Flatts. And though his friend Everett's mail-ordered marriage turned out to be the best thing to happen to the older man, *he'd* never feel comfortable attempting it again. . . .

So why not Kate?

The acid in his stomach churned, and his head swirled as if he'd had too much to drink. When his brain clouded in a liquor haze, his decision-making couldn't be trusted. Except he'd not put anything stronger than coffee against his lips today.

Could he ask her? His innards wrapped around themselves just like the time he'd shoved aside his fear and penned his proposal to Lucy. Not a pleasant memory considering his stomach had remained in knots until he'd received her reply—and he'd certainly not gotten the happy marriage Everett had.

But Kate wasn't rich like Lucy had been, and she was alone,

just like him. The only person she was attached to was Anthony . . . and he was leaving with him for Kansas.

She looked over her shoulder and caught his gaze as if she'd felt him staring. He tried to drag his eyes off her but couldn't. His lungs wouldn't even inflate at the moment.

She tipped her head and quirked the corner of her mouth in that charming way she did so often.

He'd always wanted a happy family, and seeing Anthony tucked into her side, talking and smiling . . . What he wouldn't give to see that every day.

But would she make him happy? She definitely wouldn't sulk and pout and run away like Lucy. Kate would likely tell him he'd messed up and get in his face until they'd resolved their issues. If he allowed his mind to think about Kate as more than the woman attached to his son, united as one with him . . .

Yeah, that wouldn't be a hard thing to imagine at all.

Oh, Lord. I'm going to ask her.

The sound of a faraway whistle blew.

I don't even have time to think about it anymore. It's ask or not.

At least he wouldn't have to face her again if she said no. He only hoped the sting of rejection wouldn't last too long.

He licked his lips and looked down the tracks. The locomotive slowed around the final curve, its engaged brake scraping his ears. He'd have maybe fifteen minutes before the train left.

Thrusting his hands into his pockets, he pushed off the railing and walked toward her, each step leaden as he forced himself forward despite his heartbeat trying to ram him back. When Anthony caught sight of him, he sighed dramatically and wilted against Kate. She appeared equally pitiful. The sheen in her eyes made him want to scoop her up right then to test the feel of her in his arms.

Anthony's mouth opened, seemingly ready to protest, but

he must have seen something in Silas's face to make him stop. The boy kicked his trunk. "I'll miss you, Miss Dawson. Maybe even more than I miss Mother."

Kate pulled him against her and kissed the top of his head. "You'll be all right." But the deep creases around her mouth indicated she wouldn't be. "I wish you didn't have to go already, but we want you safe."

Was Anthony and Kate's desire to be together worth marrying without love?

What was love anyway? Sacrificing oneself for another, right?

Silas cleared his throat and glanced between them. "Son, do you mind if I have a moment with Miss Dawson?"

Anthony shrugged and shuffled over to sit on the bench beside the man feeding pigeons. Silas turned toward Kate, but kept Anthony in his sight. He cleared his throat again.

The gold in Kate's hazel eyes glittered above the small, sad smile she gave him. "Keep him safe for me."

Silas pulled off his hat and ran the brim through his fingers, still rough and callused, though he'd had a month off from his farming chores. "Anthony needs you."

She cocked her head. "I told Anthony I'll write. My guess is he'll tire of writing me long before I'll tire of hearing from him. He'll—" The train whistled to signal its approach. "He'll want me to stop poking my nose into your lives probably sooner than later."

"But all boys need a ma."

"I suppose both of us would've been better off with parents, but I'm sure he'll get himself a mother one day. You're far too . . ." Her gaze ran from his head to his toes, then away. A flush stained her cheek. Did she think the train huffing to a stop kept him from hearing what she'd almost said?

His chest cinched up tight. Did she find him attractive, nice, what? "No other woman would love him as much as you."

169

"Are you trying to make me cry, Silas?" Her throat garbled his name, or maybe it was the steam engine's chuff, but it sounded as if . . .

She took a step back and gave him a curt nod, her gaze stuck to the boards at her feet, but then she peeped up at him for just a second, her eyes sad—or longing? "We should bid each other good-bye now."

"But wouldn't you want to be his ma? To . . . to marry me and be his ma?"

Her head snapped up, and her eyes went wide, but not with longing. Had what he said insulted her?

He cleared his throat again. Why couldn't he get words out? "I mean, he needs one—"

"Oh no." She looked off into the distance, her head shaking, her mouth slightly agape. "Please don't tell me you're asking me to marry you just for Anthony's sake. Once he grows up, where would that leave me?"

How could she think she'd be unneeded? "I still wish I had a mother." The steam engine's hiss escalated, and he spoke as loudly as he could without yelling. "If Anthony stays around Salt Flatts, there'd be grandchildren, and a farm's work is never done. If you took over the house chores—"

"Stop." She held out a hand, and her tongue ran between her lips. "I'll not give up my job to be a maid."

"I didn't mean that's all I'd want you for."

She raised her voice to be heard over the train. "Then what good would I be once Anthony leaves?"

Was she daft? "Do you think that after years together we'd stay strangers?"

"Strangers, no." Her lips pursed, and she pointed at his chest as if she would poke him. "But I want to be happy, even if I have to remain a poor spinster to be so. I want love. It'd be too hard—"

170

"Well, of course I want you to be happy." He slapped his hat against his leg. "This hasn't come out right at all. I hadn't enough time to think of how to say this proper." But he couldn't promise love before he actually felt it, could he?

"Exactly, you haven't thought it through." Her throat worked, and her eyes turned moist. "I understand you're worried about taking on a boy you hardly know who hasn't warmed up to you, but you can't ask me to give up my entire life because you want help for a few years. What do you even know about me, about what I want? If it wasn't for . . ."

The train's brakes' long hiss drowned out her words, but her mouth kept moving. The more she argued, the harder it was to look away from her full bottom lip, the subtle dip in the top one.

What did she mean he didn't know about her? They had a lot in common: their orphaned background, their love for Anthony, their ability to work hard. What else did they need to build on?

Whatever was special between a man and a woman.

All of a sudden, she pressed her mouth shut. Her chest heaved right along with the hissing and heavy chugging that had grown so loud behind them she must have realized he couldn't hear a thing she said.

He felt something for her, sure. Many a man felt something when the shape of a woman and the details of her face were as delectable as hers. But she needed to know if he could feel more.

They couldn't become certain of such through letters—his past was proof of that.

The train's hiss ended, and a mechanical *pop* made her jump. She crossed her arms, her expression transforming from anger to hurt. "Clearly, you aren't—"

He caught her waist faster than he could lasso a sleeping calf and cut off her words with his mouth. Her sharp intake of breath, and her eyes darting off to the side reminded him of

Anthony and the disembarking passengers, so he brought his hat up to shield their kiss from view.

But that was the last logical move he made.

He'd expected some sizzle—either from her fists or her lips—being the firebrand that she was, but the magnetic draw was an unexpected shock. The second his lips touched hers, his free hand cupped her long neck, which arched backward to accommodate his height. His thumb ran along the smooth curve of her throat as his body closed the gap between them. He dropped his hat to bury his fingers into her hair and pull her closer.

She put a hand against his chest, but she didn't push him away.

He needed to be pushed away! He was far too close, consumed with the same insatiable thirst that came when he pressed a liquor bottle to his lips. But no short kiss would tell them much of anything they needed to know. . . .

Her fingers dug into the fabric of his shirt and dragged him even closer.

He could feel the crowd scurrying past them, but when she started to move her lips against his in a way Lucy's never had, his mind closed off, as if they'd been transported to a place where not a single soul but God knew what they were doing.

And then she moaned.

Heaven help him—

Wheeeeeesh!

They jumped apart at the train whistle's blow, alerting passengers to get on quickly for the scheduled short stop.

They blinked at each other for what seemed like forever, red-faced and short of breath.

Oh, there was certainly that special feeling between a man and a woman bouncing off of them all right. They had it in spades.

Her hand flattened against his chest, which dragged in such

exaggerated breaths he was hard-pressed not to look down and take in every inch of her. He'd not really lingered over her feminine curves the past few weeks, but at that moment he wanted to rather badly, though what mattered was in her eyes.

He found his breath first. "Would you come with us?"

"Now?" She put her fingers against her mouth. "This is too sudden. I can't . . . I can't leave my job unless I'm absolutely certain you won't back out on me. You said you haven't even thought this through. Another hasty marriage proposal—"

"*I'm* not the backing-out kind." That description would belong to his late wife, his mother, the foster parents who'd given him back after only a handful of weeks.

No. Backing out was what the people who were supposed to love him did, not what he did.

"I . . . I don't know." She shook her head, but her eyes dropped from his and onto his lips. Not her feet, not elsewhere . . . She was still glued to him though the physical contact had broken. "I promised myself I'd never again make a decision like this so quickly. Yet you're asking me to decide now."

But she hadn't slapped him, hadn't run away, was still looking at his mouth.

He'd married a stranger once, and he'd thought he'd felt something for Lucy after looking at her picture, after taking her home.

That something was as cold as a blizzard compared to the heat still in his body and the fire flushing Kate's freckled cheeks.

His heart had been so focused on Anthony while he'd been living in Breton, he must have been completely ignoring his body. He looked at Anthony, who darted glances between them.

No warning bell clanged in his mind. She'd be perfect for his every need—their every need.

And he liked her. More than liked her. But he couldn't handle her coming to Kansas, then changing her mind. Not after that kiss. Not knowing how Anthony's heart would break if she didn't follow through. "I won't beg, Kate. If you come, I'll give you the best wedding I can afford."

"All aboard!"

He stooped to grab his hat, then stood. "Looks like we've run out of time."

She started to shake her head, and it was all he could do not to grab her and kiss her again so she wouldn't say a word.

They didn't need another kiss though. He already knew exactly what that would tell them. "Was Richard wrong about you feeling something for me?"

Her lips flattened as if she was trying not to flat out tell him she hated his guts. Yet she didn't say anything.

"Please think about it." He gestured for Anthony to pick up his bags.

How did one say good-bye after kissing a woman like that? He laid a hand on her stiff shoulder and let his palm run down the length of her arm until he cupped her elbow, his eyes locked on hers. He stared at her for a moment. Was she going to say something?

She dropped her gaze from his, seemingly struck dumb.

"All aboard! Last call!"

"Write me, Kate." He let his fingers trail down the rest of her arm, then tucked a loose wisp of hair behind her ear.

She looked up and blinked. He wasn't sure, but he thought she nodded.

He turned to grab his luggage and shuffled it over to the freight car where Anthony was the last person hoisting his things into the porter's hands.

Over his shoulder, Kate only stared at them, both hands now pressed against her mouth.

He hopped onto the passenger car's back platform as the locomotive's pistons started their first hard, slow chug.

He waited for her to take a step forward, hold out her hand, widen her eyes with regret—anything to tell him whether or not he'd hear from her soon. But she only stood transfixed.

When the train depot's platform and Kate's slender figure disappeared, Silas laid a reluctant hand on Anthony's back and guided him into the car. Anthony slid across the cushioned bench seat and looked out the window.

Silas closed his eyes and let his body rock with the train's gentle swaying. Was it his imagination, or had she responded to his kiss as if . . . as if she'd been pining to kiss him all along?

But then she'd said no to his awkward proposal.

So which was it? What was he to hope for?

Time. Time was what they needed.

Time for his proposal to sink in. Letters to discuss what could be. Dreams of more kisses that would stir up the undercurrent of feelings already there.

How had he not entertained marrying Kate earlier? He smiled. Just a few exchanged letters to convince her Anthony wasn't the only good thing awaiting her in Kansas, that he'd work to be a good husband, that there'd be more kisses like that. . . .

Surely she'd let him prove the spark that had just consumed them could be fanned into a flame. If she wrote, they could get to know each other better and she'd see he already respected her. Coaxing admiration into love wouldn't be as hard as nurturing crops through a season of drought—and he'd done that before.

But what if *he* wasn't enough? His smile faded. Kate was a keg of dry powder. Any flame sparked her passion, and she burned hot. Moments before kissing her, had she not said they had nothing to base a relationship on?

She knew his addiction still threatened to send him back to his darkest days, and her school contract promised her a stability she probably didn't believe he could provide after all his talk of his farm being in ruins.

She'd not been happy when he'd almost given up on finding Anthony either.

"So did you convince Miss Dawson to come?"

He glanced at his son sitting beside him before groaning and closing his eyes. Of course the spectacle he'd made of himself would plant a seed of hope in Anthony.

And if Kate didn't come, Anthony would be far more devastated than he.

Chapter 14

With her fingers pressed against her mouth, Kate stared after Silas, though the train had already conveyed him from sight.

She should've waved farewell to Anthony. Had he been waving at her while she'd stared at his father? She forced herself off the empty depot platform, putting one foot in front of the other, fighting against the heat in her eyes.

Anthony was gone.

But they didn't have to be separated long . . . if she got married right away. She fisted her hands against her skirts.

How dare he do this to me. Like dangling a carrot in front of a mule, he was trying to get her to consider the one thing she'd decided never to do again. She of all people should know not to be enticed by a hasty marriage proposal. She didn't know Silas inside and out; he hadn't courted her like a proper gentleman over months and months, couldn't possibly love her in such a short time.

However, Anthony wasn't a carrot, and the dreams she'd entertained, the feel of Silas's lips against hers . . .

Her brain still felt sluggish and dazed and . . . and . . . mind-numbingly elated.

It had been so hard to say no, but it was the smart thing to have done.

Wasn't it?

Someone bumped her shoulder. "Excuse me, miss." The man grasped her upper arm to right her before he continued on his way. She needed to clear her head if she was going to make it home without tripping and making a fool of herself.

But the kiss kept replaying in her mind. Had she been longing for a kiss from him for so long that she'd felt more than she should have? She'd been daydreaming about Silas, assuming nothing would happen. But something had.

She just hadn't expected a proposal to come with it.

What was wrong with her that men didn't seem to care if they loved her or not before they offered their hand?

And what was wrong with her that each and every time she wanted to answer with a "yes"?

But this time, she wouldn't do it. She'd pledged never to do it again.

Waiting for a buggy to pass so she could cross the last road to the Logans', she blew out a breath and tipped her head back to watch the clouds roll by overhead.

Should her opinion on quick, convenient marriages change with one kiss? One really, really extraordinary kiss?

She did want to be with Anthony, but Silas had said nothing about love—and that's what she was holding out for.

After the way her heart practically leapt from her chest and into Silas's arms, what if she married him and he never came to love her? She might as well throw her heart on the tracks and let the locomotives grind it into the rails every day for the rest of her life.

All of this contemplation only proved she was on the edge of making a mistake again. But what if refusing to marry was the mistake this time? Would she ever have another chance to leave spinsterhood behind? Was gaining a financially secure future more important than love? She might have a teaching job to rely on now, but if she crossed Mr. Kingfisher again . . .

At the Logans', Kate quietly let herself in the side door. Knowing dinner would be long over, she headed for the stairs, but the rattle of dishes in the kitchen led her stomach to hope Mrs. Logan had something warm left for her.

Drying a mixing bowl, Mrs. Logan pierced Kate with a sharp look the minute she passed through the door.

Kate cleared her throat. "I hope I didn't inconvenience you by not letting you know I'd miss dinner."

The woman's eyes didn't grow any softer with the apology. "You were with Mr. Jonesey again?"

"Yes." She straightened her shoulders despite the blush she felt creeping up on her. This time Mrs. Logan would be right to believe she and Silas may have done something inappropriate. That kiss . . . Well, it wasn't the chaste peck on the lips she'd seen a few married couples exchange in public.

Oh goodness, how many people saw them kiss like that? She pressed her hands against her cheeks and staggered over to one of the kitchen table's chairs. Trying to envision the train station, her mind blanked over how many might have seen them kissing. The whole world had disappeared, and—

Mrs. Logan's *tsk* jarred her from that memory.

Kate cleared her throat. "Anthony was almost kidnapped this afternoon so I helped him pack so Silas could get him out of town to keep him safe."

"Why would he be any safer gone than here?" The woman didn't look sufficiently appalled over a boy nearly being abducted.

"We're certain Richard had to be behind it, so we had to get Anthony away."

Mrs. Logan set down a plate and picked up another. "Was Mr. Fitzgerald arrested?"

179

"The sheriff is looking into it. Richard's gone—at least he appears to be, but why else was Anthony targeted in the middle of the day? I've never heard of kidnappers so bold."

"I suppose there won't be any more of your traipsing about town, then."

Why did she feel as if she was no more than fifteen? Kate gritted her teeth against the desire to ask if she'd be as concerned about Kate's actions if the child in question was one of the Logans'. "You don't need to worry about me being improper now any more than you had to before."

Especially now that Silas was gone.

Mrs. Logan grabbed a pie tin off the back of the stove and slipped it onto the table. "Here's leftover ham I kept out for you."

"Thank you."

Mrs. Logan stared at her, an eyebrow raised.

Kate covered her mouth with her hand, though surely the woman couldn't see that her lips still felt roughened from Silas's beard. Of course she hadn't looked at herself in the mirror before she came into the kitchen. Was it possible to tell if a person had just been kissed?

Had her lips felt like this when she'd kissed Aiden two years ago?

The late afternoon beams piercing through the Logans' kitchen curtains splintered into the shards of gaslight that danced around the memory of Aiden McGuinness's mischievous smile under the oak tree in front of her sister's house in Georgia.

He'd just given her a sweet little peck on the lips. "Things will be better with me—I promise."

Kate had smiled up at him. "Of course they will." Had he really just proposed? He was too good, too handsome, for someone like her. Had he really come to care for her during the few conversations they'd shared the handful of times he'd come to her house earlier than her brother-in-law had expected?

For years, she'd longed to get out from under Peter's abusive hand, and just hours earlier, she'd overheard Aiden regaling her brother-in-law's guests with how his stepfather had often tried to beat the Irish out of him. Not the typical story told at the grand parties Peter and her sister Violet threw for the bank employees to celebrate particularly good business months.

Though Kate had been ordered upstairs for the evening, she'd crept closer to the doorway to the dining room as Aiden continued his story about proving to his stepfather that an Irishman needn't blueblood heritage or family money to succeed in America. His voice resounded in the crowded dining room, impossible to ignore. And then Aiden glared straight at her brother-in-law as he accused any man who laid a harsh hand on his charges as worse than a snake.

The champagne in Peter's glass had shook as he took a nonchalant sip, though he nodded his head along with the other gilded guests murmuring their agreement.

He'd have to have been daft not to realize Aiden was declaring he knew how Peter treated Kate—and that he didn't approve.

She'd waited outside to catch Aiden as the guests left, hoping against hope he would help her leave—but she hadn't expected his proposal.

"I'm assuming you won't want a long engagement?" Aiden tucked a stray strand of hair behind her ear.

She shook her head. He was indeed seriously suggesting marriage. The nervous butterflies fluttering about her body clogged her throat. She stepped into his offered embrace and pressed the side of her face against the shoulder of his starched suit, trying not to think of the patched work dress she wore. The fine weave of his dinner jacket cooled the heat in her cheek. She'd never dreamed he'd propose marriage as an escape. Why would she have? A young, talented banker paired with his boss's sister-in-law, who was treated worse than a servant?

Perhaps *Cinderella* was more than just a fairy tale after all.

Aiden wrapped his arms around her, his forearm pressing against her left shoulder blade. She sucked air in through her teeth.

He backed away and narrowed his eyes. "Don't tell me there are marks on your back."

She swallowed and looked at his hand clutching her upper arm. Peter always made sure bruises from the broomstick were hidden.

Aiden placed a tender kiss on her forehead. "Why didn't you come to me before I figured this out myself?"

How could she have convinced anyone of the abuse without disrobing? No one but her sister saw the bruises beneath her shirtwaists. How would she have known he'd believe her until she'd heard the cruelty he'd himself known at the hands of his stepfather—and that he was already suspicious of Peter?

Aiden's jaw tightened. "How could anyone treat you like this?"

She'd been asking that question for years. Peter didn't even raise a hand against his Great Dane, and that beast stole food off the table and made most of the messes she rarely cleaned to Peter's satisfaction. "Maybe—"

"Hush, there is no good answer. At least I never got one that made any sense from my stepfather." Aiden's face took on a faraway angry look, the same one he often directed at Peter when her brother-in-law talked down to her in Aiden's presence. "What I wouldn't give to strangle them both."

Aiden laughed, a throaty, vengeance-filled cackle. "But we'll show both of them. We'll take away Peter's free maid, and I'll prove to my stepfather this lowly Irishman can mop the floor with him in the banking world."

"Oh no." She pressed a hand against her mouth. "What if Peter fires you when he finds out? What if he's so angry—"

"Hush." Aiden laid a gentle finger on her lips. "I once heard him say he wished someone would take you off his hands. That was what drew my attention to how he treated you in the first place."

If she could melt with shame, she'd slip through Aiden's fingers like sunbaked butter.

"Besides, I'm his best employee. I have a knack for investments none of the others have. He'll not fire me. It'd cost him more than he thinks you're worth."

Which wasn't much.

Aiden leaned down to whisper in her ear. "I'll be richer than him in no time—wait and see. Imagine how they'll squirm seeing you wearing fancier furs and riding in finer carriages than Violet." He smiled and tapped her nose. "Let's go tell him."

Within the hour, she'd been tossed out of the house. But it didn't matter. Aiden had scrambled to get her lodging at the boardinghouse, and she was drunk with thoughts of a wedding and a new home.

While she'd worked on gathering a trousseau, he'd spent his spare time deciding on a place for them to live. He finally settled on a huge townhouse, one he surely couldn't afford no matter how well his first year of investments went.

Evidently he figured appearing wealthy would gain him the affluent friends, connections, and opportunities he sought. And of course, he'd explained, she'd have to do her part and keep the place immaculate with only a cook to aid her, for they, after all, hadn't the money for more help . . . yet. So she'd run the house for him as she'd done for Peter and Violet, from sunup to sundown—minus the blows from the broomstick and any help from other servants. After realizing exactly what Aiden expected of her, Kate's future no longer looked so bright.

Oh, she'd not be beaten, at least she was pretty certain of that, but her brother-in-law had a cook, a gardener, a butler, a head housekeeper, and two maids other than herself, and she still couldn't please Peter. How could she possibly keep up a three-story townhouse well enough to impress the businessmen Aiden hoped to charm?

That night, trembling at how quickly her hopes of an easier life had fallen down around her, she'd picked up a discarded newspaper at the boardinghouse where she lived. Her fingers slid down the matrimonial advertisements. Surely some man wanted a wife who wasn't a glorified maid.

Jasper's advertisement had popped off the page: a small house and the desire for help in the paint shop he owned with his brother. She'd always wanted to learn to paint. She—

"Is there something wrong with the ham?"

Kate startled. "I'm sorry?"

Mrs. Logan stood beside the table with her hands on her hips.

Clearing her throat, Kate picked up her fork. "The ham's good. I just got lost in thought."

"Do you need me for anything?" Mrs. Logan wiped her hands on her dish towel. The dishes were all put away. No wonder her ham had cooled.

"Can I ask you a question?" She knew her hostess had questioned the time she spent with Silas, but what other woman did she have in her life to ask?

"What do you want to know?"

She swallowed and busied herself with cutting her meat into tiny squares. "I . . . well . . . Did you marry for love?"

"I find that question highly improper." She tilted her chin higher.

What did she do that this woman didn't consider improper? She wilted, but drove on. "It's just that, I've had two men . . . or well . . . three now, offer their hand to me without being in

184

love. I just wondered if there was something wrong with me, or . . . as a spinster, is that all I can hope for?"

"I thought your contract explicitly stated you can't court while teaching."

"It does."

"Then I don't see why you're contemplating your marital status."

"But what if I want to change it?"

"You can't until the end of the term."

"Right." She sighed. The hope of getting motherly advice was evidently for naught.

And Mrs. Logan was correct. She couldn't make a decision right now as a teacher anyway, didn't even have to.

This time her exhale took a weight off her shoulders.

She had her answer. She'd write Silas as he suggested and learn more about him, and she'd have the whole rest of the school year to decide. To see if the ache of missing Anthony got stronger. To see if there was more behind Silas's proposal than the need of a mother for his son.

"Thank you, Mrs. Logan. You've helped me tremendously." She lifted a piece of meat to her mouth, where she could still feel the weight of Silas's lips. The sensation of which she could experience again within days if she'd only—

Blast the memory of his lips on hers. She needed to be patient and careful for once in her life. If she ever felt his mouth on hers again, it'd be a year from now.

———

Silas groaned and rolled over. Since returning to his home-stead outside of Salt Flatts, nights on his cabin floor had not been kind. He should get to work making another bed, but the mess Peter Hicks had left drove him to do as much as possible before a cold snap made outside work even more unpleasant.

He lifted his head off the quilts he'd piled on the floor and squinted into the early morning light filtering across where Anthony slept on the bed.

His hip aching at how he must have lain throughout the night, Silas pulled himself up off the floor and onto the chair he'd dragged in. The boy's joints and muscles probably would've taken sleeping on the floor better, but it was the least he could do to help Anthony look favorably on his new home.

Taking his clothing from yesterday off the back of the chair, Silas slipped them on before heading into the kitchen to stoke the fire for coffee.

A few minutes later, Anthony came stumbling in, rubbing at his eyes.

"Good morning, son." He smiled. The cricks in his body and the weight of dread over the coming winter lessened a smidge just by uttering the word *son*.

"Can I go to school today?"

Silas pressed a hand to his complaining stomach and slid the pot onto the burner. "Maybe next week. We have pears to gather and some of the persimmons are dropping, so we need to gather those right away and make persimmon leather." They needed everything he could store considering how much of the garden had been left to rot or was eaten by wildlife. Evidently Peter Hicks had done nothing more than load as much of Silas's goods on Silas's wagon as possible and head west. The man had told him he needed a job to help him start his own homestead but had failed to explain he planned to take Silas's stuff to do so.

At least the bulk of his savings had been in the bank, but with the way Kansas weather went, he needed to keep every dime there in case next year's crop failed or the winter was harsh. So in the meantime, he'd scrounge every wild growing thing possible.

"While I fix something for breakfast, why don't you throw

the scraps to the pig?" One pig. The other two hadn't survived without being watered for weeks.

The boy groaned but worked to put his muddy pants back on.

"Maybe you could do the laundry before our clothes walk away from us. Kate said you worked at a laundry once. Could you do so without help?"

Anthony stopped pulling his boots on to frown at him. "Back in Breton you said you didn't need me for chores. That's all I've done since we got here."

He swallowed. "This isn't the situation I expected to bring you home to."

Anthony gave him a glare the orphanage directors would have clocked him for, then tromped over to the washstand and scrubbed his face.

Silas followed him out to the barn but stopped in the middle of the yard. "Right, no milk."

His milk cow had gone dry. He marched to the coop, where he had been glad to see at least half of his birds had survived, though they were thin. Thankfully Will had found them in time to give them water before they joined the rest of their dehydrated companions.

In the nest boxes, he found two eggs. The stress of their ordeal must be waning. He threw out a handful of corn and clucked at them. "Come on, ladies. Let's be happy and get back to egg laying. I'm counting on you." Though he'd saved up quite a bit of their summer production, he'd now have to pay for milk and cheese and butter, so the more eggs the better.

The jangle of a bridle caught his attention, and sticking his head outside the coop, he waved at Will driving into his yard. "Over here."

His friend searched for him and smiled when he found him.

Silas opened the yard gate to let the chickens forage and strode toward Will. As much as he wanted to talk with his friend, he really needed to work. He shook his head—he could stand to chat a little, considering the man had basically saved the livestock he had left.

But the days were growing short.

"Hey." Will hopped down from his wagon, his thick hair flopping into his eyes as usual, but with two paper bags in his hands, he had to whip his head to get his bangs out of the way. "Brought breakfast."

Silas swallowed against the shame of knowing seconds ago he'd halfway wished his friend hadn't stopped by.

"I'm headed to the Gentrys' to check on their baby. Eliza sent me off with muffins."

"Wonderful. All I got was two eggs this morning." He held up the speckled ovals. "Better than another morning of crackers and jelly though."

Will tossed him the bags and leaned into the back of his wagon. "And Eliza caught the milkman this morning and bought you a jar."

"Bless her." Will's wife seemed more concerned about his loss of milk than he was. But didn't a growing boy need milk? At least babies did. He walked to the house. "You eating with us?"

"I've eaten, but thanks for the invite."

Anthony hadn't come back yet, and after a quick look around, Silas saw him making his way to the outhouse. "Thanks for thinking of us."

"No problem. How's living with Anthony going? He didn't seem exactly thrilled the night you showed up at my house, but it was three in the morning, so I guess that's understandable."

"Well, can you blame him? His mother dies, he finds out the only father he knew isn't his real father, has to leave behind the one person he loves to live in another state with a stranger, and now he's not thrilled I've kept him from school to help with the farm." Silas ran a hand through his hair. "You don't think that's wrong, do you? Part of me's concerned he'll run off if I don't keep an eye on him, and with how Peter Hicks left my farm . . . I really need his help getting things put together. I only planned to get myself through the winter, and now I got a boy who's always hungry to feed."

He'd not even thought about the amount of food *three* people would require or the accommodations awaiting back home when he'd proposed to Kate. Even when the farm was in good shape he'd have been worried.

Heady with the feel of her in his arms, he'd asked her to marry him without taking enough time to think a lick. Should he write to explain how wrong he'd been to propose when he wasn't even sure he could keep him and the boy fed this winter, let alone her if she came?

Should he back out for her sake?

But he'd told her he wasn't the backing-out kind. He could only tell her he'd changed his mind if he was all right with being a liar.

Near the privy, Anthony kicked a stone on the well-worn path.

Of course, he could set up an account with the Hampdens' mercantile again, but he'd not had to use credit for eight years now. He liked living without that burden, but he'd do so in order to keep his son from going hungry . . . and his potential wife too. . . .

"What are you looking at?" Will was squinting off into the distance, where there was nothing but stubble left from the summer harvest.

"Nothing." He'd not told Will about his impromptu proposal since his friend would request details he wasn't ready to share. "Just worried about requiring too much of Anthony."

"Pa kept me home when there were chores he couldn't handle alone—didn't hurt me any."

"But you and your pa had a good relationship. Anthony doesn't trust me yet."

"It'll take time, I'm sure." Will waved at Anthony before holding the milk out. "I'd best be off."

Switching things around in his hands, he took it and nodded good-bye.

Anthony bounded up the porch stairs as Will turned his team to head out. "What do you have?"

"Breakfast." The milk jar was slipping. He should have put the eggs in his pocket. "Here, take this."

Anthony grabbed one of the muffin bags.

"No, the milk."

He pulled on the neck instead of taking it from the bottom. "Careful!"

The boy winced as if expecting a punch.

The gruff drained right out of him. "Sorry about shouting, but I don't want to waste the milk."

"I wasn't going to waste it."

Biting his tongue, Silas gently placed a hand on his shoulder and waited for Anthony to look up. "Even if you'd dropped it, I wouldn't hit you. You know that?"

Anthony's dark eyes looked wary. "Mother said you hurt her."

Silas resisted wishing away the past. If he'd not gone through it—hadn't messed up so poorly—he might not have a son in front of him right now. He gripped Anthony's shoulder and tried to hold his gaze. "When I drank, I manhandled your ma a bit when she . . ." It wouldn't do to tell the boy his late mother had been meaner than his Rhode Island Red rooster. "Sometimes we argued and I got angrier than I should have. I shoved my weight around—which isn't right—but I never hit her."

Anthony seemed to be searching his eyes as if he could find the truth there but then shrugged. "I'm hungry."

190

"All right." No use forcing the boy through such a painful subject unless he wanted to talk about it. Words wouldn't matter anyway—time would, just as Will said. Silas backed into the house and got to cooking.

Cracking the two little eggs, he scrambled them, but not quickly enough—Anthony was starting on the third of the four muffins Will had brought by the time he turned around.

He'd been right to worry about having enough to eat this winter if the boy could pack away three muffins without even a sip of milk. He snatched two tin cups and set them down. "Probably should've waited for me to pray first."

Anthony stopped chewing, his cheeks still full.

Silas huffed a chuckle, said grace, and poured out the milk—only half of what he'd normally drink so Anthony could have a full glass. Maybe he could stretch the milk to last three days.

He halved the eggs. Anthony inhaled his portion, then frowned at the muffin Silas had pulled toward himself.

He wanted to make sure the boy had enough to eat, but he had to have something too.

"Where's the laundry stuff?" Anthony looked as if he'd been asked to wash his clothes in dung rather than soap and water.

Silas could think of plenty of worse chores than laundry, but then, he'd not been forced to work in a laundry as a child. "You can find the tubs and washboard in the lean-to on the side of the barn. The soap's in that chest over there."

Maybe he shouldn't have asked Anthony to do the wash. But the boy hadn't been enthused about any other chores either. Was it just because he didn't want to work, or was the sunup to sundown needs of a homestead more than the boy had endured before?

Was he asking too much of him?

Lucy had certainly thought he'd asked too much of her.

Would Kate think so as well?

"Do you got any bluing?"

Silas raised his eyebrows. Maybe his clothes would be better off in the boy's care from now on, whether Anthony liked the chore or not. "No, but I can put it on the list."

Anthony shrugged and looked at the last remaining muffin, his eyes as sad as a puppy's.

"Here." Silas forced himself to tear off the top and give him the best part. "Have I thanked you for the help you've been this past week?"

Shrugging, Anthony stuffed his mouth with the crumbly mass of cake and sugar.

"I wish the farm would've been in better shape when you came so I didn't need so much help, but I'm thankful you've pitched in." Though he'd moaned and groaned. "I wish I could make things better for you. Perhaps—"

"Is Miss Dawson coming?"

So that's what would make things better for him? Silas's chest tightened. "I'm not sure. But if not, it isn't because she doesn't want to for your sake. I'm positive of that."

"You think she might not come because of you?" Anthony's glare was piercing.

He tried not to fidget under the glare of a nine-year-old. "Maybe. But it could be for some other reason. She—"

"Even after you kissed her like that?"

Silas winced. His kiss had fired up an attraction he hadn't been completely aware of and, at nine years old, Anthony appeared to expect a wedding would take place after he'd kissed Kate like that.

"Or maybe because I *did* kiss her like that." What had he been thinking? With Kate's reputation on rocky ground, how could he have kissed her in front of everybody? Was the school board disciplining her for poor public conduct at this very moment?

No wonder she'd basically told him no.

Anthony's frown looked about as heavy as the half muffin in Silas's gut. Should he stoke up the boy's hope? His own? "She hasn't written yet, so we'll wait to see what she says."

"Well, if she does come, she won't want to sleep on the floor."

Silas frowned at his wadded-up bedding he could just see through the bedroom door and clamped a hand against the heat in his neck. And he thought only women could blush instantaneously. "No, she wouldn't." And sleeping on the floor would likely start the list of things Kate wouldn't care for around the place.

"Well, I hope she comes." Anthony downed the last of his milk and walked out.

Silas nodded at the boy, but he wasn't sure he agreed. If she wrote, he'd have to admit what the coming winter would hold for them all. And with that information, as smart as she was, she'd not go through with a wedding.

He shouldn't do anything to encourage her, for her own good.

*C*hapter 15

Chewing on her lip, Kate walked out of the post office. She'd written Anthony, asking him to let her know that he'd arrived safely, but the envelope she now held had Silas's name on the return address.

Would it contain a letter full of feelings for her? The memory of his kiss played havoc with her capacity for rational thought.

But if he brought up marriage again as if he were arranging for a nanny . . .

She'd tried to write him, had even taken out her stationery a few times, but couldn't. The only questions that came to mind were why he'd kissed her, how he'd felt while kissing her, and whether he dreamed about kissing her again as much as she did. Very unladylike and inappropriate questions. And if he felt nothing much for her, how silly she'd sound.

For days she'd grappled with what to do despite having a whole school year to decide. Should she forget him, write him, go now, go later, go never? All this thinking! She'd always trusted her gut before, but hindsight proved her gut to be a sorry counselor. But her logic wasn't helping much either, because her heart fought against every impartial argument.

Being a mail-order bride had been scary but it was nothing close to this. Knowing what she did about Silas, she wanted a marriage between them to work. So much so, she hadn't slept well trying to figure out if it would.

God, if only you would tell me yes or no. When Silas kissed me, I felt that I . . . I belonged with him, but maybe it's just because I wanted to be with him, not because I should be.

What woman wouldn't want to be kissed like that again? But his previous wife had left him, he had an addiction to alcohol, and he'd not come from a good background.

All excuses. Marrying anyone would be scary, but a man she'd only known for a few weeks . . . ? She'd chosen poorly before—could she know if she was choosing poorly again?

Slipping a finger beneath the flap, she tore open the envelope. Would Silas ask her why she hadn't written him? Or had he thought better of his spur-of-the-moment proposal and wrote to rescind his offer? At least that would end her indecision.

"Miss Dawson?" The superintendent maneuvered around a young boy skipping on the sidewalk. He stopped in front of her, his frown deepening as he stared at her.

"Are you all right, Mr. Kingfisher?" She'd never seen his skin so sallow. He looked as if someone had died or he was about to die himself.

He cleared his throat. "I am not."

She glanced both to her left and right. Surely someone else should help him. "Do you want me to find your wife or a doctor?"

"Unfortunately, neither would help me with what I have to do." He held out a hand toward a bench in front of the toy store. "Let's get out of people's way."

Her heart slammed into her throat. Was she the reason for his disgruntled appearance? If so, there was no possibility of

195

this talk ending well. But she'd been a model teacher since Anthony left. No socializing, clean corners, well-performing students. She'd done everything right.

When he gestured toward the seat again, she shook her head.

"It's likely you'll want to sit, Miss Dawson."

She lowered herself onto the slats, one loose enough she didn't trust it to hold her weight, just like she didn't trust she'd leave this conversation unscathed.

"Have you been courting?"

"What?"

"Courting." Mr. Kingfisher said the word slower, as if she didn't understand.

"No." She swallowed against the film that had taken over her throat. Could a rumor take her down?

"Mrs. Logan just now told me you've been considering a marriage proposal from Mr. Jonesey."

She blinked. Considering, yes, but . . . "I wasn't courted by Mr. Jonesey. And he's gone now."

Her fingers trembled as she gripped Silas's letter. Could she put it behind her back without calling attention to his name? She flipped the envelope over in her lap without taking her gaze off Mr. Kingfisher.

"So he didn't propose to you?"

She wouldn't lie. "He did."

"I heard from more than one person that he kissed you in plain view of everyone at the train depot the day he left."

She kept her gaze on his. She wouldn't be ashamed of something she hadn't asked for . . . no matter how much she'd enjoyed it.

Mr. Kingfisher slapped his hat lightly against his trousers, shaking his head. "I cannot understand how a woman whose situation with the board is as precarious as yours would carry on with a man in front of the whole town. Beginning with

196

spending all that unchaperoned time in the guise of looking for a boy—"

"'In the *guise* of'!"

"And now accepting marriage offers."

"Accepting?"

"And kissing in broad daylight."

She pressed her lips together. She could tell him she hadn't wanted to be kissed, but that wasn't the truth—she hadn't expected to be, but not wanting it? She'd definitely wanted to be kissed. The thrill of emotions Silas created in her on the depot platform flared up again, making her flush right in front of her boss.

Mr. Kingfisher was right. Seeing a couple kiss like that in the middle of a crowd would've shocked her too.

"I know that might seem as if I was trying to defy the school board's wishes—"

"You are causing me too much grief, Miss Dawson. You might have an excuse, but frankly, dear, you've made my job exasperating. Whether you call it courting or not, that's what you did and are therefore in violation of your contract. Consider yourself relieved of your duties. You may continue to work until the end of the week unless you don't feel as if you can conduct yourself maturely."

"But you can't—"

"Please." He held out a hand. "No one, Miss Dawson, would believe that kind of public spectacle is socially acceptable for an unmarried woman."

"I—" She cleared her throat trying to loosen her restricted vocal cords. "I—"

"I know this isn't what you want to hear, but I've already consulted with the other board members, and since you didn't deny the kiss, we are severing your contract."

Her hot cheeks turned to ice. If she'd slapped Silas, she might not be having this discussion. But she'd pulled him closer, relishing the warmth he'd created all the way down into her toes, which now instantly reheated her cheeks.

"We've decided to allow you the dignity of resigning." He gave her a wobbly smile. "It'll make things easier on everyone."

"I—" Since her voice seemed unable to create anything but one short syllable, she gave up and nodded.

"Very well then, Miss Dawson—I'm relieved. Please turn in your resignation tomorrow, if you would." He stood and nodded to a passerby. After giving Kate a curt nod, he left her alone on the bench.

She sniffed hard to keep the tears and the anger back. Releasing her grip on her now-crumpled envelope, she pulled out the letter and scanned the contents, a short note written in Anthony's hand. No postscript from Silas begging her to say yes . . . or explaining he'd changed his mind. Nowhere in Anthony's tightly bunched letters did he mention his father, just assured her he'd arrived in Kansas safely.

She let the letter fall into her lap and tipped her head back against the toy store wall. Nothing tied her to Breton anymore, and the only people she cared about were in Kansas.

Well, had she not asked God for an indication of what to do? Her job was gone, and the Logans wouldn't want to continue housing her. Whether she wanted to or not, she'd have to make another quick decision in regards to a marriage of convenience without knowing what the man behind the proposal really wanted.

And since she wanted to say yes, to believe things had happened for a reason . . .

God, I'm going to work off the fact I asked you to provide me with a yes or no, and I've definitely got a no to teaching. So since the only other option I've been considering is Silas . . .

Seemed like she needed to figure out what to write.

198

———◆◆———

"Anthony." Silas gave his son a firm look—one he had to use more and more if he wanted the boy to obey. Was the boy testing him or was Silas failing at this parenting thing? Anthony got more stubborn every day, even after he'd been allowed to return to school.

Anthony rolled his eyes but climbed down from the wagon. After Silas hitched his team, he circled around to find Anthony hadn't gone into the post office as asked.

The boy stood, arms crossed, staring up at the building as if Silas intended to drag him inside and throw him into a prison cell.

"Why can't I wait outside?" Anthony muttered.

Silas flipped up his coat's collar to ward off the wind. "It's too cold, remember?" At least that was Anthony's excuse for refusing to go to the creek, explore the farm, or anything else Silas encouraged him to do after he'd finished his chores. He'd even offered to let him keep a snake if he could find one in this weather, but his son hadn't budged. The day Kate's letter came— asking only if they'd arrived safely, with no hint of her planning to follow—Anthony had started sulking.

Likely the boy blamed him for her not coming to Kansas. Though if he'd never proposed, Anthony wouldn't have hoped.

Regardless of being a fool, he wouldn't let Anthony continue to ignore him. They had to start doing things together besides chores.

He didn't have any toys or games, but surely he needed to provide his child with more than the three books he owned. He'd ordered a chess set, but in the meantime, Anthony could learn how to play with the bachelors who gathered in the post office for chess matches on Fridays. Perhaps Anthony would loosen up around the others. Plus they hadn't been in town all week, and Anthony was anxious to see if Kate had written another letter.

As for himself, he wasn't sure he wanted Kate to write again. Life was difficult enough trying to figure out how to live with one person who didn't love him.

"Are you coming in?" Anthony's voice held a hint of sarcasm as he stood on the threshold, letting the wind whip into the post office.

"You go on."

Anthony shoved at the door with a huff and disappeared inside.

Silas wiped his clammy hands against his coat. Maybe he should write Kate and tell her he'd made a mistake. He'd been reckless, out of his mind.

If only the feel of her in his arms hadn't . . .

He blew out a breath, trying to rid his face of the warmth that had taken up permanent residence in his cheeks. He needed to stop reliving that kiss every hour or so. He'd held a woman in his arms before—more intimately than for a mere kiss. But the flames that engulfed him whenever he thought of kissing Kate—

"What are you doing standing out here?" Lynville Tate stomped past him, headed for the post office door.

"Nothing." Besides going crazy. Silas lunged forward, caught the door, and forced himself inside. A gust of the north wind slammed it behind him.

The postmaster, Jedidiah Langston, grimaced. "Would you mind not breaking the door?"

Silas shook his head. "Sorry." He needed to stop thinking about Kate and focus on what he was doing. Focus on Anthony.

Oh, God, thank you for the boy you gifted me, but I need help.

200

And since I didn't ask you about Kate, well, I just don't know how that situation needs to be resolved. Should I write her or let her write me? I'd thought I needed her for Anthony's sake, and then I wanted her for mine, but maybe I'm just scared to be responsible for him on my own, especially now that it looks like I'm not doing that great of a job. I know you promise to help us through anything, and I need to trust you'll help, whether Kate's with me or not.

Silas unwrapped his scarf and draped it over the seat between Lynville and Anthony behind the long table Jedidiah used to sort mail packages during the day. Four chessboards were set up, though rarely enough men came for more than three games at a time.

"I see you've brought yourself a chess player you can actually beat." Lynville stood and punched Silas in the arm.

Silas could wipe the floor with Lynville with nothing but pawns. "Naw, I brought him for you to beat. Though he may be too skilled. He says he's played once before."

Lynville attempted to snarl, but a smile flickered underneath his curled lips. He turned to Anthony and flicked up the boy's hat.

Though Anthony's face turned dark, Lynville kept smiling. "You ready to find out if you've inherited your pa's pitiful chess skills?"

The boy shrugged and frowned at the board in front of him.

The door opened, and the frosty air sucked the heat from the room again. Ned Parker tried to catch his hat as it flew off, but missed. "Daggone wind. Hate Kansas." He kicked the door shut.

Silas greeted the grouchiest man in Salina County with a slight nod.

Ned didn't bother to return the greeting. He looked back

at Jedidiah. "You got me a letter yet?" Ned snatched his hat off the floor, then hung his bowler and slicker on a peg before marching to the back counter.

"I have one for both you and Silas."

Silas's heart tripped. Anthony lifted his head, his eyes alight with the first bit of interest Silas had seen in a few days. Who else would bother to write but Kate?

Ned ripped the top off his envelope with weather-cracked fingers.

"Here's yours, Silas." Jedidiah's eyebrows rose.

What if Kate kept writing? Jedidiah wouldn't keep his questions to himself much longer.

The letter shook in Silas's hand, so he tried to stash it quickly in his pocket, but his fingers fumbled and he had to retrieve the envelope off the floor.

He needed to get ahold of himself. The only reason Kate would write him was for Anthony's sake. She'd not quit teaching to marry him. Any feelings their kiss had created would fade over the months left in the school year. Anthony would adjust to Kansas without her help and then there'd be no need for her to come.

He let out a slow breath and went to sit.

"Ha!" Ned folded his letter with a flourish. "All done now. I'm a free man! Too bad Silas the do-gooder balks at me bringing my moonshine. I'd pass the jug around. Even let you have a swig, you little cuss." He tweaked Anthony's ear.

Anthony yanked free and glared.

"How're you free?" Lynville tried to grab the letter Ned brandished.

Ned smacked him in the back of the head with the paper before stuffing it into his chest pocket. "Done divorced her. Now who's in the worse position, eh? Helga—that's who. Who'll want her? Now I can get myself a woman to—"

202

Silas cleared his throat. "My boy's present."

With a quick eye roll, Ned dropped into his customary chair and hiked a dirt-laden boot onto the table. He leaned back with his hands behind his head. "The hag don't know what done hit her." He guffawed.

Jedidiah gave him a courtesy chuckle. The rest of them kept their mouths shut. Everyone avoided encouraging Ned to rant about Helga. Trying to talk decency into the man was a waste of breath. Hadn't done a lick of good anytime before.

Did he really think he'd pulled one over on her? Sure, most women didn't wish for the stigma of divorce . . . unless she'd been abused like his wife. Helga was probably laughing right along with Ned right now, but with joy.

Lynville grabbed a pawn and pointed it at Silas. "You gonna read your letter or play?"

"It's probably for Anthony." He looked at his son, who frowned at him. "Do you want to read it now or later?"

"Now." Anthony glanced at the four men around the table. "Not enough people for me to play anyway."

"I think Micah's coming. He's in town for a few days." Lynville turned the board to set up the white pieces on his side.

Silas tore the flap and took out two letters, Kate's flowery penmanship flowing across both pages. One for him, one for Anthony. The jitters in his stomach resembled a hoedown. He handed Anthony his and stared at the other. A good thing he'd long ago asked Ned not to bring along any more of his paint-stripping moonshine. He might have tempted fate and sacrificed his throat to the awful stuff.

With a shaky hand, Silas pocketed his letter. He couldn't read it now; the men might get curious enough to ask why he couldn't wait until home to read what Anthony's teacher wrote.

Lynville realigned his pawns, Jedidiah poured peanuts into

a bowl, and Ned stared at the ceiling with a satisfied grin while Silas worked to squeeze out the desire to find himself a whiskey, a tonic, something to take home with him to—

"Miss Dawson's coming!" Anthony squeaked.

Silas's fingers dug into the chair arms.

"Who's coming?" Lynville grabbed a handful of peanuts from the bowl before Jedidiah placed them in the middle of the table.

"My teacher."

Had he ever seen Anthony smile like that?

"To visit?" Ned smashed a peanut against the table with his fist, then swept the shell pieces onto the floor. "For Christmas?"

Anthony shrugged. "Didn't say anything about Christmas. Sounds like she's coming now."

If she was coming while school was still in session . . . Silas worked to breathe like a sane man.

Micah burst in the door. "I've brought beef!" The smell of smoked meat heavily doused in garlic from his father's butcher shop filled the room. The men flocked to Micah.

Silas tipped his head toward the men. "You getting some, Anthony?"

His son stared at him for a bit, likely wanting his reaction to Kate's coming, but he'd barely managed to utter that last question. Finally, Anthony stood. "I guess I could eat again." He ambled over to the counter and Jedidiah handed him a tin plate.

With no one paying him any mind, Silas unfolded Kate's letter and slumped in his chair to see the letter under the table. The shadows made it difficult to read, but he wasn't about to let anybody read over his shoulder.

Silas,

I've decided to come. I figured we could talk about

arrangements once I arrive. By the time you receive this letter, I should be on my way. I arrive on the 11th.

Sincerely, Kate Dawson

Micah plopped down in the chair beside him, and Silas rammed the letter under his leg.

"You not eating?" Micah waved a fork at him.

Lynville took the seat across from Micah, his plate piled high. "Mind if I play Micah first?"

Silas rolled his tongue around in his mouth a time or two to make sure it was wet enough to work. "I'll play Anthony. Make sure he remembers the rules."

Arrangements. What would she want? A wedding immediately? Where would they all sleep? He'd only just started working on Anthony's bed frame. He'd have to work faster. He smoothed his hand over his beard, trying to stem the grin threatening to rearrange his face.

While the men busily munched, he read the letter again. She hadn't said anything about marrying, just coming.

Despite the north wind snaking through the cracks in the walls, Silas wiped the sweat off the back of his neck repeatedly. Trying to focus on his game strategy.

"You going to move?" His son huffed and grabbed more peanuts.

"I'm afraid I . . ." He swallowed and tried to remember his plan for his rook.

Fear. That's what had agitated him since leaving Missouri and now wound through his belly and radiated out his every limb. Not worry over whether he should have proposed, not wondering if Kate should reject him, not fretting about Anthony turning out all right.

He was out-and-out scared. She could get their hopes up and

decide not to marry him at the last minute. She could be just as disappointed with this winter's meager provisions as Lucy had been with anything involving his homestead. She could go through with the wedding and keep herself guarded against his affections while he lost his heart.

Should he do anything to protect himself against the hurt she could cause them?

Chapter 16

"Would you mind having a seat, miss?" The young porter, his red freckles bright against his nearly translucent skin, sighed with exasperation. "The passengers are complaining about you again. They need to get around too."

Stuck on a train with nowhere to run, Kate had been compensating by pacing—for hours. "Is Salt Flatts the next stop?"

"Yes, miss."

She shook her head. How could she possibly sit when she was this close to seeing Silas again? Would she see what she wanted to see in his eyes the moment she stepped off the train? If she didn't, did that mean her plans should change or—

"Miss?" The porter's eyes narrowed. Would he dare wrestle her into a seat?

She blew out a breath and pivoted. She tromped back to sit and grabbed the armrests as her anchor.

She'd spent her savings for the train ride. Salt Flatts was her only option now. So why did her gut refuse to believe that? Her sister and husband surely never wanted to see her again, even if she groveled—which she wouldn't.

Aiden had likely taken a wife already, not that he'd want her back. And she still wouldn't marry Jasper, even if he offered her all the paint in the world.

And most importantly, Anthony needed her.

She'd been brave enough to cross the country once to marry a complete stranger, so why did her feet refuse to stay still when she was headed to a man she felt something for?

"Miss, please." The blond woman beside her squeezed her arm. "You're shaking the entire seat. I can't read."

"Sorry." Kate clamped her legs together, but within seconds her knees shook again.

The young lady huffed and glared at Kate's skirt until she got her legs under control.

What was the woman reading? Maybe if she talked to her about books, she'd forget about the shaking.

Gold letters embossed the bright green cloth cover: *Shake-spearean Sonnets.*

What did Shakespeare know about real life anyway? Romeo and Juliet fell in love, married, and died for each other in less than a week. She'd known Silas four times as long and wasn't sure what she felt for him . . . besides jitters.

A month was not enough time to know someone. Though the other times she'd run off to get married, she hadn't bothered to think through her decision longer than a day.

Where was the courage she'd possessed on her last train trip? She even knew the groom this time. Silas was caring, wanted her to raise the child she loved, kissed like—

"Are you all right?" The blond lady leaned over to see her better.

"No." Kate grabbed the cheap fan she'd bought several stations back and fanned her rapidly heating face.

Her seat partner laid her sonnets in her lap. "You're agitated about something."

That was an understatement.

"Do you want to talk about it?"

"No thank you." She couldn't even look at the woman. If she did, the lady would note the high color in her cheeks and figure out exactly what was wrong with her.

"Could you stop fidgeting and swishing, then? I can't concentrate with you all aflutter over there."

Aflutter. That was definitely the right word for the heart palpitations that took over when she relived Silas's kiss. Which she desperately needed to stop doing if she was going to make a good, logical decision this time. Though being on the way to marry a stranger again basically proved she wasn't capable of sound reasoning. Oh why couldn't she have been mature for once and found a way to wait to make a decision no one would call into question?

But he had kissed her like he meant it . . . though so had Aiden.

Maybe she should have saved her money and found a job in Breton, but who would've hired her after her public disgrace? And no one lived there whom she cared for anyway, at least not in the same way she cared for Anthony.

Maybe being on a train, headed to the boy she loved and a man she had feelings for wasn't the most unreasonable thing in the world to do.

And she really, really wanted Silas to be Prince Charming.

But what if he wasn't?

"Are you sure you're all right?" The lady's voice seemed genuinely concerned this time. "You're crying."

Blinking, Kate swiped away the errant moisture. "I'm not." She clenched the seat's arms to keep from bolting down the aisle.

She'd make sure Silas had the property he claimed to have, and if she didn't uncover any faults beyond the ones he'd admitted to—if he'd indeed told her the truth about everything—could she tie her feet down with a wedding ring for Anthony's sake and the hope of something more?

❖

"You're going to wear a rut in the planks." Will shook his head at Silas while lounging on the train depot's bench. Will had removed his suit coat and rolled up his shirt sleeves despite the cool temperature. Medical school hadn't changed his laid-back friend much, beyond giving the man extra confidence . . . though that might have come from his bride, Eliza, more than his fancy degree.

If only Silas could be certain Kate would bring the best out of him, because Lucy sure hadn't.

He pivoted at the end of the platform and shook out his hands, trying to release the tension.

Didn't work.

He paced across the platform, thankful most of the crowd was huddled inside the depot, giving him space, and Anthony was at the post office. He didn't know Kate was coming today, but he would know something was amiss if he watched his father's nerves get the better of him.

Will let out half a laugh. "One would think you've never waited in this very spot for a mail-order bride before."

"Kate's not a mail-order bride." He stopped midstride and turned his ear to the east. Yes, the rumble warring with his heart's erratic beating was the barely audible approach of a train. How long until Kate arrived? Five, ten minutes? "She's not desperate enough for that. She's too pret—" He cut off before he got himself in trouble. Will's wife had been a mail-order bride, and Eliza wasn't pretty, though she wasn't ugly either. He couldn't afford to offend his best friend just because his nerves were shot.

"Oh, Kate might be desperate, all right. After she sees you pacing like a caged wolf, she might be desperate to hightail it back onto the train." Will's face lit with amusement.

On any other day, Silas wouldn't mind being ribbed. "Not funny." Kate wasn't the kind that deserted; she was the kind that fought.

Maybe he shouldn't have told Will what was wrong this morning. He was definitely rethinking inviting him to sit with him while he waited.

Will leaned back with a stupid grin on his face. He was way too jovial for the occasion.

Silas shook his head. Here he was, possibly jumping into another unhappy marriage, and his friend found him amusing. "My nerves are so tight I'm about to explode. You should be more sympathetic."

Will acted as if he were enjoying a show. "If you wanted sympathy, you should've chosen Everett to wait with you."

"Not if I want her to arrive alive and willing to marry me." Will's friend, Everett Cline, had had the worst luck with women he'd ever heard of. Having Lucy run away wasn't nearly as bad as being jilted four times, as Everett Cline had been. Though the man had finally landed a happy marriage, with a gorgeous wife to boot.

Silas turned to watch the cloud of coal smoke billow on the horizon.

Maybe Kate would become his Julia Cline, a bride who'd stay. Bring him love and happiness and children—

"I thought you told me you didn't know what you felt for this woman."

He startled. How'd he forget Will was right there? "I don't. How could I?" Though the thought of her giving him children heated his limbs enough he could shuck his coat.

Will's grin grew wider. "I knew Eliza was The One the second

211

I saw her, though I had to ignore her, seeing how she arrived for another man."

Silas rolled his eyes. "Now you're telling tales. That's nothing but hindsight."

"Ah, but I recognize now what those feelings were, and I recognize them in you."

"I'm glad one of us is certain of what I'm feeling." He huffed, trying to find something to say to lighten the mood. "The men won't welcome a married man to play chess in their club. I need someone to play with besides Anthony—and you're lousy."

"Considering how Kate's already got you checkmated, I bet she'll prove to be an excellent chess player."

Just like a king stuck behind a wall of pawns, Silas was ensnared by the integrity he wanted to keep and half a hope things would work out. "I am indeed trapped."

"Aw, Jonesey." Will hopped up and slapped him on the back. "I'm teasing. A good woman isn't a trap, or rather it's a trap you don't mind being in."

Silas kept his eyes on the black dot of a train engine appearing under the smoke as more people wandered up from the streets to wait on passengers. "Eliza sure has you bamboozled if you're willing to lie still in a snare."

"Hmmm. Lying down in her snare is a fine place to be, my friend."

Silas groaned. One would think Will was still on his honeymoon the way he couldn't keep that silly look off his face.

His own honeymoon haze had lasted a day before Lucy found everything he did or owned unsatisfactory. "Don't you have doctoring to do?"

"You trying to get rid of me?" Will nudged him with his elbow. "You're the one who asked me to stand here and watch you pace."

"I didn't know you'd probe so much." Silas waved at an

212

acquaintance from church, thankful the man didn't come over to chat before joining the waiting crowd.

"No probing necessary, your agitation's written all over your face. I'm just amusing myself."

"A doctor's job is to calm nerves, not ratchet them up."

"Ah, but I'm not charging you for the hour, so you're just a friend, and those I mercilessly taunt." Will gave him a glare that was probably supposed to look malicious, but Will and *malicious* combined as well as oil and water.

"You're in too good of spirits for me." The hiss of the slowing locomotive would soon make talking difficult. "I'm facing potential doom and gloom right now."

"You're right, I'm much too happy for doom and gloom." He pulled a cigar from his chest pocket. "I don't smoke these, but Carl Hampden gave me a handful. Here." He poked one toward him. "I'll finally be feeling that fatherly pride you've been reveling in."

"Fatherly pride? You?" Silas let Will's smile leak onto his face, just a little. "Congratulations, Stanton."

He clamped onto Silas's shoulder. "Thanks."

What would it feel like to be Will? Having a wife he loved, raising a child who'd love him in return, being so sure things would work out.

If he hoped for such things, and they didn't come true . . .

The clamor of brakes and steam grew loud enough they'd have to yell to communicate, so they didn't talk while the engine protested to a stop.

Would this locomotive bring him the same happiness Will and Everett had found? The opposite of what he'd attached himself to last time?

While the deafening noise of released steam dissipated, more townsfolk swarmed the platform, effectively corralling Silas's fidgeting feet.

He'd asked Will to wait with him, but now . . . He turned to face Will so the man could read his lips. "You wouldn't mind if I asked you to . . . uh . . . not be here when . . ."

Will cupped his hands around his mouth and shouted. "Bring Kate by to meet the wife."

He nodded and shook hands with Will before his friend bounced down the platform stairs.

If only he felt like bouncing. The dying hiss of the train muffled the heartbeat throbbing in his ears—the only part of him that bounced. The rest of his body weighed like lead, anchoring him to the platform.

As did the memory of his impulsive proposal.

And the feel of Kate's lips on his.

Last to disembark, Kate didn't bounce down the steps. Hesitating on the bottom stair, she put a hand to her brow to ward off the sun. Her simple straw hat's tiny brim was uselessly decorative, hardly covering her auburn hair, which was prettier than the hat anyway.

He waved until she raised her hand in acknowledgment. Slowly, he wove through the crowd as did she, but he stopped before they got within talking distance. How did a man greet a woman he scarcely knew, yet had kissed like no woman he'd ever known?

He certainly couldn't kiss her like that again in front of so many people—despite having done so in Breton.

His hand clamped onto his neck. Had he completely ruined her reputation? Was that why she came with no warning, no discussion? God forgive him for his loss of sanity.

A pretty woman, a mother for his child, a family—maybe his loss of sanity wouldn't turn out so bad. Maybe he'd be as happy as Will with time. God wanted good things for him—the Bible said so.

He dragged off his hat and forged forward the last few steps. She slowed, one arm crossed across her stomach and an-

Melissa Jagears

chored to her other arm carrying a valise. She looked intently
in his eyes, making him squirm. What was she looking for?

He held out his hands as if approaching a hurting wild ani-
mal. "Can I take your bag?"

She shook her head, her eyes blinking rapidly, perhaps holding back tears, perhaps just irritated by smoke, but they were
definitely red-rimmed. "You'll need to get my trunks."

He still held out a hand. "I can come back for them."

She squeezed the bag's handle tighter. Maybe she needed it?
"I'm capable of carrying it myself—thank you."

"All right." He shouldn't let a lady carry a heavy bag when
he had empty hands, but her trunks were not yet retrievable.
His tongue stuck to the roof of his mouth. Was she reliving the
electricity they'd shared weeks ago? Was that what kept her as
tongue-tied as he?

With her feet firmly planted on the platform and her back
as straight as a fence post, she didn't look willing to move. "I
want you to know I can't promise anything until I'm certain
you've told me the truth about yourself."

So her tongue untied first to bushwhack him. Kate wouldn't
be this wary if Lucy hadn't talked so badly of him—some of
her tongue-lashings likely earned.

His hands itched to reach for Kate, to make her rigid frame
soften in his arms again, but that likely wouldn't work right now.
And he'd already ruled out kissing her. He fidgeted and ended
up putting his hands in his pockets. "We don't have to rush into
anything. We can't get married for a week or so anyway. Got
to get a license and you a dress. If you want— "

"Dress?"

"Do you have something nice already?" He'd never seen her
in anything but brown and navy wool dresses. She probably
had lighter weight outfits, maybe in prettier colors, but that
wouldn't help now since the weather had turned cold. And he

215

had promised her the best wedding he could afford. He wished he'd not said that after taking a look at his farm, but a woman would want a nice dress at least.

She pulled at her neckline. "All I have are these. I put on collars and cuffs for Sunday."

That's what he'd thought. "I arranged for you to stay at Mrs. Langston's boardinghouse. She's a seamstress. Figured you could get some material from the mercantile and work on a dress with her."

She seemed to be breathing easier and her hand relaxed on the handle of her bag. "I wouldn't feel right asking someone I don't know to work on my dress."

"I don't think she'd mind, but if she did, I could pay her something, or we could wait until you're finished." He waited until she looked him in the eyes. "When you're ready."

Finally, her shoulders loosened, and her chest rose with a deep breath. A smile even played on her lips.

He smiled back and offered his arm again. "Now, about seeing my farm. Will was right when he sent me those telegrams. It's not in good shape anymore. I hope that won't make you think less of me when you see how much money I'm going to have to pour into it to get it back to where it was just weeks ago. Anthony's at the post office, so we could pick him up and head out. But my place is about fifteen minutes north, so if we go there tonight, you'd see little of the homestead before we had to come back. It might be best if I came for you tomorrow."

She nodded. "Tomorrow's fine. What about my trunks?"

"I'll come back for them. We'll get Anthony first. I'm sure you're eager to see him."

She swallowed and nodded again. He reached for her bag, which she thankfully released this time. He threw the valise in his borrowed wagon before taking her arm and guiding her down the busy sidewalk. They walked a block of Main Street in silence. Weren't women supposed to be talkative?

With every passerby's side glance or raised eyebrow, his chest tightened, making it difficult to draw sufficient breath. The townsfolk were used to strangers coming off the train, but not one on his arm. Halfway to the post office, he cleared his throat. Guess he had to start the talking. "This is Main Street. Most of the shops you'll want to visit are here. There's Hampden's Mercantile. You'll find pretty material there for a dress—just tell them to put it on my account." He pointed to the shop they were passing. "This is the tailor."

Surely she could've read the signs herself, but it kept his mouth moving, so he kept pointing out which business was which. Hopefully talking would keep anybody from coming over for an introduction . . . or to ask pesky questions.

They passed Will's old store, now a millinery, and Silas stepped in front of Kate to open the post office door.

Anthony sat staring at a chessboard, chin held in both hands, and then reached over to move his queen. He hadn't told the boy Kate intended to come today, in case she'd not arrived for some reason.

Jedidiah glanced up from handing a woman a pile of mail. His gaze bounced off Silas and onto Kate. "Good afternoon."

Anthony looked up, and his eyes brightened. "Miss Dawson!" He stood so fast he bumped the table and several of his chess pieces fell over. "You came!" He ran over and hugged her waist.

She wrapped him tight against her. "I told you I would."

A woman who kept her word would keep her vows. Wasn't that what he'd wanted most in a wife? A woman who'd never abandon Anthony . . . though they could run away together.

He pinched the bridge of his nose to snuff out the wayward thought. His fears were messing with his logic. She'd told him in Breton she believed the boy belonged with him, but she had

217

contemplated running when the boy was in danger of going with Richard.

Even if she didn't find anything wrong with him personally, if she found life on a homestead too hard . . .

He'd just make sure to ease Kate into farm life—unlike he had with Lucy. He wouldn't assume this go-around that his wife would know how crazy planting and harvest times were, how the fields demanded they work from dawn to dusk.

Wife. Just the thought of the word sent a shiver down his arms. Kate peered up at him with a question in the lift of her eyebrow, but he only shook his head.

Thankfully, they'd have the winter to adjust to each other before the land claimed their full attention.

Jedidiah walked around his counter, wiping his hands on an ink-stained white cloth, taking in every inch of the newcomer. "How do you do?"

Silas stepped forward. "Mr. Langston, this is Miss Dawson. My son's teacher from Breton."

"Anthony mentioned you planned on visiting." Jedidiah's tone was suspicious. "But I figured you'd wait 'til winter break, being a teacher and all."

She looked between the two men, likely wondering if such direct questioning worried Silas.

"Yes, she's early. Come, Anthony." He'd hoped to have this conversation with Jedidiah later, because right now, *he* didn't even know why she'd come so quickly. And he definitely wouldn't discuss the subject in front of Anthony. "Let's get Miss Dawson's things to the boardinghouse."

The door creaked open behind them and a couple from across town came in. Thank God for customers to distract his friend. "See you tomorrow night, Jedidiah." He'd figured they could play chess after bringing Kate back from seeing the farm, not that he was eager to endure the inevitable interrogation. But

Anthony seemed interested in the game now—or rather bent on beating Lynville, since everyone else could.

Maybe with Anthony along, the men would keep from berating him for shucking the title of disgruntled bachelor. They'd already cleaned up their language in front of the boy, and a gentleman didn't talk about someone's soon-to-be momma like they would an old flame. If his marriage turned out, maybe the other men would finally see forgiveness could free them up for better things too.

At least Silas hoped he was headed for better things. If not, these men would rub his nose in his every misstep. He held open the door for Kate and Anthony to exit.

Please tell me if we're making a mistake, Lord.

But of course God didn't answer with a voice or a vision.

A peace maybe? Could you give me a peace?

But he'd already asked for that while imagining marrying her—or not—and his guts still turned with indecision.

Anthony held Kate's hand as they left the post office. "I'm so glad you're here."

Silas followed them out into the chilly air but let them walk ahead.

"I'm glad to see you too." She pulled the boy closer, wrapping her arm around his shoulders and rubbing his arm.

Though she didn't say she was glad to be here.

Hadn't she turned down his proposal in Breton? So what made her come without one letter between them? Something must have happened with her job.

He should've taken her to the hotel to eat before retrieving Anthony. Then he could've asked her what had spurred her to Kansas without the boy's listening ears.

"I can't wait to show you my kitten." Anthony practically skipped beside Kate down the sidewalk, though he'd surely claim he was too old for such behavior. "I got to pick one from

A Bride at Last

Dr. Stanton's litter, and I chose the black one with three white socks. Mr. Jonesey said I should name him Socks, but that's too easy. Maybe you could help me think of something."

"What's his personality like?"

"Well, he attacks Mr. Jonesey's old knotted sock as if it's a ferocious critter one minute and then falls asleep with it the next."

And with every step beside Kate, Anthony talked faster.

Silas walked behind them, soaking up the stories his boy told her so freely. They weren't within sight of the depot yet, and Anthony had already used more words with Kate than he'd bothered to spill since leaving Missouri.

The two of them together, conversing with such ease did his heart good, and yet, he wasn't a part of it. Would they forever shut him out, or had three decades without bonding with anyone set him up for stilted relationships for the rest of his life?

Chapter 17

Kate primed Silas's well and pumped water. The handle stuck just as he'd said it would, so she jiggled it. From the dipper, she took a long drink and then leaned against the well's edge, gazing out over Silas's land.

During the train ride, she'd tried to erase the picture Silas had painted of his place and envision Lucy's dismal descriptions.

Either he'd made a lot of improvements since Lucinda left, or her friend had exaggerated the hardships.

Some of both, most likely.

And why had Silas's friend kept sending him telegrams over the disaster Mr. Hicks had made of the place? Nothing much looked amiss. There was a large pretty yard—or it would be when spring brought back the green. The well sat between the barn and the small whitewashed cabin, which contained a bedroom, a combination sitting room and kitchen, and a loft. Several other small buildings dotted the property, likely root cellars and sheds.

She turned to watch Silas pick the rocks and dirt from the last of his borrowed horse's hooves. A borrowed wagon and a borrowed nag. Maybe that was why the men were worried about the farm. How much of the stuff she saw was on loan?

If only she'd seen that something in Silas's eyes when she got off the train yesterday. But after she'd detrained and told him he had to measure up, he'd turned aloof.

Sighing, she shook her head. Could she blame him for going quiet? He didn't need her to underline his faults when she had plenty herself. "Just ask the school board."

Silas stopped. "What'd you say?"

She hadn't realized she'd said that aloud. *Oh well, might as well get the conversation started.* "The school board." She shrugged. "They fired me."

"Because of me?"

"Yes, seems plenty of people saw us . . . at the train station."

He rubbed the back of his neck. "I'm really sorry about kissing you like that. I take full responsibility."

But her brazen response hadn't been his fault at all. What if . . . what if he regretted everything? She wrapped her arms around her middle. "Are you sorry I lost my job or that you kissed me?"

He pulled at his collar. "I regret kissing you without thinking about how it'd affect you—your reputation, I mean."

"But what about the kiss itself?" She forced herself to look up at him.

"I, uh . . ." His gaze landed on her mouth, then darted out over his pastures, his Adam's apple working harder than necessary. Was he enamored with her even a little bit? He'd certainly been skittish and stiff since she'd arrived—but she hadn't been particularly warm either, nearly implying he'd lied to her about his property the moment she opened her mouth.

He blew out a breath and looked back at her. "I'm not sure I'd do it again, but it's not that I didn't enjoy it."

They stood staring at each other for a moment. Then he pointed toward the well. "I need to wash my hands."

She moved out of his way, but not far enough away she couldn't smell the cologne and leather and musk of the man. She needed to forget fear, forget reason, and just . . . stop overthinking. Maybe if she stopped being so standoffish, he'd start acting the way he had back in Breton.

But to do that, one of their mouths ought to start moving. . . . Talking, at least. "What's that heap of rocks for?" She pointed to the haphazard pile sitting a body length away from the cabin.

"I collect them as I plow. Almost enough to make a summer kitchen, I think."

Surely no bachelor thought a summer kitchen necessary. Had he been collecting all this time in hopes Lucinda would return?

"What's that back there?" A wooden fence surrounded three towering piles of hay beside an earthen lump overtaken by weeds.

"The soddy I started out in."

Ah, the dirt hovel Lucinda had complained about. And no wonder. It certainly looked small for two people.

"You want to look at it?"

She nodded. Maybe moving would work the kinks from their awkward conversation. "What kind of wire is that around the garden?" Dead plants drooped in weary lines behind the house.

"Torn ribbon wire. Keeps the cattle and horses from eating my vegetables, though it doesn't keep chickens out. I wanted to get more wire for the cattle since they're easier to contain that way, but I won't be able to afford it for a while now."

"Eggs, beef, and vegetables." Was there anything the man was missing from being self-sufficient? "Have you a dairy cow?"

He pointed to a rust-colored lump in the nearest pasture. "Milky's over there."

"Milky?"

He shrugged. "She's not well named at the moment considering she's dry now."

"I suppose you have a cat named Cat?" She couldn't help but laugh at her joke.

"Well yeah. He's the gray shadow over there under the wheelbarrow."

She snorted, then put her hands on her hips. "Don't tell me the dog's name is Dog."

"I'm not that bad. He's Yellow Eyes."

Was he being humorous, or did he really think Yellow Eyes required more imagination than Dog? No wonder he'd suggested naming the kitten Socks. "Remind me not to let you name the—" *Children.*

She sped up, hoping he'd not notice the terrible blushing she'd been cursed with lately. Precisely how had she so quickly gotten from worrying about whether or not she should marry him to naming children?

By the time she reached the soddy's entrance, she'd breathed in enough cool autumn air that the only color that should be left in her cheeks was from exertion. She pinched the building's sagging wall made of long, thick dirt bricks and rubbed the soil between her fingertips. "How long did you live here?"

"I built the cabin seven years ago, so . . . nearly five years."

And it wasn't surprising Lucinda had complained about living in this thing. Kate ducked under the low doorway into the darkness. Only one deep, east-facing window covered by an oilskin curtain let in any light beyond what came through the doorway. White plaster crumbles littered the floor and speckled the sparse farming equipment stored inside. She tried to imagine a stove, table, bed, chairs, wardrobe, chest, and washstand stuffed inside instead of plows and rakes.

She'd never felt the meaning of the word *cramped* more keenly than now.

"I've let it fall into disrepair. Been too focused on the crops and livestock." He reached up to the ceiling, where roots dangled through a hole. He pushed against a rotten wood beam to keep from hitting it with his head as he took another step inside. "I know it looks awful. Wasn't much to live in, but it's warmer than the cabin in the winter and cooler in the summer. Though both houses have their flaws. Bugs and snakes plagued this one." He shuddered, then rolled his shoulders as if to shake off the shiver. "The cabin though, well, I've had coons holing up under the porch, and once a skunk—"

"Are you trying to make your place sound bad?"

He wiggled the rotten section of the stud until he pulled it from the ceiling. Soil rained down on him. "Figured you needed to know what you might have to deal with." He swiped the dirt from his hair.

"You've got a nice place, Silas. I can't imagine the dedication needed to build this by yourself."

He blinked at her. "I'm always behind on everything, and I'll be even more so this coming season since Peter Hicks ruined quite a bit of what I'd built up. I've lost crops, animals, and equipment."

"I'm sorry about your setback. I hope the trust you had in God back in Breton will help you get through this winter."

"He did honor that trust, didn't He?" His voice was soft, contemplative. "So He could certainly do it again. . . ."

"You should be proud of your place—not trying to make me think poorly of it just because things need improvement or repair."

"I shouldn't?" He took a step closer.

She'd thought the place was cramped before, but his nearness created a panicky feeling of another kind.

She licked her lips. "Why are you making your homestead sound worse than it is? Are you trying to talk me out of marrying you?"

Since her eyes hadn't quite adjusted to the dim room, she couldn't tell what the dark look on Silas's face signified, but the air around them suddenly felt serious—if air could be filled with emotion.

"Are you saying yes, then?"

She swallowed and her lungs quit working. What *was* she saying? Nothing she'd seen in Kansas proved he'd lied about who he was or what he had, and she hadn't money or opportunity to do much else but marry.

But more importantly, she loved Anthony and trusted Silas.

How could she have expected a declaration of love when she'd disembarked in Kansas? Of course he couldn't say he loved her; what sane person declared such a thing after only a few weeks?

She'd seen what kind of person he was in the middle of a crisis—and she thought all the better of him for it. There was respect, admiration, and an attraction to build on.

Her heartbeat ratcheted up in anticipation of voicing her reply. Once she answered, she couldn't unsay it. She took a deep breath and closed her eyes. "I'm saying, yes."

"Good. That's good." He nodded, as if trying to convince himself getting married was indeed good.

His gaze lowered to her mouth.

Or at least she thought he was looking at her mouth in the dim light.

With all the quickness of a summer storm, she wanted him to kiss her again—something she'd feared he'd do without any warning at the Salt Flatts depot, but now . . . She stepped forward, placed a hand on his chest, and tilted her head back. Tiptoeing, she left only a breath's distance between her lips and his.

And she waited.

His shaky hand came up to her jaw, tipping it back ever so slightly, then his mouth landed on hers as light as a whisper.

She had no job to lose now.

Sliding her arms around his neck, she pressed her lips harder against his until he crushed her to him like he had before. His hands came up to entwine themselves into her hair and his thumbs swept the errant tresses back from both her temples. She held on tighter and kissed back—until he broke away.

He cleared his throat. "When are you wanting to get married?"

She forced open her lazy eyelids, her head still cradled in his hands. "Um, this Sunday?"

"Then, I think—" he reached back to grab her wrists and gently untangle them from his neck—"that I should show you, the uh . . . necessary now."

She squinted. "The outhouse?"

"Well, yes, you need to know where that is, of course. You said you wanted to see everything." He released her and left the soddy as if maybe *he* needed to visit the necessary.

She'd come to Salt Flatts hoping to find an excuse to keep them from wedding quickly, but after the overwhelming desire to kiss him again had hit her like a falling soddy brick, and how her heart couldn't find a steady rhythm right now . . .

If she thought she'd be planting her feet in Kansas soil just for Anthony, she'd been so very wrong.

• ◦ •

Silas pushed his plate away and smiled at Kate across the hotel table. He still couldn't believe she'd said yes. He'd

227

braced himself for her to break off the engagement. Who didn't cut ties with him when he got close? Yet despite what his hired hand had done to his farm, she'd not once mentioned leaving.

"Would you like pie?"

He jumped at Mrs. Studdard's voice so near his ear—again. The hotel owner's wife lived to eavesdrop, and her wide, toothy grin proved she'd pieced together enough tidbits to start the rumor mill.

Kate put down the spoon she'd used to stir her coffee and raised her eyebrows in question. How could he order pie when he shouldn't have even spent the money to eat at the hotel? But how could he tell her no when he'd asked her to lunch so they could talk? Not that they'd done much of that with Mrs. Studdard constantly checking on them. "Would you like to share a slice or have your own?"

A faint blush settled on her cheeks—it seemed her cheeks were looking rather rosy of late. She wore a plain-colored dress, as usual, but with her Sunday collar and cuffs. Yet she somehow looked exquisite in mud brown.

"I think it'd be better if we each had our own piece."

Mrs. Studdard clasped her hands together. "Our chocolate pie is a dream."

"Two of those?" He didn't want to annoy Kate by ordering for her.

She nodded. Mrs. Studdard moved away, and he sucked in air.

"She likes to hover, doesn't she?" Kate watched their hostess glide to the kitchen.

He chuffed. "How else can you mine gossip fodder if you aren't close enough to unearth every word?"

"I thought you told me Mrs. Graves was the town gossip."

He held up two fingers entwined together. "Best friends."

"But why would she care about us?" Kate's confused pout made him want to kiss her again. Soon.

Not if, not maybe, not hopefully—he would indeed kiss her soon.

But he shouldn't kiss her anymore until the wedding. If he couldn't behave himself in broad daylight in front of an entire town, he certainly could make a huge mistake alone with her on his farm—especially with the way she kissed. He closed his eyes to rein in his thoughts so he could make conversation.

"For ten years, if I couldn't get home to eat, I dined here—alone." No one had ever cared much about him until he moved here, not even his mother, but in Salt Flatts everyone seemed interested in him . . . and his failings. "She's probably pacing in the back perturbed that she knows nothing more than your name."

"You must have been so lonely."

"Yes, and you? How long have you been away from family?"

"About two and a half years, but then, it wasn't the happiest of situations, so it's nothing I pine for." She wiped her mouth and looked out the window. Evidently not a topic she was comfortable discussing. "My parents have been gone for thirteen years, and I still miss them terribly."

"Were they good to you?"

"The best." She sighed and closed her eyes. "Mother never cared that I ran around and got dirty. She gave me plenty of time to get into mischief."

Leaning back against his bench seat, he settled his arm across the top and looked to make sure Mrs. Studdard wasn't returning before taking a long glance at the woman across from him. As much as he preferred to give them more time to get to know each other before the wedding, he couldn't afford to pay for her room any longer.

And she'd be such a help cooking and cleaning and caring for Anthony while he worked extra hard to make up for what he'd lost to Peter Hicks. He could chop extra firewood this winter to sell next year and maybe replace the tools he'd lost without dipping into his savings. But what could he do to make extra money for the next few months? He'd have to ask around for odd jobs.

Mrs. Studdard swept in like a Kansas breeze—knocking off his fork, stepping on his boot, her skirt dragging his napkin off the table as she plopped down their pies. "Hope you enjoy. Special night, huh?"

"Is it Tuesday?" He looked at Kate with the most confused expression he could muster.

"I believe so." Kate's eyes widened comically. "That *is* special."

"Very special. Thank you, Mrs. Studdard. Looks good."

The woman's bright face dimmed, and her lower lip popped out. "All right, then." She stomped away.

Kate giggled. "We broke her heart."

He frowned at the utensil on the floor. "Ah, but she dirtied my fork." He grabbed his spoon.

Kate stared at him a little before nibbling on her pie. Was it a terrible thing if they settled into a comfortable silence? She'd never really been quiet in Missouri, but then, she'd been bossy most of the time and was constantly worrying about Anthony. Had his mentioning Mrs. Studdard's eavesdropping scared Kate into keeping quiet? Or maybe he'd lucked out with a woman who wouldn't be upset with him for sitting on the porch, sharpening his knives, and staring at the horizon after a long day of work. Lucy had always nagged him about the slightest idleness on his part.

What if Kate didn't really like him, as Richard claimed she did? Sure the kisses were nice, more than nice, but since he'd just learned she'd lost her job over one of those . . . was she rushing into marriage only for security? And would she rush out if he didn't meet her expectations?

He drummed his fingers against his seat's back as Kate finished her chocolate pie. No, he couldn't let his past disappointments with Lucy meddle with how he viewed Kate. If she'd wanted to marry him just for Anthony, she'd have thrown herself at him in Breton, and she could have gotten a teaching job somewhere else if all she wanted was security.

Kate set her fork down on her empty plate and held his gaze for half a minute. She then looked over at the hotel owner's wife slowly cleaning a nearby table and sighed.

"Mrs. Studdard?" A maid came down the back stairs and whispered to the woman, who soon bustled away with the younger worker.

He breathed a sigh as if he'd just been let out of a box. "I'm sorry about you losing your job because of me. Are you wanting to teach again?"

She shook her head. "Teaching was just the best job I could find after I got to Missouri and realized I couldn't marry Jasper."

He blinked. "What?"

"Oh, I guess I never fully explained how I met Anthony and Lucinda. I'd come to Hartfield after answering an ad that Jasper's brother—I later learned—put in the newspaper to get him a wife."

She'd answered an ad? He could only think of one reason a woman would answer an ad saying she would marry, but he couldn't imagine Kate as a mail-order bride. She certainly hadn't acted desperate to marry him.

"I'd smelled alcohol on him when I first met him at the train station, but I told myself I'd imagined it. He seemed nice enough, but right before the ceremony I heard his brother laughing with a bunch of other men that a mail-order bride was the only way the town drunk could possibly get a wife so pretty." Her face screwed up in disgust. "I was not going to marry a drunk."

His arms turned numb with cold. She'd left a groom at the altar. One who had a problem with alcohol.

She shrugged. "Shortly after, I got a job helping the teachers at a school in Hartfield, and Anthony drew my attention—he only came to school once in a while and was always so sad when he did. One afternoon when I went to check on him, it happened to be after a night Richard had beaten Lucinda. Evidently, Anthony stayed home whenever Richard lost at the gambling tables and took his disappointment out on her."

"You do realize—" Silas swallowed hard—"that I was the town drunk."

"*Were*." She nodded at him and smiled. Why had he turned so pale? She knew about his drinking problem already. Hadn't she reassured him that afternoon with the whiskey that she didn't condemn him? "I'm not going to marry a man who needs to change. After watching my sister try to change her husband, I know how unlikely it is a spouse will change to suit your preferences, but you've already stopped drinking."

"I've lapsed before."

She swallowed heavily. Poor man could certainly beat himself up over his failures. "I know, but I saw how badly you don't want to do it again. I can help you be what you want to be, but making someone be something they don't want to be is what's unlikely."

Silas sat silently, his shoulders tight and his chest puffed as if he expected her to throw a knife at his heart.

Had she hurt him? She clasped her hands and squared her shoulders. "What is it, Silas?"

"You were a mail-order bride." His voice fell into a whisper.

"Yes." Why was that such a disappointment? Lucinda had been a mail-order bride, and he'd not thought himself above marrying her. And his proposal to her now was for a marriage of convenience, though hopefully it wouldn't take too long for him to fall in love with her. Judging by their kisses, it wouldn't.

"You left a man you'd promised to marry." If a spoon could crumple, the utensil in Silas's hand would be a wad of silver.

"As I said, I found out his brother was the one who'd written, pretending to be him. He'd not even had the gumption to write me himself. Surely you see how wrong that was."

"Oh." His posture relaxed, but he still worried his lip. "But why were you a mail-order bride in the first place?"

A vise wrapped around her heart. She'd pursued Jasper to get out of marrying another man. Somehow she doubted Silas would welcome that news. She swallowed and kept her gaze even with his. "In general, I wanted to be more than some man's housekeeper and Jasper—or rather, Leonard—assured me I'd have a maid and could work in their sign shop. He seemed enthusiastic about letting me help and promised me paint for my own use. . . . Sounds silly now."

"So you didn't know what kind of man he was."

"No. That's why I didn't agree to marry you until I came here. I wanted to be sure of the man you were." She'd lay a comforting hand on him, but he seemed so . . . distant. Were her explanations not getting through to him? "Though it was silly to believe you were anything other than what I saw in Breton."

"So why were you looking to marry someone outside of Georgia? You're beautiful. Surely plenty of men would've offered their hand."

She forced herself not to look away. What would he think

about Aiden if Jasper had ruffled him so much? "Uh . . . I was
trying to get away from my family."

"Your family?" His voice deepened dangerously.

Oh goodness. Maybe she should've admitted to Aiden
first. She hadn't been keeping anything a secret—just hadn't
thought it mattered much. "I . . . I had a fiancé in Georgia, a
co-worker of my brother-in-law's." Aiden might have provided
her with security, but he'd not wanted a family as much as
he sought help with his career. Silas longed for family—with
her and Anthony.

"A fiancé? Any more of those in your past?"

"No." She tried to reach over and grab his hand, but he sat
back, shaking his head slowly.

"Silas." She took her hand back and huffed. "Things are
different with you. There's Anthony, and I've met you. I've put
my mind to being here."

"So you hadn't met your first fiancé either?"

"Well, no." Her voice faltered. "I'd met him."

"And why didn't you marry him?"

She swallowed a couple times. What was the real answer? She
might have a good answer for jilting him now, but what had it
been then? "I was young . . . and foolish."

"How old were you?" He shoved a hand through his hair.

"Twenty-two."

"And you're now . . . ?"

She couldn't hold his gaze any longer and dropped hers to
the oil-stained tablecloth. "Twenty-five."

"Just three years."

She peeped up at him. "Can't one grow a lot in three years?"
Though she didn't feel much different than her twenty-two-year-
old self. "Perhaps I've learned running is rarely the answer."

"Do you want to run now?" He looked at her with such
intensity, she had to shift back.

He'd revealed his drinking habit, letting her see his weakness. She could hide hers, but then she'd be a liar. Hadn't she thought about running throughout the entire train ride? "Sometimes," she whispered.

He made a sound like a sad puppy dog.

"But it's just a feeling, Silas. Don't you think most people are nervous before they get married—even people who know each other better than we do?"

"What about your family?"

"My sister and brother-in-law?" At his nod, she shrugged. "What about them?"

"Do they know where you are?"

Her stomach suddenly dropped. *This.* This revelation would not help her situation at all. He was surely comparing her to Lucinda right now. "No. Though Peter wouldn't care. He hit me, Silas. Whacked me with a broomstick when I didn't perform up to snuff. I was just a kid when I came to live with them."

"Did your sister hit you too?"

"No, but I'm sure—"

"Does she know where you are?"

She willed herself to stay seated—leaving now certainly wouldn't help her win him over. "No."

"So you abandoned your sister to an abusive man without letting her know where you are? She doesn't know if you're dead or alive?"

"That makes me sound terrible." She hated the grating self-pity in her voice.

"I don't think you're terrible, Kate." He looked up at the ceiling and exhaled, his eyes moving back and forth as if calculating something. Her worth, perhaps? "Just maybe not the right woman for me."

"What? You can't mean that." She strangled the skirt fabric in her hands. "We should think things—"

"Have you ever loved someone so much you felt as if they were a part of you—even if they weren't the greatest person in the world, they were yours? The only family you had? And then they abandoned you without having the decency to tell you where they went?"

Her body trembled. Being an orphan was a little like that. "My parents' deaths devastated me."

"But they didn't leave you on purpose."

"No." She pressed her lips back together.

"But you did. You left your sister and fiancés intentionally."

"I had good reasons!" Didn't she? Jasper, definitely, but Aiden . . . ? Though offering her a better life, he had planned on taking advantage of her.

"I'm sure when my mother left me at that orphanage she thought she had good reasons, but she never bothered to tell me what they were."

If only she could tell him she'd written her sister—but she hadn't. Violet had never acted sorry for how Peter treated her, so she'd convinced herself that her sister wouldn't care about anything she did. And she certainly didn't care one whit if Peter worried about where she'd run off to.

"Pretending my mother had good reasons didn't help my five-year-old heart. There's a crack there that'll never mend, not with all the glue in the world. And then when Lucy left me . . ." He shook his head as if to clear it. "I have a nine-year-old boy to protect, to make sure he doesn't get hurt."

"I love Anthony. I do."

"I doubt my mother hated me. She kissed me on the top of the head before sending me into the boys' home." He released his grip on his spoon and nudged it onto the table.

"I might have run from an engagement, but I'd never run from a marriage. I wouldn't!"

"If you can abandon blood, your own sister, without telling

236

her where you went, then you could abandon me." He shoved his chair back and stood.

She got up and grabbed his arm, but he pulled away.

His dark eyes wavered. "I'm sorry, Kate."

The wedding. "What about Sunday?"

"I think—" He took in a deep gulp of air. "I think we should call things off for now."

"But—"

"Can I get you two anything else?" Mrs. Studdard's voice was entirely too cheerful and invasive.

"Here." Silas took out several bills and handed them to her. "Keep the change." He turned to walk toward the front.

"Is everything all right?" Mrs. Studdard looked at her with such a concerned expression she nearly gave in and blurted out everything.

She swallowed. "Hopefully." With time. Surely. She'd just surprised him. "Excuse me."

He was waiting outside by his wagon, his eyes shuttered. "I'll see you to the boardinghouse."

Kate wrapped her arms around herself. How could she endure a ride with him looking at her like that? The disappointment in her brother-in-law's eyes didn't come close to the wounded look Silas was sporting now. "I can walk, but please promise we'll talk later."

Surely when he got over the shock of her past, he'd see he was overreacting. But telling him he was overreacting now would be like telling him his emotions were meaningless. "I know you're worried about me running away, but I have no intention of doing so."

This would be the time to tell him she loved him, but she couldn't do it. She cared, she wanted to love him, but it was too soon. She wouldn't lie just to keep a man from leaving her.

Would Aiden and Jasper whoop with sadistic elation if they knew she now understood how it felt to be abandoned?

Silas gave her a long look that about tore her heart out, and then climbed up into the old wagon a neighbor had lent him. The moment he started down the road, she ran from town in the opposite direction.

If only she hadn't been so good at running throughout her life, she might now be running to someplace that felt like home.

Chapter 18

Morning light steadily erased the cabin's shadows. Silas's head weighed heavy in his palms, and his elbows protested being smashed against the table's hard wood.

In the loft, in his new bed, Anthony snored, a peaceful sound rasping against Silas's inner turmoil.

He'd need to wake Anthony soon so he'd have enough time to walk to school. He'd been trying to draw Anthony out over breakfast the last several days, but at the moment, he'd rather not talk at all. He wasn't sure he could keep a pleasant expression on his face or friendly banter going this morning.

Not that his son responded much to him lately. Anthony used no more words than necessary—with him anyway.

But he understood his son's reticence. Hadn't it taken him a long time to feel comfortable enough to talk to the adults in the mines and the mill when he was not much older than Anthony? Trust took time.

And yet, he'd trusted Kate too quickly.

How could he be certain she'd stay after what he'd learned? He might consider gambling with his own life, but Anthony's?

Beyond trying to forge a relationship with his son, he didn't want to worry about anything except his farm right now. Livestock and fences and repairs didn't hurt to think about.

His aching heart told him to let Kate go and be done with women. The single men who played chess at the post office every week would certainly champion that decision, but his mind insisted he think things through before he talked to Kate again. He needed time for his heart to stabilize.

Or maybe the memories of her fiery kisses were wreaking havoc with his decision making.

The floorboards creaked above him. No more snoring.

He sighed. He should've had the biscuits and preserves on the table already, and a lunch packed for school. He'd only just started the coffee.

"Aren't we having breakfast?" Anthony scratched his belly and yawned. His hair stood up like a rooster's comb.

"Let me get it." Silas pulled biscuits from the tin and grabbed a spoon for the jar of peach preserves he'd bought from a neighbor woman.

"When's Miss Dawson coming? I bet she'd make us flapjacks."

Yes, this question. He'd pondered what to tell him all night. Maybe he'd been too hasty. He should give her a chance to prove herself for Anthony's sake, but he wouldn't keep a quick wedding date just to make Anthony happy either.

If she stayed in Salt Flatts for a while or so, with no promise they'd reconcile, he might muster up enough faith to believe she'd stay for good. Lucy had only stayed for seven months. Should he make Kate wait that long?

He hated dealing with the uncertain future.

"I'm not sure when she'll come." There. That was true and shouldn't worry the boy.

Anthony slathered more preserves than necessary on a broken biscuit and sighed. "I was hoping for sugared flapjacks on my birthday."

240

Silas blinked. "When's your birthday?"

"Next Wednesday."

Great. The best gift he could give him was time with Kate—but only a few days after they were supposed to marry? How could he spend time with her so soon? Thankfully Anthony would leave for school in a little while, and Silas could tend animals and think. "What would you like to do on Wednesday? Maybe eat in town after school?"

"At the hotel?" When Silas nodded, Anthony's eyes grew wide. "I can't wait to tell Miss Dawson!"

Silas pressed his lips tight to keep from telling him she wasn't invited. If he could work things out in his head, then courting her slowly could help him be certain of her. Maybe she'd run before he gathered the nerve to start where he should have—asking questions, not proposing marriage.

Why had God allowed him to become attached to a woman with her history? God knew their pasts and yet hadn't warned him away until he'd kissed her two times too many.

Anthony shouldn't learn of his trouble with Kate though. If they patched things up, he didn't want Anthony anxious about her abandoning them one day. Which meant he'd have to invite her to Anthony's birthday, ready to see her or not.

"What about getting frozen custard instead?" Sitting down with Kate while Mrs. Studdard hovered around them again didn't sound fun, and ice cream would cost less. "We could get some at Frank's Confectionary."

"Ice cream?" The boy jumped from his chair, knocking it over. "I've never had ice cream before." He ran over and hugged Silas.

He crushed his son to his chest. The boy wrenched loose within seconds, then ran for the ladder. Silas closed his eyes and imagined holding him a little longer. How long had it been since he'd been hugged? He couldn't remember anyone hugging him after Jonesey had embraced him the night before he left the orphanage for the last time, and Lucy had never been very affectionate. . . .

And Anthony had only hugged him because he'd been promised an expensive dessert.

If he wasn't careful, he'd break the bank buying ice cream with the hope that Anthony would wrap his arms around him again.

Maybe they'd be all right without Kate. The boy would warm up with time . . . or at least lots of ice cream.

❖

"Miss Dawson!"

Anthony zipped in through the door into the boardinghouse's parlor, where Kate had worked all afternoon trying to attach the sleeves of her new gown. She'd already reworked them twice. A shame to leave the dress undone, even if she never wore it for a wedding.

Anthony skidded to a halt in front of her. "Mr. Jonesey said we could have ice cream next Wednesday after school."

"What?" The needle pricked her finger, and she sucked air through her teeth.

"For my birthday." He practically bounced on his toes. "Have you had ice cream before?"

And she'd thought Anthony would've been devastated once he learned they'd called off the wedding, but it seemed that ice cream made everything better for a child—if only it could make things better for her.

"Well, have you?"

She forced a smile on her face to match his—just the shape, not the joy behind it. "Once, when I was your age." After that, her brother-in-law deemed it a luxury wasted on her and never gave her pocket change again. "It's wonderful stuff, a good birthday present." She'd intended to bake him cookies. Her mother had always made her cookies for breakfast on her birthday, and she'd looked forward to starting the tradition with Anthony.

She tried to keep her face cheerful so as not to dull his excitement, but all she wanted to do was go upstairs and cry.

Especially since the boy didn't seem to care she wasn't marrying his pa anymore. Maybe he'd warmed up enough to Silas already that he didn't need her. Her breath hitched.

"It's hard to sit as stiff as a board like Mrs. Owens wants us to. Especially because I couldn't wait to come see you. I wish you were my teacher again. You never made us sit so long. Do you think she'd mind if you came to recess and ran with us? The boys don't believe that you can run faster than most anybody, even with your big skirts."

So that's why he wasn't concerned about them getting married. He expected her to stay in town no matter what. "I'm not sure your teacher would agree, especially since I'm not a school employee. How about I race you after church on Sunday? I'll wear my running boots." She wouldn't need her pretty slippers for an after-service wedding anymore anyway.

"Will you run with me every Sunday?"

She swallowed. If he wasn't disappointed that she wasn't getting married, how easily would he get over her leaving? "As long as I don't have to go away."

He cocked an eyebrow. "Why would you go away?"

"I have to find someplace to work. If I can't find a job in Salt Flatts, I might have to look elsewhere."

His face lost its joy. "Why can't you teach at my school?"

"It's a long explanation." She took his hand and gave it a squeeze. "But I promise I'll try to find something in town."

"If you got married right away, would you be able to stay?"

Did he not care to whom? She nodded, her heart feeling a tad bit lighter. At least he still wanted her around.

"Well, then, why don't you just get married?"

Thankfully Silas hadn't bad-mouthed her if Anthony thought someone else would want her now. "I don't think I can marry anybody fast enough to keep me from needing a job." And even if she could, she'd never get suckered into contemplating a quick marriage again. And this time she meant it!

"You'd marry someone besides Mr. Jonesey? But I wanted you to be *my* mother." He yanked away from her, a snarl on his lips. "That's why you came."

"Don't blame—"

But the boy had already pivoted and run from the parlor. The front door slammed, rattling the knickknacks on the shelving.

Fannie, the boardinghouse owner and the postmaster's estranged wife, shuffled in, drying her hands on a towel. She looked out the window. "Why's he running off like his pants are on fire?"

"Grown-ups aren't as fun as he wants them to be." She fingered the sleeve draped over her chair's arm. She wasn't ready to explain things to Fannie right now. She'd not told her about Silas calling off the wedding, hoping he'd come around.

Fannie picked up the bodice and frowned at the uneven gathers in the sleeve. The woman had been gracious to help her sew a wedding dress and likely couldn't stand the substandard work her guest was doing on the simple, but elegant pattern she'd pulled from her box. "We don't have much time to get this right. I need to make sure everyone's lamps and water pitchers are filled first, but I'll come back to help. We're so close."

So close. She'd been so close to having her life settled.

The desire to run coursed through her and came out in the quick tapping of her toes. But she wouldn't disappoint Anthony, no matter how difficult it'd be to celebrate his birthday with his father—to stay in the same town knowing Silas would've held her in his arms if she hadn't left so many others.

244

Running had never made life easier, not really. She was in this mess because she was good at running.

She stilled her foot, took up her sleeve, and cut out the thread again.

Silas slowed his team as they entered Salt Flatts, directing them toward a small opening near the lone tree shading the church. He maneuvered the wagon through parked carriages, buggies, and the congregants heading inside.

Once stopped, Anthony climbed down the wagon wheel without a shred of enthusiasm.

"Hello, Silas!"

Silas raised a hand in greeting to Will, who stood near the church's side steps with Eliza on his arm.

When Anthony trudged up the stairs, Will tried to put his arm around the boy. Anthony moodily shrugged from his embrace.

Silas had seen many men light into their sons for such disrespect. He'd have to have a serious talk with him tonight. But would talking be enough? Nothing he'd said this morning had helped his son's mood. He'd almost had to carry him to the wagon. For a moment, he'd considered leaving the boy at home, but since he'd run away in Breton without much thought, he might take off here too, and that'd be even more dangerous.

After taking care of his team, Silas joined Will and Eliza, who were waiting for him. He sighed. He'd have to tell them he didn't need them to stick around after services anymore. "Sorry about Anthony's attitude."

Eliza smiled, causing the small pale-pink scar at the corner of her right cheek to bunch. "He's got a lot of adjusting to do."

"So do I." Silas pulled off his hat before they entered church. He scanned the pews and found Anthony up front with Kate.

She'd turned in her seat, her eyebrow raised as if to ask if Anthony's decision to sit with her was all right.

He nodded his permission, and followed Will into his pew.

His friend scratched his head. "You're sitting with us?"

"Yes." He moved a hymnal off the seat, thankful for something to mess with. "Miss Dawson and I called things off. No need to stay after services with us today."

Both Will and Eliza paused mid-sit but lowered themselves the rest of the way once Silas thumped down and deposited the hymnal in his lap.

Will glared at him. "Why's that?"

He focused on the reverend's wife starting the music. "She's got a history of running off I didn't know about."

"You've got a history of drinking."

Silas gritted his jaw. He wouldn't deny it, but did Will have to say it so loud? Some in the congregation weren't as forgiving about past mistakes as God was. "I got a boy to consider. I could live through being abandoned again, but I won't put Anthony through it."

Will nodded toward Anthony. "Looks like you're putting him through it by not giving her a chance. Is that why he's upset?"

Silas set his jaw. Anthony had barely talked to him since he'd learned from Kate that they weren't marrying, but he needed to consider what was good for his son in the long run.

A woman who couldn't commit was not a woman he'd pine over, no matter how nice she'd felt in his arms or how much he wished things were different.

Reverend Finch drowned out any further questions with the first verse of "The Solid Rock." Silas stood and sang, and they soon reached the third verse.

> His oath, His covenant, His blood,
> Support me in the whelming flood;

When all around my soul gives way,
He then is all my hope and stay.

On Christ, the solid rock, I stand;
All other ground is sinking sand.

He kept singing, but with less gusto than usual.

All other ground is sinking sand.

He quit and closed his eyes.

Jesus, I need help. Everything is giving way, the storms have hit, and that's a dangerous place for me. I've got Anthony to look after now. Thank you for entrusting me with him, though I'm uncertain I'll be a good father. Please be my hope and stay—I need your stability.

He tried to pay attention to the pastor once they'd all been seated, but his eyes kept wandering three pews up and one across. Just to be certain Anthony was all right, of course.

But he didn't look all right. The boy hadn't uncrossed his arms since Kate had pulled him close. How could he deny his son the love of a mother?

It was all Silas could do to keep from standing up and giving in.

Of course, Kate didn't have to be the mother, but Anthony warming up to another woman would likely take just as long as it was taking him to warm up to a new pa.

Not that there was another woman in town—or one he'd ever met in his life, really—that he admired so much.

Or at least had.

No, he still admired her. Couldn't lie to himself. He was just appropriately leery now.

At the end of the service, Kate walked toward him, her arm around Anthony.

Silas looked to his left, but Will and Eliza had vanished. He tugged at his tie. He'd promised they'd talk later, but he still wasn't ready. He needed to be certain he was level-headed enough not to change his mind if she flashed him a pretty smile.

She stopped in front of him, her smile more sad than pretty. "Anthony said we're meeting for ice cream on Wednesday?"

"Yes, ma'am."

Her eyebrows raised at his formality, and then her eyes turned wounded.

He crushed his hat in his hand. Wounded eyes were a whole lot worse than a pretty smile. He pressed his lips together to keep from babbling nonsense in case he said something to give her hope he didn't feel at the moment.

Why wasn't anyone coming to talk to them? The church had emptied faster than usual. Or had they been standing staring at each other for longer than he realized?

"Go on outside, Anthony." Kate pushed his son forward. "I'll be out to run in a minute."

He forced himself to stop crushing his hat and clamped it against his leg.

"Fannie asked me if I was still going to be at the boarding-house next week."

Well, of course she was. He'd called things off. He nodded.

"I don't have money, Silas."

He closed his eyes and swallowed his groan. He didn't have money either, at least not if he wanted funds to buy a wagon and tools come spring. "All right, I'll pay for next week."

"And to compensate, I'll come to your place and help you with the garden or whatever else I can do." She blinked her large, earnest eyes at him.

No. That wouldn't do at all. He stuck a finger into his collar and tugged. He was already far too attached to her, and the last time she'd come, he'd found her too easy to kiss. "I don't think that'd be good for Anthony."

Her gaze fell. "Won't you even think about . . . *us?*"

What did she mean? That's all he was thinking about. "I can't promise anything, but we can talk later." After he had himself put back together and knew whether he should pursue her or not.

If he distanced himself for a while, wouldn't he know whether or not he could or should live without her? "But the reason you can't work for me is you'll need to find a job since I don't have enough money to pay for your boarding indefinitely."

Her hands slid up to her hips. "Where do you propose I look for work?"

At least he was stoking the fire back up in her. This Kate was easier to deal with than the one looking at him as if she were lost. "The school?"

"I don't have a proper license."

Right. "You could ask Will's wife, Eliza. If any woman can help you find a job, it'd be her. She's a bona fide businesswoman."

"And if I still can't find one?"

He ran a hand through his hair. Could he promise her anything? "I don't know."

"I love Anthony, Silas. I've got nothing to go back to. I'm not leaving."

"What about after Anthony grows up and heads out on his own?" He swallowed hard. Hadn't she asked him about that when he'd proposed?

Her body went soft again. "Depends on where I am."

The front doors of the church creaked open, and Anthony poked his head in. "Are you coming?"

"Yes," Kate called. She turned back to look at him. "I'm going to run with Anthony now. But I'm not running any farther than the churchyard."

He exhaled the moment she left the room, and he glanced up to where the stained-glass window of Christ praying in the garden bathed the front of the church in red and amber.

I know I'm not in a tougher spot than you were, but I wish I knew as clearly as you did what I'm to do. I want to believe her. . . .

He turned to look out the window and saw her holding her arm out in front of Anthony as if he'd try to get a lead on her before they both shot off together and out of sight.

I really want to believe her.

———•◦•———

On Wednesday afternoon, with her arm around Anthony's shoulder, Kate followed Silas inside a shop that smelled of spun sugar. What could she talk about that wouldn't upset Anthony? Eating ice cream in silence was no way to celebrate a birthday.

"It smells heavenly in here. Seems a shame you only get to have one bowl of ice cream." She snapped her fingers and squeezed his shoulder. "You know what? I hadn't the time to get you a gift or paint you a birthday card, so why don't you choose a handful of something to take home."

Anthony smiled, but not as brightly as usual.

Silas cleared his throat. "Are you sure you should be spending money on—"

"A dime or two won't break the bank." Not that she had a bank to break. She owned a very small coin purse with a lot of air in it.

Silas nudged him. "What do you tell Miss Dawson?"

"Thank you, Miss Dawson."

She smiled and squeezed him again.

At the counter, an old man in a pink-and-white-striped apron held up a big flat spoon. "Strawberry or vanilla?"

"How'd you know we were coming in for ice cream?" Anthony gaped.

"I can just tell." The confectioner winked at him.

They all chose strawberry and made their way to a corner booth. Silas had been nothing but polite since picking her up from the boardinghouse, but he'd yet to really meet her eyes.

Anthony's eyes were downcast as well, but he hummed after his first spoonful of the frozen treat. She smiled at the melting cream on his upper lip, then frowned at the way his shoulders sagged.

Silas couldn't really believe she'd leave Anthony. Surely he was worried about himself—which only led her to believe she had a chance with him if she was careful.

She took a bite and let the cold sweetness coat her tongue. Anthony would recover from his disappointment over her broken engagement to his father, and if she saw him occasionally, she could endure most any job. Tying herself down to take care of this boy had never been in question, and he needed her now just as much as before. "So are you going to race me again next Sunday?"

Anthony looked up, but only nodded since his mouth was full of cream.

"You better practice. I don't intend to let you win again." She glanced at Silas, who'd finally looked at her, his face devoid of any telling emotion.

Last night she'd prayed for help with her attitude. Though hurt, she still wanted to be here with them. If she could keep from acting anything like Lucinda, perhaps Silas would rethink putting her aside.

Had he not felt for her what she had for him? Maybe he'd kissed her like that back in Breton to entice her to Kansas to be his son's caretaker, and now that he'd deemed her unreliable, his interest had disappeared.

She regretted her running ways, but if she hadn't jilted the other two men or left her family, she wouldn't have known either Anthony or Silas.

Lord, I don't regret refusing to marry Jasper, but I do regret leaving Aiden without a word. I'd viewed him as nothing more than a way out from under my brother-in-law's thumb, and then when I deemed him imperfect . . .

Just like Silas now deemed her imperfect.

She needed to send a letter and apologize to Aiden. It wouldn't help her current situation, but it was the right thing to do.

"We can't be long, Anthony." Silas looked back at his ice cream, took another bite, and stared out the window. "We gotta get home before dark."

They were in no danger of having difficulty doing that. She huffed and took another bite of her dessert.

Silas's gaze weighed heavy on her, but the moment she turned to look back at him, he looked away.

The time to give up on him definitely wasn't now.

Chapter 19

Kate squeezed Anthony's hand at the edge of the first farm road outside of Salt Flatts. On the horizon, three columns of smoke pillowed toward the clouds. Likely none of them Silas's chimney fire—his was probably too far away to see. "How long does it take you to walk home?"

"I have to leave forty-five minutes before class to make sure I have time to get a drink and warm up. If I'm not in my seat exactly at nine, my teacher marks me tardy, even if I'm just taking off my coat."

She ruffled his hair. "She'll help you mind your p's and q's, then. Maybe she'll be the one to help you figure out math."

"I hate math."

"I know." She tucked a wisp of a curl behind his ear. He desperately needed a haircut, but who was she to mention it? "Go on home. I'll see you another day."

"Tomorrow?"

"I'll be looking for work again tomorrow. If I'm near the school, I'll walk with you again. But maybe, if you get your pa's permission, we can paint this coming Saturday morning." The streams around Salt Flatts were more mud than anything, so he'd actually have to try his hand at painting since murky brown water wasn't as fun to poke around in as crystal-clear creeks.

He shrugged. "Why won't they let you teach? I can tell them what a good teacher you are."

"They don't need me." Though they did need another teacher—the first-year class was enormous—but the moment she'd mentioned she had no certificate, Mr. Scottsmore's smile had faded. She'd figured the school board member who was also a lawyer would be the toughest man to convince, and so she'd started with him. And she was right. He'd dismissed her quickly.

She gave Anthony a gentle shove, and he sighed and walked away. At about fifty yards, he turned to wave and she waved back before returning to town. Thankfully Silas hadn't forbid the boy from visiting with her, but after the night he'd treated them to ice cream, she'd not seen him again.

If only she could make herself walk to his place without invitation. She understood his hurt. Hadn't she run from people when they'd disappointed her? But instead of running, Silas shut himself off. Was that how he always dealt with problems?

She kicked a rock that had the audacity to be in her way. What to do?

Salt Flatts sprawled out in front of her, but the hope of finding a job in this town had dwindled after another week of looking. She'd tried to find work but instead received two offers of marriage. One from the livery owner, the other from an old man spitting tobacco outside Lowry's Feed Store—and he didn't mean for his son. A shiver ran across her shoulders.

She'd also had a less than proper solicitation to work for Mrs. Rosemary Star, who evidently ran a new brothel on the south side of town. Kate hugged herself as she turned onto Maple. Perhaps hasty marriages of convenience weren't the worst option in the world.

She made her way to the boardinghouse, a three-story build-ing on the edge of town. Tall yellow prairie grasses waved their way up to the building's eastern garden full of spent rosebushes. The fancy boardinghouse had a wrap-around deck swathed in a variety of soft green colors, its many gables and dormers painted maroon. At each corner, rain gutters ended inside a goldfish statue, its mouth wide open to spew water away from the foundation.

If only she'd be so lucky to work here for room and board. But Fannie already had cleaning girls, and the job wouldn't merit board in such a fancy place anyway. Was there somewhere in Salt Flatts as dilapidated as Mrs. Grindall's back in Breton? Maybe she could afford to board in a place like that.

Kate forced her feet up the stairs and into the boardinghouse. Thankfully Fannie was nicer than Mrs. Grindall and hadn't kicked her out yet, despite Silas paying late for the upcoming week. She knew he couldn't afford it—and making him pay for her when he was so worried about his homestead likely wasn't making him any fonder of her—but what was she supposed to do?

In the parlor, she pushed the center table to the wall, making room for the large quilting frame the women worked around every Monday. Kate lowered herself onto an embroidered cush-ioned chair and stared at the quilt. She hadn't come down to sew last Monday because she couldn't face the women. They would've asked her about the wedding since they'd helped hem her wedding dress the previous Monday.

But she couldn't stay holed away forever.

The front door opened, and Kate busied herself with the thread spools.

Rachel Stanton, the mother of Silas's doctor friend, came through the parlor doorway and gave Kate a great big smile. "How are you Mrs. Jon—"

"Miss Dawson." She shrugged with embarrassment. "Still Miss Dawson."

"Oh dear." The older woman came over and wrapped her arms around Kate as if they'd known each other their whole life.

Tears welled in Kate's eyes as the feeling of Rachel's body registered soft and warm against her. She'd hugged Anthony many times, and Aiden had held her occasionally, but the last comforting embrace she remembered was her mother's the morning before she'd died.

She gave Rachel a gentle squeeze and stepped back, refusing to swipe at the tears on her face lest she draw attention to them. She turned to occupy herself with the spools again.

"What happened, love?"

Kate located a needle that needed threading and dug out scissors. "My past happened."

"Now, who doesn't have a past?" Rachel looked fierce with her hands planted on her ample hips.

"My past happens to make me the kind of woman Silas wants to avoid. But my real problem is finding a position in town so I can stay near Anthony." She folded her hands in front of her. "I have to support myself somehow."

The front door opened again, and Nancy Wells came into the parlor, followed by her daughter Millicent. The lady's red hair was wild and poufy in contrast to her stepdaughter's limp brunette braids. Millicent's gaunt cheeks and sallow skin indicated an ailing young lady.

"Life could be worse." At least the only sickly thing about Kate was her broken heart. She tried a smile. "I'll figure out something."

Rachel patted her shoulder, and Kate could almost see a speech composing itself behind the older woman's kind brown eyes, but with Nancy and Millicent finding their seats, Rachel must have decided to keep her words to herself.

Nancy pulled a container from her needlework basket. "I made blackberry crumb bars. Had to make Mother's group some too or they'd have followed me here." She winked and set the cookies on the end table by the sofa. Fannie had mentioned another quilting group met in town, but it was more an excuse for Nancy's mother, Mrs. Graves, to gather women for gossip.

Had Mrs. Studdard informed them all about how quickly she and Silas had gone from flirtatious glances to cold shoulders?

At least here, if she had to explain why she was still single, the details shouldn't go past the door. Nancy and Fannie couldn't stomach the tittle-tattle, so they'd started this group, wanting to focus on sewing stitches over sowing scandal.

Nancy came over, wrapped an arm around her shoulder, and squeezed. "I heard Mr. Jonesey gave your marriage license back to Reverend Finch. I'm so sorry."

Kate's lungs deflated. So much for keeping things within these four walls. "I suppose your mother knows?"

"Yes, that's how I know."

She sighed. "And here I'd hoped if Mrs. Stanton hadn't heard—"

"Gossip doesn't make it far through corn fields, despite all the ears." Rachel smiled and settled herself in a blue upholstered chair. "I'm usually the last to know of anything important. I rarely come in for the quilting, but Dex is helping Everett haul more lumber, and they've been kind enough to schedule their trips so I can attend."

"Lumber?" Kate latched on to any information that could shift the topic off her. "What are they building?"

"Julia—Everett's wife and my neighbor—insists they need more space. One room for boys, one for girls. She's certain she's got a girl coming." Rachel turned to Nancy. "Kate told me she needs a job. I'll ask Julia if she needs help since she's been so sick lately, but that wouldn't be a permanent position. You know of anything?"

She shook her head, her lip bowed in pity. "I've looked a time or two myself, but haven't had much luck. Eliza would be the one to ask."

"Ma's sparking with Micah Otting." Millicent grabbed a bar cookie. "Grandmother says marriage is the only business a woman ought to pursue."

Nancy gave her girl a warning glare, laced with mirth. "Yes, that seems to be the surest way to gain 'employment.' Don't worry, Kate. Mother'll be happy to help you pursue that avenue the next time she sees you. Make sure you have a pen and paper handy for the list of bachelors she thinks will suit."

"But she doesn't even know me."

Rachel and Nancy both laughed.

"Doesn't matter." Nancy winked.

"Did I hear Millie say you're attaching yourself to Micah?" Fannie came into the room with a tea set. "Isn't he one of the regulars at my husband's *all women are bad* meetings?" She chuckled, but the sound was not as merry as Nancy's and Rachel's laughter had been.

Fannie had stayed up late last night commiserating with Kate over men not honoring their end of the marriage bargain. Evidently, she'd been put aside by her husband, Jedidiah, many years ago after he'd learned their firstborn wasn't his. When they'd met, she'd been desperate to cover her pregnancy and latched onto him after an attempt to obtain a husband through a mail-order-bride service failed. Years later, she'd thought Jedidiah loved her enough to reveal the truth, but the man only seemed to harden toward her with each passing day.

Was Silas's current cold shoulder saving her from being rejected and discarded years from now like Fannie? No, she just couldn't believe Silas was like the post office manager she'd met, who eyed her with suspicion every time she was in his presence.

Nancy shrugged. "Micah only attends because Lynville's there. He finds them amusing and likes to play chess, though he doesn't go often since he's busy with his surveying and railroad work."

"Silas is a part of that group, right?" Rachel's frown deepened.

"Yes, but I haven't gotten the impression from Micah that Silas was as adamant about avoiding marriage." She cast an apologetic look at Kate. "Though I'm sure Lynville isn't. He'd shuck his bachelor status as soon as an available lady accepted his court. If you want to marry a homesteader, Kate, Lynville has a nice farm. He's younger than Silas, so his place isn't as nice, but it's a good spread. I don't have anything bad to say about him besides he's often overeager when pursuing a girl—so you'd have to be firm with him. Otherwise he might plant a kiss on you the first night he came calling."

"I'm not looking to marry." No one but Silas anyway. If only the women knew how she'd reacted to the first kiss he'd laid on her without even so much as a *May I walk you home from church?* "I tried to get a job with the school, but Mr. Scottsmore was disappointed with my lack of credentials."

Fannie passed around teacups and saucers. "Mrs. Crismon should be along soon; she's on the board. Maybe we can convince her to give you a chance."

Kate shrugged. No reason to get her hopes up. "Men always hold more sway."

"Won't hurt to mention it," Nancy said as she scooted her chair to the quilt block she'd worked on last week.

"I guess." But even if Mrs. Crismon didn't care about a state certificate, if she wrote Mr. Kingfisher to get a teaching reference, he surely wouldn't respond with anything that would make them want to hire her.

The front door opened again, and ladies' voices came in all aclatter. Kate busied herself with her thread.

As the women shared good-natured stories about children and neighbors, Rachel's motherly gaze wandered to Kate often. Was she worried for her? Who wouldn't be? If Nancy couldn't find work in a town she'd grown up in, who'd bother to hire an outsider with no skills?

What she really needed was for Silas to take her back. Would these women think her pitiful if she admitted she still wanted the man who'd rejected her?

This past week, Fannie had turned away two long-term boarders because of her, so she had to find somewhere else to live soon. She couldn't sit around and hope.

She'd written her sister to let her know she was alive, but could she stomach writing her abusive brother-in-law and begging to return?

Surely there was something else she could do.

⁕

The whack of ax against wood from the other side of Silas's cabin grew louder with each step Kate took. He'd not had a wife for more than ten years, but he'd kept a flower bed, which flanked both sides of the front door, though it held nothing but dead plants at the moment. The yard wasn't a trash heap like one of the homesteads she'd passed on the way out of town, and the fancy little coop looked newly painted, red with white trim. Surely he'd make up for Peter Hicks's negligence quicker than most, considering he cared diligently for his property.

She walked past the barn, surprised Yellow Eyes hadn't yet barked at her arrival. Taking deep breaths, she forced herself closer to the steady crack of firewood splitting.

She found him on the other side of the house, his back turned as he heaved his maul above his head. She'd wait for him to no-

260

tice her, so as not to disturb his work. But the wind was chilly in the shadows. She crossed her arms tighter about herself.

Silas stopped to wipe his sleeve across his forehead. With his maul safely on the ground, she cleared her throat.

He startled and turned to face her. His chest expanded with a deep breath, the corner of his mouth jumping a little. "I didn't know you were coming."

"I hope you don't mind the visit."

"I don't mind seeing you, Kate." He pulled a handkerchief from his pocket, then wiped at the back of his neck. "I don't hate you or anything of the sort."

"Well good, though I'm afraid you won't like what I'm here to talk about."

He leaned his maul against the house, then wiped his hands. He seemed broader than she remembered. Maybe it was the way his shirt wasn't buttoned up to his neck, or how the damp fabric clung to his muscles, or maybe it was because he'd filled her dreams every night and her visions hadn't done him justice.

"What do you want to talk about?"

She dragged her gaze off his chest and stepped back so she wasn't close enough to smell the lye soap and the woodsy air that smelled so good on him. "I can't find a decent job in town. Most everyone wealthy enough to hire housemaids already have them. One older man did offer me a cleaning job . . . or his hand in marriage, but I didn't like how he leered at me."

"Old man—Old Man Carson?" He croaked.

"If he's the one who spits tobacco outside the feed store—"

"Yes, that's him." Silas's eyes turned hard. "You were right to turn him down."

"He's not the only one offering marriage. I've—"

"You're considering marrying someone from around here?" Silas's eyebrows hiked.

"It's a possibility." She crossed her arms and stared at him.

Silas wiped his hands with his handkerchief again, though there couldn't be anything left to wipe off.

"So what're your thoughts on me marrying?"

He looked off in the distance for a bit, then closed his eyes. His face contorted, and he seemed to have difficulty swallowing. "If Ned Parker offers, don't choose him. He's . . . He wouldn't treat you right."

If he was having difficulty thinking of her marrying this Ned fellow . . . "Fine, I won't consider him."

"Good." A muscle in his cheek twitched as he shoved his handkerchief into his pocket.

She gave him a long look. "I can't sew well enough for the seamstress, the school isn't hiring, and Mrs. Star—"

"No." He grabbed her arm. "Tell me you didn't set foot in her place." His eyes shot daggers toward town.

"I didn't. She overheard me inquiring about a job."

Silas remained silent, and Kate let whatever was going on in his mind churn uninterrupted. Maybe she wouldn't have to say anything more. If he thought she might have to turn to something so horrific to support herself . . .

He looked back at her, more intense than she'd ever seen him, and his hold tightened. "Tell me you'd never take a job with her."

"No." But if he thought she'd consider another man, could she get him to reconsider by starting a flicker of jealousy? "But what do you think about Mr. Arnett?"

"James?"

"The nice-looking livery owner?"

He closed his eyes, and she kept from mentioning that his grip on her arm was too tight. "Yes, he's a good fellow. He'd—" Silas's black dog barreled right in between them and jumped on her.

"Down, Yellow Eyes." Silas let her go and grabbed the mongrel by the ruff.

She smiled at the dog's clunky name but sobered quickly. "Sorry about that. He likes people too much."

The dog settled next to Silas's feet, his tail thumping wildly, his tongue hanging out of his mouth as if asking for permission to jump on her again.

If only the dog hadn't broken Silas's train of thought.

But she had time to wait—unless a letter from her sister came with a train ticket for her to return home. Because if Peter spent money on a ticket, he'd expect Kate to return to Georgia to be their housemaid—an unpaid housemaid.

No, she'd do almost anything to keep from going back—maybe even marry someone else.

No! What was she thinking? She might threaten Silas with the mention of proposals from other men, but she wasn't about to accept one.

She could endure a few months at her sister's while she looked for somewhere else to live. But then, she'd be nowhere near Anthony . . . or Silas, who needed to realize what he was doing to her.

She puffed her chest and tilted her chin up. "You owe me money, Silas."

He looked to the sky as if he kept a tally of debts there. "Come again?"

"You told me if I came to Kansas, there'd be a wedding."

"But—"

"I used my savings to get here—not to mention your kiss at the train station caused me to lose my job."

He rubbed his brow with his thumb and fingers as if trying to squeeze away a headache. "I'm sorry, but my finances aren't in good shape. I had the trip to Missouri, the extra ticket for Anthony, the man I hired to watch my place who also stole my wagon, my plow, my—"

"I'd need more than the cost of a ticket to Breton to compensate. You've made it impossible for me to go back there."

"But the cost of going to Georgia—"

"Then you should continue paying my room and board until I find a job."

He licked his lips. "But you said you don't have many prospects."

"Exactly. Or you could pay until you . . ." She would not beg, she *would not*. "Until *I* marry someone."

He groaned so quietly she barely heard him over the dog's panting and then ran a hand through his hair. "Mrs. Langston's costs too much. Maybe someone from church could offer you a spare room until you find something."

Was it wrong to want to kick him in the shin? Except she was fairly certain Silas cared about her far more than he was letting on. She probably shouldn't ruin that by doing something she'd regret. "Sure. You find me somewhere cheaper to live, and I'll move." As long as she could stay in Kansas long enough for him to realize he was a dope and he and Anthony needed her. But how would that happen if she was out of sight? Maybe there was another option. . . . "Since I can't find a job, I think you should hire me, then I'm paying for my own lodging."

He shook his head. "I don't have the money to pay you indefinitely. And when you someday leave for another job, another man, another state, don't you realize what that would do to Anthony? It'd be better for you not to be so close."

"But I don't intend to leave him. I love him."

His fists clenched, though it seemed not so much from anger, but more from an internal struggle. "I know you do, but—"

"How is that not enough?" If he didn't look so conflicted and heartbroken, she'd spit in his eye.

His Adam's apple bobbed, and his shoulders hung as limp as wet clothing on a line. "I hope you know I'm only trying to look out for Anthony."

"I do." She tried to smile but failed. Which hurt more—that

he continued to refuse her though he seemed to be wavering or that he thought she wasn't good enough for Anthony?

Silas let out a shuddery breath. "I'll have enough money to get you a train ticket to Georgia at next harvest."

Anthony's lithe form poked his head out from behind the barn, but the second she looked over at him, he disappeared.

"Or maybe even in the spring, after we've made it through winter and—"

"I still need somewhere to live until then, Silas. You can't leave me floundering." She stepped closer and put a hand on his arm.

He closed his eyes, as if her touch would make him cry.

Who knew such a strong man would have such difficulty getting over the ache inside? "You're stubborn—you know that?"

One eyebrow raised, popping one eye open to look at her.

"And stubborn's good. It'll help you stay sober, but it'll also keep you from good things too, just as much as it'll keep you from the bad."

Whether he liked it or not, she'd be back. He wasn't the only stubborn person in Salt Flatts.

Chapter 20

"Anything else for you, Miss Dawson?" Mrs. Hampden put Kate's three spools of thread into a small brown sack.

"A job." She forced herself to look the mercantile owner's wife in the eye—to make it harder for the woman to say no again.

"I'm sorry, but I still haven't need of you. My children are old enough to do most anything I need done." The petite older woman scooped the change off the counter. "You've put your advertisement on the board, yes?"

Kate flicked a glance toward the flyers posted at the front of the store. How often were those looked at? "I have. Has anyone asked about mine?"

"No." She handed Kate the sack of thread. "Would you like me to ask the out-of-towners when they're in? You might have to live with them depending on how far out they are."

"Just as long as it's not a single man." Nowhere had she advertised herself as a bride, yet she'd still garnered two more proposals in the last week.

"Of course." Mrs. Hampden gave her an odd look.

"It's just . . . Aren't there enough women in Salt Flatts for your men to court? Why are so many proposing without asking me a single question?"

Mrs. Hampden grimaced. "I guess they've heard you came here to get married for convenience, and since you're pretty, they must hope you'd be willing to consider another."

"Well, if you hear about anybody else wanting to ask me, tell them I'm only interested in a job."

Mrs. Hampden smiled. "Of course."

Considering there was another woman in line, Kate moved out of the way, but stopped to look at the woman dressed in a coarse blue silk with a matching feathered hat. Surely she'd overheard—might she have pity and offer her a job?

But the lady plopped her canned goods on the counter without even a glance toward Kate.

Trying not to slump as she walked out of the store, Kate pursed her lips. She'd have to do as Eliza suggested and start a business of her own to have any hope of staying. But there were already two seamstresses and a tailor in town—who all sewed better than her—three laundresses, and no hope from any of the school board members for a position until she got a proper school license.

"Excuse me, miss?" A gruff voice sounded behind her on the sidewalk, so she turned, offering the blond stranger tipping his hat a tentative smile.

His face lit with more than the pleasant expression of a man welcoming a woman to town. His roving eyes made her shiver almost as much as when she'd waded into the cold waters of Dry Creek with Anthony and Silas.

She glanced down at the bag of thread she'd just bought but couldn't think of how to use it as an excuse for not responding. "Good afternoon, sir."

He pulled off his dingy, sweat-rimmed hat and held it in front of him. His posture appeared solicitous, yet his eyes were unnerving. "I hear tell you're looking for work."

She took in his shiny boots and his clean—though not pressed—suit. "I'm sorry, I didn't catch your name."

"Ned Parker, ma'am."

She crossed her arms. Wasn't that the name of the man Silas told her to stay clear of? "You know of someone hiring?"

"I know you've had difficulty finding a job since Silas hasn't made good on his promise to marry you."

Instead of her body flushing, she suddenly grew colder. Why couldn't this town keep sensitive information to itself? "Yes, but . . ." Did she really want to expand on her situation? "So do you know of an open position?"

His gaze took in the top of her head, moved down, lingered where it shouldn't, and hit the bottom of her feet before he looked her in the eyes again.

She hugged herself tighter and searched the street for a familiar face.

He rubbed his scruffy jawline. "I figured I could use a woman about my place."

"*A woman*?" The iciness that had resided in her limbs melted with the uptick of her heart. Did he really think such a proposal would be enticing? "I do not need a position as your woman."

"Now, hold up, sister." He crammed his hat onto his dirty blond hair. "You might not like how I said it, but I've got as much to offer as any other man around here. Maybe more." He leaned over to spit. "And if you're so uppity you won't consider marrying, I could just hire you as my cook."

"Cook?" She bit her lip. If she couldn't find a job, would cooking for this man be a bad idea? Working for a rake would be leagues better than seeing him at Mrs. Star's. Not that she'd ever work for Mrs. Star, but cooking was better than nothing.

"I'd pay you a dollar a day for three meals."

That's about what she'd made teaching.

"The problem is, I live two hours out of town. I doubt you could afford to pay for a horse along with a place to stay, so if you stayed with me—"

She took a step away. This was definitely the man Silas had warned her away from. "So you're offering me a job I can't take without ruining my reputation? And somehow you think that'll make me reconsider becoming your 'woman'?"

His upper lip curled. "Marrying me ain't that bad of a deal. You can even keep the thirty dollars you'd earn working for me each month. I know men who give their women allowances. Thirty's generous."

He'd pay for a wife? Silas jilting her looked rosy in comparison.

She jammed her hands onto her hips. "No thank you, Mr. Parker. Don't bother asking me again."

"I don't think you understand how you ain't gonna get many offers for work." He stepped closer—the smell of hair cream and a hint of alcohol invaded her nostrils. "Your best bet is marrying, and since Silas ain't gonna do it, who else is going to—"

"Mrs. Crismon!" She hollered and waved to the older woman thankfully walking out of the tailor's across the street. "Excuse me. I'm to meet up with her." Without bothering to give Ned a last glance, she skirted him and did her best not to run across Main.

"What's going on, Miss Dawson?" Mrs. Crismon, the gray-haired school board member she'd practically begged for a teaching position, frowned over Kate's shoulder, then back at her.

"I was getting thread for Fannie when Mr. Parker offered me, uh . . . a position." She grimaced at the thought of expanding on what that entailed.

"I hope you said no." Mrs. Crismon shot a right-frightening glare across the street.

"Yes." She gulped and took a calming breath. "You were a good excuse to leave him. I hope you don't mind me walking with you to the boardinghouse."

"Of course not, dear." Mrs. Crismon took her elbow, laying a comforting hand on her arm. They strolled down the block before Kate had the nerve to look behind her.

"He's slunk off." She let out a long exhale.

The women walked in companionable silence toward the boardinghouse. She'd hoped to have gotten back to Fannie's before the quilting women arrived so she could hole up in her room, but now that Mrs. Crismon knew she was available, sequestering herself would only invite them to talk about her in quiet, pitying tones.

So once they reached the boardinghouse, Kate set out the snacks Fannie had prepared as the women came in.

She was soon sitting behind her quilt block as small talk floated gaily around her. Her stitches from last week had veered to the left. Should she pull the thread or wander back to the middle? She rolled her needle between her fingers.

Starting a business that dealt with any kind of sewing should be stricken off her list—that was certain.

"Are you all right, Kate?" Fannie held up a kettle. "Do you want tea?"

She shook her head.

"Do you want to talk about something? You've been awfully quiet." Nancy's lips plumped with worry.

Nancy, Fannie, Rachel, and Mrs. Crismon stared at her from around the quilt. She'd rather curl up in a ball than admit in front of near strangers how much trouble she was in, but then, they might be able to help her figure out what to do.

Because she was definitely in trouble.

"I need to find someone in town desperate enough—or maybe generous enough—to let me stay with them in exchange for being a housemaid. I'm not looking for wages anymore, just a bed."

Mrs. Crismon—who sat on the edge of the divan with the posture of a queen—threw a glare at Fannie.

Kate shot an apologetic glance toward her hostess. "Mrs. Langston has been kind to let me stay without being assured of payment. However, she's turning away boarders because of me, so I need to find other accommodations for her sake as well as mine."

"I wish I could afford another maid." Fannie frowned and poured Mrs. Crismon tea. "But my two are good workers—it'd be unfair to fire them. And I've already got a cook."

Mrs. Crismon pointed her needle at Kate. "Did you put up an advertisement at the mercantile?"

Kate nodded.

"The post office?"

"I—"

"I'm afraid my husband isn't being helpful there." Fannie apologized for cutting Kate off, then sighed. "I've heard Jedidiah's warning people away from her when he catches them reading her advertisement—says mail-order brides are as unreliable as they come."

"I'd like to knock some sense into him." Mrs. Crismon's shoulders shimmied with indignation.

"Me too," Fannie muttered.

Mrs. Crismon crossed her arms and continued, "Your Mr. Langston and that dreadful Mr. Parker and all the others stewing in the post office, talking badly about spinsters and old maids and single young ladies . . . Well, I haven't seen anybody near as bad as they are since I was in California with my daughter, who was giving birth to her fifth. That Bachelor's Club of Grass Valley was just about as vindictive."

Fannie's shoulders slumped. "If it hadn't been for me—"

"Nonsense." Rachel interrupted. "You made a mistake more than twenty years ago, from which you repented, and since then you were a good mother and a good wife. You're not at fault for Jedidiah choosing to baste himself in his own bitter juices." She tied off her thread and reached for another spool. "Maybe the proprietress at the millinery might have a job. Have you tried her for work, Kate?"

"Yes." Who hadn't she tried?

"Did you talk to my daughter-in-law, Eliza? She could find a position for a woman even if there weren't any to be had."

"I did." Kate swallowed against the warmth creeping into her throat and reaching up to heat her eyes. Eliza had given her a whole list of people to ask after, but the second she'd given her name, many of them cocked their head with suspicion. At least now she knew why her name had caused such a bad reaction with some of them. It appeared that Mr. Langston had been talking her down something fierce.

"Have you talked to Silas recently?" Nancy threaded her needle with a long, brilliant piece of indigo. "Maybe he's got his head back on straight."

"I asked him for work or money until I found a position. He said he didn't have enough—"

"Like you do." Mrs. Crismon scowled.

She pressed her lips firmly together. As much as she wanted to lash out at him herself, she didn't want the ladies to think terribly of him. "He's looking for somewhere for me to stay and paid Fannie for the week."

"He needs to be taken down a notch, considering how he jilted you." Mrs. Crismon placed her empty teacup on her saucer with a clank. "Perhaps if his name was sullied like yours is by the men at the post office —"

"Oh no, I don't want to destroy him." She swallowed hard. "He's a good man. He's just—"

"Wounded?" Rachel reached over and clasped her hand. "He's made a lot of mistakes—and he'll admit it—but underneath it all, he's afraid, not malevolent, right?"

Kate nodded. "He thinks he's doing what's best."

"What's best is giving that boy a mother and living up to his word." Mrs. Crismon clucked her tongue as if admonishing Rachel and Kate for letting him off. Then she straightened and snapped her fingers, her face alight. "You should sue."

"What?" Fannie and Kate chimed together.

"Sue?" Nancy scoffed. "What could she sue for?"

"In '81, I think, one of the members of that Bachelor Club I was talking about ordered a mail-order bride. But as soon as she came, they talked him out of it. So he refused to marry her. She was a smart one, though—sued him for breach of contract and won two thousand dollars, if I remember right."

Kate's mouth slowly dropped open. She'd never had that much money in her life. "But I'm not a mail-order bride." Not this time at least. "I don't have a contract with him."

"Verbal contract, honey. I'm sure you wouldn't have spent your every dime coming to Kansas unless you had a promise of some sort." She frowned. "You did have a promise from him, right?"

She licked her lips and thought back. His kiss was almost all she could remember about his proposal. "He said if I came there'd be a wedding, the best he could afford."

"Ha! That's a promise if I ever heard one." Mrs. Crismon snipped her thread with enthusiasm.

Rachel fidgeted as if her seat were made of upended nails.

Kate's hands trembled. Could she sue Silas? He'd promised her a wedding, and she wouldn't have come unless he had. But how could she take his money when she'd be taking from Anthony as well? "No, I wouldn't do that to him or Anthony."

"Can you go home?" Nancy questioned softly.

"I wrote my sister." She shrugged. "But I've not heard from her yet."

"If you're looking for a bed, well, I don't have an extra bed, but I've had visitors stay overnight in my barn." Rachel shrugged. "Never had them sleep there through the winter, though—not sure it would be pleasant."

"Thanks. If I truly can't find anything, I might have no choice, but I'm hoping to remain in town so I can visit with Anthony." She'd be nothing but a burden to the Stantons, since they had plenty of children to do chores. "But if I wasn't able to earn money or be near Silas, I'm not sure what good it would do me."

Rachel folded her hands in her lap, her quilt block forgotten. "You'd rather work things out with Silas than go elsewhere." She said that with more conviction than Kate could've mustered.

She nodded and kept her eyes off the others, in case they were pitying her for wanting to reconcile with him. But it was true. She wasn't ready to give him up. Finding a job would only free her up from taking advantage of Fannie's good graces. She'd still be praying for Silas to change his mind . . . unless he held out so long she changed hers first.

"Then what about some good old-fashioned courting?"

She shook her head as she let out a sad chuff. "We didn't do any of that in the first place, so—"

"Exactly." Rachel patted her legs. "Force him to spend time with you . . . in a manner he can't resist. Sort of like my husband did with me. Though he wasn't officially courting me, the reading lessons he asked me for forced us together long enough to admit our feelings."

"I saw Silas look at you at church." Nancy smiled. "I bet you could win him over with a little feminine wile."

"But he's told me he doesn't need my help on his farm."

"Doesn't mean you can't find plenty of excuses to be there." Nancy batted her eyelashes.

Could something as simple as forcing Silas to spend time with her work? "I might as well try it." She laid down her needle and folded her hands. "Got any good ideas?"

"Excuse me." Fannie stood and rubbed her hands agitatedly on her skirts. "I should check on something in the kitchen. I'm sure I couldn't come up with anything to help you anyway."

Frowning, Kate watched the older woman slink out of the room.

Jedidiah refused to trust Fannie because of a past mistake, so if Silas couldn't trust her for the same reason now, would he ever? Would whatever these women came up with change the heart of the problem?

Was she foolishly pining for the trap Fannie found herself in now?

After collecting her last basket with mittened hands, Kate waved to the stable boy who'd brought her to Silas's as an excuse to exercise one of the livery's stabled horses.

She marched toward the door and took in several deep, icy-cold breaths. Before knocking and disturbing their morning routine, she waited until the buggy disappeared. If there wasn't an easy way to send her back to town, perhaps Silas wouldn't try to suggest she leave.

"Kate?"

She jumped at Silas's voice behind her and turned. What was he doing outside this early? His hair wasn't combed, and his face was red and sweaty. His long wool coat was unbuttoned as was the top of his plain white shirt. The laces on one boot undone.

His breath swirled like locomotive steam in the morning cold. "What're you doing here?"

"I'm sorry, I hadn't expected you to be working outside so early." And in such a disheveled state.

"The pig got out." He set his hands on his hips, letting his shoulders roll forward with a sigh. His chest worked hard, his lungs attempting to return to a normal breathing rhythm.

Hadn't he said he'd lost all but one pig to Peter Hicks's negligence? "I hope my arrival didn't thwart you from capturing him."

"Her. And no, I ran her back into the pen before you unloaded your first basket." He eyed the assortment at her feet. "Whereas I know what she was doing—trying to get into my compost—I don't know what you're doing."

Oh, if he only knew, he'd send her back. "Did you forget it's Thanksgiving?"

His cheek muscle twitched. "Anthony reminded me last night."

"So no plans, then?" What if he did have plans? Rachel said she couldn't ever recall him eating with anyone in the area and that he'd declined the few invitations she'd extended throughout the years.

"Only to figure out how to make a sweet-potato pie, but nothing beyond that."

"How does one 'figure out' how to bake a pie?"

He shrugged. "I've got sweet potatoes and the knowledge that such a thing exists."

"Well, I happen to actually know how to make one." She smiled and stooped down beside her smallest basket. "I also have a chicken." Pulling back the cover, she showed off the pale-skinned bird Rachel had her husband bring into town yesterday.

"I thought Thanksgiving was supposed to be turkey?"

Yes, because if he was going to be forced to celebrate Thanksgiving, the menu should be perfectly traditional. "It's got wings and it used to have feathers. I say it's close enough."

He swallowed hard and stared. "I suppose Anthony will be ecstatic to have you here."

Why did he say that so sadly? "You two are the closest thing I have to family. I felt I should be here. Even if uninvited."

"There's nothing to be invited to. I've never done Thanksgiving before." He shoved his hands into his pockets.

He had to be getting cold. And though she'd invited herself onto his porch, she wasn't bold enough to order him into his house and follow him in without being asked. Of course, some of the things the ladies at the quilting circle had planned for her to do today would take more brazenness than that.

She pulled her muffler up to hide her cheeks, likely reddened by the wind just as much as by her flush. "Well then, let's start some traditions . . . for Anthony anyway." She huffed at herself. She shouldn't have softened her statement. She wasn't doing this just for Anthony.

The misty swirl of Silas's breath increased.

She pulled out a letter Fannie convinced her estranged husband to hand over and took a step toward Silas. "I brought your mail."

His body blocked the wind and the heat of him drew her closer.

Despite wearing mittens, her fingers were numb. She held out the letter until he took it. If only she had enough nerve to slip a hand into his empty one. She settled on cupping his upper arm with both of her hands, though his warmth didn't seem to penetrate his sleeve enough to help her fingers, but she was closer to him, and that was good.

Nancy had suggested she stay as close to him as possible, not letting him forget she was nearby—and could be nearer if he'd let her—so she tucked herself against his arm even tighter. He stiffened but didn't jerk away.

She stared at the envelope he'd yet to open. "Ezekiel Jones— isn't that the man from the orphanage you took your name from?"

He held the letter in front of him with both hands, but she could feel his gaze on the top of her head. Too timid to tiptoe up for a kiss he might turn away from, she settled on pretending she didn't notice how he'd yet to breathe after she'd sidled in so close.

After a few seconds, he cleared his throat. "Yes, Jonesey." He stepped away from her, and she released him reluctantly.

He tucked his letter into one of her baskets, picked up that one and then another, and rammed his body through the door, hollering, "Anthony, you've got a visitor!"

Invitation enough. She grabbed the remaining basket and forged into the warm, serviceable cabin. She moved straight to the table—only steps from the door, given the close quarters—and set the baskets beside the linens he'd carried in.

Descending from the loft, Anthony turned a smile on her that was worth staying for all on its own.

"I didn't know you were coming!" The ten-year-old bounded over and hugged her. He was still in his pajamas and sockless. His cowlicks were mussed in opposite directions, just like his father's.

She gave him a hard squeeze. "You don't mind having Thanksgiving with me, do you?"

"Really?" He released her and headed straight for the baskets on the table. "What did you bring?"

She pulled the nearest basket away from his eager hands. "Go wash up. I'll need your help getting dinner ready on time."

"Right." He flew through the doorway on the left into Silas's room.

She couldn't help smiling at the boy's enthusiasm and glanced toward Silas, who evidently did not find the boy's eagerness as charming as she did. His face was serene, almost pained, as he watched his son.

"Are you all right?"

He shrugged before crossing the room to pull a trunk out from under a small table. "I have to feed the animals." He took out a muffler, gloves, and a stocking cap. Stalking past her, he muttered, "Send Anthony out when he's dressed. I need him to help clean stalls before he cooks with you."

Anthony would likely look as enthused as Silas sounded when she told him about his chores. "All right."

After the door swung shut, Anthony came out grumbling. "I heard him." He plopped down on the tiny sofa with his boots. "I'm going."

"Don't be sour." She winked at him. "We'll be making pie in no time."

When he passed by, she ruffled his barely brushed hair and stood still until he exited. She looked around the cabin. She'd only been inside once, on the first day she'd come here with Silas. Though small, the house was neat and large enough to hold a cookstove, hutch, table, chairs, and small sofa in the living area—plus it had a separate bedroom for Silas and a loft above for Anthony. She glanced away from the cookstove and tried not to think about how it would feel to stand there every day cooking while Silas and Anthony were out choring, tried not to contemplate the way her heart stuttered a little at thinking about living in a house belonging to her and a husband.

She took out a box of lavender and baby's breath from the first basket. While Anthony was outside where he couldn't ask questions, she'd make Silas's cabin look more homey, as if she were already living there.

The women in town had donated things for just that purpose—though it'd felt a lot less sneaky coming up with a plan than actually following through with it. With jittery fingers, she arranged the dried flowers in the two vases Fannie had found in storage. Taking one of the vases, she darted into the bedroom and set it on the bedside table. She plumped Silas's pillows, enjoying the musky scent of his hair and the smell of soap in his pillowcases before going to retrieve the rosewater Mrs. Crismon convinced her to bring.

Could she do it? It wasn't near as bold as Ruth sleeping at Boaz's feet, but the audacity of sprinkling her perfume on Silas's pillows made her feel as wanton as Mr. Kingfisher had accused her of being back in Breton.

Unscrewing the cap, she settled on rubbing some in her hands and then making the bed, smoothing her hands along his sheets and plumping the pillows again. If he cared anything for her, Mrs. Crismon believed the smell of Kate's perfume would keep her predicament in the forefront of Silas's mind.

She smoothed out the last wrinkle. Was the smell too much or was it just because it was on her hands? She closed her eyes, nothing she could do about it now. He could wash his sheets if the smell bothered him.

After slipping the doily Nancy had given her under the vase, Kate returned to the front room and kitchen area. Working as quickly as possible, she set out the tablecloth, table runner, throw pillows, curtains, and other items the ladies had helped her collect. Why did she feel as if she were a thief? She was leaving things behind not taking things away.

Once everything was out, she rushed to wash potatoes, trying to compose herself so if Silas walked in, he'd not notice the heat in her cheeks. Would leaving this stuff all over his house do any good, or would he think her a crazy woman?

She glanced at the things around the living room. She hadn't set out too much.

Maybe she was crazy.

Anthony hollering at the dog outside the window made her snatch up her knife and start peeling her first potato. She had cooking to worry about now. A man's heart was supposed to be won through his stomach.

She was about to put that saying to the test.

———— ✦ ————

"Oh no!" Anthony covered his eyes and flopped back against his chair. Silas looked up from where he sat in the corner reading.

Kate brandished Anthony's captured black queen. "Try to stop me now, bub."

"I'm going to win again anyway. Just watch!" Anthony got up and swiped her rook with his bishop.

Kate groaned, but the sound turned into a cute little growl that clearly indicated she wasn't about to throw the game for the boy. She wasn't the best loser, as evidenced by the last two games.

Silas shook his head, a smile fighting to rearrange the placid expression he'd been trying to maintain throughout dinner, dessert, and now their lively game. Though he'd stopped working at two that afternoon, he'd not been able to completely relax with her in his house. However Anthony couldn't have been any more at ease than he was right now. He'd become an entirely different kid in her presence.

Silas turned to stare out the window, where a powder so light it almost couldn't be considered snow swirled in the pale sunlight that would disappear in about an hour.

How could he have forgotten Thanksgiving? Of course, he'd rarely ever celebrated it, but with a son, this year was more meaningful than any other. He'd been too focused on making up for what Peter Hicks had cost him to stop and be thankful for what he'd gained. The man hadn't stolen anything that truly mattered.

"Ha!" Anthony swiped a piece off Kate's side of the board, and she frowned comically.

Of course, if he could figure out how to keep this lighthearted boy around every day, he'd have even more to be thankful for.

Having Kate around more often would be the way to ensure such a thing, but how could he have her work on his homestead and not kiss her again? And if she came here every day, what would happen to her reputation? To his resolve?

He swallowed hard and pulled out Jonesey's, or rather Ezekiel's, letter to take his mind off Kate.

Though the only thing that was likely the man's actual writing was the misshapen signature at the bottom of the letter, his eyes devoured the words.

Silas Jonesey,

Forgive me for not remembering much when you came last. My memory's not what it used to be, and some days are far worse than others. I've been thinking about you. I remembered something a few days ago. Pretty sure you were the boy who had a hard time sitting still long enough to eat anything—not that the gruel Mrs. Oldstein ever made was any good. Always had a good bit of energy, you did, and a shy smile you rarely used. I was surprised that first family brought you back since you were always so eager to please me whenever I asked you anything. I hope things worked out better for you later.

I also remembered you're the boy whose sister came looking for you after you left for good. Her name was Jewel, a right pretty name, that. So I found out where the Oldsteins live now—well, only the Mrs. since the man's passed on—and I asked about you. She said she gave your sister the name of the folks you went with but you'd run by then. All Mrs. Oldstein could remember was the girl— well, she was a woman, really—said to send word of you to Raytown on the other side of Independence should they hear of you. Mrs. Oldstein said you came to the orphan-age without a name, and she don't remember what the girl called you—said it was something she'd never heard before. Wish I remembered more, but I likely never had more information than that.

Ezekiel Jones

Folding his letter, Silas let his head tip back against the chair's high back. If only he hadn't run. . . .

He sighed and sunk in against the chair's cushion. Someone had come looking for him. What would his sister have done or said if she'd found him? Would his life have turned out any better?

He looked over at Kate. If she hadn't run from her previous fiancés, this rift between them wouldn't ever have happened. They'd be a family already.

No, if she hadn't run, he'd never have known her.

"Can you come back tomorrow?" Anthony's head lay against his palm, smashing his cheek up into his eye, waiting for Kate to move.

"Unfortunately, no." Kate tapped her last remaining bishop as she contemplated the board. "I'm still looking for a job."

"What if you can't find one?"

"I don't know. I'll have to move to Rachel Stanton's house." Kate moved her piece forward but dragged it back before releasing it. "Or rather, I'd be bedding down in her barn."

"The barn? But it's cold!"

She shrugged, but it was quite evident she didn't relish the idea of cold either.

He rubbed his arms. What kind of man was he to let Kate sleep in someone's barn? But marrying a woman just so she could sleep somewhere warm wasn't a reason to call up a preacher. A man shouldn't randomly marry a woman because she needed somewhere to stay.

Not that a woman living in poverty had ever made him feel guilty for not proposing before.

Or rather, feel guilty for not proposing again.

How long was he going to force himself to ignore the real reason lurking behind his fear of committing to Kate?

Marrying her for his son's sake meant he put himself on the chopping block.

He ran his fingers through his hair and then down along his neatly trimmed beard. He needed to pray before he ended up proposing to her again without thinking things through.

Kate plopped down her chess piece.

Sitting up straighter to see the board, Anthony quickly slid a pawn forward. "Are you going to stay in their barn all winter?"

"I'm afraid I'll have to once my boarding fee is no longer paid." She looked over at him as if to ask how long that would be.

Silas pulled on his collar. How had he thought to make her wait all the way until harvest to send her home if she couldn't find work?

Anthony sighed. "How much money do you need to get to Georgia?"

"I haven't gone to the train station to ask yet."

Was there anything Peter Hicks left behind that he could sell for the price of a train ticket? He had to help her return home or propose. One or the other.

His stomach churned despite the good food residing there.

"Checkmate!" Anthony whooped as he jumped up from his chair.

Kate groaned, but the smile in her eyes made him wonder if she had thrown the game. Collecting the mugs she'd made hot chocolate in earlier, she came over and grabbed Silas's mug too. "You keep rereading your letter. I hope it's good news."

"I have a sister." He stared at the words, not really seeing them. "She came looking for me."

"Really?" Kate face brightened. "That's wonderful news."

"More than a decade ago. I don't know if she's still around."

"You should try to find out." She looked at him with big concerned eyes, but once he dropped his gaze back onto his letter, she crossed over to the sink and picked up the dishcloth.

She'd acted all afternoon as if it wasn't strange to cook, clean, and dust for a man who'd jilted her. He looked at the throw pillows, doilies, and other frilly things she'd strewn about. He understood the table decorations, but he'd yet to figure out what had possessed her to put fripperies in every corner of his house.

"Did you hear that, Anthony? Your pa has a sister. You've got an aunt."

The boy shrugged.

"Maybe you'll get to meet her sometime." Kate stopped washing to look at him. "I guess that depends on where she lives."

"Raytown, Missouri."

"Why, that's not far from Hartfield."

Anthony's smile died. "You mean she lives near Pa?"

Kate winced, and Silas's stomach knotted.

"Silas is your pa, Anthony." Kate's reproach held authority despite its softness.

"I know, I just . . ."

Silas cleared his throat. "It's hard to remember to call Richard something else when you've called him Pa your whole life. I understand." And yet, the comfortable family-like mood Kate had created now seemed shallow. "And yes, I'd like us to go back to see her if possible." But without a last name, how would he begin to find an address for her? At least Jewel wasn't a common name. Maybe he might get lucky. Though if he did find her, would he ever feel comfortable enough to travel after how his homestead had fared with Peter Hicks?

Outside the window, a wagon turned onto his road. Silas put a hand against the glass to erase the low-lying sun's glare. The livery boy again? He frowned. Anthony would not be happy. He'd assumed they'd have to take Kate home.

Sighing, Silas folded his letter. "Kate, your ride is coming."

"No." Anthony groaned and slumped in his chair, the chessboard halfway reset.

She wiped her hands and crossed the room to press Anthony's dark head against her side in a makeshift hug. "We can play another day."

"Tomorrow?" he whined.

She laughed. "You have school tomorrow."

"Even worse." With a big sweep of his arm, Anthony knocked the pieces back into the wooden box.

"I'm sorry I didn't get the dishes done, Silas." Kate folded the towel and set it beside the dish basin.

He couldn't even form words to tell her she needn't have done any of them.

She packed the candlesticks and some of the cooking utensils, then took her coat off its hook.

He stood and looked around at all the things she'd brought. "Can I help you gather your things?"

"No, I've got everything."

He frowned at the stuff he knew wasn't his. Then realized he should've been helping her into her coat, but she already had it on.

"Come on, Anthony." Silas grabbed the back of the boy's chair. "Let's see Kate out."

Kate pressed Anthony to her side as they both squashed through the front door. "I'll walk to the edge of town with you after school like always—no need to be so glum."

The livery boy stopped in front of the porch, and Anthony trudged down the stairs with one of Kate's empty baskets and tossed it into the buggy.

"I had a good time, Silas." She came close, almost as if she were going to go up on tiptoe to kiss him on the cheek, but with a glance at the driver, she stepped back to a more respectable distance. "Thank you."

"I wish I'd done something worth being thanked for." He shrugged, trying not to pull on his collar anymore today, lest it hang loose on him forevermore. "I should be thanking you."

"Maybe we can do it again next year?" She raised her eyebrows, and the way she tilted her head to look up at him . . . was she flirting?

No, surely not. What woman would flirt with a man who'd jilted her all because he was worried she might follow in Lucy's footsteps?

Might.

He followed her down the stairs. When she grabbed hold of the side of the buggy, he helped her up.

Once seated, she didn't let go of his hand. The strength in her grip made him certain she held on to him on purpose.

He shouldn't have proposed to her back in Breton—he was still right about that.

But did that mean he'd proposed to the wrong woman? He worried about her, thought about her, wished she could've stayed longer, wished he didn't have to let go.

He lowered his hand once he realized she'd released him at some point.

"Good-bye." She smiled a little at him, then winked at Anthony as the buggy pulled away.

And he envied his son that wink.

His heart had clearly lied to his brain. He'd never truly been worried about her leaving Anthony—but rather her staying and him failing at marriage once again.

What would happen if he let himself kiss her again? The first time, he'd proposed; the second, he'd thrown all caution out the soddy's window. There'd be no way he'd not fall hard for her once they were wed.

So what if he married her and she never came to love him back? He'd been unable to capture Lucy's heart, and now he was having difficulty winning his son's. How could he be sure he would win Kate's?

The second she stopped waving and turned to face the road, Anthony reassumed the slumped posture and sour expression he'd been sporting for weeks.

The same expression Jedidiah had sported for years.

Silas paused. He'd always thought Jedidiah a fool. His wife had gotten pregnant with another man's baby before they'd met and kept the information to herself. Not a secret any husband would be happy to learn about years later, but nothing she'd done while married to Jedidiah indicated she was or would be unfaithful again.

Nothing Kate did now indicated she'd run. Despite the difficulty he'd put her in, she seemed determined to stay for Anthony's sake—as she'd said she'd do all along.

Was it wrong to want to gain the boy's affections without Kate's help though? "You know, Anthony, I wish you didn't act like this every time Kate left. I don't expect you to love me like you do her just yet. I know I'm little more than a stranger to you, but I'll only stay that way if you don't get to know me—if you don't give me a chance."

The boy didn't so much as flinch.

"I want you to stop calling me Mr. Jonesey. If you don't want to call me Pa, that's fine, but at least call me Silas. I know your ma didn't have much nice to say about me, but

I'd like you to judge me for what I do now rather than what I did years ago."

"But aren't you mad at Kate for something she did years ago?"

He swallowed hard. No wonder he was getting nowhere with his son if he was modeling the very thing he wanted him to stop doing.

He put his arm around Anthony, and though his son didn't wrap his arm back around him, he at least didn't shrug him off. "It's hard to risk our hearts, isn't it?"

If it weren't so cold, he could've stayed out here with his arm around his boy for hours, but his numb fingers protested. "Let's go in and have the last of the cocoa Kate made."

"All right . . . Silas."

He smiled and kept his arm around his son as they walked back into the house.

"Can't you hire her to work around here?" Anthony grumbled.

"I can't afford to." But maybe he'd take his own advice and risk his heart—for everyone's sake. If not, was he not as foolish as Jedidiah, wallowing in a bitter bog of his own making?

But he wouldn't tell Anthony he wanted to shuck all his misgivings and chase after joy. Because if Kate wouldn't have him—and he wouldn't blame her if she wouldn't—he didn't want Anthony to think she'd chosen not to be his ma.

But maybe he had a chance, if he could find the right words to say.

*C*hapter 21

"Oh, Kate." Julia Cline dropped the apple she'd been cutting and put a hand to her mouth again. "I need to—" She ran out the door and little Gabriel started whimpering at the table.

"Don't cry, Gabriel." Six-year-old Matthew patted his three-year-old brother's hand. "She'll stop getting sick someday. Papa says so."

"But I want my apple cut." He picked up the apple, twice the size of his hand, thrust out a pouty lip, and blinked his big, sad eyes.

Kate fought a smile. "Can I cut it for you?" She wiped her sudsy hands on a towel and grabbed Julia's abandoned knife. Though Rachel had told her Julia's husband could only pay her a small amount for helping his wife through the early stages of her pregnancy, at least she was doing something to pay for her boarding.

Gabriel hugged the apple to his chest. "I want Momma to cut it."

"She might throw up on it." Matthew stood with his hands on his hips as if lecturing someone who should know better. "Miss Dawson won't."

She couldn't help her grin now. "I promise I won't throw up on it."

"All right." The little boy reluctantly held out the green fruit.

She cut the apple she'd brought in from the root cellar that morning and put the slices on his plate.

"That's not enough," the boy whined.

She frowned. "But I gave you the whole apple."

Matthew peeked over Gabriel's shoulder. "Momma cuts it into eight pieces."

She shook her head and made eight pieces. No wonder Julia struggled to get things done while sick and sleepy. Doing anything for these two took five times longer than necessary. "Maybe you should learn to eat an apple in four pieces."

The boy looked at her as if he'd never agree to such a horrible proposition, but at least he didn't complain about how some of the apple pieces were smaller than the others.

The door creaked behind them, and Julia leaned heavily on the doorknob. Her hand pressed against her still-flat stomach. Julia was beautiful, with her delicate features and thick dark hair, but her sickness seemed to have drained her of all color. How could a baby so tiny cause so much discomfort?

"I was looking forward to having children, but now I'm not so eager." Kate handed the woman the tea Rachel had suggested for queasiness.

"This is worse than either of the boys."

"Maybe you're having more than one?"

Julia's eyes grew wide. "Oh, heaven help me! I was hoping it meant I was having a girl."

"I don't want a girl." Matthew crossed his arms. "Girls are bossy."

Julia rolled her eyes, but Kate couldn't tell if it was in response to Matthew's declaration or another bout of dizziness. She pulled out Julia's chair. "Have a seat. You look ready to fall over."

"I'm not so sure . . ." She put a hand to her mouth, spun around, and dashed back outside.

"Why does she have to be so sick?" Matthew slumped in his chair. "She said she'd read to me this morning, and it's already after lunch."

A man's throat cleared behind them. Everett, Julia's husband, gave his boy a stern look as he stepped inside. "We're to be understanding, Matthew. We talked about this."

The young boy sighed, and Everett came over and pulled him into a hug, ruffling his son's dark hair.

Kate grabbed her discarded dishcloth. "And your parents hired me to help, so as soon I dry these glasses, I'll read to you. All right?"

"I guess so." He mumbled against his father's shirt.

Everett let go of Matthew and leaned over to pick up the apple slice Gabriel had knocked onto the floor. The little boy's mop of dirty blond hair and deep blue eyes made him unmistakably his father's son. Everett popped back up and planted a kiss on Gabriel's little forehead before turning back to her. "Miss Dawson, you'll want to hold off on the dish drying and the storytelling."

She took in Matthew's pout. He'd been very patient, and Julia had promised him a story hours ago. "Do you want me to check on your wife?"

"No, I'll do that, and I'll see to the boys. You've got a visitor."

She took a towel and dried her hands. "I'm sure Rachel wouldn't mind me telling him a story first."

"Not Rachel. Silas."

She stopped rubbing her hands against the towel and strangled it instead. "Oh." With nearly useless fingers, she hung up the towel, then reached behind her waist to fumble with her apron strings. "I can't imagine why he'd come all the way out here since—"

"I bet you can once you get a look at him." Everett gave her an all-encompassing, handsome grin, as if her nerves amused him.

Hurrying to avoid any questions from the boys, she deposited her apron on a chair and walked through the door Everett held open for her.

Silas paced on the other side of his wagon, head down, hands clasped behind his back. Surely his agitation didn't bode well.

She stopped at the front of his cart and waited for him to pivot.

When he turned, he caught sight of her, and his mouth twitched. Not a smile, but not a frown either. "Good afternoon, Kate."

"Likewise." *Except not really.* Her back ached after cleaning all morning, and now her stomach threatened to visit Julia's misery upon her as well. "Is Anthony all right?"

"Yes." He walked straight to her, as if he meant to plow her over, but he stopped short and reached into his pocket. "I came to give you enough money to cover your lost school-year salary—what I cost you." He pulled out a thick, clipped square of bills. "Two hundred dollars."

She closed her eyes and all the muscles in her body threatened to give up. She reached for the side of the wagon. Two hundred dollars was more than adequate, but goodness, she'd let herself hope. *Stupid.* Had he felt nothing for her?

She shouldn't have let herself feel anything the times she'd thought of him, looked at him, imagined what being loved by him might've been like. She tightened her grip on the wagon's sideboard to keep from walking away without his money.

"Is that enough?" He held the cash out between them. "I'm sorry I expected you to fend for yourself when I was responsible for your predicament. That was wrong of me."

"Yes, it's enough." She couldn't open her eyes to look at him. "But I thought you didn't have enough to even hire me."

"I sold a parcel of land to my neighbor, Mr. Thissen."

"Sold?" She had to look at him now. "But you took so much pride in your spread; you had plans for it all once you got everything back in order."

"Well, yes. But I had no other way to get enough money to make things up to you without depleting my savings."

She pressed the heel of her hand to the corner of an eye, hoping the pressure would keep her emotions at bay.

"But I have something else I hope you might consider." He placed the money on the wagon's seat, then leaned over into the back and hefted a small crate over the side. Inside the box lay a single dark bottle propped in a corner.

She frowned. "What is it?"

"Wine. A man who once lived near me gave this to me after Lucy and I were married. Can't remember what year he said it was, but he'd brought it from Scotland and was saving it to celebrate his firstborn son, but he'd only had girls." Silas smiled. "He gave it to me for my first boy, but of course, I didn't know about Anthony." His countenance lost its happiness for a second. "That was before the state's prohibition."

Did he expect her to want wine instead of money? Surely not. The idea was laughable, but he didn't look like he was trying to be cheeky. "Did you bring this for me to pour out?" Surely he could've given the bottle to someone else instead of driving two hours to have her do it.

"No." His laugh was little more than a huff. "I'd been keeping this because I never truly believed I'd conquer my addiction. Maybe I still don't. So since I expected to fail at staying sober, I'd figured I'd keep this to enjoy someday."

She swallowed and wrapped her arms about herself. Was he here only to confess to someone in an attempt to take weight off his shoulders? "Are you certain you don't want me to pour it out? Think of Anthony."

"I am thinking of him." He stared at the wine bottle in the crate but didn't take his hands off the box. "I've quit drinking plenty of times, as you know, but I never had enough faith to believe I could stay sober. After Thanksgiving, I considered my reasons not to marry you, and I remembered this bottle."

Not to marry her.

"I'd forgotten about it and went to the barn to hold it again."

"Holding it's not good for you."

"I didn't have much of a problem this time, since I was thinking of you and Anthony. As I rolled it between my hands, I prayed God would help me stay sober."

He set the crate down between them on a patch of dirt. "Then I realized I was viewing your past the same way I viewed mine, believing that caving to our weakness was inevitable. I believed someday you'd run again, because I believed someday I'd drink again." He pointed to her worn boots. "Anthony says you only run in your old boots."

She hooked the toes of one foot behind the heel of the other. "Yes, they're the best for it." What did that have to do with anything?

"How long have you had them?"

She shrugged.

"Since before you jilted the first fellow?"

"Yes." She'd never had money to spend on anything but necessities.

"I still think of drinking almost every day, Kate. Whether I dream of sipping moonshine, or I suddenly recall the bottle of aged wine in the barn, or get a random memory of how a good whiskey burns, the desire doesn't seem to leave. It might grow weaker, but I'm not sure it'll ever go away, so I can't promise I'll never drink again, even though I wish I could." He shifted his weight. "Do you think about running a lot?"

She relaxed her grip on the wagon. Hadn't she just anchored

herself to keep from running away without his money? "Sometimes." She'd never thought of running as an addiction, but it was certainly a bad habit, a knee-jerk reaction to situations turning sour. "I guess I couldn't completely promise anyone I'd never leave when life got difficult."

He nodded as if that was a good answer. Days ago she'd have been certain he'd have considered that the worst possible answer.

He smoothed his beard as he drew his fingers down his jaw. "My other fear—if I were to marry again—is that I wouldn't be able to shake the dread of being abandoned physically or emotionally. I worry I may never feel free enough to love a wife as much as she deserves, to love her with no reservations. So I decided to give you this." He poked the crate forward with his toe. "I . . . I do want to marry you, Kate. Not because Anthony wants me to, but because I realized this week that I want to risk loving you, though I'm afraid to."

"Love?" Her voice was barely louder than a whisper.

"I might not love you as much as Will does Eliza or Everett does Julia—not yet, anyway—but I don't see any reason why I wouldn't love you as long as I let myself. I've actually been rather certain you'd steal my heart and run away with it. So I closed myself off the second I had an excuse. I was so hurt when Lucy left, and I didn't feel nearly as much for her as I already do for you."

He shoved his hands in his pockets and stared at the ground between them. "To save myself from pain, I kept myself from joy as well. It felt safer to deal with the wilderness." He huffed and looked out over the Clines' hay fields. "I'd always thought the Israelites were stupid for wanting to go back to Egypt when the Promised Land was . . . well, promised. But it seems I'm not that much smarter than them."

She swallowed, but he seemed intent on turning himself inside out before her, so she held her peace. Her heart softened as she watched him struggle for more words. When Silas Jonesey decided to talk, he clearly did a thorough job of it.

His cheek twitched, but he'd yet to turn and look at her. "When you told me about your past, I figured you'd ruin my future like Lucy had, but as I held that bottle yesterday, I realized she hadn't ruined my future. She gave me a son and led me to you. God worked good from the bad—for what other way would I have met you?"

He turned to face her, his eyes piercing, his throat seemingly trying to swallow a lump. "But if I've lost you . . ." He closed his eyes, his whole body tense. "It's my fault, not God's. I didn't trust Him with my future, and when I realized you couldn't promise me that you'd stick around and ensure me lifelong bliss—"

"I sure don't sound like the most desirable bride when you put it that way." She could have pointed out that she hadn't run these past few weeks—but was that because she'd been trusting God regardless of the outcome or because she'd been stuck?

"And I'm not the most desirable groom. That wine bottle indicates how easily I could fail you. So all this to say, I want to shed my fears and not pin my hopes on a person—as I hope you will too—but rather trust God for the future He wants to give us."

She clasped her hands together, her gut shaking again. So did he want to marry her or not? "What am I supposed to do with the wine?"

"It's yours, a symbol of the risk you'd take if you marry me, but also that I commit to vanquishing that stronghold. You and Anthony are worth fighting every vice I have. But I figure if you're willing, and if you thought God wanted you with us, then you could add your boots to the crate."

"But I don't have another pair." She cringed at her hasty response. "I guess that's like giving up a good wine."

"You don't have to do it." He let out a steady, controlled breath. "But I figured we could hand the symbols of our weakness over to Reverend Finch as a way to commit to keeping our flaws from undermining our vows. . . . If we were to wed, that is."

To hand over her boots and promise to never, ever run . . . Why wasn't she giddily saying yes? She'd wanted him to propose again, but what if none of her dreams about marrying him turned out as she'd imagined? What if he did start drinking again? She'd refused to marry Jasper because of his drinking. She'd been beaten by her brother-in-law when he was drunk.

"Please don't decide right now, Kate. I want to know you've thought everything through. But no matter what, I don't want the wine back, and here." He picked up the money and held it out for her.

She stared at it. "What if I don't choose the money?"

"It's yours to do with as you please. Either way."

"Either way?"

"It's for you, especially since I made such a mess of things . . ."

When she didn't reach for it, he shrugged, a self-deprecating smile on his lips. "God tried to bless me with you, yet I pushed you away. I care for you too much to tie you to a man who'd do such a thing unless the promised land God wants for you has me in it." He moved closer and placed the money in her hand, wrapping her fingers around the wad of cash with his own. "And if that promised land isn't with me, you could get there with this."

He trailed a finger down the side of her cheek, his lips pressed together to form a stressed smile, his eyes a mixture of sorrow and warmth. "I wish I hadn't let you down. I wish I could promise I'd never do it again." His thumb ended up on her lower lip, his eyes lingered for seconds, maybe minutes, and then his hand dropped. "No matter what you decide, would you pray for Anthony, at least?"

She felt herself nod, but she couldn't get her lips to move. She was doing well enough to breathe.

He let his gaze run over the features of her face as she tried to think of something worth saying. But what could she say that had been thought through with the care and time he asked her to put into an answer? "I'll think about it."

"Good." The corner of his mouth lifted in a slight smile, and his gaze dropped to her mouth again, but before she could step closer, he turned and with one stride, grabbed the wagon's side and swung himself up into his seat. He put a finger to his brow in good-bye and called for the team to giddap.

In minutes, he disappeared into the untamed prairie.

She stared after him, head whirling. For all her pining, what if she'd been grumbling through a wilderness of her own making, forcing her way toward a promised land that didn't exist?

Chapter 22

With a groan, Silas yanked out the huge sandstone he'd been digging around for the past few minutes. He pushed the hair from his face, but the malicious wind only threw dirt into his eyes. Though his lips and cheeks were already chapped, he had to clear this field. He needed it arable by spring to make up for the land he'd sold—because of course, Mr. Thissen hadn't wanted this overgrown section cluttered with rock.

The frosty wind blasted Silas again and would have toppled him if he were a few pounds lighter. He kept his head down and feet planted until the gust weakened. Days like this were never pleasant for working, but with Anthony at school, he hadn't enjoyed sitting at home sharpening knives in silence. His mind kept wandering to Kate, to what he should have said yesterday, or what he shouldn't have—

"Silas."

He looked around, but saw no one. And now he was imagining her voice even out here. The wind blew more grit into his eyes. Blinking and rubbing, he turned his back to the wind. Time to give up and find something to do in the barn. He marched home, blowing warm air into his icy hands.

If he walked fast enough, maybe his heavy breathing would shut off his brain.

Was there any man who could propose to a woman worse than he? Why had he talked about himself as if he were some terrible wretch? He wasn't Richard Fitzgerald or even Ned Parker. Thinking back over yesterday's proposal—where he'd basically told her there was no hope he'd remain sober—how could he expect a positive response?

And why hadn't he told Kate the things he liked about her? Like how she was so caring and tenacious. A feisty woman like her could survive Kansas, provided she didn't blow away.

He tried to catch a feed sack tumbling past but missed. The fabric snagged in the blackberry bushes. He tugged it free, then crossed to the barn. With the wind whistling through the slats, he put the bag on the pile and leaned his shovel against the stack for good measure. He squatted beside Yellow Eyes, huddled in the corner, and scratched behind his ears. "I don't blame you for hiding today. Your skinny little body'd get blown into town out there. You'd think a storm was coming, but I don't smell one or see one. Just a bunch of dumb wind."

The mongrel barely opened his eyes to acknowledge him.

"Silas?"

He jolted up and turned to the barn door as Kate blew in, most of her hair hanging loose, her pins jumbled inside her tresses like brambles. Her skirts whipped around the crate she held.

He rushed over to shut the door.

She plopped the crate down and attempted to smooth her wild hair behind her ears, pulling pins as she went. "And I thought it was hard to keep my hair up in Missouri."

He wanted to fix the pin sticking straight out from behind her ear but wasn't sure that'd be acceptable. "I didn't expect to see you until Friday or Saturday when Everett usually comes to town. You didn't walk all the way here, did you?"

She shook her head and finally dislodged the wayward pin bothering him. Her dark auburn hair hung thickly to the middle of her back. No wonder she couldn't contain it.

She shoved the pins in her pocket, then gathered and twisted her hair over her shoulder, nervously running her fingers through the tangles. "Mr. Cline came into town early."

"I didn't mean to steal you away from Julia."

"She was all right with it."

They stood staring at each other. Did she know how uncomfortable she looked? She'd stopped messing with her hair and now wrung her hands, transferring her weight from one foot to the other.

Wait. Bare toes stuck out from under her skirts. "Where are your boots? It's not exactly warm outside."

"They're in the crate." She pointed to her boots flopped over the wine bottle he'd given her. "I only have one other pair of slippers, and they wouldn't have lasted the walk out here."

His heart kicked up a notch. She'd chosen him? Without him telling her how much he admired her, and after he'd basically insisted he was a good-for-nothing? Or had she chosen to sacrifice herself for Anthony? His flesh turned hot, then cold. She'd come here for Anthony in the first place, not him. No reason to think he was the main reason she'd choose to wed.

Kate stepped forward, hands behind her back. "You were right."

He blinked. According to the men at the post office, that might be the first and last time he'd hear that from her.

"Nearly every time I've run, I didn't ask God where He wanted me."

He was almost too afraid to ask, despite her boots lying in the crate. "Do you know where He wants you now?"

"With you and Anthony." She ran a bare toe across the barn's dirt floor. "But I'm scared of the future, just like you."

He'd probably scare her even more if he swallowed her up and kissed her like he had at the train station.

"But I still put my boots in there." She pointed to the crate. "If you'll risk marrying me, I can risk you disappointing me, if . . . well . . ." And all of a sudden she flushed bright red.

"If what?" He tilted her chin up until she dragged her gaze off her bare feet.

She blinked and swallowed, her heartbeat quick against his fingertips. "If our marrying could be more than a convenient solution to my predicament."

Ah, so she cared for him more than he'd dared to hope. He ran his thumb over the blush high on her heated cheek, then brushed his lips against her warm cheekbone and whispered into her ear, "There's no such thing as a convenient woman in my house."

Her short and fast breathing feathered his neck. "I'm sorry I didn't tell you about running away from so many—"

"Nothing to apologize for." He placed a kiss against her jawline. "My reaction wasn't your fault."

She shuddered.

But that reaction was definitely his fault.

"And I'm sorry I pinned all my hope on you instead of trusting God."

He waited for her eyes to open. "Absolutely no need to apologize to me for that."

"Well then, I'm sorry—"

He stopped her with a feather-soft brush of his lips. Her eyes widened for a second, then slammed shut. He kissed her softly again, pulling her into an embrace, her body relaxed and weighty in his arms.

He broke away and took his time looking at each freckle sprinkled across her cheeks, her long eyelashes, the swirl of greens and gold in her soft, peace-filled eyes. He smiled. "Got anything else you don't need to apologize for? I'd like to stop you again."

"No. But maybe I'll have to apologize for this." She pushed up on her tiptoes and hit his lips hard. She wrapped her arms around his neck and moved her mouth against his with determination.

He groaned and kissed her like the ravenous man he was. Oh, how she felt good in his arms, the chemistry they'd had at the train station blooming sevenfold. She was his this time. His. He wrapped her up tight, then broke off for air and held her back a little. "No apology needed for that either, unless you have something against marrying me today."

Her eyelids fluttered. "How did you refuse to marry me after kissing me like that in Breton and in the soddy?"

How had he, indeed? "I told you I don't always make good decisions."

She laced her fingers into his. "But you'll try?"

Her warm hand in his felt even better than her kisses. He squeezed her fingers. "I'll try. But what will you do when I do something stupid again?"

"Stick around and help you stop being stupid."

"No running?" He tightened his grip.

"Maybe to cool off for a while, but not forever." She wrapped her other hand around his arm and tried to pull him closer.

Oh, how he was tempted to sweep her up again. But they shouldn't. "So what was your answer to marrying me today?"

She tiptoed up to kiss him.

He smiled against her lips, kissing her back a little but refusing to get entangled again. "I'll take that as a yes, because if not, you're going to get us in trouble."

She went back down onto flat feet and sighed. "Today will have to be soon enough, I suppose."

Not soon enough at all. He kissed her on the forehead. "Let's pick up Anthony from school. He'll be ecstatic. He's been put out with me over you."

"He'll see soon enough he's got no more reason to be."

She hadn't seen how grumpy Anthony had been lately. "Taking him out to ice cream would probably help."

"Again? I thought you had no money."

He started for the door, her hand still nicely tucked into his. "I know a pretty lady who happens to have a couple hundred dollars. I'm hoping she'll part with one. I bet Anthony would agree she should."

She laughed. "I'm sure he would."

"But first, you need some boots." He let go of her hand to pick up the crate she'd dropped inside the barn door.

"I thought you wanted me to give them up?"

"What would the townsfolk think if I let you walk down the aisle barefoot?" He forged out into the wind, threw the crate into his wagon, and charged toward his cabin.

When he came back outside, she was hanging over the wagon's side, pulling the crate toward her, hair flying everywhere.

"What're you doing?"

"You forgot I put my boots in there." She stopped short and pulled hair away from her eyes. "What do you have?"

He held out the new pair he'd purchased for her. "Boots."

Her lips turned up in delicious confusion. "Those aren't particularly feminine. They look—"

"Good for running?" He handed them to her.

"Yes." She smiled as she ran her hand along the polished leather. "What would you have done with these if I'd chosen not to marry you?"

"Put them on the mantel as a reminder not to judge anyone for their past—just as I don't want to be judged for mine. But if you choose to stay, Anthony would never forgive me if you couldn't race him anymore. He's still convinced you can outrun me, even after watching me beat you to the buggy to save him."

She straightened, plunking her fists on her hips, her skirts flailing wildly about her. "I could've beaten you if you didn't have a head start."

He couldn't help the smile that spread across his face. "Put them on, Kate. Let me chase you down."

With her hand tucked inside Silas's, Kate tried not to blush while fighting the urge to slide across the wagon seat and snuggle into his side. Sitting in the school yard holding hands—not yet married—was probably too much already for any gossipers, even if Silas would make an excellent windbreak, and they'd arranged to get married after they picked up Anthony.

Why was she more nervous to recite vows in front of him today than when she'd first come?

She peered up at Silas, whose gaze roamed the school yard as the first class let out.

Did he notice how her hand trembled in his? Not from dread but anticipation.

More children poured out with hoots and hollers, and Silas squeezed her hand. "You ready?"

"For ice cream?" She licked her lips. "Can't wait."

He laughed and raised the back of her hand to his lips again for a quick kiss.

Oh, to slide closer and lean against him, especially with this wind whipping her hair about. She wiggled her toasty warm toes in her new wool socks and stiff boots—one place the cold wind's icy fingers hadn't penetrated.

She slid closer to Silas anyway. Did she really care about reputation over warmth right now? They would be married within the hour.

A little girl in pigtails and a blue pinafore skipped out of the door behind what appeared to be an older brother. Then the door shut.

After a minute, Silas frowned. "Wonder if Anthony's talking to the teacher?"

"Has he mentioned having trouble with schoolwork?"

"He's told you about Mrs. Owens, right? Maybe he's in trouble."

She nodded. "She doesn't sound especially endearing."

Silas's hand tightened around hers with every child that left the yard and moved out of sight. "Too bad you aren't still his teacher."

She might not have been as tight-laced, but . . . "I don't know if I was a good teacher or just kind, with so many children in one room with different abilities—"

"I'll go in and get him." He let go of her hand and jumped off the wagon.

Kate pulled her coat collar closer to her throat, the wind battering her from the other side now as well. Too bad Silas didn't have a covered wagon. What if she used her two hundred dollars to buy him a carriage? No, he needed a farm wagon first and whatever else had been stolen from him that needed replaced.

Or maybe she could get Mr. Thissen to give Silas back his land.

Silas disappeared into the schoolhouse, and she shivered again. She should've gone with him or at least had him help her down so she could shelter beside the wagon somewhat.

She hooked her newly booted feet into the wagon wheel's spokes and climbed down.

Just as she leaned against the wagon's side out of the wind, the schoolhouse door slammed and Silas rushed down the stairs like a charging bull, his head swinging one way, then another.

Her body seized. "What's wrong?" she asked once he was closer.

Silas hastened to her and held out his hand to help her climb back up. "He didn't show up today."

"What?"

"The teacher doesn't know where he is." He ran around the back of the wagon and yanked himself up onto the seat. "I thought we were good." He strangled the reins as he turned his team and started them toward town. "After Thanksgiving, he'd been quiet, stopped being rebellious. I thought that was an improvement."

"So you think he's run again?" She grabbed on to her seat as the wagon jolted forward.

"Why else wouldn't he be in school?"

She scanned the sidewalks. Though if he'd not come to school that morning . . . "Has he missed school before? Maybe he went looking for snakes."

"It's too cold for snakes." Silas's jaw was as hard as Anthony's attitude had been the last few times she'd seen him. If only the boy wasn't so fool stubborn, his anger would've melted away as he watched them get married this afternoon. But Silas was right—he'd seemed happy at Thanksgiving. Surely there was some other explanation.

She latched on to Silas's arm, willing him to slow as she dug her fingers into his muscle. "Maybe he thinks he can find snakes anyway. We can look around the ponds and the creek near your place. Did the teacher mention anybody else missing?"

He shook his head. "Didn't think to ask."

"Maybe he's with a friend. Do you know of any boys he's bonded with?"

"He talks about the Harrisons and the Moores down on Mud Creek."

The wagon veered sharply next to the church, yet he didn't turn into the yard.

Her heart sank. There would be no wedding.

Oh, Anthony. Why did you run again?

Wait. She clenched onto Silas's tense arm. "I don't think he'd run with me still in town."

She waved apologetically at Mrs. Graves, who gave them an evil glare from the sidewalk, likely for going too fast—or maybe sitting too close.

"Then what do you think?" Silas skirted the ice wagon and swung around a slow-plodding carriage.

She swallowed, wishing she didn't have to voice the thought that was turning her stomach. "Maybe Richard wanted Anthony badly enough to come out here to get him? I didn't think to hide where I was going when I bought my train ticket."

"No." Silas shook his head, his eyes glazing. "Surely not."

"Hey! Watch out!" A man jumped out of the way as Silas's wagon wheel missed him by inches.

"Sorry!" she yelled over her shoulder. Then she turned and squeezed Silas's arm with both hands. "Be careful. Getting us killed won't help us find him."

But then, if it hadn't been for Myrtle, they'd not have found him when he ran away in Missouri. What hope did they have of finding him this time?

Chapter 23

The cold wind followed Silas inside the crowded sanctuary. Several people turned to look his way, but not a single face gave him any hope. Sure it was a blessing to have so many people help search this time around, but the inevitable "There's nothing more we can do but pray and keep our eyes open" speech would only come that much sooner.

He trudged toward the front and slumped onto the first pew, trying not to listen to the worried murmuring filling the room.

Kate's cold hand slipped into his. Where had she come from? He squeezed her fingers harder than he ought, but with Anthony gone and the two hundred dollars in her possession, what if she was rethinking her decision to marry him? Would he lose her again, this time for something out of his control?

Over the last two days, they'd knocked on doors and walked across pastures with about a hundred Salt Flatts's citizens—plenty of time for her to rethink things.

He let go of her and jammed his fingers into his hair and squeezed a handful, pulling at his scalp. What should they do next? Salt Flatts was tiny compared to Breton; they'd combed every corner of the town already. The world was too big to search every field and tree and farmstead, though he just might try.

Someone sat on his other side. Out of the corner of his eye, he saw Reverend Finch's solemn face.

Then Will sat down on the pastor's other side.

Great. They were about to tell him what he was trying not to think about.

"I'm sorry, Silas." Reverend Finch's slim hand squeezed his shoulder. "No one's come in with any information."

He shook his head, wishing he wasn't too old to plug his ears with his index fingers.

"Perhaps Miss Dawson's suspicion about the boy's former pa needs to be explored more fully."

Will leaned forward, his elbows on his knees, and peered around the reverend. "Have you received any telegrams in response to the ones you've sent?"

Silas rubbed his brow. "The Hartfield sheriff said Richard's wife claims he's in town, but he didn't personally see him. And since there is nothing but suspicion on our part, he wasn't planning on doing anything more than that."

"All he's willing to do is ask Mrs. Fitzgerald about Anthony and accept whatever response she gave?" Kate's voice cracked.

He squeezed her hand as if he could keep her from despair. "Apparently."

The double doors behind them sucked the body heat from the room. Silas turned to see the last group of men come into the sanctuary—without Anthony.

Will's pa, Dex Stanton, the tallest of the bunch, caught Silas's eye and shook his head.

The reverend stood and cleared his throat. "Thank you, everyone, for looking again today. My wife put several pots of hot cider over on the communion table. Warm up before you head home. For those available tomorrow morning, we'll meet at eight to discuss where else to look. And of course, we'll pray at tomorrow night's meeting."

Silas pushed himself up and forced a smile. "Yes, thank you for taking time from your jobs and families to help us look. I'm grateful." But he couldn't bear to listen to each of them offer their condolences, so skipping the hot cider, he strode quickly through the empty pews toward the pastor's office. Once inside, he dropped into the cushioned chair he'd sat in many times after Lucy had left, when he'd struggled to let go of the anger he'd fortified with liquor.

The door swung open, and he sighed, though he'd not mind Kate or even Will. But Dex Stanton ducked to enter the cramped office. Behind him, his youngest son, John, ducked under the doorframe as well. The boy was barely a man, yet he'd beaten his father's uncommon height by an inch.

Dex's cheeks were still red from cold, his frown still as hopeless as when he'd stepped into the sanctuary minutes ago. "I'm sorry we haven't found him, Silas."

This was exactly why he'd tried to escape into the pastor's office. How many times could he respond to the unnecessary apologies before he snapped?

Taking off his hat, Dex managed a smile. "My daughter Becca's got all the kids giving up their recess to pray for Anthony—thought you'd like to know that."

John cleared his throat. "Miss Dawson said you're going to Missouri. Is that correct?"

As much as he hoped the sheriff would do more than ask Richard's wife a question, he'd seen how little the Breton sheriff had done to find Anthony a month ago. If Richard had indeed abducted Anthony, the only person who'd care enough to actually look was him. But who could he leave his homestead with this time and have any hope of having a farm worth coming back to?

"I want to, but I'm not sure how." Of course he had to go, even if he had to beg an outlaw to use his place as a hideout. But what if he didn't have enough money to survive once he came back?

Kate came in from behind them. "I checked the train schedule earlier. There's one leaving in an hour."

He rubbed his forehead. "I couldn't possibly go in an hour."

"I've already packed for you."

Dex's face lit with amusement. "You snagged yourself a bossy one."

Kate's eyes narrowed.

Silas sent her a warning glance. "If you don't want to be teased, you should probably ignore anything that comes out of his mouth."

"But what fun is there in that?" Dex winked at Kate, before turning back to Silas. "But in the interest of time and seriousness, John and I talked about him watching your place. I don't need much help this month, so he can stay out there for a week or two."

Silas closed his eyes and let the tension in his shoulders melt. He trusted John. The boy had grown up homesteading, and being the only Stanton boy interested in farming, he was building himself a place near his parents to help expand the property and take over one day.

"However, I must warn you. He'll empty your cupboards," Dex added.

The seventeen-year-old rubbed his belly. "I hope you have plenty of bacon."

"That's about all he knows how to cook." Dex laughed. "So your jerky, crackers, preserves, and whatever else you got that don't go in the oven or a skillet will need restocking once you come back. We think that's the real reason he's not finished his cabin—can't have his ma cook for him way out there."

313

"Oh no, even when I finish, I'm coming over for supper. That is, until I convince Lillith to marry me."

"Would it be all right for John to watch your place, Silas?" Kate raised her eyebrows, her bottom lip held hesitantly between her teeth.

Though John wouldn't steal anything and would probably improve his place while he was gone, that didn't help Silas afford the train ticket. And the bank was closed already. "I can't get a ticket in time for tonight, maybe tomorrow—"

"I bought our tickets already."

"*Our* tickets?"

Dex put a hand on his son's shoulder. "I think we'll leave you two alone. We'll wait outside by the cookies. Or rather, the soon-empty plate of cookies."

The second they disappeared, Kate put her hands on her hips. "Yes, *our* tickets. You don't expect me to stay here, do you?"

"If people thought it inappropriate for us to search for Anthony together in town, they sure won't find it appropriate for us to travel together."

She rolled her eyes. "Not a problem after the reverend marries us. We have an hour."

An hour? He swallowed against his tight collar. "Married?"

"Yes." She said the word slowly, as if his brain wouldn't understand otherwise.

But it wasn't his brain that was worried—it was his heart. "Anthony could be gone forever, Kate."

She shrugged as if that meant nothing.

"I know you're hoping he's in Hartfield, but unlike last time, he has no friends here that we haven't checked with, so if he's not with Richard, we might not find him—ever."

"And that's why I haven't quit praying for the last two days, but why would that keep me from going?"

Surely she hadn't thought this through. He straightened,

tightening all his muscles to keep him from sagging once she realized what the future likely held. "If he never comes back, Kate, all you'd have is me."

She came over, took one of his hands in both of hers, and shook him a little. "I'm not marrying you for Anthony. I'm marrying you because I love you."

He blinked.

"I don't know enough of Salt Flatts to be of any good here, but I do know Hartfield. And with John at your place, you don't need me there—not that I know anything about farming. He—"

"Say that again."

She frowned, her right eyebrow raised in question. "John knows more about farming than I do?"

He swallowed. What if he'd heard her wrong? "No, the part about why you plan to drag me to the altar in a few minutes."

"So we can go to Hartfield together?"

His lungs deflated.

She put her hand to her cheek. "Or that I love you?"

"Is that a question?" She hadn't said she loved him when she'd accepted his proposal.

"No, it's the answer." She shook her head and smiled, placing her hands on his shoulders. "I love you. Anthony or not. But he'll need both of us when he returns."

Silas blew out a shaky breath. Despite the dreary day, a ray of sunshine was trying to break in through the thunderclouds cloaking his soul. He anchored his hands in the crook of her arms. "And if we're not lucky enough to find him this time?"

"Then I hope you'll pray with me every night for God to bring him home. Besides, I don't feel like worrying about my reputation this time around. If we get married now, there's no need for anyone to gossip about how much time we spend together."

He pushed an errant strand of hair back behind her ear.

"You're really not worried about getting married without Anthony?"

She flushed prettily. "I said I love you, didn't I?"

He let his thumb run across the color in her cheeks and down to her neck, which was just as pink. "A woman's supposed to fuss over her wedding day. If we're marrying in an hour, it'll be nothing more than a recital of vows, with me in mud-splattered trousers and you in your everyday dress."

"I run about town in men's boots, Silas. I think I can handle getting married in plain navy wool."

"God love you, Kate, and so do I." He took her jaw in his hands, pressed a fast kiss to her lips, then swung open the door. "Reverend? We've got some marrying to do!" He whistled sharply to stop Will, who was halfway out the door. "Will!"

His friend turned around and gave him a stern look. Perhaps whistling like he was calling for his dog wasn't the most appropriate thing to do inside a church. He beckoned him with his hand until Will started back.

The pastor walked over, scratching his head, his wife following behind him. "You're doing this now?"

"Yes, sir." He walked back in and grabbed Kate's hand. "We're doing this now, right?"

She nodded.

Will entered the office, a smile tickling his lips. "I suppose I'll be telling John he's to watch your place."

"Yes."

Reverend Finch scrambled through the pile of things on his desk, muttering under his breath about people making up their minds. He pulled out a well-worn book and flipped it open to where the spine was broken. "I suppose there's no need for frills."

Silas looked at Kate again, but she only blinked at the reverend. She might not have been worried about flowers and rings, but surely she had enough feminine attributes to have wanted something more than Reverend Finch's messy desk as decoration.

The pastor came around the front to stand by his wife and looked at Silas an uncomfortably long time, though it was likely less than a handful of seconds.

Then he turned to Kate. "Marriage affects your life more than most anything else in the world. Are you sure this is what you want to do, for reasons beyond making it easier for you to look for the boy?"

"Yes."

"In a few minutes, it'll be too late to change your mind."

She smiled, and something lit her eyes. "My intentions in regards to Silas haven't changed since the last time you talked to us, before Anthony disappeared."

"All right." The pastor shoved his glasses onto his nose and started with, "Dearly beloved . . ."

Though Silas tried to keep his focus on the pastor's words, all he could do was take in Kate's profile and worry over the amount of fidgeting she was doing, her skirts more than slightly swishing in response to her restless legs. Though she hadn't moved farther from him, her arms were tense despite him rubbing the back of her hands.

". . . if any persons are joined together otherwise as God's Word doth allow—"

"Wait a minute." He pulled Kate to the corner and, taking both her hands, drew her closer. He leaned down to whisper. "I know how badly you wanted to avoid a hasty marriage, and this is the epitome of one. I promise if you back out today, I won't act like I did earlier. We can figure out something—"

"No, Silas. I'm fine."

He took a pointed look at her legs, still twitching. "You going to tell me you aren't feeling like you want to run right now?"

"I don't want to, it's just—" She took one of her hands from his to flutter it near her chest. "Nerves. A jumpy energy I can't seem to control right now."

"Maybe your nerves are telling you something."

"What about you?" She lifted her eyebrows. "You going to tell me you wouldn't like a drink right about now?"

He laughed. "If I were still drinking, that's exactly what I'd do—but not in front of the preacher."

"But you're not going to go looking for a drink, right?"

He shook his head.

"Nor am I going to run."

"Did I tell you I love you already?"

Nodding, she beamed at him and then tugged him toward the others.

Hand in hand, they walked back in front of the pastor, who'd leaned against his desk as if he expected to sit there all night.

Will stood beside Reverend Finch, arms crossed, with a stupid grin on his face. Mrs. Finch was looking between the two of them as if she wasn't sure she shouldn't speak up and stop the whole thing.

But there was no reason to stop them at all. "You can continue, Reverend, if you would."

The man straightened, shoved his glasses back up his nose, and rattled off the vows for Silas, which he answered with a determined "I will."

When it was Kate's turn to respond to the recitation of vows, she looked down at her feet, her lips pressed together.

Trying not to squeeze her any harder or let go, Silas closed his eyes, worried his heart could actually break. He'd just told her she didn't have to go through with the wedding, that she could run if she needed to, but evidently he hadn't really thought she'd do it, otherwise his body wouldn't feel so heavy and his stomach slightly nauseous right now.

"I just . . ." She exhaled through her pursed lips. "I wanted to add to the vows a bit."

He opened his eyes and stared into hers.

Squeezing his hands, she nodded. "I vow not to disappear for more than a few hours without making every effort to let you know where I'm headed. And I do intend to stay, 'til death do us part—not Anthony's, not anyone else's, but yours or mine." She smiled up at him. "Anything else you might be worried about that I should address?"

He couldn't help the joy inside him from bubbling up onto his lips. "No."

"Then all those things, I vow."

Slipping his hands against her jawline, he kissed her softly on the lips, his heart warming even more with the way the tension left her body and her knees stopped knocking.

Reverend Finch loudly cleared his throat, making him pull away.

"I haven't told you to kiss the bride yet." The laughter in the pastor's voice was barely contained. "You're messing up my speech, here."

"Sorry."

"No, you're not." Will snickered, and Kate covered her cheeks with her hands, not that anyone could miss the fact she was blushing—as usual.

"Shall I continue?" The reverend grinned.

Silas shrugged. "I almost feel like maybe you should go back, so I can promise some extra stuff."

Grabbing his hands again, Kate shook her head. "Go on, Reverend. He's got a long train ride to promise me whatever he wants to."

After Reverend Finch pronounced them man and wife, he shut his book with a loud thump. "Here's where I would normally tell you to kiss your bride, but I don't want to force you to do such a thing twice."

"What about thrice?" Silas wrapped her up in his arms and kissed her once for a second, and then again.

Will clasped on to his shoulder. "You got a train to catch, my friend. Plus I got to get home to my wife. Can't sit around here watching you smooch all day."

Kate looked at Will sheepishly before following the reverend to his desk, where he handed her a pen to sign the license.

"And I'd told Eliza just last week I was about to write you up an official diagnosis of insanity for not marrying your woman. I just didn't know what to prescribe." Will's amused voice sobered with a quick clearing of his throat. "I'm sorry for the boy's disappearance, but Kate will do you good. I'm sure of it."

Silas thumped Will on the shoulder, too choked up to say anything to him, then walked over to take the pen from Kate, who'd signed her name: *Kathryn Anne Jonesey.*

"I wish I had my real name to give you."

She laced her hand through his left arm. "We're not letting the past affect our future, remember? Jonesey will do as long as it's attached to you."

Will was correct. He'd been insane not to marry this woman the moment she stepped off the train. "You're right. I need to let go of the unknown, painful parts of my past before they hurt me anymore."

But had his fear of repeating his past already cost him the future with his son?

———◆◆———

Trudging past Richard's house, Kate scanned the sidewalks for Silas. She'd left an hour ago to intercept the teachers leaving the Hartfield school Anthony had once attended, but only received blank stares from teachers who'd never met the boy.

For all her desire never to enter into a hasty marriage, she'd

320

thrown herself into this one thinking Anthony would certainly be in Missouri.

Not that she wouldn't have married Silas yesterday or any day after that, but she'd been so sure coming here would be the answer.

Surely Richard wasn't desperate enough to kidnap Anthony, knowing they'd foiled him once and would suspect him again. If Anthony wasn't here, would Silas be upset she'd wasted money to appease her ridiculous suspicions?

Sure, they were using the cash Silas had given her when he proposed, but they could've used the money for so many other things. Would his inability to purchase replacements for what Peter Hicks had stolen cause them to lose the farm along with Anthony?

Would Silas regret their hasty marriage if that happened?

Leaning against a clock post at the intersection, Silas smiled when he caught sight of her, but his smile, though genuine, didn't quite reach his dark-circled eyes.

The poor man had hardly slept at all on the train. Every time she'd been jolted from her sleep when her neck rolled forward, he'd been awake praying.

She held up the bag of sandwiches she'd purchased. They hadn't eaten since they'd detrained early that morning, when the sky was barely gray enough to see the steps the porter had plopped down in front of them. "I'm sorry if you don't care for corned beef, but I don't know what you do or do not like yet."

He took the bag from her. "At the moment, I'd kiss you even if you handed me boiled cow tongue."

She couldn't help the laugh, though the weight of Anthony's missing presence snuffed it quickly. "If you're that easy to please, I'll have no trouble keeping you happy."

He let his gaze roam her face and then strayed to her mouth

for so long her lips practically begged her to kiss him despite being in the middle of a street.

He dragged his gaze up to her eyes, his pupils, dark and captivating.

The shiver that ran through her warmed her body despite the November chill.

"Oh, Kate." He pulled her to sit with him on the bench by the clock post. "This is not how I wanted to spend the day after our wedding."

What could she say to that? Though she'd claimed not to be a romantic, eating lunch with frozen fingers on a bench in a strange neighborhood was surely one of the worst honeymoons she'd ever heard of. "I'm fairly certain eating on the street will make us appear more suspicious than we already are."

He scooted closer to her, wrapping his arm around her. "We can't leave this spot until we've seen Richard either coming or going."

Tugging up the collar on her coat, she wished for the hundredth time she'd packed hats. Frowning at Silas's reddened ears, she wanted to apologize for her lack of foresight.

Hadn't he promised to stop any future apologies with a kiss? The heat of a blush might warm her up.

"Why are you blushing?"

Goodness, just thinking about kissing caused her to blush—but considering the tips of her ears and nose were still cold, blushing was no match for today's weather. "I was trying to come up with something not worth apologizing for so you could stop me with a kiss again."

He kissed the top of her hairline and sniffed her hair with a little groan. "There's been a sad lack of kissing since you became my wife." His stomach rumbled. "And a sad lack of food apparently."

She took the bag back from him and handed him a wrapped

sandwich. "I can take care of the second problem, but the first should probably be taken care of elsewhere."

"Right." He sighed and took the corned beef. "I figure you can stay and watch the house while I look for Richard at the taverns and find us a place to stay."

"Hopefully nowhere near any of those taverns."

He let out a small chuckle. "No." Taking a bite of his sandwich, he stared out at the empty street.

How long would Silas want them to keep an eye on Richard's house? Until dark?

The dread of repeating the weeks of searching for Anthony, not knowing where to look next or when to give up, made her want to curl up into a ball and cry. If Richard didn't have him . . .

Kate took a bite of her sandwich before tucking her fingers under her arms to try to warm them. She'd not cry here in front of random passersby.

Keep Anthony safe, Lord. Show us where to go.

Out of the corner of her eye, a flash of navy appeared in front of Richard's house. A woman with dark, graying hair shut the front door, then stalked toward the sidewalk with purpose— glancing their way every few steps.

"Silas, I think we're about to have a visitor."

The woman's face was scrunched with suspicion, and one of her arms awkwardly stayed stiff and hidden behind her skirt as she walked.

"And I think she's got a weapon," Kate whispered. Her heart thumped wildly. It was one thing to watch a house; it was another to stand face-to-face with one of the people they were spying on.

Silas stood, his napkin blowing away in the breeze. "Good afternoon, ma'am." He held out his hands as if he were surrendering.

Stopping a few feet away, the woman didn't appear to be

the least bit intimidated by Silas, who stood at least half a foot taller than her. "Why do you keep walking past my house? I've caught you staring at my windows more than five times now."

"I'm sorry to disturb you." Silas kept his hands in front of him. "But we're looking for Richard Fitzgerald."

"Then why don't you knock and ask?"

Silas blinked, his mouth moved, but he shut it without saying anything. Would he admit they wouldn't believe her no matter what she said?

"He's not here. You aren't the only one he owes money, so he won't be coming home until he's won enough to satisfy at least the lenders willing to kill him." The woman's arm tensed at her side, her eyes narrowing. "And I don't have money to give you neither. A woman's got to eat."

"Oh no, ma'am. We don't want money. I'm actually searching for my son, Anthony Riverton. Richard, uh . . . used to think Anthony was his son, and—"

"The dark-headed boy the sheriff asked me about?"

"Yes."

"I already told him—the boy and his mother moved away years ago."

"Yes, well, did your husband tell you he saw Anthony in Breton last month?"

The woman raised an eyebrow. "You think a man who keeps a mistress informs his wife where he is when he doesn't come home?"

"I suppose not, ma'am."

Kate brushed bread crumbs off her lap and stood up next to Silas. "It turns out Anthony wasn't your husband's son, and he didn't react very well to that news. We think he might have tried to take him. We'd not blame you at all if you were caring for him."

The woman sighed. "As I already told the sheriff, as far as

I know, Richard's in town but not here, and I have no boy. If I let you look inside, will you stop pacing in front of my house?"

Putting a hand to Silas's arm, Kate nodded. "If you wouldn't mind, it would set our minds at ease." Maybe a little anyway.

"Fine." The woman pivoted and marched away.

"I don't know if we should go traipsing around in her house." Silas's steps were slow to follow.

Kate tugged on him. "She invited us in, and it'll free us to look elsewhere."

Mrs. Fitzgerald swung her door wide open. "Come in."

They ducked inside, and Kate caught a glimpse of the small pistol she was hiding in her skirt.

"Go on and look, but I'm not going to bother going with you. I got nothing worth stealing with the way Richard gambles."

"This is kind of you, ma'am." The resignation in Silas's voice indicated he figured searching was a waste of time, but he slipped into the parlor anyway.

"Want coffee?"

Kate looked between Mrs. Fitzgerald and Silas opening a door in the darkened room. "No thank you, we've already inconvenienced you enough. I'm sorry we didn't feel as if we could take your word for things. If it wasn't for Mr. Fitzgerald trying to—"

"Honey, I was a headstrong seventeen-year-old who married a charmer I'd known for a few weeks. The loan sharks, the sheriff, and all manners of scum started showing up on my front step soon after. I don't blame you for not trusting anyone associated with Richard."

Silas came out of the room and ducked into another. Mrs. Fitzgerald motioned for her to have a seat.

She'd do whatever a woman carrying a gun told her to do, so she sat.

Mrs. Fitzgerald settled into a chair across from her and they both watched Silas as he trudged up the stairs. A clock ticked loudly from somewhere behind them, counting off the minutes Silas walked around the second floor.

She shouldn't have refused the coffee—at least she'd have had something to occupy herself with. "Do you know of a decent place to board in town? I once stayed at Mrs. Levett's, but she's no longer in business."

"The Blue Lantern's run by a Christian woman. It's on Pine and Lookout."

Silas's slow, heavy tread descended the stairs. His frown was deeper than before. "As she said, he's not here."

Mrs. Fitzgerald's face was blank, seemingly not too offended by them thinking she'd been lying.

Silas stopped in front of her, holding his hat in front of him like a chastened schoolboy. "You wouldn't happen to know which tavern your husband frequents?"

"This week?" She chuffed. "I don't keep up with that anymore, but Gordon O'Connor, the bartender at the Lucky Devil, tends to know everything going on in that part of town. He's the one I talk to when I have to track Richard down myself."

"Thanks." Silas shifted his weight. "Could I ask your name?"

"Why?" The woman's body stiffened.

"I'd like to pray for you, figured it'd be good to know your Christian name."

Kate smiled at her husband. She may have married just as quickly as Mrs. Fitzgerald, but she'd definitely not chosen a man who'd run amok like Richard.

"I don't know what good it'll do me unless you pray my husband kicks the bucket, but the name's Muriel."

"I appreciate you letting me look through your house, Muriel. We'll bother you no longer." Silas held out his hand to help Kate up.

"Wait." She glanced at the table beside her. "Do you have

a pen and paper? I'd like to leave our information in case you hear something."

"Sure."

After she'd written down their name and address, they awkwardly took their leave.

Kate frowned at the birds pecking apart their sandwiches on the far-off bench. "What's the plan now?"

"Get you settled somewhere."

"Mrs. Fitzgerald recommended the Blue Lantern on Pine and Lookout."

He turned them around, heading toward Pine. "Let's go there first and find something to eat before I start looking for Richard. Once I find him, I'll trail him to where he's bedding down for the night. If Anthony's not there . . ." He shrugged and tucked her arm into his, his voice low and defeated. "We go home."

She wanted to insist on looking with him, but her fingers were icy and the sleep she'd gotten on the train hadn't been enough. With how little he'd slept, she could imagine how tired he must be as well, but how could she insist they both rest with Anthony missing? "You don't sound too hopeful."

Silas shook his head. "I don't think he's here, though I'll check as well as I can to be sure. But since Muriel said Richard wasn't home because he owes money, I doubt he would've had enough to travel to Kansas."

She played with the button on his cuff as they walked toward the busier part of town, trying not to let Silas's quiet resignation steal her hope. Turning onto Lookout, she pointed to the green two-story building with a blue lantern painted on its hanging sign.

He led them across the street and opened the boardinghouse's front door.

The heat was welcoming, though no one greeted them. At least the place looked sturdy enough to withstand a strong

327

wind, unlike Mrs. Grindall's. As Kate pulled off her mittens, she caught Silas's eye and gave him a smile.

Though he attempted to smile back, his lips didn't turn up enough to hide his worry.

"I wish I could make things better for you, Silas."

He looked at her the way he had after he'd kissed her at the Breton train station. "Maybe we can figure out something when I return."

Her heartbeat accelerated. "Don't tempt me to wish you back quickly, since one of us needs to find our son."

He tapped the bell on the front desk. "I like the sound of that."

The bell sounded fairly ordinary. "Sound of what?"

"*Our son.*"

She shrugged. "I hope you don't mind that I claim him."

He bent down to kiss her neck right below her ear, and whispered, "As long as I get to claim you later."

She closed her eyes and prayed for Anthony, so she didn't selfishly pray for Silas to stay behind with her.

———

As their rented coach slowed to a stop, Silas tightened his arm around his sleeping wife to keep her from falling forward. Kissing her hair, he breathed in the scent of her. "We're here, love."

She mumbled something incoherently, and her head rolled over onto his shoulder.

He'd stayed out until three in the morning last night, waiting for Richard to go to whatever place he was currently calling home. When Richard and another drunk had stumbled all the way from the Dirty Goat to a dilapidated house, he'd returned to the boardinghouse to catch a few hours of sleep only to find Kate still awake. When he'd chastised her for not sleeping, she'd said she felt guilty for being warm and comfortable when he had to be as tired as she was. So she'd roused herself with several cups of coffee and had prayed the whole time, just like she said she was sure he'd have done in her position.

He shook his head at himself. How had he ever worried about her following in Lucy's footsteps?

He'd gone back out at dawn to make certain Anthony wasn't in the shack with Richard, which he wasn't. But if Anthony hadn't been abducted, where could he be? Maybe he hadn't been the best pa, but he couldn't have been as bad as Richard. He loved his son, not for what he could do for him, but for the simple fact that he was his. So why had the boy run?

He'd not stop looking for him until there were no more stones to overturn. So back to Salt Flatts they would go, see if the townsfolk had discovered anything helpful, and then decide where to go from there.

But when he'd returned to the boardinghouse wanting to scramble back under the covers with Kate, she'd already packed their belongings and then convinced him to go to Raytown. She'd guessed he'd not spend the money to come to Missouri again just to look for his sister, so she wanted to do so before leaving.

Raytown's sheriff had known of one Jewel in town, a woman who'd once taught at the grade school. Evidently she'd come into his office many years ago, after an older student hadn't been thrilled with her for punishing him for excessive tardiness and had given her a black eye in protest.

The school's superintendent had told them which church Jewel used to attend, and one of the deacons gave them an address. The man hadn't given them much hope that she'd be the correct Jewel since he said she looked nothing like Silas.

The coach stopped, and the driver hollered that they'd arrived.

Silas kissed Kate's forehead again. "Gotta get up."

She yawned and shook herself. "Maybe you were right. We should've slept in before we left."

"Too late now." His chuckle came out more nervous than he'd anticipated. Looking out the window, the large house they'd stopped in front of easily dwarfed every building back in Salt Flatts. A wrap-around porch stretched across two sides of the two-story house, with a small third-story crow's nest peeping up above the top gables. Balls scattered around the yard and a porch swing decorated with ribbon indicated children. What would it have been like to grow up in such a fine place? He'd wanted to find some relatives, but could he have much in common with people of such wealth?

Getting out of the carriage first, he told the driver to wait, then helped a wobbly, bleary-eyed Kate out of the vehicle. He stood, blowing out his shaky breath, wishing he knew of something besides alcohol that could settle his overreacting heart.

Kate grabbed his hand and pulled him toward the house. "Standing outside for hours won't change what you'll find."

Oh, but it had with Lucy—he'd missed asking for her forgiveness by about fifteen minutes. Not a regret he wanted to deal with again, so he shoved his feet forward. At the door, he knocked, and Kate tightened his tie as if making him presentable would determine whether or not his sister would accept him—if they'd found his sister.

A woman old enough to be his mother opened the door, and he couldn't find his voice. He'd only thought to find a sister, but what if they'd found his mother as well?

The older woman looked between the two of them. "Are the Coopers expecting you?"

Silas shook his head. He should've realized by the woman's attire and the huge house that she was a servant of some kind. "I'm sorry to show up unexpected, but someone who knew I was looking for lost family members told me I had a sister named

Jewel in Raytown. I was hoping to visit with Mrs. Cooper today to confirm or deny such a thing."

"Mrs. Cooper's at home, so I'll see what she says." The lady opened the door wider and bustled toward another open door. "Please take a seat in the blue room. May I get you some tea or water while you wait?"

Silas shook his head, but Kate asked for water for the both of them.

The dainty blue chairs all looked too weak for a farmer like him to sit upon, but he followed Kate to a settee where she sat smiling at him, patting the spot beside her. But his nerves wouldn't let him sit.

"You look like you've never seen furniture before."

"Not anything like this. You don't see such finery in orphanages or farmhouses."

"Silas?" A lilt of a voice made him turn around. A dainty blond woman of perhaps forty looked at him with bright blue-green eyes. She didn't look a thing like him, and yet, had he given the housekeeper his name?

"Yes?"

She came over with arms open wide and embraced him. He brought up his arm awkwardly and patted her. She didn't look like his recollection of his mother either, yet she acted as if she knew him.

She tipped her head back and smiled. "My, you're tall."

He was five ten—nowhere near Dex Stanton's height, though this lady appeared to be barely over five feet. "Jewel?"

"Don't you remember me?" She stepped back and put on a small pout. "I guess the last time I saw you, you were only three, maybe four."

He cleared his throat. "Are you sure I'm the Silas you know?"

"Yes, you look just like your father."

For some reason, having someone know what his father

looked like and that he bore a resemblance made him want to cry. He had family! He cleared his throat again, hoping his words didn't crack. "So you must look like our mother."

"No, I look like *my* father." She smiled and patted his arm. "Let me check on the tea and cookies I told Mavis to put together, and then I'll tell you all I know. I'm so glad you found me."

Watching her scurry away, he staggered over to Kate, whose smile was as big as her face. "Oh, Silas. I'm so glad something's going right for you."

"What?" He grabbed one of her hands tight between his and squeezed hard, bringing her knuckles to his lips for a quick kiss. "This isn't the first thing. You and Anthony are. No matter what Jewel tells me, you're my life now."

"Tea's here." Jewel almost sang as she came back in through the door trailing Mavis, who carried in a large silver tea set.

Too bad. The shine in Kate's eyes had promised him a really good kiss if they hadn't been interrupted.

Jewel lowered herself into the dainty chair across from them. Her blue silk dress made her eyes shine like her name. "Your wife, I presume?"

"I'm sorry." Where were his manners? "This is my wife, Kate." He couldn't help the smile at saying those words. "And I'm Silas Jonesey, but you already knew that."

"Jonesey?" She huffed with interest and picked up the teapot. "I figured they'd probably change your name to something easier to say, but that certainly isn't anything close."

"My name?" His throat dried. "What's my name?"

"*Shuh-bel-ski* spelled P-r-z-y-b-y-l-s-k-i."

What had she spelled?

She laughed. "That's the exact look Ma always got after introducing herself during the years she was married to your pa. I find it fun to spell at least."

"But you're not a . . . a *Shubbel-es-key*?"

"No. I'm a Marchman, though my father was actually a Mumstedsman. And if a Mumstedsman thought he ought to change his name when he came to the United States, you'd think your father's father would've changed his name too."

Kate squeezed his knee and leaned forward. "Why don't you start from the beginning? Silas tells me all he remembers is the day his mother left him at the orphanage."

"You remember nothing more than that?" At the negative shake of his head, Jewel straightened and began passing out tea. "Then, of course. Our mother's name was Grace, though she didn't seem to have found much of it in her life. She married my father, John Marchman, when she was barely sixteen, had six children, four surviving infancy. I'm the eldest. When I was ten, my father was thrown from a horse and died. Though he'd been a good husband and father, he wasn't rich. Mother couldn't afford to remain single and your father, Peter Przybyl-ski, was willing to marry her, but . . ." Jewel shrugged and gave a sad sigh. "He had particular views on how family ought to be. He was willing to be a provider . . . for his own children. He wouldn't marry Mother unless we were farmed out to Father's siblings. Since my father had seven brothers and two sisters, that was easy enough. Though your father was a bit rough around the edges, he still let Mother see us. He sent us a gold dollar on our birthdays, and when we came over for Christmas, he gave us each a peppermint stick. You had an older brother named Lawrence, but he died of the flu along with your father when you were three."

"I knew I had a brother." That one memory of a sibling had torn at him—he'd wondered why his mother had loved his brother more than him since she'd not taken them both to the orphanage.

"Mother needed to marry again—and this time, she chose

333

poorly. The man's name was Rooney, and he insisted that if she could give up her first four kids, then she could give up another. But she'd been an only child, and your father's brother, who lives in Chicago, already had eleven of his own. So she put you in the orphanage."

Jewel stopped stirring her tea to look up at him and frown. "I was seventeen then. I wish I would've known where you went much sooner. I married at eighteen and, as you can see, my husband came from money. I could've kept you, but once your father died, Mother as good as disappeared. I saw her once at the market, sporting deep circles under her eyes I could've sworn were bruises. I asked her about you and she told me she'd given you up. I sent a letter to the Hall's Home for Boys but didn't get a response."

"Do you know if our mother's still alive?"

Jewel shook her head, her eyes downcast. "She died falling down the stairs a few months after I saw her last. I don't believe it was an accident."

A blond-headed boy of about eight poked his head into the parlor and eyed the tea set. "I thought I'd smelled cookies."

Jewel laughed and held one out for him. "Go get your brothers and sisters."

"We're already here." A girl of about ten with long dark curls came in. "If Jacob says there're cookies, we believe him."

A taller version of the ten-year-old girl came in along with a boy around the same age.

"Children, I want you to meet your Uncle Silas. The two oldest here are Christopher and Catherine, my fourteen-year-old twins. Then there's Isabelle and Jacob. I have two older boys named Randolph and Maxwell, but they're already married."

Each of the children came over to greet him, and he had a hard time finding his voice to greet them back. What a wonder to go from being an orphan to learning he had more relatives than the six people in the room with him.

"Do you have any children?" Isabelle's hazel eyes were shaped so much like his own that he blinked to make sure he wasn't just imagining them being so similar.

"I have a boy, about your age."

"Is he here?"

"No, that's why we're in Missouri—we're looking for him." At her frown, he added, "He ran away."

"Why?"

"I'm not sure." He looked at Jewel, afraid of what she might think of this news, but not wanting to elaborate in front of the children. "I just learned about him myself two months ago."

Jewel gave stocky Jacob a cookie. "If we can do anything to help you locate him, add money to a reward, write to—"

"Oh, the driver!" Kate jumped up and looked out the fancy-curtained window. "What do we tell him? He's out there pacing."

Silas set down his cookie. "Could you tell us where there's a decent place to board near here?"

"Upstairs." Jewel sprang up and rang the bell near the door, and an older man appeared almost instantly. "Please inform the driver to pull up to the carriage house and unload their luggage. We have overnight guests!" The way she clasped her hands as if it were Christmas stifled his protest. "Go on out and wash up, children." She spread out her arms as if she were herding cattle through the door instead of people. Jewel looked over her shoulder. "I'm going to tell the cook to make something special. I'll be back in a few minutes."

The moment she slipped out the door, he closed his eyes, wiping at the hot moisture he'd been trying to keep at bay.

Kate swiped the corner of his eye with her thumb. "I hope these are happy tears."

He shook his head. "Not entirely."

She squeezed his hand tight and tucked herself in close but said nothing. But he knew she was waiting for him to explain.

When he swallowed enough to speak, he opened his eyes, but couldn't look at her lest he cry and ruin his sister's happy day. "They're wonderful, of course, but knowing Anthony may never know them, that I might have lost my chance at being a father when I've only just become one . . ."

"I think you forgot about me." Kate kissed his cheek. "I can't replace Anthony, of course, but we can certainly try to outdo your sister if a bunch of siblings for Anthony is what you'd like to entice him home with."

"Maybe we just might try that." He slipped his arm around her and pulled her closer, forcing himself to smile despite the sorrow. "It's certainly a tactic I doubt I'll tire of."

Her fingers combed into the curls at the nape of his neck. "Tonight?" she whispered.

Despite hearing the tread of fast-approaching feet, he leaned over and put his lips a breath away from hers. "I think that might work." He kissed her for a fraction of a second before his sister's throat clearing made him pull away.

Even if he'd never found Jewel and learned he indeed had family, the promise in Kate's eyes of creating his own would've been enough.

Chapter 24

With his hands in his pockets, Silas leaned against the Salt Flatts post office, his head tilted back until it rested against the siding, enjoying the sun and the unseasonable warmth that came out of nowhere.

Once they'd returned to Kansas and more carefully checked the cabin, they'd discovered the bag Silas had bought for Anthony in Missouri was missing, but their son hadn't packed much—the only other things they'd figured he'd taken was an extra set of clothing and a few pantry items. If he was still in the area, the boy had someone he was depending on, or he likely hadn't survived the cold snap.

In the week since returning home, they'd traveled the roads, taken the train to five stops both coming and going, and called until their voices were hoarse in the fields surrounding his farm. No sign of Anthony anywhere.

Silas would have to give up his homestead to keep searching. But what if Kate didn't agree? She'd be back from her last attempt to question the school children soon, but after that?

The post office door beside him opened, but no one came out. He tilted his head to the side to look.

Jedidiah stood in the doorway. "You got business here, or are you trying to scare people away with your scowling?"

He rolled his eyes. "I'm sorry my mood's affecting your business."

"If people scare so easily, they don't deserve their mail." Jedidiah let the door slam behind him. "I take it you've had no luck?"

Not wanting to voice a negative response, he simply shook his head.

"You look like you need a drink."

"I do." He shook his head. "But I won't."

"That's what a woman will do to ya." He crossed his arms over his chest and sat on the short tree stump he had on his porch for a stool. "How's life with the missus?"

Silas smiled, more amused than anything by the disdain in Jedidiah's voice. "I was an idiot for ever joining your woman-hating club."

"Yeah, well, so was I."

"What?" He looked at the older man askance.

"Don't look at me like that."

Silas kept his mouth shut. If Jedidiah wanted to spill something, he would.

They watched the pedestrians walk by for a minute or so. Silas scanned the crowd for Kate, though he was pretty certain he'd know the moment she was within eyesight.

"What if Lucy hadn't died?" Jedidiah's voice held none of its usual scorn.

Silas licked his lips and swallowed. And here he'd thought Jedidiah'd be spilling his guts, not asking him to spill his. "I might not be as happy as I am now, but I'd have worked at our marriage—I was more miserable when she was gone."

"Yeah." Jedidiah's shoulders slowly deflated with a long, loud exhale.

Silas kept his gaze on the passersby. "Fannie's a good woman. You don't deserve her."

"I'd say she doesn't deserve me."

He wasn't about to argue with the man since that's why Jedidiah and Fannie were still separated—no one could change his mind for anything.

"How I've treated her, well, she shouldn't have to be strapped to me." Jedidiah squirmed in his seat. "Told her that a year ago, yet she still sticks around."

"Ah." So he meant *he* wasn't worthy of *her*. Now he definitely wasn't going to argue. "So you've chosen to let your pride steal your joy."

"I don't deserve joy."

"But it's nice to have." He pushed himself off the wall. "What's Fannie want?"

"Me, for some reason." And yet the man's arms stayed stiffly crossed over his chest, like a stubborn, chastised boy.

"If you hadn't just told me you've been waffling about this for more than a year, I'd have thought you'd finally smartened up. Why are you hanging on to being so dumb?"

Jedidiah sniffed and continued staring out into the street. "Well, you're no help." He stood and shoved his way back through the door into the post office.

A flash of ordinary brown far down Main Street caught his eye. Kate. If he could only outfit her in nicer things. He fingered the sales notice he'd penned while waiting for her. Maybe they could afford to replace her worn dresses soon, though she might not let him buy one after taking such drastic measures to get more money.

Her eyebrows lifted the moment she caught sight of him, and he shook his head. Her frown seemed to slow her pace. When she made it to him, she clomped up the stairs and went straight into his side embrace. Oh, if only they were home, he could bury his face in her hair, pull her body against his, and lose himself in the joy of loving her.

But he had to talk her into something that would take away the comfort of home.

He kissed the top of her head and stepped away to hand her the paper. "I thought of something after we split up this morning."

"What is it?" She eyed the paper in his hand suspiciously.

"I can't let my place keep me from going after Anthony like it kept me from finding Lucy."

"You tried your hardest to find her. She didn't want to be found."

"Neither does Anthony, apparently. But nothing's going to make me give up again."

"But your farm . . . It's your life."

"Was." He took her hand and rubbed his calloused thumb over her knuckles. "You two are my life now. I don't want to continually fret between searching for my boy or keeping my homestead, like I did in Breton."

"And if you don't find him before the money runs out?"

"I won't put you into poverty, but we could search longer this way. I'll pick up work wherever we want to take our time looking, and if we decide there's nowhere else to look or the money's running low, we can settle somewhere. As I can't put my trust in you for happiness, I can't trust my land either. I can only trust God will get me wherever He wants me, and I'm sure He'd rather I go after my son than hold on to a patch of dirt. He brought me to Anthony before—He can do it again."

The sweet smile on her face felt almost as good as the kiss she was considering giving him—if he was reading that look in her eyes right.

He took hold of her wrist and pulled her close enough to whisper in her ear. "Too bad there's people around or I'd take the kiss you're offering, sweep you off your feet, take you inside, and—"

"Silas," she hissed as a man in a dirty Boss of the Plains hat passed by on his way into the post office.

Silas lifted Kate's hand and kissed her palm, giving her a look that produced exactly what he wanted: Her cheeks turned scarlet.

The door shut behind the dusty cowboy, and she gave Silas a sorry excuse for a chastising glare. "You're going to get us into trouble. No telling what that man thinks of us now—"

"What could he think that ain't true?"

"Come on." She pulled on his arms and opened the door. "You have an advertisement to hang."

That was certainly one way to stop his teasing. "No argument?"

"As you said, family matters more than possessions. Though I'm going to miss having an orchard—you have so many beautiful trees." She sighed. "Wherever we settle, promise we'll put trees in first thing."

"Well, that depends on the state of the fields we end up buying, the type of soil and time of year, and the amount of money we have left—"

"Just say, 'Yes, my love.'"

"Ah, so now we're starting the bossy-woman part of the relationship."

Jedidiah glared at them as they entered—as if Kate's laughter was a hardship.

"Ignore the grumpy man behind the counter; it's an act," he stage-whispered.

Jedidiah pretended as if he hadn't heard and grabbed another handful of mail to sort.

Kate dropped his hand. "Can't ignore him. I've got to check for mail unless you have already?"

"No, go ahead." Silas went over to grab a thumbtack off the advertisement board where the cowboy stranger stood reading the flyers. "You don't happen to be in the market for a homestead?"

"Nah, looking for work. You know of any?"

"Not off the top of my head. How long you looking to work?"

"Up to a month."

Silas pinned up his handwritten sales announcement. "Have you checked anywhere already?"

"A few places."

"Are you looking for a good job or just money?"

The man looked at him warily.

He held out a hand to ward off suspicion. "Just that I know Ned Parker's always asking for hired hands. He pays well, since people willing to put up with him are scarce, so if you just wanted cash—"

"Already tried him. He hired my brother. Said he didn't need me with the kid he's got doing the grunt work."

"Kid?" Silas's heart sped up. There'd been no kid at Ned's when he'd stopped by when Anthony first disappeared. "Boy? Girl? What age?"

"I'd say a boy of nine, maybe. Didn't see him but from afar. Mucking stalls."

"Dark headed?" At the man's nod, Silas refrained from grabbing the man's upper arm and squeezing information from him. "How was he being treated?"

"Don't know. Kid was working hard though."

"Thanks." Silas strode over to the counter where Kate waited for Jedidiah to finish going through a stack of unsorted mail. "I have to go."

"Where?"

He shook his head. What if it wasn't Anthony? They'd al-

342

ready asked Ned if he knew anything about the boy and he'd answered negatively. But Ned wasn't trustworthy. What if he was treating the child like he treated his ex-wife or the hired hands he'd had over the years? He treated people no better than his oxen, and his teams never lasted long.

Silas fisted his hands. If Ned had hurt Anthony, he didn't want Kate around when he gave the man a lesson with his fists.

Kate cocked her head. "What are you thinking about? You look . . . murderous."

He tried to smother the rage that had taken over—he wasn't even sure Anthony was the boy the stranger referred to. But if he was . . . "I want you to go to Fannie's and stay there until I get back."

"What's wrong, Silas?" She reached for his arm.

He cupped her chin. "Trust me." He shot a glance at Jedidiah. "Maybe you could walk her to your wife's place after you close up?"

They all knew Kate didn't need an escort, but would Jedidiah take the opportunity?

Jedidiah shrugged. "Sure."

Kate's face turned stubborn. "But I can come with—"

"No." He didn't need more than one person to worry about. "Trust me." He charged out of the post office and jumped into his wagon. What other kid could it be? No parent in Salt Flatts would allow their child to work for Ned.

As much as I don't want Anthony to have endured Ned's heavy hand, please let it be so. And keep me from murdering the man if he's indeed working my boy into the dirt.

Before his team came to a complete stop, Silas jumped from his wagon and charged toward Ned and the stranger setting a corner fence post.

His tense muscles made his whole body tremor. "Where's the boy? If I find one bruise on him, just one—"

"You got a problem, Jonesey?" Ned straightened and leaned on his sledgehammer. "Threatening me on my own property?"

"Where's Anthony?"

"I'm not about to answer a man who's got no respect—"

"So help me, Ned." He charged toward him, fists raised.

The stranger slid between them and held out his arms. "I think both of you better shut your yaps and talk *to* one another instead of *at*."

"He knows why I'm here." He hadn't denied having Anthony. "I can't believe you'd steal him away."

"I didn't steal him. The boy said he didn't want to talk to you. Who am I to tell him otherwise?"

"If you were a decent man, an adult, instead of the scum—"

A sharp whistle stung his ears. The stranger glared at him. "I said talk *to*."

To, *at*, what did it matter if Ned refused to let him see his son? One more minute of Ned's belligerence and his anger would avalanche. "He's ten years old, Ned." His teeth clenched so hard his jaw ached. "He doesn't get to decide where to go without telling his parents."

Still draped on his sledgehammer as if he were only taking a breather, Ned leaned over to spit. "My parents never gave a rat's tail what I did. I was fending for myself by the time I was eleven. I didn't need or want my parents, so if the boy says he doesn't want to talk to you, I'm not forcing him."

Silas clenched his jaw. Was that where Ned's meanness came from? "I'm sorry your parents didn't care, but I care for my son and I need to see him."

Ned shrugged and gave him a dismissive wave with the back of his hand. "He's in the barn. Take him off my hands." He hefted his sledgehammer with a warning in his eye.

344

The barn? Silas left Ned behind. Just thirty yards away, Anthony could've heard them arguing and bolted already. Silas picked up his pace. He wasn't dumb enough to go after a man with a sledgehammer anyhow.

Shoving the big barn door aside, he stared into the sunny haze, where bits of straw and dust and fur stirred in the updrafts. The air hung heavy with the smell of droppings.

In the corner, Anthony tossed manure with a pitchfork too large and unwieldy for his slender body.

Silas blew out the breath he didn't realize he'd been holding.

Anthony stopped in midtoss, hay and muck falling and splatting beside him. He scowled at Silas.

Staggering over to a stall, Silas gripped the short wall, giving his lungs time to work like normal again.

Thank you, God.

No bruises he could see, and if the boy still had an attitude, his spirit hadn't been beaten out of him.

Anthony heaved the rest of the manure off his pitchfork and stabbed the tines into the dirt with a peeved huff. "How'd you find me?"

No apology, no look of guilt or shame? "Have you any idea what we've been through the past two weeks? Looking everywhere, not knowing if you were dead or alive . . ."

He sputtered and took a calming breath. He had to be composed, be the adult, be the parent, especially given that he had no notion why Anthony had run from him in the first place.

The boy rolled his eyes to the ceiling and sighed. "You didn't have to come looking. You could've left me alone."

"I can't leave you alone. You might not care that I'm your pa, but I am, and God wants me to protect you from here on out. And Mr. Parker's is *not* a good place for you to be."

"But Madam Star's place is good for Miss Dawson?" The boy's eyes narrowed, his voice filled with contempt.

Silas straightened and blinked. "What do you know about a place like Madam Star's?"

He shrugged. "Heard Ned talking about how Miss Dawson might end up there, and Jedidiah acted as if that'd be real bad."

Silas let out the breath he'd been holding. "I wouldn't have let Kate go anywhere bad."

"But you weren't marrying her or giving her any money, so I had to do something."

He had to do something? "What are you doing besides running away?"

"Miss Dawson paid for Mother and me to stay at Mrs. Grindall's, so I figured I'd pay for her train ticket to go back home."

Silas's body felt numb. "Why didn't you tell me?"

"I figured you wouldn't let me work for Mr. Parker instead of going to school."

"No, I wouldn't have."

"See?" Anthony grabbed the pitchfork and scooped another shovelful of manure, throwing a glare that dared Silas to stop him. He tossed a cow chip into a waiting wheelbarrow.

"How long did you expect to work here without anyone finding out?"

"Mr. Parker said I could earn enough for a train ticket in three months." The boy heaved a forkful again, the long handle too much for him to move with grace, but most of the mess landed in the barrow.

Three months? Looked as if Ned was working him like a full-grown man. "How many hours a day are you working?"

Anthony scooped up some more litter. "All of them."

Silas's hands fisted and he took a calming breath despite the rancid dust clogging his nose. Ned had Anthony doing a man's job for a boy's pay. "After you got Kate a train ticket, then where were you going?"

"Back home."

"To Missouri?"

Anthony's face screwed up, and his eyebrows folded in bewilderment. "To you."

He suddenly couldn't breathe, and his heart raced up into his ears. "To . . . to me?"

"Of course. You're my pa."

Silas's knees went soft and the weight on his chest lifted. He grabbed the stall's wooden wall again to steady himself. "You were coming back to me?"

Anthony set the hayfork against the wall and crossed his arms, but not before Silas saw the blisters covering the boy's fingers. A surge of pride over his son working so hard without complaint threatened his eyes with moisture.

"You weren't helping Miss Dawson much, but you've been good to me." Anthony coughed and waved away whatever he'd inhaled. "Mother never cared much for me except for the times Richard was around."

"I'm sorry you didn't feel as if she cared." Seemed Anthony wouldn't have learned anything new from Lucy's journals.

He shrugged again. "Miss Dawson has always been nice though. Just wish she didn't have to leave."

"She's not leaving." He couldn't help but smile at the certainty filling his voice and his heart.

Anthony frowned. "When I get her enough money she can."

"She won't—not now that she's married."

His frown grew deeper. "Who'd she marry?"

"Me."

Anthony swallowed hard.

The utter relief and joy crossing his son's face made him shake his head. "I told Kate I made stupid decisions. I thought not telling you about our problems would keep you from worrying or getting your hopes up or throwing fits. But here you are, being the man I wasn't." He took off his hat. "Will you forgive me?"

Anthony ran over and squeezed his middle. "Only if you take me to see Miss Dawson."

He smashed the boy's head to his midsection and ruffled his soft brown hair. "She's not Miss Dawson anymore."

Anthony tipped his head back and smiled. "You're the best pa in the whole world."

Oh, he certainly wasn't, but he couldn't tell his son otherwise when his face glowed like that. Maybe, with God's help, he could spend the next decade living up to his son's opinion. "I love you, Anthony, more than I knew was possible."

Chapter 25

"You sure you don't want a cookie?" Jedidiah shoved the platter of snacks Fannie had brought into the sitting room toward Kate. "They're delicious."

Fannie's mouth screwed up as she looked at Jedidiah askance and refilled Kate's tea.

Since they'd arrived, Jedidiah had complimented everything from the boardinghouse's décor to the food. For a man who'd dragged his feet as he escorted her to Fannie's after closing the post office, he seemed ready to admire anything and everything about the building and its owner.

Silas had abandoned her to Jedidiah hours ago without an explanation, and it ruffled. He wasn't running away certainly, but it annoyed her not knowing where he was.

Had her sister felt the same when she'd left with Aiden?

No letter had come from her sister yet, even though plenty of time had passed for a reply. Were they well? Were they still in Georgia? Would she ever know?

"Where do you think Silas went?" Fannie sat tentatively in the chair next to the sofa her husband had deposited himself on. She kept giving him sideways glances as if to check if he was still there.

"I don't know." Kate took another sip of her tea. "I read all the advertisements, trying to figure out what triggered him to rush off. Something must have given him an idea of Anthony's whereabouts, though I don't know why he couldn't waste the breath to tell me."

"Women—always needing explanations when they're just supposed to submit."

Kate joined Fannie in giving Jedidiah a withering glare.

He shrank a little. Good.

"Sorry, I'm used to, uh, . . . saying whatever I'm thinking." He held up his hands, palms out. "Now, I know you ladies probably think it's necessary to know everything, but if you trust the man, why you worrying?"

"Easy for you to say," Kate muttered.

"Not all men are trustworthy," Fannie muttered, her gaze glued to her teacup.

"No, they aren't." Jedidiah smashed his hands between his knees. "But I trust Silas."

Yes, she trusted Silas, but she still had the irrational urge to leave Fannie's and go search for him, or go to the creek and sit and stare so when he returned he'd get a little panicked over her leaving with no explanation too—which would be terrible to do to a man with Silas's fears and something she'd vowed not to do.

She rubbed the top of one new boot with the sole of the other. Even with what these new boots symbolized, the urge to run when life was tough pulled at her.

But she wouldn't run. She could talk to Fannie about curtains and cookies while waiting for him to return. And once he did, she'd explain how she felt rather than bottle her emotions inside until they pushed her to disappear.

If Silas was trying to be a better man, she'd work to become a better woman.

She grabbed a gingersnap and nibbled. Running while eating would be poor manners. She took another bite and chuckled at her attempt to anchor herself with a cookie.

The front door opened, and a burst of Kansas wind knocked it against the wall. "Kate?" Silas's voice called.

Throwing the cookie back onto the plate, she rushed to the foyer and fell to her knees. "Anthony!" She held out her arms and he ran into them. She planted kisses along the part in his hair and squeezed him tight. Then she held him out at arms' length and scowled. "Don't you *ever* run away again. How many times do I have to tell you this?"

He hung his head, his neck coloring. "I didn't run away. I went to work."

Silas pulled off his hat and clamped it against his leg. "Sorry about running off on you, but when the stranger in the post office said there was a boy at Ned's, I wasn't sure it'd be a good idea to take you with, and well, I didn't want to get your hopes up."

"Ned Parker's?" The nasty man who'd asked her to be his *woman*? Hadn't they gone by his place last week? "He knew where you were this whole time?"

Anthony nodded. "I was working for him so I could buy you a train ticket since Pa didn't have the money to send you back to Georgia."

She pressed the boy's head against her heart. Not just because he'd been worried about her, but the word *Pa* had rolled off his tongue so easily. "Silas gave me plenty of money to get home the day you disappeared."

"He did?" Anthony's chest deflated. "But I thought he said you'd got married?"

"We did." She couldn't help but smile over Anthony's shoulder at the man she'd rather run to than from. "But he gave me money just the same."

"Then you don't need mine?" Anthony's shoulders drooped.

She gathered his hands, noting the blisters and depositing a kiss in one of his reddened palms. "Well . . . I don't have enough for ice cream. How about you take us out for a treat?"

Silas clomped forward. "Now, wait a minute, aren't we spoiling the child with two ice creams in a year? Especially since he left without telling us where he was going."

She frowned up at him, making her eyes as plaintive as she could. "But he missed the wedding, and we didn't have cake."

"Ned said you'd leave just like every other woman." Anthony's voice tripped with emotion. "But you're really staying?"

Warmth flooded her chest at the look of adoration in Anthony's eyes. "Yes."

He threw himself at her, almost knocking her over with a fierce hug. "I love you, Miss Dawson."

"I love you too, son." She squeezed him tight, then broke away to stand and beckon to Silas. "But I'm not Miss Dawson anymore. In fact, we're thinking of changing our name as a family. Though Silas wants to keep Jonesey as his middle name, he found out his real last name last week, and unless you want to play stump the teacher for the rest of your life, we thought we'd decide on a brand-new surname together—once we found you."

Silas came over and wrapped his arms around both of them. "I'm thinking something easy, like Shelby or Presby, or maybe we could just spell my crazy last name like it sounds."

Anthony shrugged and looked up at Kate. "I don't care what it is, as long as you're happy with it . . . Ma."

"I'm more than happy." She hugged him tighter and looked over his head at Silas. Her husband looked as content as she felt.

"So, after we change our name, then can we get ice cream?" Anthony stepped back, sporting a big, proud grin on his face.

"I have plenty of money. I could buy you more than just ice cream. What else do you want?"

"Oh, well, how about some paint from the Five and Dime? I've run out of several colors and I'd love to start painting with you again."

"Now, wait a minute." Silas's fingers rubbed a lazy circle at the nape of her neck. "Don't you have him spend all his hard-earned cash when you got plenty for paint. I think he should save it."

"But I don't have any money left."

Silas's brow descended. "I know you paid for our tickets and our lodging, but that couldn't have been all of it."

"I convinced Mr. Thissen this morning to take what I had left as a deposit on the acreage you sold him. He'll let us split the profit from the crops we grow on it until he's paid off." Good thing they weren't selling the homestead now since their stubborn neighbor probably wouldn't have appreciated her changing the deal yet again. "I don't need anything but the two of you anyway."

Silas tightened his hold around them both and pressed his face into her hair. "Oh, Lord, thank you for a wonderful family of my own . . . at last."

Epilogue

Rachel Stanton breezed by Kate Presby, stealing the platter of butter mints from her hands. "You sit. This is your day to enjoy."

Kate shook her head. As if Rachel shouldn't be enjoying the day just as much. Her daughter Becca was marrying Anthony—but the older woman wasn't toting around a huge watermelon in her stomach either. Kate pushed against an elbow or a knee attempting to escape through her belly button. Twins again, she was sure of it. How could she endure another set of twins with five other children to manage—no, just four, since Anthony would be moving out to live with his bride. But a departing eighteen-year-old wouldn't make twins any easier. That thought alone made her want to cry.

She awkwardly lowered herself into a chair beside her two youngest playing on a blanket. Two-year-old Glenn and four-year-old Heidi had roped Everett and Julia's eight-year-old Naomi into playing tea party with wedding cake.

Kate looked up at the rows of pear trees heavy with blossoms under which the bride and groom had recited their vows half an hour ago. She took in a deep breath of crisp spring air. Thankfully no frost or wind had destroyed the blooms before the wedding, so now she'd hold her breath and hope the buds would survive until tiny green fruit clustered along the branches.

Joy filled her every time she had the chance to be in the orchard Silas babied and added to over the years for her. Though he always pined for more buildings or new equipment, he never failed to add new fruit trees—just for her—every year since they'd been married.

"A perfect day for a wedding." Julia Cline walked over with her youngest boy, who held onto her hands, taking hesitant, jerky little steps.

Kate sighed. It had been perfect. "I was afraid yesterday's cold would keep everyone home."

"It's pushing the other end of the thermometer today." Julia plopped Paul down on the picnic blanket and fanned her neck. Though the older woman was sweating, she still looked prettier than most of the younger ladies milling about. "That's April in Kansas for you."

Everett walked up, placed a hand on his petite wife's shoulders, and smiled over at Kate. "Silas says you think you're having twins again."

She nodded. She didn't like discussing her condition with any man other than Silas, but there were two again. Silas had teased her for months saying she was just having a big baby until he felt the two different set of hiccups last night.

"Or maybe triplets?" Everett said. His smile grew bigger when Naomi and Heidi happily jabbered over the thought of three.

Oh, dear Lord, please no.

Julia playfully punched her husband's side. "No need to worry her until it actually happens."

Shy, lithe Naomi came over, her gaze stuck on Kate's belly. "Do you know if they're girls?"

"Sure don't."

"Will they look the same, like Lawrence and Lucas?"

Kate twisted around looking for her six-year-old boys who were rarely apart. Ah, there they were in the apple trees with a slew of other boys. "I don't know that either, but it'll be a fun surprise, won't it?"

She nodded and then wandered back to the little tea party.

Nancy walked over from the bride and groom's table, a bright smile on her face. "I saw the paintings you and Anthony did for Becca's kitchen. They're cheery."

Kate's lips couldn't keep from curling up in a half smile. "I suppose that's one way to put it." She and Anthony had decided years ago that painting wasn't their gift, but every now and then they'd work together on a canvas, filling it with splotches of colors and swirls while they talked.

"No, really, I like them. Micah thinks they're a bit . . . silly, but I told him I want some for our kitchen. Could we buy three canvases in greens and blues?"

Kate sneaked a glance over to where the paintings she'd given to the new couple leaned against the front table. They were some of their better ones. "Really, you want to buy something like that?"

"Well, why not?" Eliza Stanton came over in her no-nonsense outfit—no cuffs, no piping, no ribbon. A plain navy day dress with just a little bit of white lace at the neckline. "I think they'd do well in my store on Maple."

"Goodness, I never thought we'd be any good, and now we've got buyers!" She smiled. "I could probably do something for your kitchen, Nancy, but knowing you, Eliza, you'd want handfuls of them for better profits."

"Yes, are you willing? I'd give you sixty percent."

She laughed full out. "Oh, Eliza, I'm too swamped with children and the farm. But if I ever get in the mood to paint any more, I'll let you know."

A spoon clinked against glass. "If I can have your attention, I'm going to toast the bride and groom." Silas held up a Mason jar of lemonade—he'd insisted they set out filled glasses so no one would spike a bowl of punch with illegal liquor. His gaze sought hers, and she shook her head. She'd rather sit than waddle in front of everybody and stand with a giant ache in her back. These babies were due in a few weeks, but her back and legs would thank her if it were only a few days.

The crowd swelled toward Silas, obscuring Anthony's head full of dark hair tilting close to Becca's pile of curls.

Fannie, hand in hand with Jedidiah, waved at her as they passed on their way to toast the couple.

Silas evidently climbed onto a stump and beckoned people closer. "Grab yourselves a drink. I want to tell you how proud I am of my son. I missed a lot of his growing-up years, but the time we've had together makes this a sad day for me. I love you more than you know, Anthony, and I'm so happy Becca is joining the family. You've chosen well. The Stantons have been a great influence in our lives, and you couldn't have better grandparents for your children."

"You're talking as if we're the only ones old enough to be grandparents," Dex quipped. Being a head taller than most of the crowd, he was easily heard. "They'll make you a grandpa as fast as they'll make me one."

Silas shot Kate a wide-eyed look as if he'd just realized the truth of it.

"Hey, I'm not nearly as old as you all. Don't be looking at me!" Kate hollered.

The crowd laughed, and Dex looked over at his wife. "I think Kate's calling you old, Rachel."

Kate pressed her lips together to keep from teasing Dex back. He'd not let up—especially with an audience—until he'd twisted her words up so badly she'd blush. He'd found out early on how easily she did so.

"Despite the gray hair he's given me and will soon give Becca . . ." Silas paused while their friends laughed. "I wish I didn't have to part with my son so soon, but I'm happy to gain a wonderful, godly daughter-in-law. May you two have a marriage as happy as that of your parents." He raised his glass. "And thanks to everyone here for influencing their lives for the better. Cheers."

The crowd echoed him back, most gathering around the front to give the bride and groom their congratulations before they left.

Will broke away from the well-wishers and came toward her. "You're to the point of miserable, aren't you?"

"I think I passed that weeks ago." She smiled big despite the twinge in her side. The discomfort was always worth it in the end.

"Anything concerning about how you're feeling?"

"No, just tired and ready."

"Dr. Stanton!"

Lawrence and Lucas, along with Will's only child, David, jumped on him from behind.

He growled and pulled Lucas up over his shoulder like a sack of potatoes. "Now, hold on a moment—I'm asking your mother how she's feeling."

David shook his head. "You said you'd play with us. If you

start asking people doctor questions, you ain't never going to come."

"Go on, Will." Silas sat beside her, his hand sliding across her neck and squeezing her right shoulder, his thumb pressing in a circular motion against her tight muscles. "My wife won't pop right here and now . . . hopefully."

"All right, then. Come on." Will gestured for the boys to follow. "Seems I'll have to race you, since your ma uses her condition as an excuse for losing."

He sprinted off with the boys but took a quick side trip to Eliza to kiss her on the cheek. She shooed him away from what was likely some business conversation she was having with the bank owner.

Kate smiled when Will kissed Eliza again anyway, and then ran to catch the boys. "That man needs more children."

Silas quit his massaging motions, slid his hand to her non-existent waist, and pulled her closer. "I don't think it's for lack of trying."

She pushed on some tiny limb diligently working to separate her ribs. "So *that's* what we're doing too much of."

"Oh no, we're succeeding."

She smiled at her husband, but he was looking toward Anthony and Becca, who were finally coming to see them.

"How are you doing, Ma?" Anthony sat down and gave her a peck on the cheek.

"Just fine." She patted Anthony's hand resting on her shoulder. "No need to worry about me; you focus on your wife." How odd to say that to her son. *Wife.*

Becca leaned over and kissed her on the cheek. "You looked lovely today, Mrs. Presby. . . . I mean, Mother."

Anthony pulled Kate up as if she weighed nothing. His height always surprised her when she looked up at him. "Thank you for paying for our trip to Boston. Becca's excited to see her grandparents for the first time."

He squeezed her awkwardly around her inflated middle, then kissed her on the cheek again. "Love you, Ma." He turned to Silas and clamped him into an embrace. "You too, Pa. Thanks. We'll gather up all the news from Aunt Jewel to share when we get back."

Silas made some strangled reply, which she wouldn't ask him to repeat since her own throat wasn't cooperating.

After the crowd swallowed up the newlyweds, Kate wiped away her tears. "I can't believe he's old enough to leave us already."

Silas laced his fingers into hers as they walked toward the buggy Anthony had bought for his bride. "This is the day I feared you'd leave me, remember? The day Anthony left."

She tipped her head toward the children playing in the orchard. "I think you've provided me with enough children to anchor me for a while longer."

"You've certainly done your part in giving me the family I've always wanted—above and beyond, I'd say."

"I hope you realize I plan on sticking around."

He rubbed her side but then moved his hand to massage the little baby limb trying to pop out of her belly. "Just for the wee ones, I'm sure."

"Well then, we'll have to work at having more so I'll never have reason to leave you."

His silly grin changed into a sly smile, and his eyebrows went up. "What a temptress you are. We've got guests crawling around every inch of our property and our eldest to send off into the world and you're teasing me with more baby-making." He pulled her against him and kissed her behind her ear, making her shiver.

A swift kick inside her belly hit her so hard, Silas's eyes flew open wide. He stared down at where he must have felt the kick against his own side and laughed. "Thank you for making me a daddy—five times over . . . or maybe six."

"Thank you for loving me so much I've never felt like running anywhere but into your arms."

"My pleasure." He pulled her close again, inhaled the scent of her hair, and placed a kiss to her temple. "So very much my pleasure."

Much to her introverted self's delight, **Melissa Jagears** hardly needs to leave her home to be a homeschool teacher, day-care provider, church financial secretary, and novelist. She doesn't have to leave her house to be a housekeeper either, but she's doubtful she meets the minimum qualifications to claim to be one in her official bio. Her passion is to help Christian believers mature in their faith and judge rightly. Find her online at www.melissajagears.com, Facebook, Pinterest, and Goodreads, or write her at PO Box 191, Dearing, KS 67340.

Subscribe to Melissa's Newsletter

To be certain to hear of Melissa's new releases, giveaways, bargains, and exclusive subscriber content, please subscribe to her email newsletter located on her webpage or at http://bit.ly/jagearsnewsletter.

More Romance to Enjoy

You May Also Enjoy...

After Shannon Wilde literally follows mountain man Matthew Tucker over a cliff, can these two learn to live together—for better or worse?

Now and Forever by Mary Connealy
WILD AT HEART #2
maryconnealy.com

Millie and Everett are eager to prove themselves—as a nanny and a society gentleman, respectively. They both have one last chance . . . each other.

In Good Company by Jen Turano
jenturano.com

When a new doctor arrives in town, midwife Martha Cade's world is overturned by the threat to her job, a town scandal, and an unexpected romance.

The Midwife's Tale by Delia Parr
AT HOME IN TRINITY #1